GREAT APES

GREAT APES
Will Self

GROVE PRESS
New York

For Madeleine
AND WITH THANKS
TO D.J.O.

Originally published in Great Britain in 1997 by Bloomsbury Publishing Plc.
Published simultaneously in Canada
Printed in the United States of America

FIRST AMERICAN EDITION

Library of Congress Cataloging-in-Publication Data

Self, Will.
Great apes / Will Self.
ISBN 0-8021-1617-5
I. Title
PR6069.E3654G73   1997
823'.914—dc21   97-14802

Grove Press
841 Broadway
New York, NY 10003

2 4 6 8 10 9 7 5 3 1

'An ape, a most ill-favoured beast.
How like us in all the rest?'

Cicero

'When I come home late at night from banquets,
from social gatherings, there sits waiting for
me a half-trained little chimpanzee and I take
comfort from her as apes do. By day I cannot
bear to see her; for she has the insane look
of a bewildered half-broken animal in her eye;
no one else sees it, but I do and I cannot
bear it.'

Kafka, *A Report to the Academy*

Author's Note

HoooGraa! We chimpanzees are now living through an era in which our perceptions of the natural world are changing more rapidly than ever before. Furthermore, these same perceptions are being distorted by the ways we, as chimps, now live. Some thinkers describe our current way of life as 'unnatural' – but this is too simple, for chimpunity has often been defined as just this adaptive trait – the capacity for social evolution. Suffice to sign, these 'unnatural' ways of living do themselves impact on global ecology.

This is a bewildering state of affairs: our capacity for judging our own objectivity is circumscribed by itself. Is it any wonder that in such circumstances the chimps who have given the whole question of animal rights their fullest attention have dared to consider enlarging the franchise of chimpunity to admit subordinate species, such as humans?

It is worthwhile at this point representing the signs of Dr Louis Leakey, the pioneering archaeological palaeontologist. On learning from his protégé researcher, the celebrated anthropologist Dr Jane Goodall, that she had observed wild humans fashioning twigs and then using them to probe termite mounds, Dr Leakey remarked, 'Now we must redefine *tool*, redefine *chimpanzee* – or accept humans as chimps!' He referred of course to the traditional definition of chimpanzees as *pongis habilis*, the tool making ape.

My intention in writing this novel has not been to make

any simple-minded plea for human rights, or the welfare of humans. I personally believe that, despite the apparent inchimpunity of the way humans are employed for scientific purposes: held in large compounds, isolated, diseased, in pain, malnourished etc. etc., these experiments will continue to be necessary, particularly as regards CIV and AIDS.

The issue of CIV corrals us once more in the vicious moral circle. If humans are genetically close enough to us to be infected with CIV (and the most recent research suggests that humans share as much as 98% of our genetic material, and are closer to chimps than they are to gorillas), then surely they are worthy of some small measure of our sympathy?

To this the answer must be a qualified 'yes'. Humans should be preserved. The dying-out of the human species would be an incalculable loss, and it is one that seems more than likely as bonobos[1] encroach further and further on their habitat[2].

But don't bonobos need our sympathy as well? Aren't bonobos more important than humans? Yes, of course, but the utility of preserving humans goes further than the search for a cure for AIDS, or any other medical research. The humans have much to teach us about our own origins and nature. Chimpanzees and humans had a common ancestor who lived as recently as five to six million years ago, an eye blink in evolutionary terms.

Furthermore, if humans were to become extinct in the wild, what would be the fate of domesticated humans? If, as anthropologists like Dr Goodall suggest, humans do indeed have some form of culture, then this would be effectively

[1] Throughout this book I have used the term 'bonobo' and its variants to refer to chimps of African origin. I appreciate that some bonobos prefer the ascription 'Afro-American', or in the case of the British, 'Afro-Caribbean', but on the whole 'bonobo' still seems – to me – to have the widest application.
[2] It is estimated that there are now as few as 200,000 wild humans left. A shocking state of affairs when you consider there were probably several million as recently as fifty years ago.

wiped out. It may even transpire that the behaviours of domesticated humans which reinforce this theory are in fact dependent on some form of morphic, resonant association with wild populations. Wipe out the wild humans and even the domesticated ones who have learnt to sign (some humans have a lexicon of five hundred or more ES signs) may fall motionless. Gesticulation between our two species will be at an end.

But let not the above be taken as an attempt to primatomorphise humans. Humans are what they are because of their humanity. Humans in the wild are very very different from chimpanzees. Human social organisation may be impressively complex when viewed through the lens of scientific enquiry, but stripped of this the raw facts are brute. Humans often consort – and therefore mate – for life! Instead of resolving conflict in a simple manner concordant with dominance hierarchies, human society appears horribly anarchic; bands of humans gather together to propagate their own 'ways of life' (perhaps primitive forms of ideology) on their fellows.

And while humans may display as much regard for their offspring as chimpanzees do, their perverse adhesion to the organising principle of monogamy (perverse because it confers no apparent genetic advantage) means that the gulf between 'group' and community ties is a large one. Old humans are disregarded and neglected far more than old chimpanzees.

But perhaps most significant of all is the human attitude to touch. It is this that appears so acutely inchimp. Humans, because of their lack of a protective coat, have not evolved the complex rituals of grooming and touch that so define chimpanzee social organisation and gesticulation. Imagine not being groomed! It is almost unthinkable to a chimpanzee that a significant portion of the day should not be given over to this most cohering and sensual of activities. Undoubtedly it is this lack of grooming that renders human sexuality so bizarre to us.

Humans commonly seek privacy to mate. The male usually effects penetration by lying on top of the female (one possible anatomical explanation for the peculiar formation of human buttocks); offspring are not encouraged to participate in mating. Females are mated whether or not they are in oestrus, although once again such behaviour clearly confers no adaptive advantage. Once a human infant has been born it is often passed around the community within days of its birth, and may be weaned as early as three months.

Is it too fantastical to imagine that it is these traits – which I stress are in no obvious way adaptive – that have contributed to the human evolutionary cul-de-sac? That humans may be afflicted with some kind of species neuroticism? Such speculations may not accord with the discipline of anthropology, nor with ethology in general; however, I am not a scientist but a novelist, unconfined by dry empirical considerations.

Like Dr Goodall, who, when she first went to the Gombe Stream area to observe humans in the wild, did not know enough to avoid the primatocentrism of giving humans names, I have gone against many of the tenets of dispassionate science. I do not mean to imply for a moment that I really believe wild humans to have consciousness of the kind I ascribe to Simon Dykes, rather I have tried to imagine what it might have been like if hominids instead of pongids had been evolutionarily successful.

I am, of course, not original in this. Ever since the first description of the human reached Europe in 1699, humans have had a particular fascination for chimpanzees. Early theorists positioned the human midway between the chimpanzee and 'brute creation' in the Chain of Being. Latterly, in the wake of Darwin, some supposed that the human might prove to be the 'missing link'. For others the existence of the human confirmed their desire to deny chimpunity to the bonobo. Many writers have seen in the human a paradigm for the gentler as well as the darker side of chimpanzee nature. From *Melincourt* to *My Human Wife*, from *King Kong* to the *Planet of the*

Humans films, writers have flirted with the numinous dividing line between man and chimp.

But however we choose objectively to define humans now – and *pace* Dr Leakey, there do seem good reasons for a blurring of distinctions – the subjective response to humanity is never unproblematic. One has only to go to London Zoo and observe the humans in their caged enclosures, sitting, not touching one another, their oddly white-pigmented eyes staring out at their chimpanzee visitors with what can only be described as a mixture of sadness and entreaty.

How much worse to imagine the condition of humans kept for experimental purposes in large compounds. The human hates to be entirely unconfined, and in the wild will build quite complex structures in which she can hunch motionless for days at a time. Forced out into the open and unprovided with materials for shelter construction, the human soon falls prey to a form of agoraphobia that induces a condition that might be termed a psychosis. Experimenters say it is important for scientific purposes that humans be kept in such conditions, but why exactly? Surely only to conform to scientifically defined paradigms that have their root in just this hard dividing line between our species?

One final and personal sign concerning this text. In the past my work has been much attacked for its apparent lack of sympathy. Critic after critic has signalled that I treat my protagonists with a diabolic disregard, spraying misfortune and ugliness of character on their fur. In *Great Apes* I have – purely coincidentally – constructed the only possible riposte to these idiotic objections, the fruit of a chronic misunderstanding of the meaning and purpose of satire – I've made my protagonist human!

H'hooooo
W.W.S.
Back in dirty old London, 1997.

Chapter One

Simon Dykes, the artist, stood, rented glass in hand, and watched as a rowing eight emerged from the brown brick wall of one building, slid across a band of grey-green water, and then eased into the grey concrete of another building. Some people lose their sense of proportion, thought Simon, but what would it be like to lose your sense of perspective?

"Disastrous for a painter –"

"I'm sorry," Simon blurted, imagining for a second that he had spoken aloud.

"They're disastrous for a painter," reiterated George Levinson, who had come up by Simon's elbow and now stood beside him, looking out of the plate-glass window that faced on to the river.

"By that I take it you mean they're disastrous for *the* painter." Simon half turned towards George's ruminant profile and swept an arm to encompass the white space of the gallery, the big oblong canvases, and the posing private openeers, who stood about in loose groups, arms cocked, as if they were some tableau vivant intended to exhibit human social interactions.

"Hardly." George slurped some Chilean wine out of his rented glass. "Sold the lot. Sold the lot, every one shot with a little red dot. No, I mean the technique *could* be disastrous for a painter such as yourself, this idea of silk screen laid over photogravure. I mean, I know it isn't that – um – remarkable

1

in and of itself, but you have to admit that the finished result does have something . . . something of the heft –"

"Of oils? Of painting in oils. Fuck off, George. I'll fire you if you say another word." And painter turned away from dealer to resume staring out through the ravine of buildings, across at the *mélange* of modernist apartment blocks and Victorian mansion blocks on the Battersea side of the river.

The outer eddies from the opening reached the two men, a skirl of chamber music nouveau, a waft of Marlboro smoke, a couple of youngsters, who leant against a nearby pillar, the girl's sateen-hosed thigh gently rubbing her companion's corduroy crotch, while sheep-like they cropped on one another's faces. Islanded, Simon and George stood together with the quiet assurance of men who have stood thus many times before, the mood that held them unforced.

Another rowing eight nosed out from the brown brick building, hovered on its glaucous cushion in the masonry frame, the cox at the back clearly visible – baseball hat, loudhailer – and then slid into the grey concrete like a vast hypodermic powered by eight hearty junior doctors. "No," said Simon. "No, I was thinking when you came up . . . thinking, looking at this" – he poked a finger at the square of Thames, the oblongs of building, the garnishes of green to the side – "what a terrible thing it would be for a painter to lose his sense of perspective."

"I thought that was the whole point of a great swathe of abstract art this century, the attempt to view without preconceptions, cubism, fauvism, vorti –"

"– That's loss of perspective as an intellectual assumption. I'm talking about real loss of perspective, a sort of perspective *blindness* where all depth of field is eradicated, where all that can be grasped is form and colour mutating within a single plane."

"You mean like some sort of neurological disorder? What do they call it, agnopho –"

"– Agnosia, yeah, I suppose . . . I'm not quite sure what

2

I mean, but I'm not talking about a Cézanne-inspired viewing-of-the-world-anew, but a diminution. It's perspective that provides the necessary third continuum for vision and maybe consciousness as well. Without it an individual might no longer be able to apprehend time, might ... might have to relearn time in some way, or be left in a sliver of reality, imprisoned like a microbe in a microscope slide."

"It's a thought," Levinson replied after some seconds had elapsed, including himself out of it.

"Simon Dykes?" A woman had approached during this speech and stood, hovering between diffidence and assertiveness, hand forward, body leant back and away, as if the latter were the appendage.

"Yes?"

"I'm sorry to interrupt –"

"It's OK, I was just –" and George Levinson was gone, heading back across the lack-of-industry white floor-covering, an adipose wader of a man, dipping his bill into knots of people as he went, dropping one name here and picking up another over there, amply justifying a recent glossy magazine article which had described him as 'the most proficient room-worker in the London art world'.

"That's George Levinson, isn't it?" the woman said. She was round-faced with wavelets of black hair tossed about on the top of her head. Down below her clothing encased rather than draped her small, gibbous body.

"Yes, that's right." Simon didn't want to sound as off-putting as he knew he did, but the opening fatigue was upon him and he didn't want to be there.

"Does he still handle you?"

"Oh no, no no, not any more, not since we were at prep school together in fact, then he would often handle me in the locker room after games. Nowadays he just sells my paintings for me."

"Ha-ha!" The woman's laugh wasn't forced – it wasn't a

3

laugh at all, more an allusion to the possibility of humour. "I know that, of course –"

"Then why did you ask?"

"Look." The woman's face puckered, and Simon could see in that instant that petulant resentment was her natural cast of mind, all the rest a tremendous effort of will. "If you're going to be rude –"

"No, I'm sorry, really ..." He raised a hand, fingers outstretched, and then tamped down the thickening atmosphere between them, patted it into the shape of niceness, patted it and even patted her wrist a little. "I didn't mean to sound so sharp, I'm tired and ..." He had felt her wrist, the band of her watch, steel, the edge of her wrist bone sharp as his tone, *bird bones, sparrow bones, splintered bones.*

His eyes slid to the window even as he patted, and there in the notch of river swirled a thrown handful of birds – swallows presumably – fusing into flock then fissioning back into individuals, like thoughts in a disordered mind. Simon thought of Coleridge, and then drugs. Funny that, like a synaesthesia of concepts, some people 'hear' the doorbell as green, I think Coleridge as drugs, or birds as Coleridge, or birds as drugs ... And Simon thought then of Sarah, her pubic hair specifically, and only then of the woman walking into his mind, under his very eyes, in through his very eyes – no perspective, you dig? – and looking over its contents to see if there was anything to use. "I don't mean to be so rude. I'm tired, ope –"

"You must be, what with your new show opening soon. Are you good on deadlines?"

"No, not really. I tend to be painting the day before an opening, and then stretching and framing most of the ni –" He faltered. "I'm going to be rude again. Before I say anything more I ought to know who I'm talking to."

"Vanessa Agridge, *Contemporanea,*" She flipped her bird-like claw under his hand and didn't so much shake it as scratch the palm. "I came to this, but I don't think there's much I can

4

write about her, so it's a bit of a result for me ... seeing you here. ... out and about – so to speak – in the week before the new show ..." Like a faltering engine, she died. The pause hunched between them in unequal space.

"Her?" queried Simon after a decent while.

"Manuella Sanchez," Vanessa Agridge replied, tapping him on the arm with a rolled-up copy of the catalogue in a way she imagined to be flirtatious. Simon looked at her with his new perspectiveless vision: blob-shaped muzzle, slashed red, topped with blackish fur, blackish fur below. It swelled some, slash gaped to show canines, and she continued. "She's meant to be so *outré* – anyway, that's what her people said – but she isn't. Just dull. Nothing to say for herself."

"But the work, isn't that what you're here to write about, her work?"

"Hngfh'" she snorted, "no, no, *Contemporanea* is more of a featuresey thing, artists' lives, lifestyles and so forth. My editor calls it 'Vasari for the venal'."

"Catchy."

"Isn't it." She lifted her rented glass to her lips, sipped, and viewed him over the rim. "So, your show, figurative work? Abstracts? A return to your conceptual stuff like *World of Bears*? What can we expect?"

Simon put on his perspective again and looked afresh at Vanessa Agridge. Her thickly applied pancake was almost friable when zoomed in on; her face not blobby, beaky in fact, her eyes rather on the raw, ducty side. Simon made weird assessments of volume, mass, weight, alcohol-by-volume, then flared his nostrils and caught primitive whiffs of her, then with remote sensors traced the webbing beneath the pouching of her clothes, sent one psychic probe into her anus, the other into her left nostril. He turned her anatomy inside out, sockwise, and in the process quite forgot who the fuck she was, what the fuck she had said up until now, and so told her.

"Certainly not abstract. I think non-representational painting has finally gone the way Lévi-Strauss predicted, 'a school of academic painting in which the artist strives to represent the manner in which he would execute his paintings if he were by any chance to paint some.' "

"That's very good," said Vanessa Agridge, "very . . . witty. Could I use it, do you think – credited, of course."

"Credited to Lévi-Strauss, it's his observation, as I said."

"Of course, of course . . ." a Dictaphone had appeared in her, bird-like, prestidigitated, on. Simon hadn't noticed. "So, they're portraits then, still lifes –"

"Nudes." *He remembered smoking a stolen cigarillo in a marsh, his mother's world-girdle, his father's penis, stubby, circumcised –*

"Are they sort of Bacon-y, or maybe" – she tittered – "Freud-y. You know, peeling away the bloom from a woman's body, externalising her anatomy, sort of –"

"They're love paintings." *Piss-in-pants, piss-on-floor. That very bilious bead. Piss lives with lino. Or maybe Piss Lives With Lino. Titlewise that is* "Sigh".

"They're what?" Vanessa Agridge had the Dictaphone up by her pig-like – crushed, flat, bristly – the way some other jerks held cellular phones.

"Love paintings. They're paintings that in a quite straightforward, almost narrative way describe my love for the human body. My thirty-nine-year affair with the human body."

In the minutes they had been at contraflow with one another the opening had begun to close. The openeers swam towards the doors of the gallery, sluiced here and there into little whirlpools of further sociability. George Levinson floated by them and slowly revolved to face Simon. "Are you coming on, Simon?"

"Excuse me – where?"

"To Grindley's first, then maybe the Sealink later."

"I may see you at the Sealink, I have to see what Sarah's doing first."

"Right-o."

Levinson disappeared downstream, flirting with a youth he'd picked up, a boy like a puma, with slim hips, violet eyes and

6

a black coat. And, in the wake of seeing-George-and-him-go, bobbed the recognition of what had preceded it. Simon straightened up, pulled himself into the present. In a life where every third person he met assumed an expression that showed they recognised him, was it any wonder that he constantly found himself talking to strangers as if they were friends?

All of this, and then Simon said to Vanessa Agridge, who had a Dictaphone – as he now saw – in threatening evidence, "You must excuse me –"

"I just did." She was catching his style – it happened.

"No, I mean now. I must go. I have to work."

"To meet Sarah?"

"She's my girlfriend –"

"Model?"

"Girlfriend. Look, I'm going." And he started off, out of the trap.

"One thing . . ." she called. He turned, she was a shadow now, exiguous, wavering against the summer evening.

"Yes?"

"This Lévi-Strauss fellow."

"Yes?"

"You haven't got a number for him, have you? It's just that I thought I'd run that quote by him – if I do the piece, that is."

There was a small rank of pay phones by the main doors of the gallery. Simon levered his phonecard out of his cardholder and fed it into the slot. He punched Sarah's number at the artists' agency where she worked and waited in a virtual aviary with the chirrupings and tweetings of connection. Then her lips grazed his cheekbone, her voice breathed into his ear: 'I'm not available to take your call right now, so . . .' Not her voice. As close to her voice as the voice of Hal in *2001* was to a human voice. Not her sparky tone either, but horrifically measured, every word a spondee.

7

"Are you there?" he queried after the peep, knowing that she would be.

"Vetting, yeah, I'm call-vetting."

"Why?"

"I dunno," she sighed. "I just don't feel like talking to anyone. Anyone except you, that is."

"So, what's the plan?"

"A few of us are meeting up –"

"Where?"

"At the Sealink."

"Who?"

"Tabitha, Tony, I guess – though he hasn't confirmed. Maybe the Braithwaites."

"Shiny happy people."

"Yeah." She laughed, very briefly, their shared laugh, a kind of lip-smacking hiss. "Shiny happy people. When will you get there?"

"I'm *en route* now." He hung up without further ado, then negotiated a flurry of final 'Catch you later's, 'We must get together's and 'Next week's – that ought to have been 'Next year's – before taking the cast-iron stairs down to the street.

Summer London on the far cusp of the rush hour. The gallery wasn't in Chelsea Harbour, but it might as well have been, for all the relevance that the opening had to the world outside. Simon set off along the Embankment, occasionally peering back over his shoulder to look at the golden ball atop the central tower of the development. Someone had once told him that it rose and fell with the tide, but as he couldn't tell whether it was low or high tide he was unable to make sense of the balls.

He felt tired and his chest slopped with the sweet phlegm that comes either at the onset or the demise of a lung infection. Simon couldn't decide which as he gurgled and gobbed his way past the cars crammed in the crook of road leading up to Earls Court. The Braithwaite brothers. Shiny happy people. The Sealink Club. It all meant a late night of shouting, laughing and flirting. A production mounted with a shifting cast of name-less but recurring minor characters. And it all implied getting in at three, or four, or past five, dawn coming in prismatic beams, the world's furniture haphazardly rearranged by the clumsy removal men of narcotics.

Drugs, he sighed, drugs. Which drugs? The crap London barroom cocaine that managements turned a blind eye to the sale of, knowing that the only effect it had on its snorters was to make them buy more marked-up booze? Yeah, definitely some of that. He could already picture himself chopping and crushing, crammed into some dwarfish toilet stall. And he could already see how it would end up, Sarah and he fucking with the dismal end-of-the-world feel that the crap cocaine imparted. Like two skeletons copulating in a wardrobe, their bones chafing and stridulating. And tomorrow morning, disembodied, ghost-like, he would find himself at the cashpoint, a rime of white powder worked into the embossed numerals on his credit card.

Or perhaps there would be some of the ecstasy that Sarah got hold of, presumably from Tabitha although Simon hadn't asked. Ecstasy had initially seemed a fraudulent description for the drug, as far as Simon was concerned. The first couple of times he had taken it he'd said to Sarah, "If this is ecstasy, then a drug which produces mild pique could justifiably be called 'rage'." But he'd got the hang of it. Learnt to stop regarding it as a psychedelic, akin to the acid and mushrooms he had – more or more – taken as an art student at the Slade, and understand that it only worked on the interfaces of people's minds, their relationships with one another. It was a drug of vicariousness, of using another person's emotions as a prop, a route to abandonment. All conversations on E acquired an adolescent intensity, a titivation of the very possibility of intimacy.

It also had other weird effects. Even with a gut full of liquor and a few honks of crap cocaine on board, a white dove still made Simon feel like penetrating every body in sight.

Male, female, whole, crippled, it hardly mattered. What he desired was a flesh pit full of writhing naked bodies, smeared with glycerine; or better still a conga-line of copulation, where a cock-thrust here would produce a cunt-throb way over there.

E-ed up, Simon's body, like some rain-swelled river, breached its banks and flowed all over the place, all over the people. But Sarah would take him in hand at this point. Like some proficient hydrologist she would enact lightning-quick embanking and canalising work, until he flowed into her.

Yeah, ecstasy. And then they would get home to the Renaissance, home to the golden bower of her bed, where they would pluck and strum upon one another's mandolin bodies, until they eventually, belatedly came. Eventually, belatedly slept.

I don't want to get loaded. Simon thought, turning into Tite Street. I don't feel exactly *hot* at the moment and there's a full day's work to do tomorrow, no shirking. And in the contemplation of the night ahead, with its slalom of toxicities, he assayed his own body, its fit between mind and metabolism, metabolism and chemistry, chemistry and biology, biology and anatomy, anatomy and protective clothing. His toes scrunged in semi-sweat-stiffened hosing, and he felt their fungal deterioration, the gritting of their webbing. His hands felt numb at their finger ends. Simon thought about peripheral neuralgia, and thought of the half-bottle of whisky he skulled most nights, but then again considered it unlikely. Physical addiction to alcohol, that is.

His stomach was inflated now – as if the Chilean wine were still fermenting – so that his walk was counterpointed not simply by the harrumphing and spitting – neat that, between the two front teeth, so that a dash of phlegm hit whichever paving stone he aimed at. He remembered learning it from lads at school, upsetting his fastidious older brother with demonstrations – but also by poot-pooting from between soft-clenched bum cheeks. Like some cartoon, Simon, thought, fart-powered, 2-D.

Simon's bum exercised him nowadays, as if his arsehole was haltingly learning to talk, in order to inform him that his days were numbered.

He remembered now the business of getting to know new lovers as a young man. How intimacy was defined by sexual interaction: the shared, tacit acknowledgement of the refusal to be embarrassed by a vaginal fart or a premature ejaculation. And how that intimacy was then broadened, given further substance, by a willingness to include the other's shit and piss and furtive secretions. It all reached a climax with childbirth, with her swollen vagina stretched to tearing, voiding a half gallon of what appeared to be won ton soup on to the plastic sheeting. And the placenta, organ-that-was-hers and not-hers, maybe even partly his. But no, they didn't want to fricassee it, on any of the three snacking opportunities, with onions and garlic, so it was removed for incineration, borne in a take-away, cardboard kidney dish.

And now he could no longer face that kind of getting-to-know anyone. He and Sarah had been gasping into one another's napes for nine months now, but he didn't want to share the bathroom with her. Not only did he not want to share the bathroom with her, he didn't even like the idea of her being in the house when his bowels moved. He wouldn't have minded going to another town to do a shit. His arsehole was sending him internal memoranda on his own mortality – and it leaked. Bowel movements were no longer discrete, his bowels seemed to move all the time, telegraphing him fart bulletins, and faxes of shit-juice that soiled the gussets of his pants in hideous ways. And thinking this Simon paused to hoick at the girding of his waist, trying to give his persecutor a little more air to foul.

Whenever he stopped to contemplate his relationship to this body, this physical idiot twin, it occurred to Simon that something critical must have gone wrong without his noticing. He was bemused to awaken to this insistent reminder of his corporeality. He seemed to recall – within the memory banks of the body itself – those unconstrained, atemporal afternoons of childhood, twilight playing, parental calls to return home like hooting apes in the suburban gloaming; and accompanying that memory, suffusing it like the sunset, a sense of his body as also unconstrained, not as yet inhibited, hemmed-in, by the knowledge of the future, which became like a thermostat, regulating any enjoyment or ease of action, ease of repose.

And now, turning into the King's Road, past the Duke of York's barracks where mobile artillery stood immobile, Simon wondered if he could pinpoint the moment when it had all gone wrong. For now his bodily awareness was one solely of constraint, of resistance, of a missing fit between every ligament and bone, every cell and its neighbour. How could it have happened? He thought again of acid trips – they were still there, salient in the three-minute memory defile he was traversing. He remembered the contrived astral trips he and other psychic venturers had taken under its influence. Perhaps in one such he had departed his physical body, but on reentry failed to achieve an exact fit, leaving the psychic and the physical ever so slightly out of registration, like a badly reproduced photograph in a magazine. That's how it felt, at any rate.

There was that lack-of-fit, and there was the amputation of his children, which had caused another confusion in bodily perception, another more profound discorporation. When his marriage to Jean had collapsed in on itself, like a tower block demolished with carefully placed charges, his children had been five, seven and ten, but his physical relationship with them was unbroken; conscious cables plugged their snot noses and wipeable bums directly into his nervous system. If they nicked or cut themselves the pain was grossly enhanced, amplified, so that Simon felt it as a Sabatier to the intestines, a scalpel to the tendons. If they swooned in babyish fevers, hallucinating concepts and visions – 'Daddy, Daddy, I'm Iceland, I'm Iceland' – he hallucinated with them, climbed alongside them the shoddy Piranesi of the nursery wallpaper, hoicking up a leaf to gain a toehold on a flower.

No matter how much he saw them now, how many times he picked them up from school, how many times he made them oven chips and fish fingers, how many times he petted them, kissed them, told them he loved them, nothing could assuage this sense of wrenching separation, their disjunction from his life. He may not have snacked on the placenta, but somehow the umbilici still trailed from his mouth, ectoplasmic cords, strung across summertime London, snagging on rooftops, car aerials, advertising hoardings, and tied him to their little bellies.

Simon pulled up by a newsagent's on the brink of Sloane Square. Shiny unhappy girls walked past clad in tabards, chaps, and yokes of leatherette material. He thought briefly of a woman he had fucked in Eaton Square. Fucked in the dead zone between Jean and Sarah. Jean and Sarah, so silly, the caesura: JeanandSarah. Anyway, this woman appeared to Simon now, in Sloane Square, the ghostly set of her flat arranged on the pavement.

Big divan, glass-topped coffee-table, abstract paintings and their two bodies, each selling the other figurative insurance. Touching one another up, in the same sense that a stretch of land might be sung up, created by allusion. Here are breasts, here are hips, here is a cock, there a cunt . . . Simon wormed her out of her leggings, the leggings like worms pulling away from her shanks, the ankles cheekily rough with stubble, hers and his. He buried his drunk head in the folds of her white belly, the folds slack, skinlaps. They giggled, honked coke, half-naked, his pants round his ankles. They swilled vodka, warm and nasty. When he came to fuck her he had to poke his cock into her with his finger, but she didn't seem to mind, or didn't have a mind. One or the other.

Simon struck the set and looked to his right where a freestanding rack of newspapers stood. He scanned the headlines: 'More Massacres in Rwanda', 'President Clinton Urges Ceasefire in Bosnia', 'Accusations of Racism in O.J. Simpson Trial'. It wasn't, he reflected, political news, it was

13

news about bodies, corporetage. Bodies dragged by thin shanks through thick mud, bodies smashed and pulverised, throats slashed red, given free tracheotomies so that the afflicted could breathe their last.

There was some fit here, Simon realised, between the penumbra around his life, the darkness at the edge of the sun, and these bulletins of disembodiment, discorporation updates. His imagination, always too visual, could enter into these headlines readily enough, but only by casting Henry, his eldest, as Hutu; Magnus, the baby, as Tutsi; then watch them rip each other to shreds.

Simon sighed. "It's a lack of perspective . . ." and then coughed as a face inclined towards him, for he had involuntarily spoken aloud. He thought of Lucozade, but lacked the energy to broach the shop. He thought of sending the kids a postcard, but all there was on display were cards depicting chimpanzees in humiliating poses, dressed up in tweed jackets, carrying briefcases, with captions underneath reading 'In London, thinking of you'. So, instead, he fingered out the joint he had rolled earlier from the breast pocket of his jacket. Simon held the thing in the palm of his hand; it was wrinkled and curved like the penis of a paper tiger. Then he lit it, hoping to fumigate his mind, send the visions scuttling away.

Chapter Two

S arah sat at the bar of the Sealink Club being propositioned by men. Some men propositioned her with their eyes, some with their mouths, some with their heads, some with their hair. Some men propositioned her with nuance, exquisite subtlety; others propositioned her with chutzpah, their suit as obvious as a schlong slammed down on the zinc counter. Some men's propositioning was so slight as to be peripheral, a seductive play of the minor parts, an invitation to touch cuticles, rub corns, hang nails. Other men's propositioning was a Bayreuth production, complete with mechanical effects; great flats descending, garishly depicting their Taste, their Intellect, their Status. The men were like apes – she thought – attempting to impress her by waving and kicking things about in a display of mock potency.

She sat, a small blonde eye to this storm of impersonality. A young woman who believed, when it suited her, in defying expectation. This evening she was dressed in a little black suit, little black toque, little black veil, black heels, black tights, cream silk blouse with long pointed collar. She shifted a little and sensed silken surfaces move around her, accommodating her in a sheeny embrasure. She felt very much present on the barstool. Beamed down to it, the molecules of her still fizzing, delighted to play a part in assuming her form.

Perhaps, Sarah thought, it's this that really whistles up the men, this call of the urbane. But she knew that more likely it was the feline physicality, the blonde kittenishness of her. Nose, fine-bridged, tipped up at the end to expose nostrils pink and veined, advertisements for less random access. Mouth narrow, but full-lipped, especially the bottom which would be described as pouting in a more flippant face. The chin vulpine, sharp, a chin for delving with. The eyes, violet, truly so, a startling colour for eyes to be, their points of pale fire lustrous above cheekbones with a point. These features introduced a mineral cast to what would otherwise be an animal face. A mineral hint that would become an adamant certainty if she would only remove the toque, show the way her narrow forehead mounted to a widow's peak.

Women's faces are all too often described as heart-shaped, but Sarah's face wasn't heart-shaped, it was diamond-shaped, top triangle formed by peak and cheek, bottom by chin and cheek. And like a real diamond it was a face that contained faces, subsidiary countenances, depending on who was observing it.

The choppy, force-six sociability of the Sealink Club whirled around the stool this jewel sat on and crashed against the bar itself, allowing time in the undertow between waves for Sarah to sip her cocktail, light her Camel Filter, swap remarks with Julius the barman, watch herself multiplied and bisected in the facets of the mirror-backed shelves.

"Simon coming in?" asked Julius, pirouetting with a shaker, rattling the chunked concoction, pouring off the essence in a spiritous stream.

"Yeah, he's been at some opening . . . I expect he'll be here soon –" She broke off, a handsome young man was approaching the bar. He stared at Sarah, raked her pillbox hat with his gaze, and said to Julius, "Um."

"Um what? Umbongo?" the barman replied.

"Um . . . err . . ." He was definitely flustered. Flustered in canvas trousers, something not quite right there, thought Sarah. Flustered and sweating under the high noon of his own good looks.

"I'm not sure I know that one, sir, is it grenadine-based?" Before the young man could answer, Julius was gone, transporting his tall, lithe body to the other end of the bar in a kind of shuffle that made it appear as if he were atop a concealed conveyor belt.

"He's . . . he's very witty, isn't he?" said the young man to Sarah. It was a proposition that for once wasn't a proposition.

"Yes," she sighed, "and wasted here, wasted. Wasting his life away, and he could have been a real contender, really, a contender." She sighed again, shook her head dolefully, stirred her drink with her finger.

"Why'd jew say that then?" the young man asked; but before Sarah could answer, draw him a little tighter into her ridiculous noose, the swing doors to the barroom did their bit and Tabitha, Sarah's younger sister, sashayed in.

With her were Tony Figes the art critic and the Braithwaite brothers, an unholy pair of non-identical twins who regarded all of their life together – which was all their life – as a living, breathing, moving artwork. Needless to say this introduced an axiom: the closer the Braithwaites were to a performing context the less interesting they became. Whereas in social circumstances they were spontaneous and often downright bizarre.

"Fuck me sideways," said Tabitha, coming up to Sarah and planting a Twiglety kiss on her pointy cheekbone, a kiss so Twiglety that a bit of Twiglet remained glued to the cheek, "here you are all on your lonesome." She half hugged her older sister, digging her nails in under Sarah's breastbone.

Sarah struggled, slapped Tabitha, said, "Fuck off."

"Fuck you." Tabitha wasn't recoiling, she was leaning into Sarah, scrunging silk, cotton and flesh; she was hunting for a little nipple to tweak. The bag of Twiglets in her other hand waved about erratically.

"Fuck off!" She'd found it – she twirled away down to the end of the bar to say hello to Julius.

17

Tony Figes stepped forward and presented himself saying, "Good evening." He took Sarah's hand in the most provisional of ways, then returned it. Tony Figes smiled, and the long, L-shaped scar that made a seam across cheek, between chin cleft and lower lip, furled up to become a second mouth. A queer, bent little man, brown all over like a sheet of parcel paper, with a browner label of hair pasted on his shiny brow, this evening he was gift-wrapped in a cream linen suit. Tufts of unfortunately grey hair struggled up from the open neck of his shirt. "Hmm." He turned from Sarah, ran an eye over the room, its racks of suits, then turned back to her. "If I'd wanted an insurance quotation I'd have stayed in and called Freefone." Sarah laughed and he took his twin-smiles to the bar, signed for Julius.

The Braithwaite Brothers moved up to Sarah. They were humming under their breath. She couldn't make out the tune exactly, but it could have been 'The Grapes of Wrath'. They stood either side of her, one thin, the other fattish. But both faces lean, yellow-black. They stuck their hands out in front of their chests, palms down. Like robots, Sarah thought, or humanoid fork-lift trucks. She looked from one to the other; both sets of brown eyes were turned in on themselves, or possibly turned in on the other's. Then, without any signal being given, all four hands began to dart around her head, as if the brothers were playing a game of conceptual patty-cake, or signing for the partially sighted deaf. They boosted the humming, then let it fade, the four hands fell to their sides. They moved off without saying anything, heading for the toilets.

"Body space," Tony Figes said while lighting a Camel Filter; he was by way of being their exegetist. "They're doing something on the space the body occupies."

"I see."

"They've said that they intend to use their bodies from now on solely to define the space that other bodies occupy, in order to draw attention to the way modern existence destroys our faculties of extroception." Tony held his head cocked to one side and his martini cocked away from it. Sarah didn't think he could tell himself any more whether he was being ironic.

"How long do you think they'll keep it up?"

"This evening?"

"Yeah."

"Too, an hour maybe. They're holding some excellent coke. Fucking excellent. A couple more lines and they'll hopefully give the whole thing a rest."

Tabitha gambolled back from the other end of the bar. More drinks were ordered from Julius. The Braithwaites returned, eyes and noses wet, as if they had been doggily retrieving some cocaine which had been shot down in the gents'. Sarah sat and appreciated the warm bicker about her, the sarcasm and irony, the satire and ridicule, the delightful, cosy inwardlookingness of it all. Each snide aside she felt as a light caress, each barbed remark as a hortatory pat.

But it wasn't always thus. This brittleness had once been nothing but brittle, thin social ice failing to support her flailing sense of herself. Only ... what? As little as six months ago this early evening in the club, this prelude to her own abandonment of her child's body, would have been purgatory, a recrudescence of loathing. Now everything about it was redefined by the fact of Simon. More specifically by the fact of his body.

If she concentrated, honed down the sound, cut out the shards of light from glasses, mirrors and spectacle frames, she could imagine his approaching body as a low thrum of tangible solidity winging towards her through the shades of evening. A bomber group of a body in close formation, collarbone, rib cage, hips, penis. Feet, calves, thighs, penis. Hands, shoulders, elbows, penis. 'Sarah Loves Simon's Penis'. She should carve it on the bar with her hatpin, it was such a true, romantic belief.

The fade from neck stubble to chest hair, the long hardnesses of muscle, like flexible splints. And the paradoxical softness of his pale skin. Like a boy's skin, a skin that would always be sensual, always cry out to be touched. A skin that smelt wholly of him, him boiled up in the unpuckered bag of it. Sarah wanted to slash this skin of his, have him gush into her. She chafed her thighs together at the thought of this and wished he were there already. Why did they bother with going out at all? Why did she want to drag him out this evening? She didn't really. She would have far rather stayed in and let him peel her and peel her and peel her again. He could get her going, crank up the galvanic heart of her so that she came and came and came, each dizzy orgasm more vertiginous than the one that preceded it.

Why did they go out? Why did they do drugs? Because this was *too* much for both of them, because, Sarah sensed, this was something that could be atrophied rather than toned by exercise. Something that might be worked out of them in the working out. She had not read Lycurgus, but had she done so she would have recognised the beauty of the Spartan law on adultery. In Sparta adultery was without sanction, but woe betide the man caught making love to his wife, for certain death would ensue for both parties. This imparted a dangerous tension to marital relations, kept them forbidden, truly sexy. So it was for Simon and Sarah, the Sealink, the drugs, the gaping lacuna was their Laconia.

There was this, but more locally there were his ex-wife and his ex-girlfriends. The many many ex-girlfriends. Unpack Simon and there wasn't just Simon there, there was also a series of Russian dolly-women, his reified memories of lovemaking with them packed each inside the other. He was a cyclopaedia of clit-rubs, a compendium of cunt-sucks, and a Britannica of breast-caresses. If Sarah caught herself thinking of this as they made love it was enough to make her cry, burst out crying with him inside her. Sometimes she thought of this on the very brink of coming, the very teetering edge. Then she would be wracked by two kinds of sobs. As she subsided,

Simon would hang on to her, bewildered by this perturbation he had wittingly produced.

Where was he? Why wasn't he there already, so she could grab hold of the mast of him, hang on in the watery flux of the Sealink? Once Simon was there the whole evening would become a tipping deck, the two of them sliding down it towards bed, like a pair of hands entwined in practical prayer, then clenched in pleasure. Where was he?

He was in Oxford Circus, standing outside Top Shop sucking on an unfiltered Camel, looking across the arena of tar towards the reef of Regent Street, which curved away to the south. He was standing back from the pavement, against the plate-glass window. His temples thrummed and he felt claustrophobic. The tube had been bad enough, had been, in two words, a mistake. Or rather the joint he had smoked in Sloane Square before getting the tube had been a mistake. He had hoped for a little respite from his body, a mental excursion whilst it was transported into the West End. But instead the hash with its heavy predictability, like a bulky butler, ushered in more unpleasantness, more bad feeling.

It began on the escalator down, which was packed with a commuter crowd. I have been looking at these descending ranks of people all my life, it occurred to Simon, robotic, not touching, but moving in tight formations along tunnels and up stairways. They are like the proles in Lang's *Metropolis*. *Exactly* like the proles in Lang's *Metropolis*. This glancing observation, quite slight, nonetheless pulled up a deeper memory, depth-charged it, so that it shot up into Simon's consciousness streaming bubbles. He had seen *Metropolis* as a child, been appalled by Lang's vision of an inhuman, urban future, ruled by the Moloch of machinery, but had not, aged seven, seen it as dark fantasy at all. Simon thought it was a documentary – of sorts.

And it had been. A fly-on-the-tube-wall report of shuffling anonymity, every body reduced by the Frankensteinian future

21

to no more than the sum of its fellows' parts. And by the vending machine Simon blanched, and under the train indicator Simon sweated; he felt the ridging of sweaty cloth cut into his perineum – *visceralupdatevisceralupdatevisceralupdate.*

He had also lied to the woman at the opening, the pushy hack from *Contemporanea.* It wasn't true about the forthcoming exhibition of his work. It wasn't true about his love affair with the human body. He hadn't painted pictures that displayed the ideal couched within the real flesh, the real bone, the real blood. He had painted the unreal, the twisting and distressing of that body by the metropolis, by its trains and planes, its offices and apartments, its fashions and fascisms, piazzas and pizza parlours.

A year or so before, in the dark age between Jean and Sarah, Simon had lunched one day with George Levinson at the Arts Club and then sliced his way down through the cake-and-icing streets of Chelsea to the Tate. He knew why. He was blocked again, badly blocked. He not only didn't want to paint, or draw, or construct, or carve. He felt like some frontal-lobe fuck-up, incapable of remembering why it was that anyone should paint, or draw, or construct, or carve. The world seemed replete with its own imagery already – too like *itself* already. In this mood he forced himself in the direction of the gallery, urging one foot in front of the other. He had arrived for lunch stoned, and left drunk.

The visit to the Tate was a bit of masochism for Simon. Worse than that – a failed bit of masochism. Simon felt himself to be a middle-aged JP with a taste for birching, picking up a boy in the Charing Cross Road with the sure knowledge that his money will be taken by the pimp, and that the police will pass him on to the tabloids.

He scuttled up the wide stone stairs and entered crab-wise, skirting the main hall, ducking past the arch leading to the contemporary galleries, eyes averted, lest he catch sight of one of his peer's works, or worse, one of his own. He escaped into the Renaissance and hung out there a while, feeding deer and goats in the blue distance of Umbrian panelling. It meant nothing to him, the colours, the positioning of figures, the lines of sight, the religious iconography. Every aspect of the paintings he stared at had been traduced and traduced and traduced again by the glossy and matt betrayals of photography, of advertising. Simon wouldn't have been surprised if a *putto* had driven out of the frame of a Titian in a Peugeot 205.

He wandered on, trying to lose his bearings, but not trying too hard, because then he wouldn't – for he knew the gallery too well. Remembered being there aged sixteen, on the verge of a first kiss with a girlfriend. The two of them, palms cemented and oiled with childish sweat, had moved along, making up conversation, while his eyes took in the cornices, ventilation grilles, fire extinguishers, light switches, everything but the incandescent Blakes they had allegedly come to see. Such training – brain labouring while thin sixteen-year-old cock was straining against thin pants, and thin fifteen-year-old chest acted as crucible for the consuming heart of lust – was enough to stamp the floor plan on his neurons.

But he was lost, or at any rate unknowing, when he looked up and saw the two canvases by John Martin, the apocalyptic nineteenth-century painter, *The Plains of Heaven* and *The Fall of Babylon*. In the former a conventional enough view of romantic upland – bluer and yellower peaks and valleys, receding to a hazy horizon – was reviewed when Simon saw that what he had assumed initially was a plume of smoke or spume, issuing from a rocky cleft in the foreground, was in fact a great tumult of angelic beings in close, but irregular, formation. There were so many of them that they altered the scale of the picture entirely. What Simon had thought a horizon of some thirty or forty miles seen from a peak perspective became an unreal hundred to two hundred miles of nonlocatable nirvana. An impossibilist realisation of another planet, leaning towards the spray-guns and computer manipulations of Now, rather than the layered, mannered evocations of Then.

The other canvas, *The Fall of Babylon*, was both a complement and a corrective. A massive vortex of stone, wood, water, fire and flesh, gurgling down an invisible plug hole of destruction. Grey-robed Babylonians were caught up in this, flung holus-bolus, arms and legs cartwheeling, their disordered whipped-cream beards froth to the maelstrom. Martin seemed to be saying . . . what? Saying nothing, only carried away by the sheer mechanics of the graphic destruction he had wrought. The painting was about this: that Babylon contained this moment of explosion, this blastosphere, latent in all its solidity, its municipality.

And if not Babylon, why not London? And if not the plains of heaven, why not the moors of cumulo-nimbus? The smudged cotton wool that kissed the curved undersides of aircraft as they powered across the sky. Why not, why not indeed? Simon distrusted epiphanies. He'd been sent scampering down blind-alleys of endeavour far too many times to give credence to those moments of believing something was instinctively right. But he knew a good trope when one diverted him. He recognised an inspirational scaffold which would support him, if only for do-it-yourself.

So it had been with the series of modern apocalyptic paintings he had embarked upon the following week. In Martin's canvases the body was violate, or inviolate, but always violable. In Simon's the human bodies would be scarcely viable: the massed termites of Lang's city, their bodies uniform, their uniforms body-like. Insectoid humans – all carapace, all exoskeletal. They would sit in ranks, in an aircraft the size of a lumbering Chartres, whole choirs and transepts of them, reading blocks of wood with the pages delicately carved out, and playing Donkey Kong with twitching thumbs, tossing off the miniature plastic clitorises.

Simon conceived of a large canvas showing the interior of a Boeing 747 as its nose explodes on the Earth's crust, as its deathly decal – winged defeat – destructs in a thirty-two-feet-per-second/per second ram-raid on the concrete floor of an empty reservoir near Staines. The ripped up rafts of human figures flying actually *inside* the disintegrating plane, achieving true weightlessness at last, just at the point at which their burial anticipates their burial.

And once this canvas had come to him, the others had followed. They were all depictions of the safest and most urbanely dull of modern environments, but subject to an horrific destructive force which shook, stirred and ultimately shredded their human cargo. The interior of the Stock Exchange beneath a tidal wave; the booking hall of King's Cross tube station on that November night in 1987, at the very instant the fireball erupted; the car deck of a ro-ro as the green gush rolled in, and the red and blue cars were flushed out; instant Ebola attacking Ikea, the processing hordes of young newlyweds purchasing flat-pack furniture liquefying, still hand-in-hand. And so on, twenty canvases in all.

And while at the point of conception Simon had imagined that these paintings would be satiric, concerned with the futile impermanence of all that was held likely to last, as he worked on them he saw that this was not so. That the paintings had nothing to do with the settings, the backgrounds. That these were little more than montages, depictions of crude massifs and underwater reefs, on to which children might rub celluloid transfers of suitable human figures. And that it was those figures that were the real subject of the paintings.

The human body had – Simon felt – been pushed out over a purely local void, an overhang of time; it dangled there, a Navaho on a steel girder, pitting its head for heads against the sheer cliff of just-constructed, concretised techno. The wind had changed and left Simon's human subjects distorted in the attitudes required to live in this world of terminal distressing. A crick had run through the Tower of Babylon, leaving language communities on all five hundred floors with wrenched shoulders and necks. This was what he wanted to express, but had the deregistration of his own body preceded, or followed from this? He could not tell.

At around the same time he had met Sarah. But he wasn't

sure that that was working, or that the working was working. All that he knew was that in the last year the days had got longer, had been filled with painting and the new people she introduced him to. That the hangovers had come, a hopeful sign because before – in the caesura, the and between Jean and – there had been no over, only hang. Further, that his children had in some way come back to him, felt comfortable with him once again. Sensed that the parasites eating him from within were, at least for the moment, sated.

Where was he? He was in Oxford Circus, standing outside Top Shop smoking an unfiltered Camel, looking across the arena of tar towards the reef of Regent Street, which curved away to the south. He was standing back from the pavement, against the plate-glass window. His temples thrummed and he felt claustrophobic as he envisioned the whole scene dumped upon by a giant ape. A post-imperial Kong who smashed the windows of the department stores and pulled out wriggling handfuls of humans, twined between his digits and caught like the termites they were in the cable-thick fur on the back of his huge hands. These people were finger food to the god, sushi for the divinity. He disentangled them from his fur, eyed their knotted faces, and then popped them between his teeth, each of which was the size of a dentist.

Mmmm . . . ! Crunchy . . . and yet chewy. The clacking and gnashing of this car-park of a mouth filled the precincts, bio-noise greater than mechanical tumult. He paused, spat out a traffic warden whose reflective bandoleer had caught between his lower seven-and-eight. Inappropriate dental floss. He flexed his mighty arms, drummed on the roof of Hamley's and let out a massive "HooooGraaa!", which seemed to mean: I am body. I am *the* body. Sod the Father. Sod the Son, and piss on the Holy Ghost.

This pantagruelian pongid then paced around the block, kicking up cars like metallic divots, eating double-deckers as if they were Double Deckers, and then finally squatting in the very centre of the Circus itself to strain, push and deliver a turd the size of a newspaper kiosk, which wavered, lengthened from stub to cigar, before plummeting fifty feet from Kong's arsehole on to the shaven heads of a posse of style-victim cycle couriers, who, like cattle in a thunderstorm, had taken shelter in the open.

Simon shook his head, the vision cleared, shaken into motes and flecks of humanity who scurried now at ground level. He checked his watch, saw that he was late, and turned in the direction of Sarah, to the Sealink.

Chapter Three

D r Zack Busner, clinical psychologist, medical doctor, radical psychoanalyst, anti-psychiatrist, maverick anxiolytic
drug researcher and former television personality, stood
upright in front of the bathroom mirror teasing some crumbs
from the thick fur under the line of his jaw. He'd had toast for
his first breakfast that morning and, as usual, managed to get
a fair amount of black cherry conserve into his coat instead
of his stomach. He'd washed his fur thoroughly around the
neck area – using the watercomb the Busners kept for just
that purpose – but the crumbs obstinately refused to dissolve
along with the jam. And the more he attempted to dig them
out, the deeper into his fur they seemed to dig in.

No matter, he thought, turning his attention to dressing,
Gambol can cope with it on the way into the hospital. Gambol,
Busner's research assistant, was waved upon to groom his boss
a great deal. Of course, so were all the junior doctors, nurses
and auxiliary workers at Heath Hospital, whether attached
to the psychiatric department or not. Nowadays the more
senior medical staff – and sometimes even administrators –
would cluster around Busner as he swung into the hospital
and attempt to get their fingers in his fur. If they couldn't
give him at least a cursory groom of deference, they would
present to him and then scamper off about their business.

For, Busner, while a nonconformist and even zany psychiatric practitioner in youth and middle age, had on the

cusp of old age begun to acquire something approaching respectability. The doctrinal excesses of the Quantity Theory of Insanity, with which he had been associated, fresh from his analytic training under the legendary Alkan, had long since been forgotten. The theory was now viewed – if chimps thought about it at all – as a piece of amusing wrongheadedness, a kind of socio-psychological version of Logical Positivism, or Marxism, or Freudianism. Obviously the predictions it had been designed to make had been disproved fulsomely, and yet, a second wave of apologists had sprung up to defend the theory, pointing out that the empirical verity of a hypothesis may not be the sole criterion on which to judge its significance.

Busner took the freshly ironed shirt from the hanger dangling on the back of the door and slipped it over his rounded shoulders. His fingers were still as nimble as ever. He fastened the buttons speedily, his thumbs managing to locate the knuckles of his index fingers to effect torsion, despite the arthritis that now plagued him. When he picked up his habitual mohair tie, looped it round his thick neck, knotted it, and folded down the collar, he was further reassured by the blur of motion in the mirror.

He left the collar unbuttoned and the tie knot slack – the better for Gambol to get at the crumbs. Meanwhile, one of his feet had, without any thought on his part, snatched a curry comb from the glass shelf underneath the sink, and he now found himself absent-mindedly combing his muzzle while squinting at his own reflected features.

Pronounced eyebrow ridges with a light coping of silver-grey hairs, deeply recessed nasal bridge, neat, almond-shaped nostrils, no bagging of the muzzle, just a series of wriggling lines scored at oblique angles across the smooth skin of his full and froggy top lip. His lips were as moon-crescented and thinly generous as when he was young.

Not bad for a chimp nearing fifty, he mused, fluffing up into a halo the long tufts of grey fur surrounding his balding pate. No sign of goitre or mange, no ulcers either. At this rate

I might make it to sixty! He thrust out his broad chest and flexed his long arms. While it's true that in motion – which they almost always were – his features projected an impression of barely contained energy, in repose they slumped somewhat, slid into fleshly landslip, epidermal erosion. But Busner didn't notice this. Distinguished, that's what I am, he decided, and turned to remove a tweed jacket of uncommon tuftiness from a second hanger.

Busner's return to the popular media role that he had filled with such assurance – some might say bumptiousness – while a young male had been tempered by maturity. In the previous five years he had published three books[1] that had enormously augmented his reputation. While ostensibly collections of his patients' case histories, they had performed the unusual feat of making quite difficult themes and theories in the fields of psychology and neurology accessible to a wide audience. Further, this had not been achieved by in any way trivialising. Busner prided himself on not condescending to his readers.

The other noteworthy aspect of the books had been the dedication with which Busner had attached himself to his unusual patients. He had hit upon an observational and expository method that synthesised the objectivity and rationalism of his medical training at Edinburgh in the sixties, the imaginative flare and creative discipline imparted by his analytic training under the legendary Alkan[2], and the existential phenomenology of his work at the Concept House he had run in Willesden during the seventies. His patients were thus both studied under clinical conditions and also taken out into the wider world by Busner himself.

'The important thing,' Busner would sign his students and acolytes, 'is to achieve an inter-subjective "chup-chupp"

[1] *The Chimp Who Mated an Armchair*, 1986; *Nestings*, 1988; and *A Primatologist Recounts*, 1992. All published by Parallel Press, London and New York.
[2] For a full discussion of Alkan's analytic method see his 'Implied Techniques in Psychoanalysis' (*British Journal of Ephemera*, March 1956).

approach, somehow to enter the "euch-euch" morbid consciousness of the patient and see the world with his eyes. It is no longer sufficient to adopt a hard physiological attitude to certain disorders, or to view them as motivationally based, and therefore solely within the purlieus of "hooo" <pure> psychiatry . . .'

While this 'inter-subjective approach' had obvious and sound credentials, both intellectual and ethical, certain wags couldn't help noticing, and remarking upon, the bowdlerising tendencies of the practice. Like morbidly ebullient chimpanzee interest stories, Busner's case histories made great copy and highly entertaining television. In pursuit of his patients' distorted phenomenologies Busner would go waterskiing with paraplegics, to the opera with chronic epileptics, to acid-house raves with hebephrenics. It had even become somewhat *de rigeur* in publishing circles to have Busner and one of his protégés present at parties.

Thus chimps who barked involuntarily as they succumbed to the tics and spasms of Tourette's syndrome, or Parkinsonian chimps whose arms and legs undulated weirdly from the effects of L-dopa, or brain-damaged chimps whose gesticulatory sallies were imprisoned within the tape loop of acute amnesia, became a familiar social sight beside more conventionally behaved agents, authors and literary journalists, jostling for canapés and free drinks. 'It is,' Busner would sign to the little groups who congregated around him at such events, 'a practical demonstration of the "gru-nn" chimpunity of my approach to these disorders. By bringing these chimps into such settings' – and at this point he would usually have to break off and administer some emergency grooming to the chimp in question – 'I am "chup-chupp" actively deconstructing the ideological categories that surround our notions of disease.'

Busner finished dressing and jumped up to pull the rear-view mirror down on its retractable arm from the ceiling. Is my anus clean? he mused, sending one exploratory hand round his broad back to grope in its folds and pleats of yellow-pink ischial skin, then bringing it up to his flared nostrils and waggling lip. But despite the ghastly bout of the shits that had afflicted him when he got back from L'Escargot the previous evening, everything about his rear looked well sluiced. Gambol can go over it again on the way to the hospital, he decided, and straightening his jacket to ensure that the hem was above his magnificently effulgent arsehole, Busner snapped off the bathroom light, took a sprightly swing off the handhold at the side of the door, and bounded off down the corridor, his big balls swinging this way and that.

Busner's reappointment as Consultant at Heath Hospital had come midway through this popular renaissance in his career. And although he was still required to do some of the day-to-day grind of actually treating patients, it was more or less understood by the Trust that his presence there was as an elder stateschimp of the psychiatric fraternity, adding lustre to the hospital's reputation. He was allowed Gambol as a researcher, could pick and choose which patients he decided to concentrate on, and further, was able to cruise the intakes of other hospitals in the area, seeking out the kind of cases that would make good copy for his books.

Between projects at the moment, Busner was not looking forward to the day. A grindingly dull departmental meeting was scheduled for that morning, and in the late afternoon he was due to go into Univerity College to deliver the second of his public lectures on autism. This series, entitled 'Chimpanzees Who Groom Alone' was set to be immensely popular. Vaulting on to the podium to commence the first lecture, Busner was pleased to see that as well as the gaggle of – mostly bonobo – foreign students he had expected, there were a lot of lay chimps, as well as psychology and primatology students from the university faculty.

Nonetheless the whole subject of autism had rather palled. He had expressed most of what he wanted to in his book *A Primatologist Recounts*, and the prospect of going over it all again, even to a large and receptive audience, was not particularly exciting. What I need, he reflected as he bounded down the stairs, alternating between the handholds at different levels, is some new case history, exhibiting a syndrome or symptomatology never before encountered in psychiatry or neurology. Something unprecedented that hints at broad reevaluations of the very nature of chimpunity!

He paused before the door to the kitchen and summoned himself for the fray of his group, before leaping up to grab the lintel and swinging in.

The sight that met the distinguished doctor as he dropped to his feet and stood erect in the doorway was much as he expected. The Busners were a large group, and advancedly traditional as befitted their medical and academic bent. They were more subject to flux than most middle-class professional groups, with a core of some ten to fifteen members in residence at the Redington Road group home at any given time.

Zack Busner put great emphasis on the virtues of patrolling in the young, and would often physically eject sub-adult male members of the group from the house, occasioning raised eyebrow ridges and enquiring pant-hoots from their lippy neighbours in the tree-lined environs of Hampstead. Sub-adult females could get into trouble as well – if their alpha thought they were wasting an oestrus solely on endogamous mating, he would go up to Hampstead and round up some suitors for them himself.

But by the same token, as his reign as alpha male had extended, first to five, then to ten and now to almost fifteen years, so the fusion of the group had come to seem as important to him as its fission. At times, such as now, when two and possibly even three of the Busner females were in oestrus simultaneously, Zack accepted the influx of male group members with good grace. Even though he would find himself having to stump up for air fares for those of his adolescent wards who insisted on flying back to London from Bali, or the Côte d'Azur in order to mate endogamously.

When this happened the house would be packed to the seams with chimps of all ages, perhaps thirty in all, squabbling, scrapping, grooming and copulating. But it all made for the kind of good-natured rambunctiousness that Busner associated with his group, and he took it in his stride – even early in the morning.

The first chimp Busner noticed was Charlotte, the alpha Busner female, who was crouched on the flight of three stairs that separated the eating from the cooking area of the room, being mated by David, the gamma male, with his characteristic extreme nonchalance. David hadn't even troubled to discard the morning paper before effecting penetration, and Busner saw that he had it folded open on the ledge of Charlotte's back, and was scanning the leader page whilst thrusting. A gaggle of infants was trying to get in the way, leaping on David's back and shoulders.

Busner could only recognise one individual, his youngest infant Alexander. Spunky kid, he thought, for Alexander, although only two, had managed to get hold of the light fixture which dangled over the two trembling bodies, and was hanging from it by one arm, his tiny frame gyrating while he kicked David in the muzzle.

Busner took in the rest of the room with a glance, infants chucking second-breakfast bowls of sloes and custard apples about, sub-adults moodily and sulkily grooming each other in the corners, a couple of young mothers suckling, a couple of others up in the eating area preparing more second-breakfast bowls. The whole scene was well lit by the sunlight streaming in from the open french windows that let on to the garden, and through which a pair of the ubiquitous Busner lap ponies now trotted, tossing their heads and neighing reedily.

"HoooH'Graa'!" Busner pant-hooted, and drummed a little on the doorjamb, as befitted his status. He signed to Paula, one of his younger daughters, that she should prepare his second breakfast, then swaggered over to the mating pair, his fur half-erect.

34

On his arrival in the doorway the other adult males of the Busner group had all pant-hooted, saving David who was squealing his way towards climax. As the patriarch traversed the room all the members of his group, old, young, male, female, presented to him, and upon each of them he bestowed a touch of tenderness and hortatory greeting, here a kiss, there a caress.

There was a loose queue of males trailing down from the cooking area, more or less in correct dominance order, Henry behind David, Paul behind Henry. Busner wondered idly why David had been allowed first crack at Charlotte, but then as he rounded the breakfast bar at the top of the short flight of stairs, he saw that Dr Kenzaburo Yamuta, the distal-zeta male, was vigorously mating his daughter Cressida by the dishwasher, while Colin Weeks and Gambol awaited their turn.

'Morning "chup-chupp", Zack,' Kenzaburo signed, withdrawing from Cressida. 'Fancy a "huh-huh" fuck here?'

'No, no,' Busner signed in the process of delivering an affectionately brutal cuff to David, 'I'll just – "huh-huh-huh" ' – he broke into a satisfied pant as he smoothly entered Charlotte, who pushed herself backwards to ease him into her still further – 'give the old "chup-chupp" dear one first.' Busner juddered and shuddered, panting, squealing and then loudly tooth-clacking with satisfaction as he felt the soft, damp cushion of Charlotte's sexual swelling mush against his groin. But it took him almost a minute of thrusting before he achieved climax, one of Alexander's feet banging into his forehead the whole while, and a couple of the older infants leaping up and down on his broad back, their little hands entwined in his scruff.

Not like the old days, he reflected ruefully, withdrawing from Charlotte and wiping himself with a cloth that Frances, the epsilon female, had thoughtfully handed him. I remember mating Charlotte for the first time, I must have shot-off in less than ten seconds! Hoo how exquisite it was; truly youth is wasted on the young. He signed his gratitude to Frances and

35

remained resting by Charlotte for a few minutes, grooming the fine auburn fur around her ears, while Henry mated her, his big yellow teeth chattering.

He looked up to see that Cressida had finished with Kenzaburo and was presenting to him, a half-smile of encouragement on her gentle, liver-spotted muzzle. Busner laughed, panted, smacked his lips, and mated her in under thirty seconds, the pair of them squealing with delight. Cressida had always been his favourite daughter – although he couldn't have pointed out quite why. She certainly didn't have a swelling to match Betty or Isabel's, but there was something deeply affecting about her joyful submissiveness and overprotective mothering. Busner, although by no means a crass male chauvinist, was nonetheless fond of signing to his colleagues on the infrequent occasions that he went to the Flask with them for a drink after work, 'She's the one of my seventeen offspring that I feel most tender towards ... the seventeen "h'hee-hee" I know about, that is!'

Busner was aware of Gambol signing to him under his right arm as he was mating Cressida, but he didn't pay it much attention. Now, however, as he was wiping himself down again with a fresh cloth provided by another female, he did fully register Gambol's enquiring pant-hoot.

"H'huu," Gambol called, then signed, 'Something's come up, Zack, something that sounds very interesting –'

' "Euch-euch" can't it wait, Gambol, I haven't even had my second breakfast yet,' Busner countersigned, leaping clear over the breakfast bar out of a mixture of post-coital high spirits and irritation. He settled himself on one of the chairs surrounding the big circular pine-topped table that dominated the eating area, and indicated for Isabel, the delta, to approach with the two laden bowls of custard apples and sloes.

Busner picked up a copy of the *Guardian* that was lying on the table and began to leaf through the foreign news section, idly scanning the headlines: 'More Bonobo Massacres in Rwanda', 'President Clinton Urges Ceasefire in Bosnia', 'Accusations of Bonobism in O.J. Simpson Jury Selection'. Misery, misery, all is misery and aggression, Busner hooed to himself as he read. Perhaps it is as Lorenz suggestures, and the current woeful condition of chimpunity is a maladaptive response to overcrowding, to the loss of our natural lifestyles?

'Boss' Gambol had wormed his scrawny body under the kitchen table and was fingering Busner's dangling left foot. 'This really is something "gru-nn" exciting, something I feel we should ges –' Busner cut him short by jerking his foot away. With an agility and strength that immediately accounted for his long reign over the group, he pushed himself back in the chair and directed an accurate and forceful cuff to the back of Gambol's head. This blow temporarily stunned the hapless research assistant and he sprawled full-length on the sea-grass matting. Busner then followed up the lightning attack by vaulting off his chair and planting both his large feet full in the small of Gambol's back.

"Wraaf!" barked the eminent psychiatrist, and then bending down and grabbing him by the scruff he signed on the muzzle of the epsilon male with his left foot, 'Shut the fuck down, Gambol, you little piece of shit. When I want you muscling in on my second breakfast, you miserable subordinate creep, I'll ask you to, but for now just shut the fuck down! "Waaa"!'

'I'm sorry, boss, I'm sorry,' Gambol flourished frantically, his darting hands emerging from the pod of his crouching body. 'I didn't mean "eek-eek" to annoy you so much, please don't beat up on me, please.' He half squatted and presented to Busner, his scut quivering.

'That's all right, honey-bunny, I didn't mean to hit you so hard, wassums,' Busner gestured, grunting softly. 'You're still my favourite itty-bitty research assistant.' He reached out a hand, still roaring with pain after the blow he had inflicted, and tenderly stroked Gambol's ruffled back fur. For a while Busner groomed Gambol, removing some particles of what looked like solidified correction fluid from the thick fur between the epsilon's shoulder blades.

Typical young intellectual on the make, Busner thought as he opened up parting after parting in Gambol's fur. Doesn't groom enough, doesn't mate enough. Why, without his position as my factotum I don't think he'd have any designation in the hierarchy, let alone epsilon. He finished off this purely formal groom of reassurance with a tweak of Gambol's nape hair.

Gambol moved away from the table, still presenting, his hands flickering from behind his back. 'Thank you, Zack, thank you, I acknowledge your suzerainty. I admire your eminence, I revere your reign over the group, your anal scrag enfolds us all "grnnn".'

'Get the car out of the garage, Gambol,' Busner snapped. 'We'll go to the hospital in about twenty minutes, as soon as I've finished my second breakfast.' Busner pulled himself back up on to his chair and resumed munching on some sloes, mashing the bitter juice of the berries through his strong molars, savouring it. He turned once more to the *Guardian,* and with an ease borne of long experience, shut his large and gnarled ears to the hubbub of the kitchen, the squeals of infants, pants of copulating adults and neighing of lap ponies.

It took quite a lot longer than twenty minutes for Zack Busner to finish his second breakfast. The milkmale dropped that fortnight's bill in, cause enough for another round of mating, as was the arrival home of Dave 2, another of Busner's offspring, who worked for a bonobo community organisation in Hackney. By the time all the males present had covered Charlotte and Cressida again it was getting on for ten.

'I'm off now, dear,' Busner signed to Charlotte, who was still crouching on the stairs, her vagina bleeding a little. 'Try not to overdo the mating, remember what happened last oestrus. "Grnnn" I shouldn't be too late. In fact, I think I'll come back after my lecture, I'd like to do some reading at home this afternoon. "H'huuu"?' he enquired.

'OK, Zack, but you know how hard it is to refuse them, and there's so many sub-adult males in the house, what is one to d –' She stopped wringing her hands. One of the sub-adult males in question, William, was waving a couple of tea towels around, trying to get Charlotte's attention with this pathetic courtship display.

Busner considered William. The young male was shaping up very nicely, sleek brown-black fur, fine eyebrow ridges,tidily recessed nasal bridge, pale muzzle – every inch the Busner. "HoooGrnn," pant-grunted William, his vocalisation warbling up and down the scale, and then signed, 'May I mate you, please, Auntie, please "huuu"?'

Busner moved over to William and administered a few swingeing blows to his muzzle with his left – and not so arthritic – hand. "Wraaf"! he barked, then signed, 'Leave your poor aunt alone, can't you see the state of her vagina. She's got quite enough senior males to mate this oestrus, without worrying about you whippersnappers.'

William retreated to the garden whimpering and signing, 'Sorry, Alph, sorry, Auntie.'

Busner turned to survey the room with its teaming horde of chimps. "HoooGraaa!" he pant-hooted, impressing on the gathering the force and potency of his valediction – and by extension himself. The senior male chimps broke off eating, mating and grooming to salute him, and he left the room.

Marigold, one of the Busner infants, aged around four, came scuttling down the stairs with his briefcase. 'Here you are, Uncle,' she gestured, dragging it towards him. 'Have a good day at the hospital.' Busner took the briefcase and bestowed a drooly kiss on the little female. He checked his arsehole once more in the hall mirror, then let himself out the front door.

Chapter Four

S imon barely acknowledged the receptionist at the Sealink
Club, who, recognising him as a roller who got high and
then acted it, was fulsome-ish.

The club was underground – in site only. The reception
lobby was accessed down two flights of stairs. Wide, plush
treads, ochre walls with the uplights set behind horrid metal
basketry – keeping the illumination down, taking the members
down. You could imagine a judge saying 'Take her down!' and
the cold shock of realising you've been sentenced to a lifetime's
networking.

Through the swing doors from the lobby was the club's
main room. This was dominated by a bulging belly of a bar,
buckled into its leatherette décor by belts of chrome, a corset
of mirroring and scintillating steel suspenders. The Sealink's
clientele – or members, this place was, after all, as private as
any utterly public place can be – hung off the bar, or housed
themselves in the conchate seats in the conchate seating areas;
they flipped their leather fins and floated up to the restaurant
on the gallery level, or upended and dived down to the toilets
and table-football room on the level below the bar. But mostly
they just sat there, cemented in place by their secretions of
chatter.

For, if a net were to be cast into the Sealink Club and
trawled through its corridors and vestibules – even a seine
net, monofilamented, micro-meshed, gill-slicing – all it

40

would come up with would be a few spluttering servitors, or gasping groupers who had ligged their way in.

No, to catch one moiety of the members you'd need a pot or cage, baited with publicity, or gossip, or innuendo, or money, or all four; or combinations thereof: gossip about money, public innuendo, lucrative publicity, and so on. Because this lot were bottom feeders, pure and simple, who came to the club in the unadulterated spirit of undersea exploration, to check out how low they could go.

As for the other moiety, well, you'd have to say that they were even easier to catch, if no better to eat. All that would be required to land them was a low tide – which came twice in the twenty-four, at noon and three in the morning, when the barroom was little more than a muddy flat of wrack – a dinghy which could be manoeuvred around the downlights – which were set behind horrid metal basketry – and a long knife-arm, with which to reach down and prise them from the carpeting.

For this box-load were bivalves – to an hermaphrodite. Eyeless in the gloom, de-tentacled by devolution, possessing at most one febrile limb with which to lift a glass or tote a cigarette, they reposed as the currents of conversation flowed through them, extracting sufficient nutriment simply by the act of being. Some argued – and Simon was on occasion among them, there had to be some defence – that if a grain of insight, a granule of originality, were inserted into their cloistered, sharp-edged minds, placed on the mantel where the invitations sat, it might well be cultured, swaddled in a carbonate of some kind until it formed, if not wisdom, at any rate something resembling culture. But Simon only ever said this when he was drunk and full of the world. Drunk, and so full of the world that the world must be good – or at any rate capable of inclusion – for him to be so full of it.

Sarah saw Simon from the stool where she still sat. Saw him pause in the doorway while two sumo suits squeezed by him, saw him crane his neck to scan the room, while at the same time dipping his eyes down, keen to avoid the taint of seeming to scan the room. The very sight of him lanced across the room to Sarah, every entrance he made was a penetration of her; and every time that he left, it was a slithery, warm withdrawal.

She unglued her thighs in anticipation, signalled to Julius that he was required, twirled on the stool to summon the shiny happy people, then finally turned right round to face Simon, thighs now parted, and guided him into her.

Simon and Julius arrived at the back and front of Sarah simultaneously. Simon bent down and kissed her at one side and then the other of her lips. She placed a hand on the nape of his neck, feeling the scalp beneath the hair and held him against her face until his lips nuzzled sideways to her mouth. Then their tongues slithered over and under, pink shrews blindly questing. Her small knees pincered his thick thighs. She wouldn't let him go, wouldn't let him order a drink, until she had the firm reassurance of him, that crosstown coil of erectile tissue with which she had drawn him in, and now landed him. And Simon felt relieved too. Relieved in her attraction to him – a different kind of visceral update.

His gusset unstuck from his perineum, his clothes dried on his sticky flesh as if a blast of cool, dry air had been blown up his sleeves and trouser legs. The stubble on his cheek softened to fur, the gunk on his eyes and mouth turned from sour to sweet. She sensed through his nape all the embarrassment of the kiss, and yet she still held him, challenged him to withdraw, to reject her in any way. This, naturally, he did.

"Hello, darling," he said, and then to Julius, "My man." They shook hands.

The barman stood behind his bar, all barman. White apron, white shirt, black tie tucked just-so. Behind him his reflected back was equally exact. The ranks of bottles proclaimed near-pharmaceutical alleviation of whatever ailed Simon; and Julius, the physician, prepared for the laying-on of hands. "Can I assist you, sir," he intoned, "to a refreshing beverage?"

Simon regarded Julius as if he had never before encountered such a noble barman and this was his first visit to the Sealink. He straightened up, aware of the importance, the solemnity of ordering. He yanked the bottom hem of his nondescript black jacket and placed his blunt hands in the pockets of his nondescript black trousers. If there had been a nondescript black tie knot around the neck of his unremarkable white shirt, you could have been certain that he would have straightened it before replying, "A large Glenmorangie for myself, straight up. A Samuel Adams to chase it . . . and for you, my little monkey? The usual?" The toque tilted.

Tony Figes appeared next to Sarah, ostentatiously blowing his nose on a piece of thick paper towel. "Simon . . ." he drawled, and the two men awkwardly embraced, side on; Tony's scar writhed. The drinks were placed gently in front of Sarah. Simon asked Tony if he would like something, and then widened the order to encompass the Braithwaites and Tabitha, who had sidled up and who also had the sniffles. The snotty children waited – like the good adults they were – for their drinks.

"Simon," Tony redrawled, "how was the opening?"

"Open," Simon countersigned, "partially, at any rate."

One of the Braithwaites palmed him a wrap, hip bones touched, hands stroked. Simon was in possession and even the tenth part of the law was far away from him now. He raised his eyebrow ridges at Sarah and the two of them, without further preamble, sidled away from the group, sidled across the room, out of the doors, and took the stairs down to the car-deck room.

Down in the car-deck room Simon went to where the window should have been, and under a downlight that illuminated a duff political cartoon – axes labelled 'cuts' – opened the wrap. The cocaine was yellow and lumpy. It looked good. He raised his eyebrows again, and she tilted her toque once more. He was halfway through chopping out the lines on the rough pseudo-grain of a large television, which was camouflaged so as to resemble

43

a sea locker, when he broke off, gestured with the corner of his credit card.

"Good day?"

"Mmm."

"By which?"

"Crap. Boring too."

"Talk about it?"

"Nah."

He carried on chopping, scientifically, feeling the chemical crunch of plastic on granule.

When she took the rolled note and bent her head to snort the line, perspective was re-banished; she became an ochre swathe of face with pinkness in the exposed interior of the nostril. The swathe wound back into a bolt, which turned to him, becoming a face. "Simon?"

"Umph." He took the note. The cocaine burned his nose and anaesthetised it at the same time. Alternative medicine. Like the sodden cloth of a ragamuffin at traffic lights the drug squeegeed its way over his fore-brain, both clouding and cleaning his mind. Then he was erect and erect, Kundalini currents running both ways. Perhaps I have two spines, he thought inconsequentially, backing his petite lover between the chunky furnishings. She ended up in the corner of the room, his mouth clamped over hers.

Downstairs in the bar, Tony Figes was putting the bite on a journalist.

"It's like some neurological disorder," he told the man, who wrote a column on columns. "A compulsion to say, write, do, the glibbest and most ephemeral thing possible; a kind of glibolalia –"

"Give me an example," the man replied. He was fat, with licks of vanilla hair on a conical head, but despite this – or perhaps because of it – he wasn't going to be intimidated by a faggot.

"Well." Tony's scar squirmed. "What you wrote about the raising of veal calves in your column yesterday."

"What was wrong with that?" The fat man – whose name was Gareth – moderated his tone. Even if he was to be criticised, at least he had been read.

"You added nothing to the debate. All you said was that the mental state of the animal was an unknowable thing –"

"And isn't it?"

"Possibly, but the only authority you quoted was another newspaper article."

"Drink, Tone?" This was from Tabitha, who had interposed half her long body, half her long hair. Gareth stiffened to avoid contact, the leggy girl was that sexy; and where they were standing, hard against the bar, fast becoming a thicket of arms and legs, with burning tobacco foliage.

"Thank you, Tabitha, a Stolli martini, please –"

"Straight up?" Julius fed Tony from behind the bar.

"Straight up, but then wiggle it a bit, please. Then pull it out again, but put it straight back up." Tony gave his double smile to Gareth, who shivered with distaste.

"It wasn't another newspaper article – I quoted Wittgenstein ... Wittgenstein's theory about private language." Gareth took a pull on his glass of white wine and peered down at his interlocutor's bald patch.

"Certainly you quoted what you *thought* was Wittgenstein, but actually you misquoted him, because you lifted the quote from an article on exactly the same subject that appeared on Sunday, I think you know which one I mean." And Tony snorted, realising too late that a glob of cocaine and mucus was poised on the very lip of his nostril. This shot down in a near-vertical trajectory and lodged on the rim of Gareth's shoe. Fortunately the journalist didn't notice. Although Tabitha did, and dissolved in giggles.

"So what if I did? I don't think that goes to prove anything much. Why don't you address yourself to the real questions, instead of trying to score points."

45

"Ho-hoo! The real issue. Is that it? The real issue." The critic was becoming agitated now. Animals were Tony's first – perhaps only – love. He lived in a council flat in Camberwell with his mother, who looked like an ancient Labrador; and an ancient Labrador. "So, if that's the case, under what circumstances do you feel it's acceptable to raise veal calves in crates where they can't move, where they can't do anything but slam their heads against the planks until they're bruised and bleeding? Perhaps if we could be certain that the beasts weren't in any real distress it would be acceptable, hmmm?'

Gareth was not to be humiliated. Or rather, he had been humiliated so long ago that everything which had followed was nothing but mint on the lamb of shame. He hated Figes and his little clique. The sexy girls, the two apparently mute blacks, the painter Dykes with his sniffy attitude. He looked down at his shoe and saw that a glob of whitish mucus was lodged on the rim of the toe. He discreetly smeared this off on the carpet – ten hours later this residuum was hoovered up by a Guatemalan cleaner, dressed in blue overalls – then came back at Tony: "That's irrelevant. Whether I misquoted or not, the point I made still stands – we can't know the animal's state of mind."

'Well, shrinks now apparently have the humility to admit that they don't know anything about depression. They just hand out the drugs and if the patient responds then they say that they have a depression that is responsive to such-and-such a drug. So perhaps we should do that with the veal calves, give them Prozac and if they *seem* to be happier take it as read that they are. I can see quite a brisk trade being done in the flesh of calves raised on Prozac, can't you?"

"You're being idiotic. Very silly." And Gareth contrived to notice someone on the far side of the bar, someone he needed to talk to urgently, right away. "Excuse me." He rotated his figure on its axis and abstracted it.

Tony called after him, "Or how about venison on Valium?"
And Tabitha chimed in, "or ham on haloperidol?"

The clique dissolved in forced laughter, which left them with the uneasy feeling of not-having-been-fair to the man.

"But seriously," said Ken Braithwaite, the older of the brothers by three minutes, "if we eat the meat of animals who have been physically tortured, perhaps we should be more imaginative about it."

"Whaddya mean?" Tony was dipping one of his mouths in his martini, the other one nuzzled at the side of the glass.

"Well, how about eating the flesh of animals who have been emotionally abused?"

"Hmmm, nice idea. You mean persistently sexually humiliate pheasants – and then shoot them?"

"Something like that."

"Or," Tabitha said, clutching the little ball of humour and running with it, "chickens that have been socially ostracised, maddened by the fact that they aren't invited to parties."

"Sort of free-rage chickens, you mean?" said Tony.

"Which reminds me," said Tabitha, "if *we're* going to rage, we'd better do some of these." She already had the pills, dusty with lint, secreted in her hand and she palmed one each to Tony and the Braithwaites.

"Wozzthis?" queried Steve, the younger Braithwaite, but after popping it.

"E," Tabitha slurred – she was chewing hers up for a quicker rush. "Good too. White dove."

"That's all I want to eat from now on in," said Ken Braithwaite, skulling his with a swallow of beer. "The breasts of white doves raised on ecstasy."

Beneath the basement they stood in were the kitchens, and beneath this was Bazalgette's main sewer conduit for Soho, a Victorian creation originally tiled in green, but for so long unseen that the green was neither here – nor there, where brown rats squeaked horribly. Hosts of them, crawling up and over, through and under one another, as if dimension was of no account. They copulated in passing, their long tails

47

twined in scaly knitting. And on their backs, in the filthy fur that covered their bodies – little sacs of organs – the lice trundled, excremental eggs plopping from their abdomens.

In Soho Square – where the hunt was centuries gone – two mutts mucked about with one another. The dog covered the bitch, entirely. For his legs were as long as the bitch's body. He crouched to snag his corkscrew in, and then twisted it, twisted it. The two bodies shuddered, half on the grass – half off. On-side nails scratched the paving, off-side nails found purchase in the grass. The dog's fore-paws flapped, then twitched, then spasmodically waved. He was too big for the job, his part-Alsatian body heeled over, like a shaggy yacht with too much sail on, and too late he felt his cock hook in hard under the bitch's bone. Then they were arse to arse, horribly mated, awfully fucked. They yowled and yowled and yowled.

In the green deep, off the continental shelf, where the leviathans keep only each other's company, a penis the size of a lifeboat was unlimbered, swung out on its davit of sinew, and then plunged gently into its oceanic counterpart. The two vastnesses nuzzled one another, moved closer together with ridiculously subtle movements of their tails, each the length of a suburban cul-de-sac. Their underslung mouths parted to reveal curtains of baleine, enough to stricture a school of women. Barnacles on belly grated against barnacles on back. Their theramin cries swooped and oscillated weirdly. Of such creatures it could never be said that they came, only that they had departed. Quit the earth first, now exited the sea.

In the car-deck room Simon groomed Sarah. His finger traced the soft line of her buttock, beneath the soft line of her pants, beneath the soft fabric of her skirt. She grunted, leant into him, tucked the whole of herself beneath his barbellate chin. Her fingers scampered on his flocculent chest. The cleft of her was in the corner, in line with a cleft of cornice, a cleft of carpet, a cleft of plaster. He bit her lip. His finger explored – he was almost bent double to encompass her – hooked up the hem of her skirt, blotted itself on the inky top of her stocking, and then imprinted his touch on the white flesh above. Dab and dab and dab. Leaving dabs. He explored the lightly wrapped crotch of her, hair bunching in damp flawless flaw. Her sex was gaping. He visualised it swelling. He moaned. She moaned. "Touch me," she whispered, muffled by his mouth. He did. The elastic rimmed his finger. He sunk the emissary inside, scouted the gaff, looked for a place to leave the genetic evidence. Her little paws moved down, swirling, over shirt to belt. Simon thought of an axe-shaped turd he had once extracted from where it was wedged in his son's arse cleft. "Monkey, monkey," he uttered in her mouth.

The door to the car-deck room banged open and Tabitha stood there guffawing, a drink slopping in her hand. "What have we here?" She turned up the fader switch by the door. "Love in a dim climate, or what?" Sarah and Simon broke. His hand went to his nose, he added musk to mucus, cunt to cocaine. Tabitha threw herself in a chair. She was wearing a very short skirt and her legs were hosed in something matt yet shiny, emphasising their great length, their insulting shapeliness. "There's fuck-all happening down there," she continued, grabbing handfuls of her tawny hair and pulling them upwards, a characteristic gesture "The shiny happy people and I have dropped an E, but it doesn't look as if you two need one."

Sarah still stood in the corner, she had hoicked her skirt up to rearrange her blouse and underwear. "Hoo, I dunno, Simon?"

"God, I really shouldn't –"

"Shouldn't, or don't want to?" Tabitha's tone mocked him, lassoed him with double meaning. She always fancied her sister's men, wanted them. Although whether this was out of competitiveness, or genuine attraction, was impossible to say.

"Shouldn't, mustn't, really ought not to. I've got to work all day tomorrow and it's getting edgy, I open next week."

"But, Simon." She rose and crossed towards him, came right up to him, so close he could smell her, see the saliva behind her lips. A pill appeared between her thumb and forefinger, she took it into orbit in the space between their faces. "Next week is on the dark side of this moon, wouldn't you say." The little white satellite rose again and was dropped into his open mouth. Simon turned away, picked up his whisky and washed the thing down.

They stayed on in the club for quite a while, despite the fact that there was fuck-all happening. In fact they revelled in the fuck-alledness of it. Submerged themselves in this lukewarm footbath of anti-sociability, with its froth of tragic bathos. Until the ecstasy bit Simon drank to offset the great oubliette of emptiness and self-loathing he felt the cocaine about to tip open beneath his feet; and he took the cocaine to keep him sober. His natural geniality was not yet the aberrant genitality it would become; now it was simply crushed and then extruded from between the up and the down. And so he flowed all over the bar, talking, talking, talking. And always joking, hurling witticisms, looping in people he barely knew, people he didn't even like.

The shiny happy people formed a core group in one of the seating arrangements; those moving past would prop themselves on the arms of chairs to pick up their niblets, to insinuate themselves. It was nearly eleven when George Levinson turned up, plainly drunk and smartly dressed. He had lost the boy he'd picked up at the opening in Chelsea, but managed to acquire another one over dinner at Grindley's. The good thing – as far as the clique was concerned – was that this boy had a girlfriend, a girlfriend who was even drunker than George. Drunker than any of them in fact, and as they saw it gauche as well. She lunged across the table knocking over glasses, she made jokes that fell utterly flat – providing no relief whatsoever – she lolled against the gay and inveighed against the straight, she talked about drugs, loudly. In a word, she was a *find*. A find because every clique needs to have a litmus paper on hand with which to test its acidity, its determination to dissolve and exclude foreign bodies.

Simon joined in with this, assisted George in his bantering attempts to prise the boy away from the girl. Whenever they linked arms, or showed one another any physical affection, George would butt in, crying 'Say no to hugs! Hugging is a crime!' And then Simon would take up the cry, and then the others. 'Hugging is a crime!' They all cried. It was, Simon reflected, staring moodily at the distorting lens that was the bottom of his whisky glass, a ludicrously appropriate slogan for the clique, the members of which only ever touched one another on greeting or parting. For the rest of the time – especially when in this desert of white powder – touch was a mirage.

Simon looked across at Sarah and felt this. Felt that he might never touch her again, might never hug her again, feel her bird-brittle ribs against his. There was an undulation in the air now, a distortion that pushed her still further away, across an acre of table, several furlongs of carpet. She sat, shiny-browed, blanched in chemical sweat, listening to Steve Braithwaite explain some detail of a new artwork. She was their agent, so this made sense. Indeed, the clique were really her friends, not his. George wasn't a shiny happy person, he belonged to Simon, to Simon's past, to his marriage to Jean. He was Magnus's godfather. Seeing him with the shinies felt wrong, uneasy. Like catching a favourite, jolly uncle coming down the seedy stairs from some whorish fuck pad.

Not only that, his presence showed the clique up for what they were, spoilt children, playing viciously because unsupervised.

"I'm going to walk," said Steve Braithwaite, "from the nuclear power station at Dounreay, all the way to Manchester, staying right under the power lines for the entire distance. Ken will make a visual and aural record of the whole thing –"

"What's the point of that?" the girl broke in.

"The point, young – and ignorant – lady," George Levinson

went offensively on to the offensive, "is to experience various kinds of parallax. Isn't that it, Steve?"

"Exactly. Both the parallax of vision derived from the pylons themselves – the way they march, girdered clefs stringing the notation of power across the land –"

"Quoting from my – as yet unwritten – catalogue copy are we, Steve?" Figes donated his pennyworth.

"And, of course, the parallax of power itself. As I absorb all of this incredibly damaging radiation, as my cells themselves begin to fission, so I will be gifted a true fusion, a proper perspective on the nature of power, raw power, in our society. D'you see?"

"No I don't," the girl slurred. "I think it sounds like a load of crap. All this stuff is just crap. It's not art, it's crap. Crappy crap. It's toilet art, the sort of thing *anybody* might think of sitting on the bog, but it takes a real idiot to get up, wipe himself and then actually go out and do it. It's crap."

"She seems to think our idea's crap," Steve said to his brother. Ken sucked on his cigarette and squinted at the girl, who was sexy in an overweight sort of way. Long black hair, vaguely Eurasian features, lips that looked not so much bee-stung as swarmed upon.

"She could have a point," he replied, eventually. "Mind you – it's only at the ideas stage."

Simon felt a tinge of guilt, doubly so. He agreed with the girl about the Braithwaites' stuff, it was toilet art. Suitable only for flushing away. And even after *that* the smears it left in the conceptual bowl would still need to be vigorously brushed, zapped with naturalistic Domestos. It was as terminally irrelevant as the photogravure silkscreens he and George had seen earlier that evening. He also felt guilty because he wouldn't have minded fucking the girl. No, this was incorrect, he wanted to take the girl away somewhere quiet and sequestered. Find out all about her – her thoughts, aspirations, girlish memories – and then make love to her with a virtuosity so great as to be world-beating, a timeless exploration and elaboration on the fact of love. This very deep love he felt for her. Simon was, he realised, coming up on the E.

Why now did he think about his children? Why now, when he should have been able to abandon them anew, did the smell of them and the sight of them cut in front of his vision of the girl? Where were they? In their beds in the Brown House in Oxfordshire. Asleep under flowered counterpanes, their gummy mouths stickily exhaling, stickily inhaling, the sweetness at the heart of them. In the humming bar, edged now with chemical distortion, underpinned by the sensurround of his labouring heart, he saw the three umbilici snaking towards him, festooned over furniture, the shoulders of journalists and television producers coiling across the floor, and all converging on the pit of him, threatening to turn him inside out with the acknowledgement of the longing-for-them.

What was he doing here with these children – and so clearly without his own? He looked across at Sarah, who was now listing towards the girl, casting her off still more from the boyfriend who George, all sharp suiting and blunt technique, was working over. What was he doing here – what was George doing here? Too tall and too old for this company, the art dealer was almost primly erect, his false-coloured hair smarmed down over his low brow, his oval designer spectacles, his floppy bow tie, all bespoke someone who was not cut out for this creche. Having him there was almost like having Jean here. Jean looking at Simon from under a straight fringe, eyes aglow with religious semi-fervour.

Yes, we, they, us, we are children. Children playing like chimpanzees in the jungle gym of the night. We have no application, no purchase on this present with its terminal self-referentiality, its ahistorical self-obsession. We are brothers and sisters, in a sibling society – fighting over the toy box. We are allowed to come here and behave thus, while elsewhere meaning resides. No wonder we're reduced to such pathetic expedients, excluding her, including him, in order to establish some platform from which we can swing, out, over the abyss. What if we fell? What if armed men, some band of Balkan freebooters, raided the club. Took all these lovely men and shot them, these lovely girls and raped them?

A band of Balkan freebooters raided the Sealink Club. They shot their way through reception, firing from the hip. "Members, eurghhhh . . ." was all Samantha – who was on – had the opportunity to say before five rounds from the AK gave her an impressive cleavage – although not the one she had always wanted. The gunmen fanned out. Two took the stairs down to the toilets, two burst into the main bar, one stayed in reception and guarded the door.

For seconds after the two armed men entered the barroom nothing happened. Through the swing doors the hubbub of chatter was so loud that the fracas in reception had been interpreted as just that, a minor fracas, a drunk withheld admission – or allowed it.

Having obtained temporary membership with unusual dispatch, they stood, rifles propped on hips, bandoleers sagging around sweat-stained fatigues. They were tired, so fucking tired, and the sight of so many expensively dressed people, drinking cocktails and smoking American cigarettes, stunned them. As for the members, they barely noticed the armed men. They were a little shabby for the club, and must be – or so those who *did* notice them thought – some music company execs from one of the independent labels. Either that, or maverick ad men.

So slight was the intrusion, that one plump young woman, who was sitting by the doors pleased with herself in a backless, black velvet dress, kindly asked the taller and ranker of the two, to shift the position of his rifle because the stock was tickling her spine.

The men recovered themselves and shouldered their way to the bar. Julius came along it to meet them. The taller, smellier man eyed the barman. He was barely more than a youth, but his face was mottled with the horrors he had witnessed. It was a collage of clashing colours, brushstrokes of green nausea, a wash of white fear, blotches of red anger and a tinge of blue death. His stubble had marched for ten days and was nearing beard. His breath reeked of some vile barn-distilled liquor. His eyes were loose in a string bag of veins. His brain was hot, swollen. "Can I assist you, sir," Julius intoned, "to a refreshing beverage?"

The freebooter was having none of this – he didn't understand the question, for one thing. Perhaps if he had things would have turned out differently, a few quiet drinks, a little networking; a series of articles on the conflict for the Sundays. But as it was he grabbed the barman by his neat little goatee and yanked his head down on to the bar's metallic surface so hard that Julius's jaw shattered with a CRACK! that could only mean violence.

This at last brought about silence – although slowly. Those clustered around the bar saw what had happened immediately and their jaws also fell. Others, further off, standing in the vacant spaces, heard this silence and matched it. But those in the clustered seats still further from the bar – including the clique and their hangers-on – remained oblivious, gabbing away for some seconds, until, in the stun-gap the words, "Like, what does *he* know about styling, he's never even been on a shoot . . . " lingered and then died in the inspissating atmosphere.

"Simon?" Sarah's little paw was on his knee. He looked up from the glass ball of his glass, in which he had been scrying this alternative future. "Are you OK?"

"Yeah, yeah. Fucked – I guess."

"Me too," she replied, and then, "Good stuff."

"Mmm. Yeah . . . mmm."

"Maybe . . . maybe we should go on somewhere?"

"Go on . . . ?"

"Somewhere."

Chapter Five

It took a series of phased withdrawals for Simon, Sarah and their clique to leave the Sealink. Each time they achieved a tittering quorum they discovered that a voter was absent. Someone would be sent out to scout the bogs, the telly room, the restaurant and recover the errant suspect. But by the time they'd been rounded up someone else would have gone missing. Figes kept on sliding off to try and pick up boys, as did George Levinson. Tabitha cantered up and down the bar, gathering ungentlemanly gnats around her seductive mane.

Julius was going to join them. He knew of some shebeen or other. In Cambridge Circus – or wherever. Thought there might be crap coke. Knew there would be liquor. But there were further problems – not just gathering the right people but excluding the wrong ones. And the drugs made it all so difficult. The ecstasy made their sociable instincts break out along with the sweat. Everyone was worthy of their attention – inclusion in their lives.

During this whole jump-cut episode of leaving-the-club, Simon had a fully formed interlude of near seduction, involving a girl he remembered talking to about Dada, at a party he couldn't remember attending. "Think of me as your Dada," he said to her on this occasion, on this half-landing. "I will care, protect and –"

"Molest me?" She giggled, showing wine-stained teeth,

flicked her hair back which he hated, but chose to ignore.

"Exactly."

He moved in on her like a landing module about to coyly retract its legs on impact with a porous, lunar surface, and . . . was snagged by the back of his jacket, turned to see Steve Braithwaite. "Tch-tch," admonished the self-denigrating performance artist, "we're all waiting for you in the reception. *Sarah* too."

"You aren't," Simon replied. He was managing the strange feat of backing away from the girl without giving her so much as a backward glance.

At last they left – last. Samantha was shunting the dregs of the crowd out through the main door. They revolved in its revolution and found themselves still spinning in D'Arblay Street. In the group that trolled off through the mountainous streets of London were the shiny happy people plus George, the irritating girl, her boyfriend, Gareth the hack, and three other nameless but recurring minor characters. A tall vampish woman, wearing a black corset over a grey dress – she'd taken a shine to George, presumably unaware of his orientation, but then, looking at the way she was heading it was perhaps wrong to presume anything; a show-business lawyer with a coke problem, who talked of nothing but scams scammed and scummy money skimmed; and a girl Simon had noticed many times in the club before, a very very pretty girl, silky hair, slight figure, girlie dress which twirled from the hips. She was, he thought, too young to be here, or anywhere other than tucked up in bed, next to a nightlight with a Disney shade.

The cavalcade headed down Wardour Street, words fluttering around them. Simon tasted his own metallic cud and began fully to regret the evening, regret it with deep, passionate loathing. They could have been in bed. They could have been sober. They could have made love without him having to be a poor workman, once again blaming his tool. As it was his resistance to more drink, more crap cocaine, more of everything, was all but departed. He would – he realised with the shock of the old – do almost anything, or *anyone*.

Tabitha and Sarah walked arm in arm shouting at one another. The squat machines were moving along the dawn gutters, their automatic revolving brushes and jets of water stir-broiling the trash. Fat black whores stood on the corners. 'Business?' they enquired with third-mondial weariness of the revellers passing by, as if they were Wabenzi hustling the IMF. We're a caparisoned horde of enlightened fun seekers! Simon said to himself one instant. We're a sad trickle of dysfunctional debauchees, he took on board the next. Julius's goatee was out in front. A pointless point, walking point.

The shebeen was up four flights and had as many more oddly shaped rooms stacked up stairs with too-steep treads. They got in with a Julius's say so and a clutch of notes. The crowd inside was more densely packed than that at the Sealink, and far more polyglot. Big black guys, slab-sided, grey-sheened, were holding intense conversations with each other in huddled colloquy. Elsewhere they danced with young white girls, who were tightless, short-skirted and wearing white sling-backs. The colourist in Simon appreciated the fact that even here, even with the violet, pink and blue flashing lighting, he could still make out the stippling of brown goose pimples on the backs of their calves. He considered how he might depict this. The music was needling, thudding, reverberant ragga. "Ya-ya-ya-Hi'-ya-ya-ya-Inna side you like / Inna way you like / Thass the way you like / Me to show you / Ya-ya-ya-Hi'!" Again and again and again. To Simon the music's repetitiveness might have been its actual subject: "Ya-ya-ya-Hi'-ya-ya-ya-Annagain an'again / Thass the way you like it / Again annagain . . ."

Faces moved towards Simon and passed him by. Each one seemed to contain the outline of a possible intimacy. A set of coordinates and congruencies from which five, ten or twenty years of conversations and cuddles might have been extrapolated by some computer modelling, a morphing of relationships. Sarah had been holding his hand, but she seemed to have faded now, been absorbed into the shebeen's lurid ochre. Simon struggled to the bar and managed to secure four tumblers of warm, rank vodka. Tony Figes appeared at his shoulder and took one. His stamp of hair had been peeled off in a corner that exposed the pate of an older man; his scar was deeply grooved.

"You know how they get this?"

"Wassthat?"

"You know how they get this – get *this* . . ." Tony was holding up his cup.

"N-no."

"They take those teenage girls out back, strip them down, then they sponge them off and squeeze the sponges out into a vat. Then they re-bottle it."

"Ha-ha," Simon said – he couldn't laugh, his throat was a cement mixer, and so numb he couldn't feel the viscid mortar blocking it up, choking it off.

"Simon! Tony!" It was Tabitha, gesturing to them from the stairs. They went up to the room above, and found the others chopping out lines on some kind of shelf that was sticking out from the wall at an irrelevant angle.

"Line?" Ken Braithwaite was holding up the credit card interrogatively. What a senseless go-round, thought Simon, but said, "Yeah, thanks, Ken."

"And that's your last." This from Sarah who looked now like Simon's mother, or some long-left lover, not like herself.

"Izzthatso?" He took the note from Ken, rammed it up to where he felt the paper edge snag and ground in bloody snot, like the keel of a miniature boat on granular shingle. He added a couple of milligrams of crap to this headborne midden. Simon swigged on the vodka, felt it jolt and ram down his throat, took a pull on his googolth Camel, but couldn't sense its smoke. He could go on for . . . *ever*.

"Right we're off."

"Are we?"

"We are."

There weren't even proper farewells, only glottal garbles and ape-like hoots. She had him by the elbow, and like some mahout who by subtle pressures and sotto commands can direct the amble of a vast, potentially truculent beast, goaded him down the stairs, through the long queues of youth, along the bulging corridor, past the two slick toughs in their string vests, black dungarees and holstered mini-phones, then out into the pewter dawn of central London.

"What about Tabitha?" asked Simon. The single question had been formulated so as to emerge unslurred, perhaps the only reason for saying it.

"What about her?" Sarah wasn't angry – she was in love. She wanted his body whether or not he could do anything with it. She wanted to lie in the angled crook of him and eventually sleep. She wanted sleep the way sun-worshippers long for an eclipse, piously, awe-fully, and with mounting fanaticism.

Men recently arrived from Africa were touting for minicab trade along the curve of pavement fronting Charing Cross Road. Simon imagined himself Sarah's pimp as she bent by a rolled-down window to strike a deal. Then they were heading west, the car radio keeping pace with them. A boxing match was being commentated on; Simon ducked and feinted with the stream of words, trying to avoid the knockout. They caromed down Park Lane. Funny, Simon thought, that London can be simultaneously vernal and venal, the park frothing green against its railings, the cabs and commercial vehicles bucketing along the roads at this hour conspicuously ignoring it.

Then Harrods, a crenellated hunk of Babylonian commerce, a vertical souk. Simon turned to look at Sarah. She sat, mysteriously demure, unaffected by the night of booze and drugs, save for a puckering, a drying-out of the skin beneath her eyes. She sat, knees to one side, hands resting lightly in her lap. The toque was still poised on the lappet of hair. Did he want to stroke it? Hold the neat prettiness of it? He didn't know. He was exhausted by this workout of his sensuality. It was as if his body had been taken from him while he slept and put through an extreme assault course, then returned to him as he awoke. His insides were liquid and his skin a scaly carapace. He shifted in his seat, felt the gusset of his pants pinch and grab at his sweaty perineum. Full circle, for this occurred as the cab was passing the top of Sloane Street. The visceral updates were keeping their own rhythm, their own counsel.

I'm lying down within the impress of all his other bedmates' bodies, thought Sarah, watching the now lemon beams of morning light pass across her lover's brow.

When I touch her I think only of my children, Simon thought, caught up once more in the winsomeness of her, the smallness of her.

If only there were some preparation, Sarah thought, some embrocation he could give me, rub into me, to eliminate these memories. A kind of Ret-Gel^{RM}, which would burn at first but then sink in deeper, removing the impress of their touch and its influence on his.

"Wipe my bum, Daddy ... Wipe my bum!" High tones of culpable imperiousness, the small blond head bent forward, pressed between his thighs. The curvature of the buttocks and beyond their arcs of perfection the rim of the toilet seat in a plastic bow. He tugs at the holder, tears off a couple of sheets, feeling their dryness, their rasping dryness. Bends down himself and passes fold through crack: "Ow! That hurts, Daddy, that hu-urts ..." Where are my children? Simon thought. Where *are* they? They're not here. They're in Oxfordshire, at the Brown House, with their mother. They're OK, absolutely all right. And I'll see them soon, all three of them, I'll subside under them, they'll use me as their climbing frame. I'll see them soon, two days at most.

The minicab sped along the Cromwell Road, Simon's finger-clamped Camel burned uselessly in the slipstream from the window the driver insisted on being open. In the west of London the Middle East was already awake, pallid men in sacks of khaki cotton unworriedly flicked worry beads as they wafted past their hotels. Sarah looked absently at the house-sized billboard on the junction with Warwick Road. It had an electronic display that showed the numbers of Windows computer programmes IBM had sold worldwide. As she blanked it, it blinked, recording another transaction in Seoul or Syracuse. Sarah thought: What if those were the numbers of women he has imagined penetrating? The seas of muff he's considered diving into? The mounds he's mounted? '2,346,734' the billboard proposed, and Sarah thought: Not enough, not nearly enough.

The minicab neared Barons Court. Simon could see the glass hull of the Ark, the vast, new office block that dominated the Hammersmith Flyover. Sarah's flat was in the knot of small streets behind it. They would be home soon. Home by the Ark, with its fifteen storeys of plate glass and concrete, rising up, then swelling above the tangled roofs. The Ark, with its crest of aerials and satellite dishes connecting it to the ether, ready to receive the information that a dove bearing an olive branch had been sighted on the other side of the world. The Ark, an entirely suitable vessel to sail a menagerie away from the inundation of the city. Ground it again on a greenfield shore, where evolution could begin anew.

"Come on, monkey," Simon said, but then noticed that he was too late, she was already paying the man. He was young and his long arms protruded stick-like from the wide, short sleeves of his patterned shirt.

"She'm no monkey, man," he threw over his shoulder, fixing Simon's bloodshot eyes with his own in the rearview mirror.

"Wha-ss-that?" Simon was hunching his way out on the off side.

"She'm no monkey."

"It's just a pet name," Simon replied – he was half out of the minicab.

"Where I come from monkeys ain't pets, they're meat, man. Meat or dead."

"Oh." Why am I being polite, Simon thought as he replied. "Where's that then?"

"Tanzania, man. Thass where Where I'm from, by the big lake, we hunt the monkeys, their meat ... we like it. Tasty, innit. Specially the chimps, yeah, specially dem. They eat our babies – we eat theirs."

"Is that so. I thought chimpanzees were apes, not monkeys –"

"Mon-key, ape, makes no difference, y'know. It's bush meat. We need it.' The cab driver emphasised this, as if Simon were about to argue. "Need it to live, you understand?"

"Sure, sure, of course I understand." Simon was on the pavement now, Sarah was opening the front door; he leant down to speak to the driver before closing the rear door, speak to him male-conspiratorially. "I'm the same way. I need this monkey's meat" – he gestured at Sarah who was unlocking the front door – "to live."

The minicab driver frowned, flicked the shift into drive and drove off. Simon went up the little path with its diamond-shaped tiles, in between the files of pot plants, herbs to the left, flowers to the right. He entered the house and shut the front door carefully; the thick, distorting glass rattled. He stood for a moment in the vestibule, with its trapezoid floor covered inefficiently with an oblong of beige carpet, then opened the door to Sarah's ground-floor flat, a composite wood-chip affair, magnolia in colour, and shut it after him with an indecisive whoosh.

She was standing in the main room by the music centre, petting her dog, Gracie, an old, plump golden retriever who drooled almost constantly. The dog could only just get its paws up on to Sarah's thighs; its shaggy belly scraped the floorboards, its stiff tail swept a Moroccan rug. "There-there," she was saying, "there-there ..." running her hands down over the dog's sharp muzzle, smarming the tawny scruff and then pushing a wavelet of slack flesh along its sides. "There-there."

Gracie was uttering soft grunts of pleasure, interspersed with strangulated yelps, which skidded in and out of human hearing. "There-there, there-there, there-there ..." Each picture on the wall was doubly framed; the hard shadows of a bright early morning provided salience where there was no significance.

Sarah's flat, nice, with its tones of warm wood and china, its soft blues and reds, things looped and things dangling, mementoes of an accommodated life now given their proper accommodation, was nonetheless denuded, bleached by the morning and the irradiation of drugs. Simon moved around it, pulling down blinds, pulling to curtains, staunching the light, suturing the brightness, performing triage on the diurnal in the futile hope that it might be saved at some later hour. Still she patted and smarmed, still she indicated, "There-there, there-there, there-there ..." still the soft grunts of canine pleasure.

And then elsewhere as well. "There-there, there-there," or rather, "There ... there, there ..." Simon was touching Sarah up now. She lay athwart the bed, the edge of the mattress beneath her shoulder blades. He lay athwart her, a hairy thigh across her shaved ones. He was up on his left elbow, and like a child flung down in the act – he read her like a book. One hand smoothed the blonde hair over her forehead, down to the nape of her neck, then down the small oblong back of her, while the other worked up over thigh, into arse cleft. The second joint of his thumb snagged there, then skated round to rest on the jut of her mons, the fingers scrabbling to open the leaves of her vagina. "There ... there ..." Simon was saying, "there ... there ..." not asking, but stating where each finger-fall was coming next. Her hands were on his penis, one softly tugging the dome, the other smoothly tugging the shaft. But to no avail, it was bendable, a bendy toy version of The Penis, push it over and it would spring back up again, but not up Sarah, and not for long. "There ... there ... There ... there-there-there." Should he stick his finger up

64

her arsehole, or get a tissue and wipe it? *Daddy, Daddy, wipe my bum!* It was all so stylised, an elaboration on the idea of making love, rather than making love itself. A school of love in which the lover strives to represent the manner in which he would make love, if by any chance he were able to. The day was coming back to Simon unbidden. Her body was so light beneath his arm, the careful assessments of weight retailed him disturbing information.Was he molesting her? 'There ... and *there* ...' Were his children here – or there? Sarah was uttering soft grunts and pants of exasperation. What he was doing was out of context ... out of genre ... He could no longer suspend disbelief in the genre of sex, or the medium of the body. His hand caressing her was like a boom mike protruding into the corner of a film frame depicting peasant life in nineteenth-century Lombardy. It shouldn't be "There ..." a harder grunt of exasperation. They were strangers to one another, fully in split screen. The small paws on his penis slowed and stopped, slowed and stopped, Sarah said "There-there, there-there ...!" patting Simon, reassuring him. He slept.

Sleep in the day is negative sleep. It throws up negative images, blackened faces staring out of the glare, ape-like skulls under tow hair, albino eye sockets. And drugged sleep during the day is doubly negative; especially sleep under cocaine, under ecstasy, when the brain-stem is implanted in the earth, the dead ground of Slumberland – as if the sleeper has been gifted a negative pillow, recessed into the posture-impedic mattress – leaving the twin lobes of synaptic leaves to flicker in chilly breezes of stark imagery.

They had tossed, and now Sarah and Simon turned away from one another, grabbing armfuls of blanket, sheet and pillow, wrestling them down on to the gritty surface. Their faces were contorted with the effort of thrusting their minds below the gelid surface of consciousness, then holding them there until gasps turned to snores. In sleep Simon found himself fucking Sarah with long, whooshing, regular strokes. His cock was adamant, inflexible, it oozed into and out of her with machine rhythm, oiled ease. Her cunt was tight around the base, then tight around the shaft, then tight around the dome; annagain, annagain. Tight. Tight. Tight. He felt the the sub-sonic shudder that was the beginning of her climax, a laval worm of hot liquefaction boiling deep-down in the faulted core of her. He went further up on her, so that the whole of his upper body was projecting right out, an overhang, a proud outcrop, no longer exiguous, no.

They were in a bedroom that contained the world, oceans of blanket, continents of pillow, a biosphere of billowing sheet that supported their plunging, aerodynamic bodies like piled-up cumuli. "Come, baby / Come, baby / Baby, come-come . . ." Lucidity here, or what? Simon thought to himself *within the dream*, the Ragga trope getting caught up in the thrusting, in the rhythm. Then there was some complicated limbering, some contorting within the contortion. As if Simon were a child gymnast, exercising on a bar that spanned the empyrean, he found his back arching, arching, arching back and back, while his legs did something, sleight-of-limb: This is the church / This is the steeple / Open the doors and these are . . . the people were face to face again now, but separated by the length of both upper bodies. Yet Simon was still fucking Sarah, fucking her with long, whooshing, regular strokes. If anything this new position – their upper bodies pointing in opposite directions, each the distorted *doppelgänger* of the other; his knees bent beneath her bent knees; he holding himself up on locked arms and using those cranking knees to yank his cock in and out of her cunt – made the whole process even more deliciously juicy. Squidge-squidgy-squidge, they squidged. Her cunt so firm – yet so moist; his cock solid and liquid.

Simon had another irruption of lucidity, of ridiculous dream logic – he couldn't be managing this, it wasn't physically possible; to effect this position his cock would have to be . . .

long. He looked down, it was long, very long, at least eighteen inches; and as he watched, awed, it grew still further. He was pulling it out from the outsiness of her, the pink effulgence of her, and it was lengthening and lengthening and rarefying at the same time, as if it were a stria of chewing gum being pulled by finger and thumb from the crumbling milk teeth of a child. Where was that child? Sarah seemed not to have noticed this. Her upper body had fallen back on to the mattress, but still it writhed, legs flexing as if he were still bearing down on her. She gave the stiff grunts of effortful sex, this was sex as hard labour. A late, tragic fuck? He was getting further away from her now, much, much further. She was on the other side of the ocean from him and still he scampered backwards on paws-for-hands, hands-for-paws. She was so nonchalant – or so Simon thought – crouching there while these yards and yards and yards of stringy penis uncoiled from her cunt and fell in loops and even knots, all streaked with blood, across the sheet.

Then Sarah was outside the window – the little monkey. She was scampering up the trunk of the oak in the garden, grinning at him over the downy hair on her pointed shoulder. Downy hair, or downy fur? She had scaled it and reached the first branching; here she crouched, the umbilical penis trailing from between her legs. She was utterly unconcerned, but Simon felt awfully aware of the strangeness of this, its laden quality. She must have done something – someone must have done something, because now he could feel himself running back into her. Even at this great remove – down the tree, across the gravel, up the outside of the house, in through the window – his penis was moving back into her again, being sucked up by the trap of her. She'd pressed some operative button, and now he was being retracted like a hominid tape measure into her simian casing. Truly, Simon mused, man is the measure of all things. His heels skittered and bounced across the sheet, he fell hard on to the strip of the carpet between the bed and the window, was yanked up and over

67

it. Whumph! Simon fell on to the small patio her godfather had laid for her. She was still grinning down at him from the fork as scherluppp! he came wobbling, arse above tit, up the trunk towards her. A final scherluppp and Sarah was engorged by Simon, made fully gravid. She absent-mindedly rubbed the still-wet lips of her cunt, smelt the fur on the back of her hand. Then she made her way carefully along the thick branch of the oak. One arm cradled protectively around her distended belly she dropped softly into the next garden and made off.

They woke again towards noon. The light that streaked from between curtain hem and windowsill had gone from lemon to orange. The memory of the dream, the little monkey that was Sarah sucking in his umbilical penis and then disappearing into the next garden, was still so vivid, so present, that it vied with the grittiness of the mattress, the bent pipe of his throat, the grout in his eyes, for inclusion in this reality.

It wasn't a nightmare, of that much Simon was certain. There had been no access of dread, no pounding dream heart, no paralysis of dream body, as he watched his cock transmogrify. Rather, it had been something he had wanted to happen. The sense of lucidity within the dream had affirmed this.

Simon held himself still on the mattress, appreciating the particular cramping of his shoulder, the jarring twang of his pelvis. Should he rise, attack the hangover, hose himself down? He rolled over and his blood-filled cock, stoppered off at the root by a full bladder, twanged. He ungummed his eyes. Sarah lay along the flattened length of a pillow, her upper body canted at an angle of some twenty degrees, her arms flung out any which way, her hair damp and tousled.

Simon hoicked himself up on forearm and elbow and observed her. The edge of the sheet was tucked below her breasts, and it crumpled and bulged below that. Her back was stretched in this posture and he could see the slight bunchings of muscle that cushioned her – as far as Simon was concerned one of her imperfections. There were others, the too thin lips, lips he sometimes felt the thinness of when he kissed her, and which now were half-open revealing her oddly pointed canine teeth; which – when conscious – gave her an air of workaday vampirism, as if she had been temping for Van Helsing. The breasts were neat, but her nipples were never hard enough, teat-like enough.

As he watched they rose and fell, fell and rose. Her bruised eyelids flickered. Was she engaged in the dream he had just left – or some other? He lifted his big brown hand and laid it against the outflung white arm. In his grasp it looked as small as a chopstick, and as breakable. I must stop this, Simon, thought. I do this to debase her – to devalue us. Perfection is meaningless – and worthless, a Tupperware grail. If I carry on like *this* I'll argue myself out of *this*.

His hand had knocked against his erect cock, reminding him that he had one, reminding him of what it could be employed for. His other hand went to the folds and bulges of sheet. He ran fingertips over these, as if they were the ruches and pleats of her sex. Simon swallowed and tasted the guttural grimness of his mouth, a panniklin full of cold Camel leftovers. Could he commit the culinary crime of compelling her to taste this? In the pit of the bed his cock thwanged. He could.

She woke as his fingertips made the final, fiddly assaults on her nipples, his palms having pitched camp in the col of her breasts. Sarah seemed to experience no discomfort, nor even momentary revulsion at the idea of this sodden, vodka-blanched body over-toppling hers. She turned on, turned on. Her small head rose up, the ruff of blonde split-ends giving it a clownish air. The thin lips parted, he caught a glimpse of white pointiness, and then she received him, the little slug of her tongue uncoiled in his mouth, swelled and died in his saltiness. Their upper bodies married. Simon tasted the crap of her gullet, smelt the shit on her breath – as she did his. Soon each cancelled out the other's, as more and more saliva eroded the little seams of mucus, with their worthless veins of crap cocaine.

It was hard and abrupt. A bout of love. One of his big hands went to her mons, tearing the bunched sheet away. The fingers of the other went to their sucking mouths, gathered wallow, deposited it in her juncture. His fingers plunged into her – she gasped, bit his lip. His other hand went below her back – her child's back; his single hand could almost span it. He yanked her to him. Her small claws tore at his back, almost unable to gain purchase on the sweat that had sprung up on it. "Open your legs!" he barked into her mouth: "Open your legs!" He pushed his fingers further into her, widening her; a thumb circled over her clitoris. She bucked beneath him like a trapped animal. Bucked and bucked again. He removed his hand from her back, his mouth from hers. He put two fingers into her mouth, three. Felt the sharpness of her teeth, the taut skin of her gullet. He pulled the fingers out, smarmed them across her brow, and further – grasping a handful of her hair and pulling it down to her nape, stretching her body over the form of pillow so that all of her was exposed, laid doubly bare.

Sarah's hands had found his penis. Simon gasped, almost came from that one touch. Her fingers smoothed up and around, up and around. Then down, touching his balls, cradling them, then lower, into the sweat-filled runnel of him. She dabbed and palped his arsehole; dabbed and palped his arsehole.

His fingers were hooked inside her, he could feel the whole shape of her pubic bone. Her eyes were rolled back so only the whites showed. He could sense the precise texture of this internal, membranous skin. He could almost taste through his fingers the salty gush of come that now spasmed out of her. His mouth was clamped on hers once more and it was into this cave that she shouted, so that the echoes reverberated in his head. He wouldn't release her. He kept on kissing her, chewing on her. Then he slid down her, tasting her breasts, her hips, the twistle of lint her belly button. He placed the whole of his tongue against the wet openness of her, felt the seed of her clitoris wobble on the root of his tongue. Then he moved up again. Her hands were tugging on his cock, her hands were tugs guiding the great draught of his penile vessel, bringing it into harbour. There was such urgency in this, such will on both sides to couple – it could hardly be called desire.

Outside in the narrow passageway, Gracie, the old retriever, whuffled and scratched, hearing the commotion within as a chase that she would wish to join. She heard the yelps and drummings as the paws of lapine quarry bursting from a sandy burrow. She grabbed the hem of a batik scarf dangling from a hook and worried at it with her slack lips, her meaty teeth.

The shock of their marriage pushed Sarah backwards still further on the pillow so that it ended up beneath her buttocks. Her heels were on the small of Simon's back, and he was fucking her as he had been in the dream, with great, whooshing, oiled strokes of machine regularity. She was coming ceaselessly, her vagina rippling along the length of him. Her mouth was agape, the cries torn from it with each implosion of him into her. Cry after cry after cry, until he, at last, with an internal wrench of his urinary tract, came as well, and realised that she was no longer uttering these cries, but simply crying. Crying and sobbing, with heaves that wracked her thin shoulders, ground her thin shoulder blades against his supporting hand.

Simon withdrew, slumped out of her. He then took her lengthwise in his arms, one threading through her crotch, the other cradling her neck. She sobbed – he knew – not necessarily from emotion, for this happened often enough when they fucked. No, she sobbed almost as a purely physical reaction, the way that some women sweated profusely after coming. This is how he thought of her tears, as eye-born perspiration. She sobbed and sobbed and he said, "There-there, there-there, there-there." Then they slept again. The digital alarm on her bedside table read 12.22 a.m.; and by the time it read 12.34 a.m. Simon was dreaming once more.

71

The dream picked up at a point some short time before it had left off. The bower that was her bedroom, all wreathed around with a forest that both breached and formed its walls. The tall trunks and massy undergrowth fell away in a gentle slope on the garden side. Simon was as he had been: on heels of hands and heels of feet, propped up by his back-angled arms. And there was the little monkey, squatting on the branch of a tree some sixty feet away. Squatting easily, but with legs opened so that he could clearly see the pink effluvium of her; and running from without it the red rivulet of him.

I can look at my cock, thought Simon, and then looked at his cock. I am lucid, he realised. I am in control of this dream. His cock wavered away from his groin, crossed the tangled sheet in a series of corkscrew curls. He could see some more of these corkscrews, pigtails on the forest floor, their gummy loops encrusted with leaf mould and twigs, before they vanished amidst the humped roots of the trees. Simon called out to Sarah, who was unconcernedly picking at the skin on her forearm.

"Sarah! Sarah!"

"Simon?" She looked up.

"Sarah, pull me in now, pull me in! I want to be inside you now." He gestured at the hanks of him 'n' her that linked them.

"Simon?" She was glancing around, as if trying to search him out among the trees. She was looking everywhere but at the small clearing, with its fitted sheet, where he lay. "Simon? Simo . . . ?"

Her voice trailed off. She bent forward on the branch and plucked at something. Simon felt a twinge. It was him! She was plucking at him! Sarah brought the plait of vesicles up to her mouth. She held it in her hand as casually as if it had been a rope and she some arboreal campanologist. And then without preamble, she began to gnaw at it.

Simon felt her small, sharp teeth bite into him. "Sarah!" he cried. "Don't . . . Sarah, that's me!" But she didn't seem to hear him, she kept on gnawing, occasionally breaking off to pick a bit of their gristle from between her teeth. The thing that linked them – was it umbilicus or penis? He could not say – was now almost cut through, and still she gnawed, and still he shouted out, "Sarah! Stop it! Sarah – you'll lose me, we're in a forest!" But she paid no heed, just kept gnawing. Now only a single string of pink remained, glistening in her incisors. She bit down – and severed him altogether.

I want to wake up, Simon thought. Wake up! he commanded his body, which lay coldly athwart his volition, a grave weight. Wake up! He struggled to shift it, some tiny part of it, any movement at all would be enough to release him from the dream, but he could engineer nothing. Nothing. He strained, and thought: I am here, I am lying in this nest with . . . Sarah. Sarah, he could feel the warmth of her above or below him. He swam up to where he could . . . feel it beneath his cheek. The warmth of her small breast with its fine covering of coarse blonde fur.

Simon Dykes, the artist, awoke, his consort's breast cushioning his cheek. He sighed, and nuzzled his muzzle down into the sweet animality of her.

Chapter Six

It was a beautiful, late-summer morning. Redington Road was lined with trees at their final, fructive stage. The smells of yeast and verdancy filled the air. Busner surveyed the solid red-brick villas flanking the road. Despite the mounting heat, the early mating had left him feeling zestful and before heading off down the garden path, he took a lip-funnelling breath then let out a great pant-hoot, full of *joie de vivre*. This was answered by a chorus of pant-hoots from his neighbours, some of whom he now noticed were crouched in the surrounding branches.

"H'hooo!" they pant-hooted, then waved, 'Morning, Busner.'

"H'hooo!" he revocalised, cheerily saluting them with a wave of his briefcase. This initial exchange of greetings was echoed by chimps in the adjoining streets, who pant-hooted their welcomes to the suburb, and then echoed by still more chimps at a greater remove, and still more chimps at a still greater remove, their calls dying away in the direction of Belsize Park.

Gambol had got the car, a maroon Seven Series Volvo Estate, out of the garage and it now stood idling by the front gate. Busner could see three of his sub-adult males in the back seat. They were so entwined in mutual grooming that he couldn't establish which, but he was pleased to note that Erskine and Charles were there; neither of them had been doing enough patrolling recently as far as their alpha was concerned.

Busner threw his briefcase in the boot and got in on the passenger side. 'Now then, Gambol,' he signed as the subordinate chimp powered the car away from the kerb, his hands flying as he changed up through the first eight gears. ' "Euch-euch" what on earth is it that's so important that it couldn't have waited for me to finish my second breakfast, "huu"?'

'I had a call from Jane Bowen at Charing Cross emergency psychiatric unit this morning,' Gambol signed. 'She's now working for a chimp denoted Whatley – you remember Whatley, don't you, Dr Busner "huuu"?'

'Of course "wraaaf", he's the twerp who made those ethical objections to our work at the British Psychological Association meeting last year in Bournemouth.'

'The very same. Well, I think he's going to be doing some grovelling now, because Jane Bowen signs he wants our help.'

' "Hoo" really –' Busner flagged down and turned his attention to the thick layer of shag-pile carpet on the dashboard. 'I sign, Gambol, have you had the car re-carpeted again?'

'Last week, when it was in for its service – don't you like it?'

Busner hated to admit it but the new carpet Gambol had chosen for the dashboard was a distinct improvement. It had a bold pattern of lozenges and hexagons, in alternating purple and red – a delightful incitement to fingers or toes itching to groom. Busner found himself absent-mindedly parting and reparting the thick pile; which reminded him. 'Here, Gambol,' he signed, 'see if you can get this bloody jam out of my neck fur, will you "huu"?'

'I'll do it, Alph!' one of the sub-adults in the back seat signed – actually in the jammy patch. Busner wheeled around in his seat, grabbed the culprit – it was Erskine – by his ear, and bit him hard under the eye.

"Wraa!" Busner barked, and then flailed, 'When you're old enough to groom me in the morning, Erskine, I'll let you know. Until then – dear Skinnikins – keep your darling little fingers to yourself.'

'Sorry, Alph,' Erskine signed, doing his best to appear contrite. Yet within a matter of seconds – despite the gash under his eye – he was mucking around with his brothers, the three of them heaving and whimpering with ill-concealed juvenile laughter. The two adult chimps ignored them.

Gambol wetted the fingers of his left hand and began soothingly to tease the sticky twistles of fur under Busner's jaw. Busner soft-grunted his appreciation, "Huh-huh-huh", then signed, 'So, what is it that Whatley wants "huu"?'

'Well,' Gambol inparted, 'apparently about a week ago a seriously disturbed chimp was brought into Whatley's unit –'

'Self-referring, from a GP "huu"?'

'No, it was an emergency. The chimp had had some kind of psychotic breakdown or outburst; they had to send a crash team. Restraints, tranquillisers, the lot.'

'I see.'

Gambol's fingers fell from Busner's scruff while he concentrated on the tricky turn into Hampstead Hill. The rush hour had thinned out, but there were still dense knots of traffic moving up and down the main road at speed. Gambol wound down the window, made hand signals and screamed loudly until a white BMW driven by a bonobo flashed for him to enter the traffic stream; then he resumed. 'For the first couple of days they couldn't get a thing out of the chimp – his name is Simon Dykes by the way, apparently he's a fairly well-known artist.'

'I should sign so,' Busner cut in. 'One of his photomontages is in the Tate modern collection. Big triptych, showing a lot of teddy bears working in a laboratory – you must have seen it.'

'I don't go to galleries much, Dr Busner, it's not my thing.'

'Well "euch-euch", you ought to. As you know a great deal of our work relates closely to the kinds of intuition and lateral reasoning employed by artists. We aren't looking for dry, linear or causal explanations – you should appreciate that by now, Gambol –'

'Boss "huu"?' Gambol gestured, hunching in the corner of his armchair, just in case his alpha decided to lash out at this impertinence.

'What "huu"?'

'Could I please just finish "huu"?'

'Hoo . . . all right.'

'As I was signing, when they brought Dykes in he was in a catatonic state. To begin with Bowen and Whatley couldn't figure out if this was symptomatic, or if the crash team had been more than usually enthusiastic with the tranks –'

"Wraaf!" Busner barked. He had a hatred of tranquillisers, and indeed of all psychopharmacology, all the more so since the débâcle surrounding the clandestine trialing of Inclusion by Cryborg Pharmaceuticals. A project Busner had foolhardily got entwined with, in the belief that the drug represented a sort of panacea for depressive conditions.

Gambol went on, 'When Dykes came round they couldn't get near him. He kept signing about monkeys and beasts, vocalising like a human, and attacking the staff – albeit ineffectually. Whatley and Bowen then hit upon the notion that he found simian contact itself traumatic, so they isolated him and began to correspond –'

'Correspond, what do you mean "huu"?'

'Send Dykes notes along with his food tray, asking him what was the matter and so forth.'

'And what exactly did Dykes write then, Gambol? Has he given a reason for his breakdown "huu"?'

'He showed Bowen that he was human.'

'I'm sorry "huu"?'

'He wrote that he was a human, that the whole world was run by humans, that humans were the dominant primate species, that he had gone to sleep with his human lover and when he

77

awoke the following morning she was a chimpanzee and so was everyone else in the world.'

'Including him "huu"?'

'Well, obviously he looks like a chimpanzee to us, but as far as he's concerned he's human. He feels human. He signs he has a human body. He believes that he has gone completely mad and that the world he now perceives is a psychotic delusion.'

It had taken the Volvo all this time to inch down Hampstead Hill, but now they reached the traffic lights on the corner of Pond Street and Gambol made as if to turn left towards the hospital. 'What are you doing chimp "huu"?' Busner poked.

'Sorry, Boss "huu"?'

'Pant-hoot Whatley on the mobile 'phone right away – this looks fascinating. Let's drive down to Charing Cross and see if we can find out a bit more about this mysterious delusion.' Gambol gave a wide, playful grin. He'd anticipated this and was already dialling Whatley's direct line with his hallux.

Whatley's rather mangy muzzle appeared on the dash-mounted screen. His eyes had an unpleasant white tint to the pupil that made him seem at once feral and weak. "HoooGraa'," he pant-hooted, and Busner and Gambol pant-hooted in return; Busner even drummed the dash a little just to impress upon Whatley that he wasn't going to be remotely deferential.

'I suppose your epsilon has pointed out to you something about this chimp Dykes then, Busner "huu"?' signed Whatley, his fingers, which were, Busner noted, rather on the warty side, wiggling around furtively in the very corner of the screen.

'He's given me a very brief outline. What do you make of it "huu"?'

'I hardly grasp it, Busner. The chimp has been here for a week now. When they brought him in he appeared to be in a state of severe shock – although I now concede that it may have been some sort of manic interlude.'

'What was his behaviour like "huu"?' Busner hunched

78

forward in his seat so that he could concentrate closely on what Whatley was signing.

'He would move upright to the corner of his room if any of the staff appeared in the doorway. If they entered he would try to get under the nest, or even "hooo" attack –'

'Attack "huu"?'

'That's right. The attacks were however incredibly ineffectual – he appears to have little or no physical strength, some kind of motor-functional inhibition, or possibly even partial atrophy. At any rate, even though he was clearly terrified he was unable to inflict any damage on the staff, so we haven't even put restraints on, or given him more than a mild sedative, because he's quite harmless.'

A nurse appeared in the corner of the screen and handed Whatley a clipboard. 'Excuse me,' Whatley signed. He wrote something on it, and dismissed the nurse with a wave of his hand – not even a light cuff for the impertinence.

Busner turned to Gambol and contemptuously raised his eyebrow ridges. As soon as he had Whatley's attention again he signed, 'So what about this business of being human, when did that first arise "huu"?'

'Well, he was signing after a fashion when they brought him in, according to the duty psychiatrist. He was also vocalising – but very gutturally and incoherently, all sorts of odd noises. It wasn't for a couple of days that his gesticulation became at all comprehensible.'

'And "huu"?'

'Well, he kept wringing his hands – Get away from me, you fucking ape! Fuck off, Beelzebub, you dark creature! – things like that. Bowen got involved at this point, started this correspondence, by way of attempting some sort of diagnosis. We assumed to begin with that it was either drug-induced, or a flamboyant, hypomanic outburst –'

'Does he have any history "huu"?'

'Well . . .'

'Does he, chimp "huu"?'

'According to his GP, a chimp called Bohm up in Oxfordshire, he has a history of depression and some drug dependency. Had a fairly bad breakdown a couple of years ago when his group was fissioning "euch-euch", but nothing like this, nothing so incontrovertibly psychotic. When we got hold of his notes and learnt this we tried a different approach with him, gentler, more accommodating.

'He clearly found grooming incredibly upsetting, so we made a rule that none of the other patients, or the staff, should touch him. This has paid dividends – over the last few days he's begun to gesture more fluently, while recounting to Bowen this astonishing delusion about being human. According to him he went to sleep one night a human in a human world, lying in nest with a human female, and awoke with the world as it is now –'

'What about the consort "huu"?'

' "Huu" the female he was with when he had the break-down?'

'Of course, of course.'

'She's all right. Upset naturally, but she doesn't think she's an animal!'

'Look, Busner,' Whatley signed after a pause, 'you know "euch-euch" that I'm not overly impressed by the general tenor and direction of your current work –'

'Yes, yes, I am aware.'

'But I must concede that this case not only has me held at bay, but it's also obviously right up your scrag. The most astonishing thing is the consistency of the delusion. Bowen has pursued the ramifications of Dykes's psychosis, but neither of us have ever encountered a delusional state that was at one and the same time so comprehensive – he has an answer for everything – and so complex. I'd like you to examine him if you have th –'

'I'm on my way right now,' Busner snapped, the finger-flourished 'now' coinciding with him punching the off button on the telescreen.

After finishing his pant-hoot to Whatley, Busner sat signless. Gambol noted that his boss had drawn his feet up on to the seat and was manipulating a coin, so that it moved over and under each finger, over and under each toe, around and around on a twenty-digit circumnavigation. This was, Gambol knew, a sign that Busner was deep in thought; to disturb him now would probably result in a sound thrashing, so he kept his feet on the wheel and drove. Even the sub-adult chimps in the back seat sensed their alpha's preoccupation and remained novocal.

Busner was thinking in the very clear way that he only thought when confronted with a new pathology, or at any rate a case that exhibited a symptomatology with which he was unfamiliar. His personal image for this kind of thought was that it was akin to mopping up termites. He thrust the back of a figurative hand into the confused zone of new information, supposition and conjecture, then drew it out. Attached to his conceptual probe would be tens of little hypotheses, wriggling in the fur of cogitation. At his leisure, Busner would pick these tasty hypotheses out and examine them, thus:

A chimpanzee who suffers from the delusion that he is human. Not only that, but also believes that he has his origins in a world in which humans have been the evolutionarily successful primate species. Not only that! But the chimpanzee in question is a successful artist. Could this conceivably be an organic disfunction? The business about motor-impairment Whatley marked out is promising, but hardly conclusive – it might be an hysterical conversion. If it were an organic impairment the phenomenological implications would be intriguing ... but I mustn't swing in front of myself. Wait to see the patient, Busner; maintain objectivity, dispassion for the moment.

... and yet, how funny that this should come up today of all days, when only this morning I was dwelling on the lack of interesting cases to manipulate

But there was also a deeper level of supposition that Zack

Busner found himself descending to. A level that, mezzanine-like, occupied the area in between conscious conscience and guilty unconsciousness, between daydream and nightmare. A GP called Bohm in Thame; a patient locally treated for depression – presumably with anxiolytics. Could this, Busner wondered with a wondrous lack of acknowledgement, be more of the fall-out from that bloody drug trial?

This hand-jive of thought was interrupted by Charles who began vocalising in the back seat.

"Aaaaa!" Charles cried and then inparted, 'Alph, can't we "huu" stop here for a minute, just for a frolic, ple-ease.'

"Wraaaf!" Busner barked, whirling round in his seat to muzzle three anxious, ingratiating countenances, all floppy lower lips, yellow teeth, and six hands frantically gesturing, 'Ple-ease, Alph, ple-ease, just a little frolic, just for a few minutes!'

The Volvo was standing by the lights on the corner of Albert Road; ahead Busner could make out the frothing greenery of Regent's Park. To the right he could see the topmost spars and cables of the Snowdon aviary in the zoo. "H'h'hee-hee," Busner chuckled, and turning to Gambol signed, 'We could stop off here and have a look at some real live humans, before going to visit this notional one – what do you think "huu"?' Gambol looked nonplussed, his thick lower lip twisted enquiringly. 'Just joking, you don't have to take everything I sign so seriously.' He turned back to the sub-adults. 'All right, we'll have a patrol up Primrose Hill for twenty minutes, but then we must get on.'

Gambol began to search for somewhere to park, but without much success. 'They seem to have "euch-euch" zoned this whole area now,' he indicated as they drove slowly along the section of Regent's Park Road abutting Primrose Hill for the fourth time. The situation was complicated because there were cars constantly pulling away from the kerb, and parking, as mothers visiting the playground with infants came and went. Busner began to get agitated, the tempo of his signing increased. It

82

was – Gambol recognised – the prelude to him *really* holding forth.

' "Euch-euch" what's the bloody point of living in this city any more. Look at this "wraaa" traffic! There's no rush hour now – just rush all day. When these elegant terraces were built the whole of this area was open parkland. The Regency architects and developers conceived of it as providing a bucolic, brachiating progress between outcrops of urbanity, but look at it "waaa" now! You can't even park when you want to go to the park.' Busner pointed at the file of cars, brakes squealing, that were humping their way down Primrose Hill Road. ' "Hoo" for Christ's sake, Gambol "euch-euch", I really can't stand this. You'd better drop the patrol off and circle the block for fifteen minutes until we're ready to go.'

Gambol pulled over. Busner and the sub-adult chimps tumbled out of the car. Busner squeezed between two parked cars, vaulted the railings and headed off across the grassy slope without bothering to see if the others were following in his scut. The sun had been winched overhead and the day promised to be truly hot. Busner set his sights on a bench about halfway up the hill, perhaps some four hundred and fifty-three yards' distance – or so he judged – and made for it, knuckle-walking swiftly over the tempered turf.

Primrose Hill was, if not exactly crowded, at any rate well stocked, with chimps of all ages, classes and ethnic groups. Trim, Sloaney mothers lolloped along the paths, wearing floral swelling-protectors and vocalising to one another with the extended grunts of their class, as they toted Mabel, or Maude, or Georgia, the infants dangling off the hanks of maternal fur that flared from between strands of pearls; or perching like jockeys between maternal shoulders.

A group of swaggering males, who would have been working class – saving the fact that they weren't in work – were indulging in mock displays for their own amusement, charging up and down a small rise, swaggering, with erect fur poking up from the necks of their Fred Perry sports shirts. There were some mating chains – but they were desultory affairs, with only two or three hispid, humping links.

Busner passed a group of sub-adults who were clearly skiving off school – there was no sign of an adult in their patrol. I must be getting old, he thought, because I really can't stand seeing a chimp with a ring in its nostril. Far from being a fashion accessory or an adornment, all it makes me think is can they blow their noses through the hole when they have a cold?

The sub-adults were grouped around a large ghetto blaster, playing the hit of the moment, a Ragga version of 'Human Spanner', and were grooming one another in the negligent, insolent way of sub-adults the world over. Busner paused, barked at them, and waved, 'Turn that thing down. You know tape recorders aren't allowed here "euch-euch"!' They looked up at him, dug their hands deeper into their fur and laughed, heaving collectively. Busner considered going over and giving them a thrashing. He glanced round to see Erskine, Charles, and Carlo fanned out behind him, all moving purposively. The annoying sub-adults only had three males in their number and they were mangy specimens, underweight and unkempt. No match for my lot, thought Busner, scratching his ischial pleat – and therefore no fun either.

The patrol continued on up the hill. Three dossers were sitting on the bench Busner was making for, passing a bottle between them. At ten-thirty in the morning they were already drunk, swaying and lurching although firmly seated. They appeared to be in the terminal stages of alcoholism; none of them had bothered to dress and their coats were ragged, worn, coming out in tufts. Their chest fur was pitted with cigarette burns, networks of ruptured blood vessels stippled their nasal bridges and their eyes were filmed over, almost unseeing.

Busner came up to the bench and coughed softly, gesturing for his patrol to join him. 'Now "euch-euch", lads,' he held forth when they were grouped, 'you see here one of the most lamentable aspects of comtemporary chimpunity –'

' "Hoo" Al-ph,' Erskine broke in, 'you're not going to conduct another of your lectures, are you –'

'Hold back, Erskine "wraaa"! When I want your directions I'll ask for them. Now, as I was signing, these dossers, homeless, filthy, their minds blunted by ethyl alcohol, represent a scapegoating that we collectively indulge in as a society. Unlike many of my colleagues in the so-denoted "euch-euch" <healing> professions I see no real evidence for defining their condition as pathological. Rather, I choose to see it as a syndrome, a symptomatology that –'

One of the dossers, Busner sensed, wanted to object to this gesticulation, although not semiotically. He turned to see the most battered, bemerded of the three apes rearing up, and about to wrap a bottle of cooking sherry around his ear. Busner's sub-adults began to scream. '"Hoo" do get a grip!' he flicked one-handed, while disarming the dosser with his other. He then emptied the contents of the bottle on to the path. The dosser looked as if an artery had been opened in his neck and his lifeblood were draining away.

Busner cuffed the dosser, who collapsed back on to the bench with his fellows. He then lunged forward and delivered a series of swingeing blows to all three of them, barking the while, "Wraaaf! Wraaf! Wraaf!" The dossers were suitably stunned, and even the sub-adults shrank back on their haunches. 'I'm doing this,' Busner signed sententiously, 'for your own good. Judging from the appearance of your ally,' he pointed to the third chimp along the bench who was breathing irregularly, his chest fur streaked with bile and vomit, 'he is need of medical treatment, rather than self-medication.'

Busner set his bifocals on his nasal bridge, took a notebook and propelling pencil from the inside pocket of his jacket, scribbled down something, tore the sheet out and passed it to the dosser who had launched the attack on him. 'That's the address of Tony Valuam's clinic in Chalk Farm, it's barely a crawl – so I expect you can "euch euch" make it over there. And I suggest you do. He runs a very good detoxification programme, open access, no red tape. I don't think any of you are capable of helping yourselves, so my patrol and I had better help you on your way.

'Right, patrol! "HoooGraa"'.'

The sub-adults didn't need any further instruction; Charles and Carlo were particularly enthusiastic, pulling the dossers off the bench and driving them towards the gates of the park with a series of kicks, slaps and punches. Occasionally one of the dossers would try to break away, screaming pathetically, but in the end they all went off up Primrose Hill Road, supporting one another as they staggered in and out of the gutter.

The sub-adults tumbled back obediently to where Busner squatted on the bench, rightly anticipating the conclusion of this lecture on social responsibility, but on arriving and hunkering down, they found their alpha distracted by a series of loud hoots that were coming from the north "Hoooo-Oooo-Oooooo!" and then, "Hooo-oooo-oo-Waaaaa!" The former television personality responded, "Hooooooo! Hoooooo!" then turned to his patrol, signing, 'That's old Wiltshire, I'd recognise his hoot in a hurricane. I must go over and have a groom with him. You lot amuse yourselves for five minutes –'

'Can we go and have a little hunt, Alph "huu"?' signed Erskine, who really was pushing his luck this morning.

'Hunt? Hunt what exactly "huu"?'

'I saw a squirrel in the trees down there when Gambol was trying to park the car. I'm sure we could "wraaff" get it if we work together.'

Busner showed his lower canines, and ruffled Erskine's sleek head fur. 'All right, if you really foresee it, but be back where Gambol let us off in five minutes, or I'll send the pack of you ranging by yourselves for the day.'

'Thanks Alph,' Erskine signed and then the three of them tore off down the hill leap-frogging with excitement. Busner watched them go, spontaneously pant-hooting with the pleasure the sight gave him. Then, confident they could no longer see or sense him, he levered himself off the bench with considerable care. The blows he had dealt the dossers had done his arthritic hands no good at all – but he mustn't let on to the sub-adults or they'd be all over him.

Busner continued pant-hooting as he knuckle-walked up to the top of the hill. Wiltshire was one of his oldest allies and what with the busy nature of both their lives he didn't get to groom him more than once or twice a year. It was a stroke of good luck their paths crossing this morning, for Wiltshire – as well as being a medical doctor – was an internationally famous theatrical impresario. He would be bound to have an interesting angle on the chimp who thought he was human.

The two chimps met in the middle of the asphalt apron at the crest of the hill and fell on each other's necks with loud grunts, bestowing sloppy kisses on eyes, nasal bridges and mouths. They then settled down to groom. Wiltshire seemed to have an awful lot of sawdust in his armpit fur, Busner was trying to get the stuff out – while inparting tenderness – but finding it pernickety work, when Wiltshire pulled away and signed, 'Let me get a "huh-huh-huh" good look at you, old chimp. I haven't had my fingers in your fur for what . . . must be more than six months now –'

'Nearly a year,' Busner countersigned. 'If you remember we had a session at that book launch, but we were both a bit tipsy, I dare say you can't remember any more of our gesticulation than I can.'

'By God, Zack, you look in excellent shape,' Wiltshire signed, holding Busner off by his scruff and running one of his long, sensitive hands over the eminent psychiatrist's face. 'How do you do it "huu"?' he prodded. 'No trace of "gru-nnn" mange or goitre, fur sleek, hardly a wrinkle on your muzzle. I wish I could sign the same for myself.'

Busner examined his old ally. Peter Wiltshire was a tall, gangly chimp. Especially tall given that he was Jewish, a fact somewhat stereotypically proclaimed by the sharp prominence of his nasal bridge and the curliness of his fur.

But that fur was – Busner noted – rather lustreless and dull, and Peter Wiltshire's hands trembled ever so slightly as he signed. "Hooo," Busner was concerned. 'Yes, you don't look too good, Peter, but let me show you I'm not quite as fit as I appear. There's ar-th-ri-tis in this hand, and I greatly fear I'm getting it in the other. It's all right for the moment – my beta, gamma and delta are sound enough, but the epsilon could prove very difficult if he puts his finger on it.'

"H'huuuu?" Peter Wiltshire enquired, then signed, 'No tickling, funny thing is I'm in much the "hooo" same boat.'

'Home group, or work "huu"?'

'Bit of both really. You know I set up that production company. Well, like a fool I let my work delta – the assistant producer, chimp called Franklin – come into the home group as well and he's proved very successful, very "wraaa" cunning. Popular with my females too. It's mostly because of that that he's clawed his way up to domestic beta. It'll only take one more providential alliance on his part – and I may well be out.'

'Would that affect the work group that much "huuu"?'

'We-ell, you know how it is. And now I won't see the right side of forty again ... I suppose what I'm marking is, if he really does pull it off I might retire.'

Busner gave his old ally's fur a slather of spittle before inparting, 'Really, Peter "huu"? I shouldn't have imagined you'd climb down from the tree so eas –'

"Hooooo-Hooooo-Hooooo ..." Busner broke off as there came a series of long pant-hoots from the direction of Elsworthy Road.

'There "wraaff"!' Peter Wiltshire signed emphatically, his soloist's fingers fretting in the limpid breeze. 'The bugger has the temerity to drag me away from my constitutional. Here he comes now.'

A large, heavy-set chimp in his mid-twenties, with rather long light-brown fur, was advancing towards the crest of the hill. He was still fifty yards off, swaggering along upright and humming to himself 'The Swagger of the Toreadors'

88

in a loud, affected manner. Busner was perfectly prepared to dislike Peter Wiltshire's beta on principle, and sensing the anxiety of his old ally, he made a careful survey of the approaching chimp. Perhaps he could see some weaknesses Wiltshire hadn't picked up on?

The three chimps greeted one another with stentorian pant-hoots. Peter Wiltshire drummed vigorously on the back of a bench. Busner, ready to lash out at any impropriety, was quite disarmed when Franklin presented to him with great and grovelling alacrity. The big chimp pushed his arse towards Busner, while most of his upper body was hugging the path, flicking the while, ' "Hoo" Dr Busner, what a pleasure to encounter you and your magnificent ischial scrag – I've been an admirer of yours for many years.'

Peter Wiltshire grunted at this display of sycophancy, but Busner patted Franklin's rump in a friendly enough fashion, signing 'Always "chup-chupp" pleased to meet an admirer, especially one with talent and ambition. My old ally has just been showing me how you've moved up the hierarchy with leaps and bounds.'

' "Hooo" I do try to assist Dr Wiltshire in any way that I can.' Franklin's confusion was more or less transparent. If he is such a threat, Busner thought to himself, then my Peter must really be on the wane; this chimp is hardly *that* imposing.

' "Wraaa"! Enough of this handinage, Franklin, why've you come looking for me "huu"? I said I'd see you at the rehearsal rooms at eleven.' Wiltshire was staring out over London, his eyebrow ridge creased, one hand grabbing at his head fur.

'There's been another pant-hoot from Faludi; he signs Mario may not make it for today's rehearsals. His throat isn't any better and he doesn't want to risk the flight from Milan.'

' "Wraaf"! Bugger it!' Wiltshire was definitely riled. 'There's absolutely no point in engaging the greatest "euch-euch" tenor vocaliser in the world if the bloody chimp is so delicate he can't get on a plane. I'd just as soon we'd stuck with our original casting –' He broke off and turned to Busner. 'I'm sorry, old fellow, this really is annoying and I'm afraid I'll have to cut our impromptu session short.'

'Is that Mario Trafuello you're gesturing about "huu"?'

'The same. Have you seen him vocalise, Zack "huu"?'

'Indeed, at Garsington last year, absolutely superb.'

' "Wraaf" if you can actually get him on the stage, that is – the bugger is more temperamental than any prima donna. Constantly issuing petty directives through his agent, adding clauses to his contract. I'm almost at my wits' end. But look, Zack, it really isn't good enough; I want to feel you properly some time soon – will you pant-hoot me, please "h'huuu"?' Wiltshire's fingers chopped the air.

'Of course, Peter, of course. It's also possible that I'd like your opinion on this chimp I'm going to see now. He's suffering from the rather unusual delusion that he's a human. If he turns out to be as intriguing as I think, he could be of interest to you.'

' "H'huu"? You don't sign? Well, my initial reaction would be that it's a site-specific delusion. You'll probably find out that he has some history of saving whales, or raiding laboratories. You know how paranoiacs often take their delusional content from whichever current ethical obsession preys on them. I'm sure you'll find that's the case with this chimp –'

'Dykes. His name is Dykes. Quite a well-known artist, I believe.'

'Dykes "h'huu"? Simon Dykes? Yes, he is. Very well known. In fact, I met him once. There was some possibility of him doing set designs for me, but it never came to anything. All the more reason for you to stay in touch, Zack. If you want to patrol this fellow around like you do your Tourettics and amnesiacs, I'd be as good a place to start as any.'

'I'll bear that in mind, Peter.'

'And now I must go.'

The allies embraced with considerable emotion, and when they broke both of them had tears in their eyes. 'Well "chup-chupp" it was lovely to see you, Zachary my darling. I'll miss your scrag all the more for having had this abrupt grooming.'

'You too, Peter "chup-chupp". You're still one of the most beautiful chimps that I know.'

They held one another's genitals tenderly for a few seconds and then fissioned. Busner dismissed Franklin with a cursory – but well aimed – kick to his broad backside, and he was pleased to see that Peter Wiltshire recovered some of his pride, following it up with a hail of light blows on Franklin's shoulders as they headed off down the hill.

Busner found the sub-adults clustered around the base of a tree at the Regent's Park Road exit to the park. They had cornered a squirrel in the upper branches and were throwing stones at it, but none of them so far had attempted to shin up the trunk. ' "Wraaaf"! What's the matter with you lot,' their alpha signed, coming up behind them. 'I would have hoped to see you all licking out brain pans by now, not squatting on the ground like a troop of baboons!'

'We can't get up the trunk, Alph.' Six hands synchronised. 'There's some kind of anti-climb paint on it.'

Busner felt the trunk of the tree. It was true. It was covered with a slippery plasticised coating and a notice attached by a loop of wire informed him: 'Camden Council has intiated a programme of climbing interdiction on Primrose Hill during the replanting scheme for this year.'

' "Wraaa" bloody '87!' the old chimp gestured to his patrol.

They all flicked back dutifully, 'Bloody '87!'

'Nothing,' their alpha continued, 'absolutely *nothing* has had a more pernicious effect on the lives of young chimps in our city than the depredations of the great "euch" storm of '87.' He paused, holding up an admonitory finger. In lecture mode now, he neglected to notice the three smaller admonitory fingers, that were surreptitiously held up as well, and the three sets of flying fingers that subtly mimicked what followed. 'Nothing, that is, save for the woeful "euch-euch" and inadequate response of central government. What do they expect the sub-adults of London to do if they can't even get out and climb a tree when they want to "huu"? It's no wonder that you lot are turning into delinquents. No wonder!'

There was a rather craven "toot" from the road. Gambol had pulled up in the Volvo. 'Now,' Busner continued, 'we're heading on down to Charing Cross to see about this chimp. You will all behave impeccably – is that understood "h'huuu"?'

'Yes, sir.' Charles threw a final pebble at the squirrel, who had come halfway down the trunk, then along with the others he followed in Busner's scut, as the noted authority on chimpanzee nature vaulted the railings, the car parked next to the kerb, and swung himself in through the open window of the Volvo.

Gambol put the car in gear and the Busner patrol continued on its way, in a south-westerly direction.

Chapter Seven

T he hospitals of central London exist to serve health requirements of awesome severity. Whether it be the diseases occasioned by poverty – obesity, rickets, tuberculosis, arterial sclerosis, cancer, pollution-related asthma, hepatitis and CIV; or those engendered by wealth – pollution-related asthma, hepatitis, arterial sclerosis, cancer, CIV and obesity – the hospital's problems remain the same, to make an immovable object – the determination of the electorate to compel their parliamentary representatives to place a curb on fiscal apportionment – bow to an unstoppable force, the determination of that same electorate to have adequate, free provision of palliatives for whatever ails them, whenever it ails them.

The hospitals of central London – like the prisons – are buildings sublimely out-of-joint with their surroundings. Whether recently built, or dating from the Victorian era, they all have an air of immemorial, institutional dolour. Chimpanzees may come, these edifices seem to sign, and chimpanzees may go; areas may be gentrified and areas may be de-gentrified, but still funguses eat away at nasal bridges, and lonely flyers affix themselves to neglected bulletin boards, while vortical columns of warm, smelly air commingle on auxiliary stairwells.

Charing Cross Hospital is no exception to this sad rule. Since its banishment on the grounds of size, from its previous central location, it has strutted its stuff along a block of the Fulham Palace Road just south of Hammersmith. If you drive down from where the flyover hops on its file of single piles across the heap of shopping centres, bus stations, office blocks and entertainment complexes, you come on to a road remarkable for its failure even to fail.

The Fulham Palace Road is poorly, but not poor. Run down, but not on the run. Scared, but without even the brio to be scary in turn. Past the Guinness Trust block of flats at the road's mouth there's a procession of rancid eateries and fast-food joints. Fish follows chicken, chicken follows fish – each factory-fed on the other. Global geography is discombobulated here so that the Far East precedes the Near East and Indo-China and India trade places, again and again and again.

So cooked-out is this parade of shops, that on a hot summer's day if there were an inundation of liquid fat, flowing down the sizzling tarmac in a glossy splurge, you could throw the stock of these eateries on to the road and watch it griddle into a communal paella.

The hospital rears up from this trough of low-rent troughing, pushing a façade of pure Bauhausian rationality – glass upon concrete, concrete upon glass – fourteen storeys into the chomped-up atmosphere. But something has gone wrong here – as ever in London. There is too small – or too big, the metropolis is nothing if not ambiguous in the extreme – an extent of forecourt greenery and trapped brown water. There is too heavy and too jutting a pediment above the rank of glass doors; there is too great a mash of metal in the overcrowded car-park to give anything but the impression of an institution under siege, in trouble, its very fabric annealed by the effort of resisting the diseases that assault it from within and without, diseases of the fiscal body as much as the physical.

Inside the hospital an air of corporate endeavour tries to gang up on you. There are escalators, yes. They still thread themselves continually into their hidden spindles,

94

true enough. There are also signs aplenty, pointing out the directions in which you should drag your crapulent body in search of treatment. But head up to the mezzanine, skirt the canteen with its hooting and yammering clientele – comprising one part pasty-muzzled mother to three parts pasty-muzzled infant – push on through double doors, then more double doors, and you will find yourself soon enough in untenanted space. Wards in which the ghosts of patients long departed recline on skeletal neststeads and the broken spirits of long gone junior doctors toe-tap mournfully over the linoleum. Wards in which the trailing tubes and coiling cables of the Tree-of-Life-Giving have withered, becoming rotted lianas, scraggy and dusty.

It's bewildering, this sense of being both within a hospital and within the shell of what-was-once-a-hospital. Bewildering, and a little discomfiting, for those who have carried their wheezing infants up the escalator and along the corridors, in search of a paediatrician, but finding only a series of crumbling partitions. It's not so bewildering for the staff, who after all inhabit this building and know the detail of its roominess the way an infant knows the exact green shade of the moss growing between the paving stones outside its group home. The staff move about the hospital sure-handedly, knuckle-walking from one place where work is to be done to the next; and if their ranging takes them through one of these twilight zones they barely notice. They simply delete it and reinsert themselves where appropriate.

The only thing that has flummoxed the staff at Charing Cross Hospital – and only then the staff who have some dealings with psychiatric admissions – is the fate of the emergency psychiatric unit. This service – key for an area in which the ratio of street-conductors to scurriers-past is high – has not so much fallen into decline, or been subject to a budgetary castration – in the manner of the orthopaedic out-patients' clinic, the fertility clinic and the well-female clinic – as expelled, coughed up, shat out, so that it now lies in a corner of one of the subsidiary car-parks. Here the unit crouches on breeze-block piles of irregular heights. No chip off the proud, futuristic block, merely a Portakabin.

This outpost of the psychiatric department is not however abandoned, or alone. There is too much commerce of souls for that to be the case. Up on the fifth floor of the hospital are the main wards, Lowell for the temporary admissions and Gough for the chronics – the sectioned. Between these two and the unit there is a continual toing and froing, a transposition of different degrees of disturbance. Such that the administrators in charge of the department are always in the middle of an ongoing game of draughts, their hands and feet flying from peg to board, as they shift a manic-depressive from the unit to Lowell, or a suicide from Lowell to Gough, or a sociopath from Gough back to the unit, *en route* for a special hospital.

The staff of the department, under the redoubtable leadership of Dr Kevin Whatley, MD, FRCPsych., have grown accustomed to the perpetual motions involved in their work, the toting of this loony here, the portage of that loony there. So accustomed that a whole series of in-jokes has grown up about the unit and its awkward situation. 'I'm just off to the Gulag,' they'll cheerily gesture to their colleagues, as they scrawl their initials on the requisite docket for the restraints, or the haloperidol, or the Largactil. 'Need anything from the mother ship?' they'll enquire on quitting the Portakabin, an egress that invariably results in the whole structure rocking on its mismatched supports.

The staff are also inured to the plethora of different maladjustments that they witness in any given day; and the maladjustments of those maladjustments the underfunding has forced on the department. It is not uncommon for chimps who are little more than mildly claustrophobic to be confined in small rooms with chimps who believe themselves to be alien warlords. Nor is it by any means unknown for chimps who have been sectioned for unspeakable acts involving barnyard fowl to find themselves wandering around Lowell, with no barrier to their leaving the ward, save for a couple of neurasthenic old biddies playing crib.

But in some aspects of its work the psychiatric department at the Charing Cross Hospital retains a clinical reputation second to none. Particularly as regards its 'crash team'. This team – which operates out of the Portakabin, but takes orders from the department – is the most rapid emergency psychiatric team in London. It has been known to quit the hospital, enambulance, drive to the furthest reaches of the catchment area, bag, tag and sedate a mad chimp, and have him on Gough spraying shit at the cleaners, all within half an hour.

Such a formidable track record has brought with it certain benefits, and the team attracts both junior doctors who wish to specialise in psychiatry and newly qualified psychiatric nurses, all of whose demarcated desire is to practise not necessarily thoroughly, but at any rate at great speed. Speed, they might sign, is the essence.

So, on this particular late-summer morning, when the red 'phone in the team's office-cum-cubbyhole clattered into life, and the screen first filled, then emptied of static to show the familiar features of the dispatcher at New Scotland Yard, the five members present were galvanised into activity even before they knew where they were headed. ' "Aaaa"! I've got a chimp here who's had a psychotic breakdown. It's right on your patch,' signed the police auxiliary.

'Address "huuu"?' countersigned the duty psychiatrist.

'63 Margravine Road, ground floor.'

'Any details "huu"?'

'Not really. Some kind of acute breakdown, male, late twenties. We were pant-hooted by the consort who's in a bad way herself.'

'Drugs "huu"?'

'We don't know –'

'Any idea at all of whether he's violent "huu"?'

'He has tried to attack the consort, but he hasn't managed to hurt her. She signs he's very weak.'

'Weak "huu"?'

'That's right, weak.'

'OK, we're on our way.'

The receiver was slammed back on to its cradle. The duty doctor, whose name was Paul, waved to his two nurses. 'It's Margravine Road "euch-euch", hardly worth bothering to take the vehicle –'

'What do you suggest then "huu"?' Belinda, the new female on the team, scutted in. 'We knuckle-walk round there and get him to carry us back again?'

'This is no berserker – in fact he's weak according to the consort who made the emergency pant-hoot.'

'Weak "huu"?'

'That's right, weak.' Paul looked at Belinda; her short white coat rode up exposing her nether regions. Nearly there, he thought, funnelling his top lip and sucking in the must of her; another couple of days and that swelling will be positively oozing – can't wait to mate the little creature. For the time being he filed the lust – the three other members of the team were already outside and Paul could hear the ambulance hacking and hawking into life.

Simon Dykes, the artist, awoke, his consort's hard teat cushioning his cheek. He sighed and burrowed down into the shaggy sweetness of her. The disturbing cadences of the lucid dream had faded, replaced on waking with the remnants, the cool leftovers of their lovemaking, which cancelled out the worst of the hangover, the maculate froth from the spilt beer of last night's debauchery.

Warm water, thought Simon, that's what I need. Warm water, warm salt water up the crud-filled nose. Then coffee, then juice, then work. It would all begin in the rhinencephalon, that most ancient of neural pathways, which stretched across the front of the cerebellum, jerry-rigged by selection, the very embodiment of the individual, the cultural, peeling away from the phylogenetic, the primitive, the primate-ive.

Simon sniffed, simiously. A clutch of large hairs on Sarah's teat was actually pushed up his nostril, in amongst the crapulent deposits. A clutch of large hairs that smelt indefinably – for Simon – of chimpanzee. Chimpanzee, warm, cuddly furriness. Chimpanzee post-coital smell of sweat infused through fur. In its way a lovely smell – and all the more erotic for being braided with Cacharel, the perfume that Sarah always wore. A clutch of large hairs *on* Sarah's teat . . . Simon lifted his head and looked full into the open, guileless, heart-shaped countenance of the beast he was in bed with.

And then he was on his feet, perhaps screaming – he could not have said because the whole world was roaring around him now. Roaring as he backed away from the bed where the beast lay, on its back, its initially brute, dull eyes now on him with awful interest, the white clearly visible, right the way round the greenest of pupils slit by hot jet irises.

He backed and tripped on an edge of rug, fell heavily against the windowsill feeling the hard shock of bone and wood that affirmed this was so – Sarah was gone and he had woken up in a bed with this beast, or ape, or something that was *so fucking big* that its limbs were arranged in a human attitude, the knees akimbo, the heels touching, the arms behind the torso now pushing up on the elbows to lift that animal mask towards him, the mouth opening, gaping to reveal teeth so large, canines so long –

"Wraaa!" Sarah shrieked, and then signed to the shaking figure slammed against the window, 'Simon, what the fuck are you doing, stop screaming like that! "H'hoooo"!' Which Simon simply saw as the beast flexing and fiddling its hands towards him, to grasp him, with sickening speed, while it screeched, its breath whistling into carnivorous yowls. So loud! The cries whined off the glass of the window, jarring his spine and back. So loud!

"Wraar-ah! Wraar-ah! Wraar-ah!" he cried, and then with deafening unoriginality, "Hooo! H'hooo – Help!" He wanted to turn from the beast, turn from its mouth so large, its teeth, dripping with saliva, so long. He wanted to turn and see if he could get the sash up, if he could get down into the garden. Here he was thinking so inconsequentially – yet so pragmatically – that he considered the depth of the drop to the patio; and when it moved again he was caught off a guard he never had anyway.

It moved so fast – the beast. It reared up, then using its arms to effect springy leverage leapt bipedal. "Aaaaaa!" Sarah vocalised, truly scared now; Simon's muzzle was so pale and although not horripilating his fur was drenched with sweat. It hung in sopping hanks from those long, lovable arms, which a moment ago had been embracing her with infinite tenderness, and that now beat against the window, insensate with fear.

'Simon! "Hoooo"! Point out to me, my love, what's the matter with you "huuu"?'

There was no thought of the window now, and the door had never been in the frame. The instant he had become aware of the beast in the bed Simon had gone fully, irretrievably into shock. Like a silent sitter transfixed by a harsh flutter of wings, then the "rap-rap-rap" of beak scratching wall, scratching floor, Simon had a flying bird now in the utter confinement of his head. It was the very *embodiment* of the thing that he simply couldn't stand. The very alien *embodiment* of it. The animal was upon him.

Sarah's only thought, only instinct, was to reassure, and that meant to hold, to pluck and tweak, at that sad, lank fur, to smooth her consort's disordered limbs that knocked and shook, to steady his grappling hands which were hardly making any comprehensible signs. She moved forward to the edge of the nest, intending to hug him preparatory to an emergency grooming. "Get away! Getaway! Geddaway! G'way!" Simon sank down behind his knees, in the corner – the beast was rearing above him. He still couldn't take in much of its appearance, only its full odour which filled his nostrils, obliterating the sweat-stench of his own terror.

Why was he vocalising like that? Sarah made stunned

speculations. Christ! He's had some kind of awful seizure. She thought immediately – even in the throes of this incident – could it be those fucking drugs? The ecstasy? The crap cocaine? The furlongs of Glenmorangie drunk in the depths of the Sealink Club? She hesitated, and feeling her swelling awkwardly lodged between her upper thighs, like a balloon carried by an infant in some party game, moved reflexively to shield it with one arm.

Which was just as well, for her deranged consort chose that moment to attack. "Fuuuuckooofff!" he screeched, lurching up from beneath the window and slashing at her with claws-for-hands. Sarah recoiled, bracing herself for an impact that never came. For there was something awfully wrong with the way Simon was moving – as if his very limbs were unfamiliar to him. He had even misjudged the distance from where he was slumped to where she stood on the nest's edge. Now his hands uselessly combed the air either side of her head. She caught hold of one arm and felt at once the lack of tensility. She caught the other easily enough as well. The consorts muzzled one another across a divide that was at once two feet of gaily patterned rug, and insurmountably strange.

He was still making the guttural vocalisations that Sarah couldn't understand. She brought his flapping hands back until they were between them, and stepped down gingerly off the edge of the nest. 'Simon, my love, Simon,' she signed on the backs of his hands, in his dear, distressed fur. 'What is it "gru-nn", my love "huu"? What is frightening "grnn" you so much? It's only me, me, Sarah.'

He was whimpering and keening, but in an oddly animal way, very low-pitched, growly. His pupils were rolled back exposing the whites of his eyes. His lack of horripilation disturbed her – and his febrility. His legs were concertinaing beneath him. Then, just for a moment, she felt his fingers move with something like import, and she could mark out a few signs, shaped with spiky terror. 'Beast,' Simon signed, 'fucking beast.' Then he sprayed her.

Even the greatest of shocks can be negotiated by the mind, which is, after all, a homoeostatic device, constantly labouring towards equalisation – a steady state. So it was that Simon Dykes, the artist, in a suitable pose: recumbent, covered in his own shit, slowly came round, slowly admitted the fact of where he was and what had happened, just in time for it to happen again.

The crash team's ambulance drew up in the elbow of Margravine Road and disgorged five chimps in the bright blue jackets of paramedics. Paul, the doctor, vaulted the iron gate and nonchalantly knuckle-walked up the tiled path. He noted the careful arrangement of pot plants – herbs to the right, flowers to the left – and the tattered Greenpeace sticker in the front window. Saving the whale while smoking comfrey, he mused – looks like it could well be a drug thing.

Before he had rung the bell the front door swung open, smearing the features of the young female behind it across the panes of toughened glass. Paul consulted the call sheet in his hand. ' "Huuu" Sarah Peasenhulme?' he signed.

' "U-h'-u-h'-u-h'-u-h'" that's right.' Her fingers shook as she replied. She was, Paul not so much noted as boggled, in full oestrus, her swelling a beautiful nacreous pink, the folds of moist flesh delightfully defined, scraggy at the perineum in just the way he liked.

'Where's the consort then "huu"?'

' "U-h'-u-h'-u-h'" He's in the bedroom.'

'And what's his name "huu"?'

'Simon "u-h'-u-h'-u-h'" Simon Dykes.'

Paul moved to push by her, and she cowered in the awkward vestibule. Cowered and half presented her swelling to him, but in such a way that it was apparent that she was doing it involuntarily. Paul hesitated; while not strictly against the regulations to mate when on an emergency call-out, it was felt at the department – and in particular by Dr Whatley – to be somewhat at variance with the image the crash team was seeking to promote.

This went through Paul's mind as he shouldered his way past the submissive female, bestowing a reassuring pat and kiss on the top of her blonde head. A rather old shire lap pony was trotting up and down the corridor behind the inner door to the flat. The poor beast was whinnying pathetically and drooling. In his scut Paul heard the female patting it, reassuring it, while making gentle lip smacks and soothing pants.

On the brink of the bedroom he stopped, cocking an ear. All he could see through the half-open door was one of the wooden poles supporting the tipping mirror on top of the dressing table. This was festooned with strings of beads and silk scarves. The table itself was covered with a dusty collection of porcelain figurines, ornamental boxes and other feminine knick-knacks. In the noonday heat the temporary quiet of the flat was oppressive, as were its odours of pony, excrement, perfume and mating. He paused, hearing a whimper from behind the door. The dispatcher had said the chimp was weak – did that mean not dangerous? Best not to take any chances.

Belinda had come up behind Paul, and he turned to see that she was accompanied by the hard chimp of the outfit, Al, who was carrying a set of restraints. 'Have you got the tranks "huu"?' Paul inparted softly on Belinda's forearm.

'Yes,' she replied. Paul pushed the door gently open.

' "Huuu"? Simon, my name is –'

"Wraaaaa!" The chimp's scream ripped through Paul's soft vocalisation and gentle signing. Simon was bipedal onthe heap of disordered covers mantling the nest. His fur wasn't erect, but his shoulders hunched aggressively and all his teeth were showing as he continued to scream, "Wraaa!Wraaa!Wraaa!" He grabbed hold of a sheet in one hand and a pillow in the other and waved them in Paul's direction. The psychiatrist took a step back so that he was partly hidden by the door. He'd handled enough psychotic chimps to know that this display could turn violent if he breached the invisible forcefield surrounding Simon Dykes.

' "Hooo" Jesus Christ!' Al inparted on Paul's back. 'I thought this one was meant to be harmless – do you want the tranks "huu"?'

"HooGrnnn," Paul vocalised, then gestured to Simon, 'Now, Simon, we're not going to hurt you –'

' "Wraaa"! Keep away from me, you fucking ape! Keep away, keep away, keep away!' He threw his soft missiles at Paul – they fell short, doubly harmless. Simon advanced to the brink of the nest. Paul came out from behind the door, hoping that this would push the maddened male back again, but instead Simon attacked, using the bounce of the bed to leap feet-first at the dead centre of the psychiatrist's chest. Paul took a step backwards, but too late to prevent the chimp crashing into him, knocking him and Al to the floor. Simon's hands were on Paul's throat, the nails clawing deep in his fur, signing nothing but panicide. The hands were – Paul realised with a shock – like an infant's hands. Or rather, they had only the strength of an infant's.

Paul recovered himself instantly and aimed a short jab to his attacker's belly. With a harsh clack of his teeth, Simon rolled off Paul retching and coughing. ' "Waaa"! What the fuck are you playing at!' Paul had the ape by his scruff and delivered a couple of sharp cuffs to his muzzle. Simon began to whimper with fear and pain. 'What's up with you, chimp "h'huuu"? Been at the cocaine, have we "huu"?' Paul gave the scruff, which was on the long side, a few more tugs before registering that there was no resistance at all. The chimp's head was lolling against the psychiatrist's belly. The eyes were rolled back in their sockets, showing only the whites. The clenched hands didn't so much drum as pat at Paul's belly fur, where his tunic had bunched up.

'Tranks "huu"?' signed Al, who was standing right at Paul's shoulder, and Belinda shook the restraining garment she was holding, making both her meaning apparent and the buckles of the thing softly jingle.

'I don't think either will be "euch-euch" necessary, Simon,' he signed to the chimp whose head he was now almost cradling. 'Are you all right "huu"? Poor darling "chup-chupp", did I hurt you? Are you OK? Don't worry "huh-huh", everything will be OK . . . "Huu" Simon? Simon? "Euch-euch" we've lost him.' This last flourish was to his team, for the artist's head had fallen forward, and his lanky body, the fur shampooed with perspiration, now collapsed in a frothy brown bundle at Paul's feet.

'He's gone catatonic,' Paul gestured to the rest of the team ranged behind him. 'His mind has restrained his body for us. Although there was no strength in that attack at all. None at all.'

"Climb on my back."

"What's that?"

"Climb on my back – like spoons in a draw." The soft sounds of limb and sheet smoothly rubbing. Cool hands between the shoulder blades. Then lips there. A warm arm snakes around Simon's belly, another smooths the hairs at his nape, "Mmmf'."

"Mmmf'," they grunt-sigh in unison. They hunker down to sleep.

Herbs to the right, flowers to the left. Herbs to the right, flowers to the left. Simon's prone head banged against the metal rim of the chair's headrest as the crash team's orderlies carried him down the path, past the gawping old female from next door. He stirred – went under again.

"Can I go on your he-ead?" An infant's cry, reedy but with a twang of his own sarcasm. He does not reply. Again: "Can I go on your he-ead?" It's Magnus, or Henry, or Simon – they want to be lifted, they want to be held. They need to be held. "Can I –"

"All right." The slim hips between big hands. Like holding a lover's waist. But no lover was ever so light. As he lifts the infant Simon feels the lack-of-resistance, the way its body is but poorly attached to this earth, and imagines that he could push him – Henry or Magnus or Simon, he knows not which – up and up and up, into the sky. Then small bare legs are clamped around the back of his neck. Small hands entwine in his hair, grasp, unfeeling – or at any rate uninhibited about this touch. The hands seem to speak in Simon's hair: 'My body – your body. Where's the difference? Where's the join?'

' "Hoo" dear, "hoo" dear, "hoo" dear, "hooo"' signed the old female who was watching the team chimphandle the unconscious Simon and distressed Sarah into the ambulance. 'What has happened to them "huuu"?'

'Do you know her at all well "huuu"?' asked Belinda, who was bringing up the anal scrag, leading the lap pony by its bridle.

' "Hoo" yes,' came the reply. The female's fingers went to one of the curlers in her fraying head fur. 'She's a lovely young female, always ready with a kind sign. We often have a flutter . . . I've never taken to him though, I must sign.'

'Must you,' snapped Belinda, who already had the measure of the female. 'Why's that "huu"?'

'Well, they've been consorting now for well over a year, and in my opinion that's not right for a young female. And as for him, he's been fissioned from his group for some time now. I know because she showed me.'

'Is that so "huu"? Do you know anything else about him "huu"?'

'Only that he's some kind of an *artist* – whatever that means. As I sign, I never really took to him. But her . . . "hoo", she's a lovely young thing, lovely. It wouldn't surprise me if he's got her mixed up in some awful drug th –' Belinda flagged her down. 'Watch. You don't have spare keys for her flat by any chance "huu"?'

'"Hoo" yes, yes I do.'

'Well, in that case "euch-euch",' Belinda picked the old lap pony up bodily by its bridle and plonked it down on the other side of the fence, 'you'll oblige me if you look after this old nag while she's away, "huuu"?'

The old female – who hadn't been mated in going on twenty years – watched Belinda bound off down the path and swing into the back of the ambulance with ill-concealed contempt. Young hussy, she thought to herself as she ran her gnarled toes through Gracie's mane, look at her parading her swelling like that, even though she's days off oestrus, I don't know, what is the world coming to. Then she led Gracie inside her own, furniture-polish-scented house and began looking for her mac; she'd have to go down the shops and get the poor beast some hay for its dinner.

It was impossible to separate the two distraught chimps on the short drive to Charing Cross Hospital and on arrival Sarah refused to leave Simon's side. Paul put them in the small cubicle used for assessing patients and busied himself with the necessary paperwork for Simon's admission. 'Let them cool off a little,' he signed to Belinda, 'see if she wants a cup of tea, but don't attempt to rouse him, he may not be quite so ineffectual next time. And see if you can find a gown – being naked can't be helping him to feel simian "huuu"?'

Belinda found a gown and then Sarah helped her to push Simon's stiff arms through the wide sleeves. He lay on the examination couch in a foetal position; his lanky body resisted them, tightly curled as it was. He was breathing quickly and shallowly, but apart from that there was no sign of physical trauma.

'Would you like a cup of tea "huuu"?' Belinda gestured when they'd got the thing on.

'Yes, please,' Sarah countersigned. 'I think I would.'

'Would you like to inpart a little about what happened "huuu"?' Belinda resigned tentatively, gently teasing some more of Simon's dried semen out of the blonde hairs surrounding Sarah's sexual swelling.

'I . . . I . . . "hoo", I don't know . . .'

'Not if you don't want to – but you may find it easier fiddling with me first . . .'

'It's just "hooo", well, you probably know already, we're consorts . . .'

'Yes.'

'I didn't take him away from his group – if that's what you're thinking. It fissioned some time ago. It's just, well, he's a very brilliant chimp, you know, some people think of him as a great ape, and I don't want any of this to affect his career. He's an artist, you know – he has a show opening next week.'

'Is that right "huu"?' Belinda was noncommittal. She found this posh, pretty female's animation regarding her consort distinctly unnerving.

'Yes. And it's . . . "u-h'-u-h'" well . . . I don't want anything to upset that.'

'Like what "huu"?'

'You know.'

'Sarah.' Belinda dug her fingers a little deeper into the young female's fur to emphasise the seriousness of what she was about to inpart. 'Were you taking drugs last night "huu"? Is that what you're worried about "huu"?'

Belinda didn't get a countersign to this question, because the door swung open and Paul entered the cubicle carrying a clipboard with a form attached, a ballpoint pen grasped in his foot. 'I've managed to get a secure room for Simon on Gough,' he signed. 'We need to pant-hoot his GP and his next of kine, can you help "huu"?'

'I . . . "hoo" . . . I'm just his consort.' Sarah was flustered, embarrassed even.

'This is not the time for evasiveness, young female – you'd better delineate what you know.' The proximity to the hospital, and his superiors, gave a more doctorly feel to Paul's signing, and Sarah, sensing this, sat upright and began gesticulating with greater insistence as well, her fingers forming the signs carefully.

'His ex-alpha mate is denoted Jean Dykes.' Paul wrote this down on the clipboard. 'She lives in Oxfordshire, a place called the Brown House on the Otmoor Estate near Thame. I . . . I don't have the number –'

'We can get that. And his GP "huu"?'

'Bohm, Anthony Bohm. He works at the health centre in Thame. He . . . he . . .'

'Yes "huu"?'

'He treated Simon for "hooo" well, for depression in the past.'

'Is Simon on medication at the moment "huu"?'

'Not that I know of, but he's been on antidepressants before.'

'I see. And what happened last night "huu"?'

'Nothing unusual . . .' She tailed off, her fingers fell into her lap. Paul looked at her sexual swelling with hooded eyes. He was a chunky, well-set chimp with an appealing liver-spotted muzzle who got as many females as he wanted, and he knew that despite her obvious distress this young female still found him attractive. Possibly it was the trauma of seeing her consort transformed from a composed chimp into a raving creature.

'Sarah "gru-nnn".' Paul's fingers were precisely angled to convey the maximum of caring, admixed with resolution. 'If we're going to help Simon we need to know what has happened to him, and in particular if this is some kind of drug-induced psychosis. We're not in the business of ruining chimps' lives here – we want to help. You know that everything you sign to me will remain strictly confidential.'

' "Hoo" all right, we did do some drugs last night –'

'Which drugs "huu" cocaine?'

'Yes.'

'And alcohol "huu"?'

'Of course – and some doves.'

'Ecstasy "huu"?'

'That's right –'

She broke off, a porter had entered the room.

'Is this the one for Gough, guv "huu"?' he signed to Paul.

'Yes, that's right, are you going to take him over "huu"?'

'Well, we were.' He pointed to his co-worker, who was lingering outside. 'But admin showed us he was OK to go in a chair – and that's all we've brought with – but he looks like a "euch-euch" stretcher job to me, in which case he'll have to wait a while.'

'For heaven's sake, chimp "euch-euch"!' Paul was rattled; this was just the sort of apathetic, slipshod approach he avoided by working with the crash team. 'You can prop him up in the chair or something. "Waaa", if necessary you can carry him over –'

'– I wouldn't point that up, guv, you know we're not really meant to carry the patients –' He didn't finish signing, because Paul leapt straight at him and delivered a combination of raking blows, open-handed, across the porter's muzzle. Blood poured from a gash above his eyebrow ridge.

"Eeeeek!" screamed the porter, backing away and clutching his wounded muzzle. He gestured frantically, 'Sorry, guv "u-h'-u-h'" sorry "u-h'-u-h'" I didn't mean to bother you. I know you're a good shrink, a powerful shrink, I revere your ischial scrag – I'm sorry . . .' He turned his back on Paul and presented very low.

'That's all right, porterkins,' Paul signed, while smoothing the ruffled fur on the proffered rump. 'I acknowledge your respect, I adore your obsequiousness, now just get him over there.'

'I'll feetle this,' gestured the other porter to his wounded workmate. He bounded into the room, grabbed the collar of Simon's gown with one of his large, horny feet, and pulled the paralysed form of the artist upright. He then let it slump across his shoulders. The two porters left the room, Simon lolling on the second porter's back like a broken doll.

'There you go, my lad "chup-chupp". There you go.' How can there be meaning in that touch? Yet Simon senses meaning – in the touch: 'Easy does it. Soon have you tucked up in nest.

"H'hooo" watch it – don't want another drubbing from that shrink – now do we? Watch it!'

His eyes open on a brief, upside-down snapshot of a fountain peeing into the sky. He thinks: I know this place. Turns his head to see cars in ranks, Volvos, Vauxhalls, Fords. Cars – reassuring as their manufacturers' names. Groggily he turns again to see what – or who – is conveying him. Apes. Monkeys. Like a fucking P.G. Tips advert. Monkeys in shorty white coats. Parodies of humanity. Caricatures. He cannot cry out. It's a sleeping paralysis. He loses consciousness again.

' "H'huuu"? What do you think?' Paul consulted his colleague.

' "Euch-euch" well, that's what it looks like,' Belinda countersigned.

' "Hooo" I imagine so too . . .'

'What were you signing?' Sarah looked up from her lap; she had been staring at her swelling as if it would provide some answer to her predicament and hadn't seen the exchange.

'Well.' Paul got bipedal and moved towards the door. 'I was really just confirming my own provisional diagnosis –'

'Which is "huu"?'

'I think your consort has had a drug-induced psychotic breakdown. All the symptoms are there, the irrationality, the paranoia, the lashing-out. The only puzzling thing is his lack of strength. Quite the opposite is usually the case with this kind of thing. But this is only a provisional diagnosis, we'll have to consult my colleagues and Dykes's GP – this chimp Bohm – before we can be certain.' Paul made as if to leave, but Sarah came forward submissively and began to groom him a little. It was the first grooming she had done since the crash team arrived at her flat and Paul took it in good part.

'Doctor,' she inparted, 'he will "chup-chupp" be all right, won't he "huu"? I – I feel very guilty. You see, I don't think he would have taken those drugs without me.'

Paul looked at her seriously. 'Did you give him the drugs, Sarah "huu"?'

'N-no.'

' "H'hooo" well, I find it hard to see why you feel so guilty then. But anyway, no, you shouldn't worry too much, the prognosis for this kind of thing is on the whole fairly good. He just needs to dry out for a couple of days. We'll look after him. You go home, try and get some comforting grooming, give us a pant-hoot later today.' And with this reassurance, the crash team's duty psychiatrist gave a valedictory drum on the doorjamb and quit the cubicle.

But Paul's optimistic signs turned out to be severely misplaced. He and the senior registrar on Gough Ward, Dr Jane Bowen, had no difficulty in getting Simon Dykes settled in the secure room – the chimp didn't pull out of his catatonic state at all. And they had no problem with Dykes's group either. His ex-alpha mate seemed to have been expecting this to happen. When Jane Bowen placed the pant-hoot to her, Jean Dykes appeared on the screen clutching an ornate rosary in one hand, the beads of alternate gold and amber. The whole while the two females gesticulated she fingered this devotional device, so that her signs were admixed with the prayerful fumble. She was wearing a thick, black, velvet dress with a ruffled collar, and the combination of this old-fashioned costume and the female's staring, intent eyes unsettled the psychiatrist.

There was that – and in keeping with her religiosity and her old-fashioned mores, Mrs Dykes continued to receive the attentions of two males while she was on the phone. So that the squeals and pants of mating further embellished her formal tempo.

' "H'huuu" Mrs Dykes?'

' "HooH'Grnn" yes, may I "huu" help you?'

'It's concerning your ex-alpha Simon –'

'Oh, Simon, Holy Mary full of grace, the Lord is with thee "h-h-h-h-hooo" . . .'

'Mrs Dykes I'm afraid I have some bad news for –'

'Blessed are thee amongst females "h-h-h-h-hooo", and blessed are the fruits of thy swelling ... Has he had some sort of "h'huu" episode?'

'A breakdown, my name is Dr Bowen, I'm –'

'Holy Mary, Mother of God, pray for us sinners "h-h-h h hooooeeek" ... !' The mating came to a squeaky finish. 'Well, it doesn't surprise me, he has turned away from the path of righteousness ... Now, and at the hour of our death –'

'Mrs Dykes, I'm the senior registrar on the acute ward at Charing Cross Hospital in London. We'd like to keep Simon here on a seventy two hour section – we need your consent as next of kine.'

'Of course, of course ... Our Alpha, who art in Heaven, hallowed be thy name ...' Her signing faltered a little, and then for the first time since they had begun to gesticulate the female's hands rested in her lap.

'I must sign,' Jane Bowen jumped in, 'did you expect this "huu"? Has Simon a history of these episodes "huu"?'

'Thy kingdom come, thy will be ... He has been a sore trial, both to me and to his infants, Henry and Magnus, yes, that is true. A miserable sinner, full of the bile of his own turpitude. As to his mental health, well, you would have to consult Anthony on that –'

'Is that Dr Bohm at the Thame Health Centre "huu"?'

'The same, Anthony has been a great support to us all, a great distal support –' She broke off, a young male of about nine had come into the picture, crawling over the back of the male who had just mated his mother. The young male's resemblance to Simon Dykes was strong, the same protuberant eyes, the same bouffant brown hair.

'Can't you see I'm gesticulating, Magnus, really –' She broke off and gave the young male a clip round his ear. He disappeared yowling. 'I'm sorry. You must appreciate, with a short-reigning alpha ...'

'Of course, of course. I'm going to pant-hoot Dr Bohm as

soon as I finish with you. All I need to know is that you'll be able to go into the health centre later today and put your signature on the papers I'm going to fax through.'

'That will be no problem, Dr Bowen. Now if you'll forgive me . . .' The big male with the red sideburns was seeing to her rear end once more. 'Glory be to the Father, to the Son and to the Holy "h-h-hoooo" –'

Jane Bowen broke the connection and knuckle-walked back on to Gough Ward from her office, gently shaking her head and musing. Perhaps there was more to the Dykeses' fissioning than the artist's consort was delineating.

Peering through the judas, Bowen saw that Simon Dykes was as they had left him, sitting on the nest in an odd manner, his feet dangling over the side rather than drawn up, his upper body peculiarly erect. Jane Bowen decided to risk an attack from him, although she was a small female – under eighty pounds. ' "Huuu" Simon?'

He didn't turn towards her, but his fingers moved, fumbling faulty signs. 'Geddaway, beast, foul demon, geddaway . . . So I'm mad, so what, geddaway . . .'

She took this as a good portent; perhaps he was pulling out of the flamboyant stage of the breakdown. She moved a little further into the room. 'Simon,' she inparted very softly on his shoulder, 'do you think you cou –' He whirled round at her touch, screamed and began clawing at her muzzle. But despite his size she easily fended him off, and was even able to grab his hands. ' "Wraaf"! Simon, I'm a doctor, I'm trying to help you!'

' "Aaaieee! Aaaiee! Aaaiee"! Get away! Get away! Don't touch me, you fucking ape! Get away!'

Jane Bowen retreated to the door of the secure room. Simon Dykes collapsed to the floor as soon as she released him. He sprayed, but ineffectually – mostly over his own legs – and now he slumped in the puréed excrement keening and whimpering. Jane Bowen gently closed the door, secured it, and went to find a nurse. 'Keep a close watch on him,' she signed. 'He isn't dangerous, but he may try and damage himself. Get me twenty mils of Valium, I'll give it to him intravenously. That should calm him. Then you try and clean him up a bit – but don't groom him, I have a hunch that his psychosis is linked to touch.' She adjusted her gown, which had ridden down over her ischial scrag. 'I'm going to pant-hoot his GP and see if I can find out anything more about our tortured genius.'

' "H'huu" Dr Bohm?'

' "H'hoooo" can I help you?' The features, like the signing, were rotund, the fingers plumply plopping the signs in the very centre of the screen. The male's great bum of a jaw was fringed with a white ruff of beard.

'My name's Dr Jane Bowen, I'm the senior psychiatric registrar at Charing Cross Hospital.'

'How can I help you "huu"?'

'It's concerning one of your patients, Simon Dykes –'

'Simon "huu"? What's up "huu"? I do hope nothing's wrong –'

'I'm afraid there is – he appears to have had some kind of breakdown, possibly a drug-related psychosis. We'll need his notes, of course, and I'm faxing through the forms for a seventy-two-hour section –'

'Is that really necessary "huu"? Is he violent "huu"?'

' "Hooo'Grmm" well, not exactly violent, although he has launched several unprovoked attacks –'

'Damn it, female "euch-euch"! If the chimp's not a threat to anyone why are you holding him "huu"? This isn't just anybody, you realise, Dykes is an eminent artist –'

'I do appreciate that, Dr Bohm; believe me, if we didn't feel that he was a potential danger to himself we wouldn't dream of holding him. But put it this way – his collapse has been flamboyant, to sign the least. Show me, has he much history of mental disturbance "huu"?'

' "Euch-euch" well . . . "Euch-euch" well, I suppose you'll get it from the notes anyway. Yes, he has. A lot of depression, been hospitalised for it twice, most recently a year or so ago. And before that a couple of years previously. Group fissioned – as you probably know if you've pant-hooted his ex-alpha –'

'I have.'

'"Hooo" poor female – as it happens I've been able to provide some direct "gru-nn" support for her – in a distal capacity of course. Well, since the second hospitalisation he's been on an SSRI –'

'He's on Prozac?'

'That's what I signed – yes, he's been getting a repeat prescription. I haven't seen him for over six months now – as far as I was aware he was much improved. Working again. I believe he's been mixed up in a rather unsuitable consortship, but that's hardly a matter for his doctor – or his ex-alpha's distal male either.'

'Has he a history of drug abuse, Dr Bohm "huu"?'

'What do you mean – drug abuse "huu"? If you mean does he take drugs, I'd sign the answer is probably yes – creative types and all that – but it's nothing we've ever gesticulated. Are you sure drugs are involved "huu"?'

'It looks that way at the moment, but we haven't been able to get anything concrete out of Dykes himself; he's in a fully fledged delusional state, some impairments of motor coordination, striking loss of vigour. Keeps signing things like <fucking monkey>, won't accept grooming. He sprays any of my staff who get too near, then relapses into catatonia.'

There was no motion on the screen for a while save for Bohm's fingers teasing at his ruff of beard and bum of chin. Then he signed, 'Well, it does sound serious, very serious. Do you think I'd better come down and take a look at him "huu"? He's been my patient for many years, more in the way of an ally. And now, of course, we're co-group members – of a sort.'

'That may be an idea, Dr Bohm, I'll keep you posted. Possibly a familiar muzzle or grooming attitude could pull him out of it.'

' "Hooo" I suppose so. I'm sorry I was so abrupt before, but you know how it is . . .' he flourished vaguely, as if this senseless hand movement somehow conveyed a panoply of doubts about psychiatry and its status within the healing professions.

'Please, don't worry, I acknowledge the suzerainty of your dedication to general practice, I acknowledge your equal ranking with mine and the refulgence of your anal scrag.'

'Quite so, quite so. Well, give me another pant-hoot as soon as there are any developments – or no developments, in which case I'll come. In the meantime, if you need to sign to anyone who's really close to him, I suggest you try George Levinson – his dealer – he has a gallery in Cork Street. He's been more of a support to Simon over the years than anyone, and in all confidence, the situation with his ex is not good –'

'I kind of gathered that.'

'Quite so, quite so. Well, I'll wait to see from you then "HoooGraa".' And without further postamble Bohm broke the connection.

For some time afterwards the provincial GP sat at his desk, staring sightlessly at the posters of teddy bears and lap ponies the health centre receptionist had stuck up on the walls of his consulting room. Eventually he summoned himself, and with fluttering hands signed to himself, 'Hierarchy, that's what it comes down to; every time, hierarchy, bloody hierarchy.' He pressed a button on the intervid and asked for his next patient to be sent in.

But later that day, in a hiatus between genteel hypochondriacs, Anthony Bohm found himself wondering whether Simon's breakdown weren't in some way connected with that drug trial, and that pushy, exhibitionistic chimp, Busner.

Chapter Eight

D r Anthony Bohm's assistance was pant-hooted for by the staff on Gough before too many more days had passed. George Levinson had already been, twice in fact. Which, knowing George and the stacked nature of his diary, was something of a miracle. Sarah had been back every day, two or three times, since that first awful morning. On the third day she brought Tony Figes with her, in the hope that maybe someone who Simon didn't know quite so intimately might be able to reach him where she had failed. But it was all to no avail. Whether his visitor was his consort, his dealer, or his ally, Simon Dykes's reaction was the same – he went humanshit.

Simon comes to. In nest, in secure room number six, on Gough Ward. He is reassured on opening his eyes by the sight of walls painted with institutional creaminess. He is further reassured by the nest itself, with its functional aspect, all rounded wooden edges. Nothing for a hysterical chimp to damage himself on here. The small window is too high up to see through, and it's barred anyway. But that doesn't matter – it's still reassuring. Everything has the character of wakefulness. Simon looks at the very weave of the sheet, the nap of the grey institutional blanket, and sees that it is real. He looks at the back of his hand – only this is unfamiliar. It's clearly his, but it seems somehow far off and hovering – furry as well. There's a noise from the door, and he turns to be blessed by more reassurance, by the security of the door itself. It's a hospital door with a judas in it. Simon thinks: I'll go to the hole and get some comfort. Parley with a vision and have it reassure me by being real.

He rises and walks, unsteadily upright, across the linoleum. Flotch, flotch, flotch, of sweat-damp soles on linoleum. So reassuring. Someone is looking in on him, someone . . . he sees as he approaches the judas . . . Someone with the muzzle of a beast. He collapses. The nurse enters, chimphandles him back into nest, administers ten milligrams of Valium, with sure fingers finding vein below fur.

They come by night and they come by day. Sometimes seconds after he has awoken, sometimes minutes, very occasionally hours. Each time they come it is the same; it cancels out, completely erases whatever security he has gained from the minute, intense examination of his environment. If they leave him for a long time, and then silently, surreptitiously check to see what he's up to before they come in, they may catch him intent upon a laundry mark, or manufacturer's plastic plaque, welding origination to artefact. For the artist is nothing if not painstaking in his delusion. But even if they leave him for hours and he has the opportunity as the sedatives seep out and the disastrous day seeps in fully to accept the testimony of his senses, their arrival is always the same nullifying shock. They are so fast when they enter. So squat, moving rapidly towards him in black scrimmages of fur and muscle.

They appear to be communicating with him – this much he knows. They appear to be communicating with him, as much because of the intentness of their movements, placing their hairy limbs here and there, as the meaningfulness of their meaty grunts, their sonorous squeals. There's further import in the way they grasp him when he begins – as he invariably does – to flip; grasp him when he begins – as he invariably does – to scream. Scream until the needle bites. Scream until consciousness seeps back out and the dreams flow around and under him.

In the dreams he is always with bodies. Human bodies. And the bodies are beautiful. He almost thinks this to himself, half forms the idea, How so that these bodies can be so beautiful, so ethereal? Because on the muzzle of it they aren't, these disordered recollections *of his father's stringy calves, with knee-borne clusters of grapelike varicosity; his mother's breasts dangling, the aureoles stretched ovals of brown stippling; his sister's breakable thighs, so white, so thin; her soles lifting, first one, then the other, each so wrinkled pink, newborn soles throwing up little plumes of sand as she scampers ahead of him to the sea, to paddle. Not beautiful if beauty is extraordinary, but perhaps beauty has always been very ordinary, and it was just that I couldn't see it.*

On the third day, after six or seven of these episodes, Sarah bearded Dr Bowen in her office. She drummed lightly on the door and pant-hooted a little more loudly than she normally would, in order to impress upon the psychiatrist that – appearances to the contrary – she was not a female to be trifled with. ' "HooH'Graa" may I gesticulate with you for a moment please, Dr Bowen "huu"?'

' "HooH'Graa" of course, of course.' The psychiatrist put down her pen. 'It's Sarah "huu", isn't it?' She pushed her chair back and regarded the female in the doorway. Attractive ape, she thought to herself, very handsome, wouldn't mind frottaging her myself with that fabulous swelling dangling off her. I bet she's been having fun the past few days.

'That's right. Look, I know, or at least I hope I know, that you're doing everything you can to help Simon – Mr Dykes –'

'You can be certain of that "euch-euch".'

'It's just that . . . "hoo", he doesn't seem to be improving at all . . . and I thought . . . "hooo".' Sarah summoned herself. Get a grip, she thought, looking at the female behind the desk. I may be petite, but she's positively gracile. If it came to a scrap between us, I'm sure I'd come out on top. 'There are some things that I've noticed about his behaviour . . . Things that might be significant.'

'Yes "huu"?' Dr Bowen pushed her papers to one side and at last gave the pretty young female her full attention. 'And what would these things be "huu"?'

'It's his posture that alerted me,' signed Sarah. She approached the desk and leapt up on to a corner of it. Her hands went automatically to her gingham swelling protector and rearranged it. 'He always squats in this odd way, right on the edge of the nest, never draws his feet up. And when he comes at me – I couldn't really call it an attack – he's always bipedal, always.'

' "Grnnn" yes –'

'There's one other thing, his fur. It's never erect, always dead flat. Now isn't that strange, something so ... so involuntary not happening "huu"?'

'Young female.' Bowen got up on the desk and crawled to where Sarah was squatting; they began casually to groom one another. 'You are very observant, Sarahkins, very observant indeed –'

'I'm an artists' agent, it kind of goes with the range.'

'Of course. Well, what you sign is true and it's something that we've noticed as well. To begin with – as you are aware – we were fairly certain that Simon had a drug-induced psychosis. I can show you now, although for some reason he didn't feel able to himself, that Simon was taking medication for depression –'

'You mean "huu" he was on Prozac?'

'Yes, yes, Prozac.'

'Why didn't he show me "huu"?' Sarah was dismayed, her pretty little muzzle crumpled up with distress.

'Perhaps he was ashamed, Sarahkins.' Jane Bowen's inparting was the gentlest, subtlest tweaking of fur. 'You know, many chimpanzees still regard depression as a source of shame.'

'But I knew all about his depressions. He said they were over, he attributed them to the fissioning of his group.'

'Well, possibly the Prozac played a part in that – but more to the point, we have an idea that the Prozac may be implicated in this breakdown. Or rather the Prozac in conjunction with the ecstasy he was taking.'

' "H'huuu"? How could that be?' Sarah was intrigued.

'We don't altogether know. Suffice to sign, ecstasy – or MDMA – acts on exactly the same receptors – you know, the parts of the brain which the molecules of a chemical attach themselves to – as Prozac. We think the two drugs synergise strongly when taken in conjunction –'

'But I don't understand, we've taken ecstasy quite a lot.' Sarah flushed. 'We like to . . . we find it . . .'

'I know.' The psychiatrist grinned and sniffed appreciatively. 'It's good for mating, isn't it "huu"?'

'Yeah, sort of.'

'But anyway, you may have taken it a hundred times, and then this added, synergistic effect can occur. It's idiosyncratic. Nor do we know quite what the implications are, but some sort of damage to Simon's neurochemistry seems to be one hypothesis.'

'But what about what I was signing – his posture, his lack of horripilation "huu"?'

Jane Bowen got down from the desk and knuckle-walked to the window, where she used the blind cord to pull herself upright. She was tired and much as she found the young female's pink cushion arousing, and the predicament of her artistic patient an interesting one, such cases were often more trouble for the psychiatric department than conventional complaints. She stared out of the window at her occluded view of a ten-yard stretch of the Fulham Palace Road, idly noting the posse of bonobos hanging outside the betting shop, smoking weed and drinking Special Brew. At length she grunted, turned to Sarah and gestured, 'I've no idea what these symptoms mean. We've never seen anything quite like them. I've gesticulated it with Dr Whatley, the consultant, and we both feel that what's disturbing Simon most is simian contact.'

' "Huuu"? Simian contact? What do you mean "huu"?'

'Well, we can't – as I sign – explain it, but Simon appears to have lost the ability, or perhaps inclination, to engage in the basic forms of simian interaction. Not visual communication –

he signs, albeit his signing is hysterical – but vocalisation, body signage, grooming, presenting, all of these are grossly impaired, if not absent altogether.'

'Could this be part of the psychosis "huu"?'

'It's possible. It could be what's denoted hysterical conversion – we've noticed that when he is left alone his behaviour becomes far more responsive – to his environment, that is. He examines all the furniture and fittings in the room with great attention to detail, his own body as well –'

'Why "huu"?'

'We don't know, but I have a hunch that if we deny him simian contact altogether for a couple of days, and perhaps give him access to writing materials, he may reach out to us using those.'

Sarah shook her head, still hooting with puzzlement. It made no sense to her, the psychiatrist's theorising; all she knew was that her consort was distressed, confined against his will instead of ranging freely. Locked up like some captive human, about to be employed for hideous experimental purposes. She didn't find Jane Bowen's touch, when they resumed grooming, at all reassuring.

So the following morning, the duty psychiatrist skipped Simon's medication, along with his forlorn attack and inefficient spraying. The chimp was left to his own devices and the judas employed to give him, along with his first breakfast tray, a foolscap pad and some pencils.

Dr Bowen even insisted on covering the judas with a piece of two-way mirroring, so that Simon was free from any visual contact whatsoever with the staff. 'It's this business about him signing <fucking monkey>, all the time,' Bowen showed Dr Whatley on their ward round. 'That and his loss of ordinary capabilities for simious interaction. Call it a hunch, but if it's other chimps that he finds so disturbing, if we remove all evidence of ourselves, he may begin to show us something of what he's experiencing.'

' "Huuu" you don't think that he's seeing other chimps in some weird way, do you?'

'It's possible "gru-nnn" – maybe he's having a baboon delusion. It's rare, but I have seen some clinical literature on such syndromes. Anyway, *I* think this is worth a try.'

They've stopped showing themselves. That's some relief. When Simon goes to the judas he sees only the wavering reflection of his own pale muzzle, not a hairy visage, leering back at him with slavering canines. This is a respite – but it also serves to confirm the awful integrity of his madness. Could it be the shots they are giving me? it occurs to Simon. Perhaps that explains the nagging sense of weakness, of lassitude? Then, during one of the periods when he sits, motionless, on the edge of his nest platform, there comes the tray of food – you cannot eat in a delusion, you can orgasm, but you can't eat. Sex is hardly ever about sex, but food is nearly always about food. With the tray comes paper and pencil. Simon thinks: Shall I draw something? The exhibition must have been and gone – then pulls himself up, because this is the first time he has consciously referred to his past within the delusion. The dreams have been doing the business of being the past, but now he's thinking about it and looking at the pencil and the paper. Bog-standard pencil and paper. Staedtler HB, black-and-red hexagonal type, not well sharpened. They don't want me to wound myself. Dig that for a news item: Artist Dies by Self-Inflicted Pencil Wound. I never was that good a draftsman.

He looks at the implements wonderingly and then writes.

It didn't take long. When the auxiliary went back to collect the breakfast tray an hour or so later, she found on it a single sheet torn from the pad and covered with spiky, irregular writing. She rotated the slot, recovered the tray, and took the note straight to Dr Bowen.

Without even scanning the artist's screed, Dr Bowen ran to the door of her office, swung into the corridor and opened one of the windows that looked out on to the car-park. "H'hoooo," she pant-hooted, and when Whatley's glasses flashed in the open window of his own office – which was a floor below Bowen's on a projecting wing of the hospital – she waved, ' "HoooGraa" I'm sorry to interrupt you, Kevin, but Dykes has done some writing!'

Whatley's spindly form materialised in Bowen's office and together the two of them pored over the artist's message. 'PLEASE, PLEASE HELP ME,' Simon had written in clumsy capitals at the top of the sheet, and below it, 'I am mad. I know that. I am mad. Please, please help me. They come all the time, the beasts, the monkeys. Are they monkeys? I don't know. They come, they attack me. I haven't seen any humans. Where are the humans? Is this a hospital? Am I mad? Why is there all this screaming, I can hear screaming, the monkeys screaming. Where are the humans? All I see are beasts, monkeys. Where is Sarah? Who has given me this paper? Where are my infants? Help me, please help me. I can't stand this any more. They attack me – the beasts. They bite me and hit me, are they monkeys? Who sent this paper and pencil? Can you help me. Please. Am I mad? If I see the beasts much more I will kill myself. Please . . .'

'What a lot of questions,' Whatley gestured, putting the sheet down on the desk without bothering to ask Jane Bowen if she had finished reading. 'What can they mean "huu"? This business about seeing monkeys – sounds like it *could* be a baboon delusion. I'll pant-hoot Ellchimp at the Gruton Clinic – they have a good archive there, plenty of case histories, see if they can send something over –'

'But what about the humans "huu"? He's put here twice <where are the humans?> – what the hell can that mean "huu"?'

'God only knows. He's clearly very confused indeed. I suppose it might be evidence of an aphasia – Wernicke's, possibly. His signing is fluent but ridiculous and inappropriate. Still – I wouldn't get too fixated on that, we have no image of organic impairment, and any delusion of this form is bound to incorporate all sorts of psychic detritus. Perhaps he thinks humans are a kind of monkey "huu"? Many chimps do, you know.'

'I know, of course I know,' Bowen signed petulantly – something she would never have dared do with Whatley's predecessor, who had kept a much tighter grip on the department. Whatley was an ineffectual chimp, and even a female like Bowen, despite – or perhaps because of – her sexuality, was able to challenge his dominance without fear of reprisal.

'How do you propose to follow up this gesticulation with Dykes in the meantime "huu"?'

'Stick at it "grnn". With his second breakfast I'll give him a few figs, or sloes, or something by way of a reward, and ask him to describe the monkeys. Let's establish if he's seeing baboons or humans, or whatever; it's well known that the very recounting of a delusional state can help to dissolve it.'

'How do you propose to follow up this gesticulation with Dykes in the meantime . . .' Bowen mimicked Whatley as soon as he had left her office. Her fingers making the words with an exaggerated parody of his cod-Oxford accent, every crooked finger a spire, every smoothed palm a dream. Bowen couldn't fault Whatley's approach to the mad artist thus far, but he had, as she styled it, 'a short intention span', and she could well imagine him losing interest in Dykes before too long. Bowen herself was inclining to the view that Dykes might well have some organic, neurological damage. The odd postures he adopted were almost Parkinsonian, as if the limbs he were attempting to control were not altogether coextensive with those he actually had.

Bowen would have liked to run a battery of perceptual, relational and other tests on the chimp, but there was no way it could be done while he was unreachable, uncooperative. There was little point in tranquillising him, darting him like some wild beast; he had to be whatever passed for – in the Dykes world – *compos mentis*. Bowen sighed, a slight chimp, almost bonobo-like, she found the regimen at Charing Cross hardly to her taste. The routine was wearing, the hours long, the patients often intractable – fodder for the long-stay hospitals or the street sink of crazies. She had always fancied herself as a more wide-ranging practitioner, more adventurous, more in the tradition of Charcot and the other nineteenth-century pioneers in the field. She despised the way her colleagues reduced everything to either a continuum of mind or a continuum of matter, without considering the idea that there might be another level where these two apparently irreconcilable continua commingled.

Zack Busner, her old alpha at Heath Hospital had gestured in such terms. He had inherited his semiology from the anti-psychiatrists of the sixties and signed always of the 'existential' and the 'phenomenological'. Now he had made a second name for himself, cranked up his fading notoriety with his anthologies of whacko prodigies and twisted savants. What would Busner make of Dykes? Surely just the kind of case he would like to get entwined in – if Dykes's delusion remained as promisingly coherent.

With Simon's second-breakfast tray came a plain sheet of questions typed out on the hospital letterhead, as follows.

Charing Cross Hospital
Department of Psychiatry

Thursday 15th August

Simon,

We believe – my colleagues and I – that you are suffering from a delusional state which crucially involves the very ground of your simious interaction. We are avoiding all direct contact with you until we can establish whether or not this is the case. Could you please answer the following questions for me as clearly as possible?
Yours sincerely
Dr Jane Bowen
Senior Registrar

1. How are you feeling – are you in any bodily discomfort?
2. Do you imagine someone is trying to harm you?
3. Can you remember the events that led up to your being here in hospital?
4. You keep referring to 'monkeys'. What do these monkeys look like?
5. Why do you try and attack any of the staff who come near you – myself included – and your consort, and any other allies who come to see you?
6. You refer in your note to 'humans'. What humans? Have you been 'seeing humans'?

Bowen observed Simon Dykes through the piece of fake mirror as he took the tray from the ledge and walked stiltedly upright, resolutely bipedal, back to the nest platform and squatted down. As he put the tray down on the cardboard table, Jane Bowen's note fluttered to the floor. The artist scratched his head fur with a languid hand, then bent down low so he could recover the piece of paper, using the same hand. 'Thass another thing,' signed Dobbs the charge nurse, who was watching as well, 'he never uses his feet for anything except that weird swaggering around the room. An' when he picks something up with his hand he's all cackhanded – he don't seem able to hold things with his thumb and index knuckle, see . . .'

It was true, Simon was struggling to scrabble the paper up from the linoleum, and the frustration was calling forth some of his odd, low-pitched vocalisations. Finally he had the note and proceeded to read it, his eyes flicking every so often towards the door. Dr Bowen had the uneasy sensation that he knew he was being watched.

Sarah pant-hooted in to the agency on the fourth day and signed to her boss, Martin Green, the gist of what had happened. ' "HoooH'Graa" Simon has had some kind of a breakdown, Martin, he's in Charing Cross Hospital.'

'Overwork, or overplay "huu"?' Green looked huffy as he turned to contemplate the screen; his signing was abrupt, his body hair semi-erect, his mobile, expressive muzzle creased to expose his canines.

'I – I don't know.'

'So, I suppose this means we won't be seeing you at work today "huu"?'

'I'm – I'm a bit upset, Martin, it was pretty bad.'

'How bad "huu"?'

She showed him, omitting nothing.

'Jesus Christ, Sarah,' he signed after a while 'you know I don't set much store by convention, but this consortship, the "euch-euch" drugs, I don't know . . .'

'I know, I know.'

'I'm sorry I was so sharp before "grnnn". I've already had a hell of a morning, more trouble with that "euch-euch" git Young. I'd just finished gesticulating with him when you pant-hooted. He signs he won't pay a penny –'

"Waaa!"

'Quite so. And what am I to do without you in the office "huu"? I hate to sign it, but your status in the hierarchy is bound to be put under stress –'

'I know, I know –'

'That's what you keep signing. Look, when can I expect you back "huu"?'

'I'm going down to Cobham for a few days, back to my natal group, see if I can get my nits picked. I'll pant-hoot you Monday. Look, Martin, I acknowledge your employment suzerainty, I worship your adamant penis, you are the rising scut in my ischial firmament. I savour your smell –'

'That's all right, Sarah, you're a good subordinate, you go home and relax.'

Sarah took the stopper from Victoria and got off at West

Byfleet. It was a hot afternoon and Gracie was panting; the flies circling her head annoyed her constantly and she tossed her little mane and neighed. Sarah had bought the lap pony a nosebag at the terminus, but it was long since finished and the diminutive horse was becoming impatient. 'There-there "chup-chupp-chupp" there-there,' she soothed Gracie, idly grooming the caramel mane.

Sarah squatted back in her seat and scanned the copy of *Cosmopolitan* she held open with the toes of one foot, while turning the pages with the toes of another. Advertisements for artificial swellings, swelling-enhancing clothing, swelling clinics, classes and manuals on how to get the best out of your swelling. And the confessional pieces: 'I Consorted with a Male for a Year!', 'I Joined Three New Groups in One Oestrus' and so on, and so on. Mating, mating, mating, Sarah thought to herself – that's all these female magazines are about, as if it were the only thing that mattered.

But even thinking this anti-sensual thought brought back recollections of Simon mating her. His speed that second time – the last time – had been phenomenal. She thought her orgasm might tear her in half, all the way from her swelling to her mouth, spill her guts on the disordered sheets of the nest. 'I want a lover with a fast hand / I want a lover with a rapid touch / I don't want a male who ta-akes too long / Let him come in a disordered rush . . .' The signs of the soul song came to her readily enough – it was her and Simon's tune, in a way. She used to do the signing, he the accompanying vocalisations – and she found herself absent-mindedly signing them now in the vicinity of her swelling. When the train got to the station her muzzle was flushed and Gracie was neighing louder than ever.

The Reverend Davis, the Peasenhulmes' distal-beta male, was waiting for her in the group's Range Rover. "Hooo-H'Graa," he pant-hooted as she leapt from the train. The station was alive with the pant-hoots of other rendezvous, and looking around at the green gardens of suburbia Sarah was almost glad to be back in Surrey. 'Here I am,' waved the Reverend, 'although you are ...' He consulted a fob watch he drew from his waistcoat pocket, an affectation Sarah had always found particularly annoying, 'about seven minutes late, fancy a fuck "huu"?'

He took her without ceremony, her head banging against the open passenger door of the four-wheel drive, while he used the outside handle to brace himself as he thrusted.

'Your mother's got an early first supper almost on the table,' the Reverend signed as they headed towards Cobham on the A245. 'Not a lot of the group around at the moment though; quite a few of the males have gone over to Oxshott to mate Lynn – she's in oestrus, y'know.'

' "Waaa" I know,' Sarah prodded, fingers cramped with irritation. She had in fact been pant-hooted by Lynn that morning. The silly female banging on and on about how she'd come on, and she wouldn't take the pill this oestrus, and how Giles really wanted an infant now they'd started the sub-group, and how should she furnish the nursery, didn't Sarah just *love* the new play trees that were on offer at Conran at the moment ... Sarah could hardly stand the lack of tact and had almost cut the connection while Lynn's fingers were in mid-motion.

'Not feeling "gru-nnn" left out, are we, my cherub "huu"?' the Reverend signed in Sarah's belly fur, pushing her blouse up so that he could unpick some of his own, rapidly drying semen. Sarah was glad of the tenderness.

'I'm sorry, Pete "huh-huh-huh", I expect Mum told you what's happened –'

'She did, Sarah, but you won't get any moralising out of me "chup-chupp" – you needn't worry about that. In this day and age a young female is perfectly entitled to a consortship well into her twenties as far as I'm "gru-nnn" concerned. We can't all form new groups or join established sub-groups as soon as we reach oestrus, times have changed. How is he, anyway "huu"?'

'No change *there*, I'm afraid, still ranting about monkeys and humans. His shrink thinks the psychosis may centre on Simon's actual chimpunity. I don't know' – she shook her head – ' "huuu" it doesn't seem very likely to me.'

It was one of the things that Sarah liked most about the Reverend, in addition to his typically Anglican tolerance for unorthodox behaviour – he had, Sarah knew, been an active homosexual when a young chimp – he never pushed things, or went on when he had nothing much to sign. They drove the rest of the way home with fingers scrabbling more or less senselessly in each other's fur, a pleasant post-coital reunion as they fiddled about the redecorated Range Rover, her alpha's upcoming prostate operation, a tombola the Reverend was organising.

Chapter Nine

A dull morning at the hospital. The pant-hooting of sane chimps in the street outside disharmonised horribly with the screams and fear-barks of the insane chimps on Cough, and the whimpers and hoots of the neurotic chimps on Lowell. Dr Jane Bowen squatted in her office, the *Guardian* 'Society' section cast aside, while she looked at the sheets of paper she held in her foot. The sheets Dobbs had brought her from Dykes. The writing was as cramped and crabbed as before, but the style was thankfully a bit more lucid, almost effortfully composed.

He hadn't countersigned the questions in any kind of order, rather he had written a résumé of the past few days from his point of view – if that's what it could be called. At the same time the narrative kept breaking off as Dykes crazily extemporised on what he believed to be his predicament.

I feel fine in myself. Absolutely fine, I feel no pain – less in fact than before. Less, than before I ended up in this nut house. I woke up, you know, and in place of my consort, Sarah, there was this fucking monkey, this ape, whatever. And there was a miniature horse. I saw a miniature horse. I don't expect you to believe any of this, but it's true, believe me. Please believe me. I tried to fend the bloody monkey off, I was screaming for Sarah, crying out for her. But the thing was damnably strong. It beat me. Christ, you have no idea how frightening this was. And it was absolutely real, not dream-like, not drug-like, but real. Really real. Then I don't know, I must have lapsed into unconsciousness. I didn't know what was happening. When I came to again there were more of these apes in the room. They beat me! They did. I can still feel the blows. They attacked me! They had horrible green eyes, and they were so fast! So strong. I could have sworn it was real. And then, thankfully, I blacked out again.

I don't know how long I've been here now. I know I'm in a mental hospital. Everything looks as it should look. I think I'm in Charing Cross. Am I in Charing Cross? But this delusion – if that's what you denote it – is persisting. Every time someone comes into the room to give me a shot, it's one of these fucking monkeys, or apes, or whatever these foul demons are. I haven't seen a human since I feel asleep with Sarah, in nest, four days ago. I know I'm mad. If you're a psychiatrist why can't you help me? I know I'm mad. Even these questions you've sent me (and I thank you for stopping the monkeys coming into the room, that's some relief) are somehow part of the delusion. What do you mean about humans? And baboons? I AM HUMAN. Believe me, I AM HUMAN. Please help me, please send my ex-alpha or my infants to see me, or Sarah, or someone. I don't think I can stand this much longer. I'd kill myself if there were the means here. Can't you help me? Please.

The psychiatrist did her routine with the window and the pant-hoot once again. Whatley wasn't there, or so his secretary pant-hooted back. Off in the canteen or perhaps at his club, the Garrick, lunching with John Osborne. Osborne – perhaps a surprising ally for Whatley – was to die later that year, after pissing into an electric light fitment. Whatley had seen it coming.

Dr Bowen had to wait twenty minutes before the consultant deigned to come crawling in. "HoooGraaa." He drummed diffidently on the doorjamb – Christ! How she despised the chimp. They hadn't been in touch for twenty-four hours, but Bowen got through the obligatory grooming session as quickly as possible, hoooting with annoyance. 'So,' he inparted the nape of her neck, right on top of a particularly irksome scab, 'what's with our resident creative genius "huu"? My secretary signs he's dispatched another missive.'

' "Euch-euch" read this.' She gave him Simon's note. Whatley read in novocal, except for the occasional grunt of concentration. Bowen played with the toys on her desk. They were the sort that most doctors have, given to them usually after they've qualified by parents or friends. Bowen had some phrenological skulls where you could remove and replace brain sections to form neurological chimeras; and a miniature psycho-surgery toy, complete with instruments as well as cerebella. Make a mistake performing a tiny leucotomy and a buzzer would sound.

"H'hooo"! Whatley pant-hooted facetiously. 'I like this – <really real> – great use of FS "huuu"?'

'He's a visual artist,' Jane Bowen remarked.

' "Hoo" yes, "hoo" yes. Well,' he threw the note on the desk and swivelled to muzzle her, 'doesn't look much like a baboon delusion now, "huu" does it?'

'No.'

'You read the case histories that came from the Gruton "huu"?'

'Of course.'

'A classic baboon delusion is always focused on canines, pseudo-mating displays and so forth –'

'I read them, Whatley.'

'Quite so, quite so, none of that here, is there "huu"?

'No.'

'It's all rather fumbled, isn't it. He signs that he thinks he's in Charing Cross, and yet the questions were on headed paper. And this business of humans. Are the <beasts> that attack him human "huu"? Is he seeing chimps as humans "huu"?'

'He signs that *he* is human –'

'He thinks he's human "huu"?'

'That's what I took it to mean.' Bowen was getting frustrated. She deliberately cut through one of the miniature cortices in the leucotomy toy, setting off the electronic death tone.

'Well, I don't know what to make of it. Do you have any ideas "huu"?'

'Keep on as we are for a couple more days, try and draw him out, then suggesture that we need to do neurological tests. We aren't going to get much further like this, Whatley. And his chimps may want to get him out of here. We don't necessarily have the grounds for a full twenty-eight-day section, you know – and this chimp has influential allies. His dealer and his doctor in Oxfordshire have been pant-hooting twice daily, asking about progress.'

'And the ex-alpha "huu"?'

'Not interested.'

'His consort "huu"?'

'Out of the picture at the moment. Gone to see her natal group in Surrey –'

'Yes, she looked like a Surrey female. I can just imagine her riding hounds, wearing a Barbour and a quilted "gru-nn" swelling-protector –' He grinned, tooth-clacked.

'Spare us your mating fantasies, Whatley. Please.'

So it was Bowen who went on with the programme of communication with Simon Dykes, and it was Bowen who kept Bohm and Levinson at bay when they pant-hooted for more news on his condition.

'I think we're making some progress,' she showed the latter that afternoon.

'What sort of progress "huu"? Is there any likelihood that he'll be out next week "huu"? I postponed the private view for his new show until then – but we're going ahead whatever. The canvases are stretched, the invitations sent, wine bought . . . Obviously it would be good if he were there –'

'Good for who "huu"?'

'For him, of course. This is a very important show for Simon. Very important. Could be the one that puts him right up there among the best contemporary painters in England. You know that the Tate bought his *World of Bears* last year "huu"?'

'I am aware of that, yes. Tell me, what are the paintings like in the new show "huu"?'

'Is it relevant to his condition "h'huu"? I don't like to preview in this fashion.' Levinson fiddled ostentatiously with his bow tie; Jane Bowen could just make out the signs 'tiresome, bloody tiresome' in amongst the flicks.

'I saw that "wraaa"!' She was horripilating furiously and displayed at the screen a little, throwing paper clips, biros, whatever desk clutter came to hand. ' "Wraaaa"! I'd like to remind you, Mr Levinson, that you are dealing with a physician, not some bloody little gallery female. Do I make myself understood "h'huuu"?'

'Of course, of course. Please, please, don't trouble yourself – your basal eye is a pink loveliness to me –' Jane Bowen nearly laughed. The timorous old poof was half presenting to her, his angular rump pushed up above the level of his desk. 'I have to be a bit cautious, I know you'll understand . . . the media . . . What with this breakdown, they could make a lot out of it . . . and "hoo" the paintings themselves are very graphic. Very graphic indeed.'

'How so "huu"?'

'They're essentially paintings of bodily disintegration, destruction . . . as it were . . .' He manipulated a pair of gold-rimmed bifocals on to his nasal bridge, still signing. 'discorporation. Quite shocking really. He's taken Martin's apocalyptic paintings as a starting point and produced a series of canvases that depict both imaginary and historical scenes of bodily destruction with a kind of tortured graphicism . . .' The dealer's hands fell still. The bifocals slid down his nasal bridge, he pushed them back up again.

'I see.' Jane Bowen was mollified, charmed even by the dealer's description. 'You know "grnn", perhaps they do have a bearing on this breakdown. He is exhibiting symptoms of some kind of bodily confusion, scrambling of proprioception –'

'What's that "huu"?'

'His ability unconsciously to gauge the disposition of his own body. This is normally the result of organic damage, but it does dovetail rather neatly with what has obviously been preoccupying him – it could be what we denote hysterical conversion. Watch, Mr Levinson, thank you for your confidence in this "grnn" matter. I do hope to have some positive news for you soon, but I certainly wouldn't count on him being well enough to attend the private show –'

'How about interviews "huu"?'

'I very much doubt it, he's still incredibly confused.'

After finishing the pant-hoot George Levinson pivoted himself through a hundred and eighty degrees and squatted, motionless, regarding one of the canvases he had been describing to the psychiatrist. To suggesture there was something pathological about it was on the one hand an understatement, and on the other – as far as Levinson himself was concerned – an irrelevance. The debate about madness and creativity appeared otiose when it came to Dykes's work and the work of most truly talented artists that he represented. They did what they did – that was all.

But these paintings, this one in particular which imprisoned in a thick layering of oils the very instant when the horrific King's Cross fire of 1987 had begun, was the stuff of nightmare. The commuters, mouths gaping open, tumbling backwards down the escalator as the fireball erupted from the booking hall. Two or three chimps at the head of it combusting already, their clothing and fur in a white-orange efflorescence; and an infant – actually in mid-air, falling towards the viewer. George Levinson shook his head wonderingly, for he knew that wherever a viewer positioned herself the infant was still falling in that direction – threatening the passive with the most active of requirements – to catch the mite. The infant was Dykes's equivalent of the eyes of *The Laughing Cavalier*. In the context of this painting it added worse than insult to inconceivable injury. Levinson thought back to the evening before Simon's breakdown, remembering that odd gesticulation at the opening in Chelsea. Was this the lack of perspective he had signed about? Or had the artist, even then, sensed himself sliding into the abyss? But whatever the answer there is, George mused, going to be a riot when the critics get sight of this stuff.

Surrey summers, thought Sarah to herself, leaning on the fence surrounding her parents' tiny paddock; do I miss them? Maybe, or maybe I simply miss the young female I was, obsessed by gymkhanas, the teachers at school, playing at mating.

Massy yew trees mounted up beyond the end of the paddock and between their hard green strokes of foliage Sarah could glimpse the knapped flint wall of the Reverend's church, St Peter's. 'Handy that.' She remembered Peter signing this so many times during her childhood. 'Being the Reverend Peter from St Peter's "huu"?' One of the hounds bounded over to where she leant. Her father's old hunter, Shambala, a grey-streaked Alsatian some fifteen hands high. The dog yapped and extended a forearm's length of pink tongue, slopping with drool. Sarah stroked and massaged the beast's scruff, while Gracie neighed and snuffled at the dog's ankles. 'No more hares to course, "huu" Shammy, "grnn" Shammy old fellow?' Sarah inparted his scruff.

She was interrupted by her mother who pant-hooted from the conservatory door. Pant-hooted 'Sarah' and 'Food', and also wreathed those two meanings in a sonority of reproach, "H'h'oooGraa!"

"H'hoooo!" Sarah responded. Although having called that she was coming, she felt no great desire to make her way back across the sculpted garden, with its kidney-shaped beds of delphiniums, poppies and chrysanthemums.

It was always the same after the first two days, the visits to relatives – and now, of course, because she was in oestrus the almost hourly cavalcade of mating – Sarah felt trapped in her parents' comfortable house, trapped in their comfortable world. Her parents' little turns of phrase, 'Just coming, dear' from her alpha, almost always calling forth a 'Time means nothing to him' from her mother. And their worn idiosyncrasies. Her alpha's old horn-rimmed spectacles tied round his balding pate with a length of garden twine; her mother's ludicrously unfashionable padded swelling-protectors, which must – Sarah felt – make the sweat course unpleasantly in this heat, as well as providing a hot-bed for tics and lice.

'I need them for the dogs, y'know,' Hester Peasenhulme would sign absent-mindedly, giving that impression of not really showing to Sarah, which her daughter almost always felt. 'They take it amiss if I haven't got the old familiar swelling-protector.' She had been signing this for all the years since Sarah left the natal range for college in London. For all the years since Sarah was a barely receptive female, her first swellings matching her own awkwardness about them; until now, when only the two hounds remained in the paddock at the bottom of the garden, Shambala, and her last show dog, Sugarlump, with whom Sarah had swept the board at the kennel-club gymkhana for year after year.

And if the swelling-protector was an issue between them, it was because it concealed more than her mother's now infrequent, prune-wrinkled swellings. No, it concealed a deep trauma about mating, Sarah and the Peasenhulmes in general. A trauma Sarah had felt so confused about during sub-adulthood.

'Did your alpha mate you this morning "huu"?' Mrs Peasenhulme signed, trembling as Sarah crawled in through the back door from the garden.

' "Hooo" you know he did, Mother – you were there.' She tried to keep the cramp out of her fingers, but without success.

'I'll thank you not to sign "euch-euch" like that to me, young lady, you'll never be old enough – as far as I'm concerned – to stop being respectful to your mother.'

'Mother "hooo". . . .' Sarah wanted her to get wound up, wanted her to lash out, wanted to feel the slash of old nails, chipped from weeding, against her cheek, but they didn't come now – just as they had hardly ever come during Sarah's infancy.

Instead Hester Peasenhulme merely pouted and threw a

dishcloth at Sarah, waving, 'Help me with this drying up.' As ever, Sarah found it hard to believe that her mother really cared about her, so infrequently did she attack, or otherwise practically enforce the hierarchy.

For years Sarah had wondered about this, wondered if it had anything to do with the infrequency with which her alpha mated her. While her infancy was ostensibly nurturing and secure, when she left the natal range feelings long sensed – but unacknowledged – had swum, unpleasantly, to the surface.

At college in London, doing foundation and laterly illustration and design, she had had the same kind of work crises as her peers, and the same kind of disruptive, if exploratory, consortships. She had sat up late at night, revising with the assistance of speed, then come down with the ad-dabs – just as her allies had. And like them, she had felt that her psyche was plunging into the deep end of life.

But for Sarah everything had been that bit worse, the consortships more destructive, their fissions more histrionic; the sadnesses more global, the depressions more intransigent.

When at last she could take no more and found herself sobbing for days on end, unable to attend lectures or classes, Sarah sought out the counsellor whose task it was to deal with the emotional and psychological problems of the students. He was reassuringly straightforward. Sarah had been fearing a lot of psychofiddle, a damning diagnosis, kinky therapies and the mapping of her dreamscape.

'Point out to me,' signed Tom Hansen, blond, upright, strong of nasal bridge and commanding of lip, 'did your alpha mate you when you were younger "huu"?'

'Of – of course.'

'Often "huu"?'

'I suppose it depends what you mean by that –'

'As frequently as the other natal group males did "huu"?'

'No, he didn't. More like once during each oestrus "eucheuch". I always wondered about that. And I suppose I was

141

jealous of my sister Tabitha, who he seemed to prefer. He began mating her when she was eight – and barely showing.'

Up until this interview Sarah would have been incredulous and even angry to learn that she was what was denoted 'an abused infant', but once Tom Hansen began inparting her quite how potentially damaging her alpha's neglect had been, other pieces of the jigsaw began to fall into place. Her mother's chronic diffidence, hardly ever taking Sarah on solo patrols – that surely was a function of her own guilt over the way Harold Peasenhulme had neglected his eldest daughter, refused to give her the good mating every female requires from an alpha if she's to grow up happy, well adjusted, comfortable with her very sense of femininity and simiousness.

Sarah's first inclination on confronting this hard, hurtful fact about herself was to abandon her natal group altogether, and become a lone female dedicated to pleasure seeking. But Tom Hansen coaxed her round. 'They may not fuck you – your mum and alpha,' he paraphrased Larkin, 'but perhaps you need to consider whether or not they were fucked by their parents.'

'What do you mean "huu"?'

'This kind of "euch-euch" abuse tends to run in groups, Sarah. It may well be that if you have the courage to work on this thing with me, and work at the same time to form a better relationship with your parents, that you can stop the rot, stop it going on down through the generations.'

For the rest of her time at college, Sarah went every week to see Tom Hansen, and to gesticulate over and over and over again the minutiae of her upbringing. So often did she recreate the exact circumstances of her weaning tantrums for the personable therapist that he became incorporated into the memories themselves, a benign – if disengaged – influence.

Hansen showed her about Freud, the founding alpha of psychoanalysis, and how he had been the first chimp to recognise the destructive emotional effect of a biological alpha not mating his daughter. And so Sarah came to understand herself, and her parents, if not altogether forgive either of them.

But things also changed on the home range. Although nothing was signed, Harold Peasenhulme did begin to mate her with a little more frequency – albeit with exactly the same chronic disengagement he had always evinced, sometimes taking as much as a minute to achieve climax.

And now, what with this prostate trouble, I suppose he'll never, ever give me a really sound, thorough covering, Sarah thought angrily as she took another willow-patterned plate from the drying-up rack and subjected it to a cursory wipe. The mating that her mother had pointed out took ages, her alpha heaving over her back, his flaccid penis barely penetrating her. Eventually he had given up – not even reaching climax – picked up his discarded *Telegraph* and retired to his study without bothering to groom her.

If that was a mating, then I'm Mae West, Sarah had thought, and hating herself for it, she forced Jane, the Peasenhulmes' delta female, to groom her for a good hour, although she was practically useless at it and insisted on inparting with every tweak and comb some asinine piece of tickle-slapple.

The Peasenhulmes' house, like their car, was comfortably furnished in a staid, almost inter-war style. Every room was tastefully William Morris wallpapered. In the drawing room a collection of plump sofas and tubby armchairs sat muzzling a highly polished coffee-table adorned with a cut-glass bowl, always flower-filled. In the nestrooms the chests of drawers had lavender cushions buried in their soft depths. And in the large open-plan kitchen the old Aga still squatted, although for years now it had been purely decorative, Hester Peasenhulme preferring to cook on the modern, gas-fired range that her son Giles had fitted for her.

Giles, bloody, conscientious Giles. If it wasn't bad enough for Sarah having a sister like Tabitha, who inflamed male lust when she was days off oestrus, and whose exquisitely beautiful swellings sometimes lasted for weeks, there was also Giles, the perfect son. Giles, who had gone no further than Oxshott to found his own sub-group, and who somehow managed to find time to get back to the natal range almost every day and help his poor old parents out.

The previous evening, after their last supper, with Giles and most of his simpering sub-group in attendance, Harold Peasenhulme put the finger on Sarah. 'I don't know what I'd do without Giles's help, you know.' His fingers complacently formed the signs. 'He's a lifesaver now that I find it so hard to crawl around the place.' Harold Peasenhulme had had a career in the City notable solely for its great length and even greater stolidity. Length and stolidity also characterised his signing, never using one sign where five would do, and never upping his gesticulant tempo. He had once stood upright for selection as a parliamentary candidate – Tory, of course – but been rejected by the committee with the succinct ascription: 'Dull'.

Giles grinned widely at his alpha's compliment, displaying the characteristically pointed Peasenhulme canines. He was diligently grooming his alpha. "Hooo", thought Sarah. Goody two toes is going to pack you off to a rest home, and take over the house and the group before you can sign knife, old chimp. Then she succumbed once more to guilt, which was the emotion she associated more than any other with her alpha. She almost felt sorry for the punctilious old chimp. Almost – but not quite.

After second lunch on the third day of Sarah's stay, her alpha called her into his study. "H'hooo."

She bounded through from the kitchen where she had been helping her mother make jam. '"H'huu" yes, Alpha?'

'Sarah, I need to have a gesticulation with you,' he signed awkwardly, most of his hands and feet occupied with pipe cleaners and pipes. 'Have you seen this morning's paper "huu"?'

'No, Alph.'

'Well, you'd better take a look.' He dropped a pipe, picked up the *Telegraph* and tossed it across the desk to her. It was opened at the 'Peterborough' column.

The first thing that caught Sarah's eye was Simon's. She blanched. It was an old photo, and Sarah recognised the fur casually draped around his shoulder as belonging to his ex-alpha. She felt the flush of jealousy that always came upon her when she was presented with even the remotest evidence of Jean Dykes's existence, then summoned herself and read the copy.

Despite the good weather there's no prospect of a sunny opening at the Levinson Gallery in Cork Street next Thursday. That brooding and temperamental painter Simon Dykes, whose penchant for seeking creative stimulus in the smallest room is well known to the denizens of the Sealink Club, has apparently become even more brooding and temperamental.

Is he engaging in some last-minute life sketching of the kind of brutalised figures that feature so prominently in his new paintings? Perhaps this explains his current residence, the psychiatric ward at Charing Cross Hospital, definitely the *wrong* end of Fulham.

Or possibly it's something to do with that bright young female Sarah Peasenhulme, whose absence from her normal night range has coincided with the artist's indisposition? Undoubtedly, the only way to find out will be to attend the opening and beard George Levinson, a chimp not known for keeping his fingers to himself.

' "Wraaf"! Bloody tickle-slapple columnists, who the f –'

' "Wraaaf"! Sarah, watch your vocalisation, if you please.'

'But, Alph, this is repulsive stuff. Hitting Simon when he's down like this. You can't surely –'

'As it happens this sort of drivel does lend me some sympathy for your "euch-euch" consort. Although I find the implication here that he is a drug user disturbing, and as you know I have never approved of your association.' Harold Peasenhulme picked the paper up from where Sarah had let it fall, folded it and tucked it away on his side of the desk, as if it might be required for future reference.

' "Huu" Alph, you're not going to go into all of that again, are you? Simon and I have been consorting for more than a year now.'

'I'm well aware of that. And well aware also that he's very unlikely to found a new group with you, for all sorts of reasons; reasons that I'm sure you are aware of as well. All I can sign is I trust you're taking this opportunity to do some mating elsewhere. I covered you this morning –'

'Sort of.'

'Giles will come over and bring his distal males to give you one any time you pant-hoot. Peter and Crispin are always happy to mate you. Sarah "gr-unn", I know we've never seen exactly eye-to-hand on things, but won't you consider finding a stable, polyandrous group "huu"? You must be aware of how unsuitable this consortship is, verging on monogamy as it does, and without the likelihood of any issue to justify it.' His fingers stumbled over the sign 'monogamy', as if fearful of being contaminated.

'I can't, Alph. I love him. I want to help him. He's a brilliant chimp, a great ape. I wouldn't mind being his consort ... for ever.'

With this inflammatory remark she fled the room, not even bothering to give her alpha the slightest of valedictory grooms. And as she packed her bag and readied herself for the journey she felt the dead weight of Harold Peasenhulme's indifference. Why, "hoo" why, "hoo" why can't he beat me the way an alpha should. I insult him, I challenge his authority and he does nothing. Clearly he doesn't love me – never has.

The Reverend Peter drove her back to West Byfleet Station an hour or so later. She didn't bother to give her parents a valedictory pant-hoot, she was still too angry. Peter mated her three or four times on the way, pulling over into lay-bys, twitching aside the light cotton swelling-protector she wore and entering her with surprising alacrity – considering his age, that is. 'You wouldn't "huuu" consider staying just another day or so, would you, my dear? Just so I could mate you a bit more. It does my soul good.'

'Oh, Reverend, if only *you* were my alpha. Your arseholiness is so beautiful, your spirituality gushes like spunk from your cock.'

'You're too sweet, my dear.'

They kissed each other many times on the platform and the Reverend petted Gracie as well. They had ten minutes to wait for Sarah's train, and in that time as many males displayed to her. At one point the platform contained three such suitors, strutting up and down, waving magazines or newspapers to indicate their availability for mating. 'I do wish you'd let one of them, my dear,' the Reverend gestured. 'You might even enjoy it, you never know.'

'No, Peter, if I can't have you, or Simon, I don't think I'll be mating anyone else for the rest of this oestrus. And certainly not a chimp whose courtship display consists of beating himself around the head with a copy of *PC User*.'

They hugged again. The train pulled in. Sarah leapt on and squatted at a seat in the window with the lap pony comfortably ensconced on top of her. The last thing she saw as the train pulled out was the elderly priest sitting on a bench, teasing some of her drying vaginal mucus out his groin fur, with a wistful, almost spiritual expression on his greying muzzle.

But while she may have been defiant to her parents, and direct with the Reverend – who was after all the Peasenhulmes' beta and had been for many years – alone once more Sarah continued to brood on her consort's breakdown, and consider whether or not it might be time they fissioned.

In the few days that Sarah had been away, a voluminous and unusual correspondence had built up between the occupant of the secure room on Gough, and the senior registrar. Dr Bowen continued to ask her troublesome, if talented patient what it was that ailed him, and continued to receive remarks which substantiated a picture of such clinical oddity that at times she wondered whether or not it was she who was suffering from the delusion rather than Dykes.

'When you say you are 'human', what do you delineate by this?'

'I am a member of the human race. The Latin name is *Homo erectus* or *Homo sapiens*, something like that. Why are you asking me these questions, aren't you human?'

'No. I am a chimpanzee, as are you. You are not human. Humans are brute animals only found in the wild in equatorial regions of Africa. There are some humans in captivity in Europe, although they are mostly used for experimental purposes. Humans cannot sign, or effectively vocalise, let alone write. Which is why I know you aren't a human. Humans are also largely hairless. You have a fine coat – if I, as your doctor, may sign so. Why do you think you are human?'

'I am human because I was born human. Christ! I can't believe I'm writing this. You know I think all of this is a part of my madness, these notes I scrawl in response to your insane questions. Where is Sarah? Why won't you send her in to see me? Or get hold of George Levinson, my dealer. They're both as human as I am.'

'Both Sarah and George have been in to see you. They, like everyone else who is fully sentient in this world, are chimpanzees. I understand your fear, Simon, and your confusion, but you must recognise that something is profoundly wrong with you. I believe you may well have incurred some organic damage to your brain. If you will allow me, together with my colleagues, to do some neurological tests and assessments on you, we will be able to ascertain whether or not this is true and try and devise some way of helping you.'

And so it went on. But every time this unusual epistolary relationship looked like it was getting somewhere and Simon signalled that he would be prepared to allow Dr Bowen to enter his room and gesticulate with him muzzle-to-muzzle, he would relapse into the state of bestial fear and catatonia in which he had been admitted to the hospital.

"HoooGraa," Jane would vocalise as gently as possible, sidling in through the door. The bent figure of the chimp with his back to her was pathetic, slope-shouldered, the evidence of his Parkinsonian weakness written into every lineament. The smell of despair in the secure room was palpable to the psychiatrist's questing lip and flared nostrils.

"H'hooo?" he would vocalise, showing perfect awareness that it was she he was recalling – Jane would then sidle quietly up to him and inpart as gently as possible on his back, sniffing and grooming him the while. 'Don't worry, Simon, I'm here to help you, to psychically preen you.'

Each time this happened, the artist would allow it to go on just that little bit longer before turning his head to catch sight of her – then: ' "Wraaaa"! Get away from me! Get away, get away, get away!' He would back mewling and bellowing into the corner, his hands barely able to shape the signs.

Initially Bowen kept to the instructions she had laid down for the staff. She refrained from administering the reassuring blows, followed by the even more reassuring grooming that she would have given any other disturbed chimp in the circumstances. But as the days went by and his response remained just as aberrant and uncooperative, she did resort to cuffing him lightly around the muzzle as he backed away from her. However, this didn't pay any dividend either, save for nonsensical accusations of ill-treatment when they resumed their contact via letter.

"HoooGraaa!" Bowen drummed on the door of Whatley's office and entered at a bound, throwing handfuls of Dykes's correspondence at her boss. She continued the display for two or three minutes, plucking books from the consultant's shelves and hurling them in the general direction of the desk.

' "Hooo-Hooo-Hooo" what's all this in aid of, Jane? Trying to mount some kind of *coup d'état*, or what "h'huu"?' Whatley waved at her, the signs percussively emphasised as he deflected the squall of printed matter.

' "HoooGraaa"! What this is in aid of, Whatley, is that we aren't getting anywhere. I've been sending you daily reports on this chimp Dykes, and as far as I can see you've been doing nothing.'

'Well, what can I do "huu"? You don't seem to be able to help him. You don't even seem able to diagnose him. All we have now that we didn't have a week ago is a lot of balderdash from him about being human and humans roaming the earth; and a lot of balderdash in response from you, telling him the way things are in fact. It hardly seems like "euch-euch" psychiatry to me at all.'

'Perhaps that's the point.'

'I don't follow you.'

'Maybe we need to consider a different approach to Dykes. We must do *something*, Whatley.'

Whatley got up from behind his desk, where he'd taken shelter from the hail of books, and crawled round to where Bowen squatted. ' "HoooGraaa" now, Jane, I don't honestly think we can prevent the chimp if he insists. You haven't got any fresh ideas despite having demarcated the extent of his "hee-hee-hee" <humanity>, now have you "huuu"?'

Whatley was suprised at this stage to feel Dr Bowen's hands teasingly grooming the fur in his groin area, and even more suprised when she began, albeit with enormous, ironic playfulness, to mock mate him. 'There is one possible course of action left to us "chup-chupp", Whatley,' she inparted somewhere in his lower belly.

' "Hee-hee-hee-h'eugh". Now what's that then, Jane – Jane! Really!'

'Busner.'

' "H'huuuu" what?'

'Busner. Let's ask Zack Busner to take a look at Dykes. He might have some images.'

Chapter Ten

The long blue Seven Series Volvo pulled off the Talgarth Road and bucketed along under the Hammersmith Flyover. Inside the car the Busner patrol was exhibiting its usual behaviours, compounded in equal parts of uproariousness and pedagogy. The sub-adults in the back were gigglingly grooming each other, footling around with the car's interior decoration, and squealing as they shucked out of the way of their alpha's blows; which were aimed with equal ferocity and inaccuracy.

'"Wraff"! Now lads,' signed the eminent natural philosopher – as he liked to style himself, 'we are nearing the hospital where this poor chimp is incarcerated.' Gambol waltzed the car through a chicane; limp chip wrappers furled in the Volvo's wake. 'Observe the white latticework of poles that compasses the hospital blocks.'

The sub-adults did as they were shown, tipping their heads back so that three sets of eyes were aimed up through the sun roof, and three ruffs of fur fluffed up over the collars of their T-shirts. 'D'you see them "huu"?'

'Ye-es', Alph,' chorused the young males.

'The architect that designed this "euch-euch" place doubtless imagined that he was conforming in some way to the functionalism of the Bauhaus, the brutalism of Le Corbusier, yet all he has really done is what "huu"?' There was signlence in the back seat. '"Huu" well?'

Erskine twitched a finger. ' "H'huu" yes, Erskine?'

' "HooGraa" put bars on it, Alph "huu"?'

'Very good, very good, you are a good lad, c'mere.' Busner squeezed his head between the seats and gave Erskine a sloppy kiss on the muzzle. 'That's "chup-chupp" right. Those aren't poles – they're *bars*. Perhaps only decorative, but for all that a potent symbol that the chimpanzees in these thirteen storeys are cut off from the group, denied either territory or the opportunity to range freely.

'Now,' Busner went on conducting, 'as you lads are doubtless aware it has taken many millennia for chimpunity to conquer its instinctive dread and revulsion for any form of injury or disease – yet I sometimes wonder if in fact we have conquered it at all. These vertical holdingbays,' he gestured, letting the signs fall like confetti from his upflung hand 'are towers of moaning rather than signlence, in which the redundant bodies of our conspecifics are systematically stripped of their dignity – like state-subsidised carrion – by vultures in white coats . . .' He paused, just long enough for Gambol to interject.

'HooGraa lovely image, Boss, lovely image.'

' "Grnn" thank you, Gambol, you may kiss my arse.' Gambol did as he was bidden.

Having let the Busner patrol out under the portico of the hospital, Gambol went off to park the Volvo. His mind was – quite naturally – full of anger, full of aggression, full of the Will to Power. An alliance, he thought to himself, all I need is an alliance and I can begin to put my plan into action. I'm fed up with kissing Busner's arse, no matter what his past achievements are. This absurd case is the one I've been waiting for. If I believed in providence, or some opportunistic deity, whose aggressive image we had been made in, I might imagine Dykes had been given to me by destiny. But as it is, it's merely the most stupendous, cachinnating coincidence of my career. An alliance – an alliance – Whatley could well prove sympathetic, and the old male doesn't think I know about his arthritis, but I do, yes indeed and much else besides.

The Busner sub-adults were, despite themselves, impressed by the number of chimps who presented to their alpha as he swaggered through the ground floor of the hospital. They'd been with him on patrol to Heath Hospital many times, but had never quite believed the deference shown to him was anything but reflex, a hangover from the past. But as doctor after nurse dropped what they were doing, rushed over and backed towards Busner, arses and noses twitching with humility, the sub-adults felt a new respect for him.

The patrol took the lift up to the psychiatric department. ' "HooGraa" now stick close, you lot,' Busner signed as they whooshed upwards. 'The chimp who runs this department is not well disposed towards me. It's a situation that may well call for some forthright action, and therefore an opportunity for *you* to learn something.'

Whatley was there to meet them when the lift doors opened – someone must have given advance pant-hoot. Together with him was Dr Bowen. So quickly it could barely be seen by the eye, Busner flicked fingers at Bowen, then drummed loudly on the clanking lift door, while vocalising with tremendous ferocity, "Wraaaaaaff!" Bowen gave voice as well and the two of them charged towards Whatley, who dropped the clipboard he was holding, scampered backwards, tripped, fell and was overwhelmed by his colleagues, who jumped clean over his prone body then went racketing off down the corridor.

' "Hooo" I see your alpha hasn't changed much,' Whatley signed to the Busner sub-adults who were huddled by the wall. 'Still likes to get his displays in hard and fast "hooo"! Here they come again –' Whatley rolled over to the other side of the corridor, with considerable agility for a chimp of his age, just in time to avoid the windmilling arms and stomping feet of the senior registrar and her ally, who were kicking a miscellany of objects in front of them, cardboard boxes, a washing-up bowl, some empty blood and saline bags – while they advanced, fully horripilated and barking with exceptional violence. Busner's penis was erect – a pink spike in his groin. Both he and Bowen were spraying urine and saliva.

Chimps – both staff and patients – had gathered in small knots at both ends of the corridor and were gesturing on the finer points of the display. Up and down Busner and Bowen stamped, ramped and sprayed. A drugs trolley got mixed up in the incident and before the participants could collect themselves, a hail of pills peppered the walls and floor. Sharps, both used and unused, flew through the air closely followed by flights of ampoules. It was at this point that Whatley, wisely, called a halt. Next time the two aggressors made their run, they found his angular, tufted rump, its ischial pleat effulgent, stuck up like a sleeping policemale in the path of their four-limb drives.

Busner stopped short, shaking. ' "Wraaaa"! What's this, Whatley "huu"?'

' "H'Grnnn" it's my arse, "hoo" Mighty One.'

'So it is "h'huuu"? What do you think, Jane "huu"?'

'Looks like he's prepared to capitulate,' waved the slim female, smoothing down her own ruffled fur.

'Is that right, Whatley "huu"?'

'Yes, esteemed inheritor of the mantle of eminence – bearer of the most tattered and dangly scrag in London.'

' "Gru-nnn" good, good, you're not a bad chimp really. In fact I *quite* like you. Come on, let's adjourn to your office for a groom and a fiddle. Your subordinates and my patrol can clean this lot up.'

The three senior psychiatrists picked their way through the wreckage wrought by the display, towards Whatley's office. Outwardly Zack Busner was swaggering, puffed-up, his leg fur like swishing chaps, testosterone trousers, but internally he was raging with pain. His hands – particularly his left – burnt and fizzed, as if fireworks had been poked beneath the skin.

Whatley waved at his secretary that he was not to be disturbed, they swung through the door of the office and arranged themselves in a companionable huddle, Whatley lying atop his desk, legs dangling over the edge, head cradled by his in-tray. Bowen sat on the floor at his feet, and used her thin fingers and still thinner tongue to probe the departmental head's toes, searching for fragments of glass, pill dust and so forth. '"H'h'hee-hee",' Whatley giggled. 'Do be careful there, Jane, make sure you spit out the pill fragments, don't want you "chup-chupp" tranked up for the rest of the day.'

'"Grnnn" don't worry, sweetums "choo"!'

Busner took a squat in Whatley's Parker-Knoll recliner, and amused himself for a while playing with the innumerable little levers and knobs that altered the position and tensility of just about every part of the chair. Then he recovered and set to, running his fingers smoothly through the whitening fur that grew low on Whatley's brow. As he did this he inparted 'Good Whatley, kind Whatley, ethical Whatley . . .' and Bowen was, of course, indicating much the same down below.

This touchy-feely session went on for some time, before with a final tweak of Whatley's ear Busner broke off grooming. Whatley squatted up on the desk and crossed his legs. Bowen went to the door of the office and pant-hooted Whatley's secretary. '"H'hooo" bring the file on Simon Dykes in please, Marcia,' she gestured at the female.

There was signless and novocal until the file arrived, and then signless while Busner read it, his eroded features betraying no emotion as he scanned the missives between Dykes and Bowen. Eventually he passed the file to Whatley – who dropped it on the desk top. Busner hunkered back still further in the recliner and began to roll and unroll his hank of mohair tie, using only the toes of one foot.

"H'huuu,", Busner vocalised, then signed, 'Well, Whatley, if you're amenable to my taking on the case I think I have an image of how we can get Dykes to do the tests. It's clear that until we've done EEGs, scans and so forth, we'll have no way of establishing if there's any organic damage. By the same token, until we have muzzle-to-muzzle communication there's no way of establishing . . . how can I point to it . . .' The great ape's fingers faltered, he changed tack. 'You know, sometimes I find English signage altogether inadequate to blazon some of the more complex images we work with –'

' "Grnn" I know what you mean.' Bowen flicked in.

'It looks preposterous when you sign it, but I almost imagine that if there were some other form of signage, if gesture were the complement rather than the given, it might be possible to reach deeper into chimps' souls . . . but I waver –'

' "H'hooo" no, no.' Bowen was keen for more, being in the presence of her old mentor was proving as exhilarating as she had hoped.

'I waver, Jane,' he cuffed her – Busner wanted no discipular sycophancy at this stage, 'we need to gesticulate with Dykes, but he finds the presence of other chimpanzees disturbing. How about if we sign with him when we're not present "huuu".'

'What do you mean, Busner "huu"?' Whatley was entwined.

'Well, why don't we set up a 'phone link? Perhaps he'll find that less disturbing, worth a try "huuu"?'

Simon was sitting in secure room six. Seven days of madness, seven days of terror. Like any prisoner he had attempted to mark the days of his confinement, but because of the drugs and the fights with his bestial keepers, he had often scored three scratches in the paint of the window frame where one would have served. Now he squatted and wiggled his toes. He had dispatched another of the mad communicados to Jane Bowen since awaking, and now he waited for a reply. But instead of the judas click he expected there was a scraping of key in lock. Simon eased himself off the nest and keeping his muzzle averted knuckle-walked to the far corner of the room. He could hear the shuffling of their hideous, naked paws, and almost smell the meat-extracting breath of his oppressors.

They were making those noises, those noises that almost meant something. Snufflings and gruntings, that seemed to include comprehensible bits of "speech". Now, after some days of listening to them with ears steadily less fugged up – Bowen had been reducing his dosage of Valium – he heard the snuffle-grunts as: "Hooobecareful 'Grnn", or "HoooIdon'twanttoscareyou 'Grnn". Could this be so? He laboured to decipher the sounds, his muzzle crammed in the corner, hoping that coarse-haired fingers wouldn't yank him around, hispid hands wouldn't administer blows or needles.

They had gone. Simon turned to see a telephone on his cardboard table. Well, almost a telephone; as he drew closer to examine the thing he found that tacked to the side of the conventional, bog-ordinary device – white keyboard, flimsy, plastic receiver – there was a small screen. It was obviously meant to be part of the thing, and yet at one and the same time it wasn't right, wasn't right at all. But before he had time to consider this strangeness – it rang.

It rang the way telephones always ring, prosaically and yet with full import. The "trrring-tring-trrring-tring-trrring" signalled to Simon: 'This is the world pant-hooting, the workaday world of plumbers and quickly fitted exhaust systems' as it always had. He squatted, dully contemplating the mechanism, and savouring the possibility that if he were to snatch up the receiver quickly enough a clerk in a bookshop would show him something he had ordered had come in, or a dental secretary would inpart he was due for a check-up.

The sound of the ringing reverberated in the confined space, creating a split-second echo, a distortion in sonic registration that Simon connected with his own sense of dislocation from his body, of the mismatch between psychic and physical. He was, he realised for the first time, wearing an indecently short green hospital gown, made from thick cotton fabric, and nothing else. Simon stared at his feet, concentrating on the familiar pattern of scratches and nicks on his toenails, the knobble on the knuckle of his big toe. His feet seemed far away, as if observed through the wrong end of a telescope.

"Trrring-tring-trrring-tring-" The telephone with the screen tacked on to it went on ringing. The flex coiled away from the instrument, ran across the lino and disappeared beneath the door. The flex reminded Simon of the hideous umbilicus in his dream. He couldn't help suspecting that it had only recently been yanked, just-in-timely, from the womb of some far larger telephone. "Trrring-tring-trrring-tring –" Without quite knowing how he had got thus, squatting, feet either side of it, sensing the volar vibration, Simon found himself lifting the receiver and placing its inveterate prong against his naturally cauliflowered ear.

The little screen fizzed in time with the click and splutter of connection. White dots joined themselves into a pattern of light and dark. The muzzle of a rather old, rather fat chimpanzee appeared. The beast was drinking a cup of tea held in one hand, while the other clutched a similar prong to a generous ear. Simon collapsed in an involuntary bout of hysterical laughter, falling back on to the cushion of his scut. The image was so ludicrous, so Disney. It was like a novelty photograph, a crude bit of anthropomorphism, rendered cruder by the expression of bafflement on the animal's muzzle. Simon, through distorting lenses of salty water, saw it put down its tea cup, cradle the receiver between its shoulder and its ear, and gesture to someone off-screen.

'Well, he's picked it up,' Busner signed to Bowen.

'That's a start then –'

'Yes, a start. He appears to be laughing at me.'

'Sounds fairly positive. I haven't got so much as a tooth-clack out of him.'

'D'you think there's some athetosis? Has he dropped the 'phone "huu"?'

'Could be athetosis of some kind. We've certainly noticed inappropriate hand movements.' Bowen was squatted alongside Busner in the nurses' station. Dobbs stood behind them, picking his nails with a multi-bladed penknife. Busner had sent the sub-adult males off to range the hospital, and Gambol was with Whatley photocopying Dykes's notes.

' "H'hooo" here he is again, he's back in range of the camera. Simon, can you see and hear me "huu"?'

Simon could see and hear him, and if he had known what it meant *he* would have diagnosed the elderly chimpanzee with athetosis. For, as far as Simon was concerned that's what he saw, the animal – now with the receiver tucked between cartilaginous ear and unshorn shoulder – wiggling the fingers of his two free hands, as if going coochy-coo to the air.

Yet the finger-wiggling was doubly strange to Simon, because as with the noises his keepers made he could – without quite understanding why or how – recognise within the movements the chimp's thick digits made, the presence of comprehensible signs. And without quite knowing that he did so, Simon squatted over the videophone – which is, of course, what it was – and cradling the receiver as his interjector was, wiggled a reply: 'Beasty-beast,' he signed, 'wiggly-waggly, beasty-beast,' he continued, 'pooh-pooh, ca-ca beast . . .' Interspersed with this baby talk came muted, distorted vocalisations, of the form: "Geddaway" and "Fuuuckooooff".

Busner paid great attention to these utterances and fumblings. Out of sight of the 'phone's camera, he gestured to Bowen, 'Has he shown any evidence of coprolalia before this "huu"?'

' "Huuu",' she recalled, 'not that I'm aware of.'

'Well, he's certainly coprolalic now!' Busner kept his eyes on the screen, where Simon was now signing, 'Pee-pee beastie pee. Pee-pee beastie pee . . .'

'If he's "grnnn" coprolalic it will make things a damn sight simpler –'

'I want to "hee-hee" pooh on your heady-head, "h'hee-hee" pooh-pooh on your heady –'

'After all catatonia – as Ferencenzi remarked – is the opposite of tics; and he has been catatonic has he "huuu" not? –'

' "Fuuuckooooff" pooh-pooh in your bum-bum, pooh-pooh on your heady –'

159

'He's a bit on the old side for a flamboyant onset of Tourette's, isn't he, Zack? And none of his other symptoms are exactly consistent with such a diagnosis.'

'Well ye-es, strictly signing – Now, Simon "HoooGraaa"!' Busner broke in forcefully. 'Pay some attention here – this is important.'

Simon spasmed into attention. This noise in his ear he understood. It meant 'Pay attention', just as surely as the shapes of the letters that spell 'pay attention' would have meant the same. He stopped mouthing and wiggling. He scrutinised the brute countenance on the absurd little screen, the zoic figure that had just signed to him. Signed to me? What does that mean, signed to me? *Signed* to me? Surely I should have signed something else, not 'signed', but something which means –

'Simon, can you visualise what I'm signing "huu"?'

'I – I can "hoo".' Could he? How did he know that he could? Who-he? "Hee-hee!"

'Is something funny, Simon?'

'You're *bloody* funny – you're a chimpanzee "hee-hee"!'

'So are you.'

'No, I'm human. Oh "Hoo-waaa"! This is ridiculous! I've been over all this with the other fucking monkeys, the "hooo" beasts that come in here. "Hoo" Christ! You don't, you don' –'

'Know what it's like "h'huuu"? You're "chup-chupp" right, Simon,' Busner's signing was fantastically well styled at this point. Bowen looked on in admiration, the old chimp still had the 'fluence, the ability to reach even the most severely disturbed patients. 'And I don't want to gesticulate about that now anyway. Let's just accept that the fact that I appear to be like a chimpanzee is part of the problem, shall we "huu"? And then "huh-huh" see where we can "chup-chupp" go from there "huu"? If it disturbs you, squint at the screen, "huu" distort my features, and maybe I'll seem a bit more human "huuu"?'

Gambol and Whatley were forming their alliance in the Café Rouge, across the road from the hospital. Whatley had suggestured they squat at one of the tables outside on the pavement – so as not to appear, if seen, to be seeking any form of sequestration.

'Don't be "euch-euch" ridiculous,' Gambol signed as they scampered across the busy road. 'If we squat out here we'll get more lead in our bellies than a Bosnian in a safe haven!'

'"Wraaaf"!' Whatley barked, then thumped his subordinate hard on the head. 'Cut it out, Gambol – just because we're working on an alliance here, it doesn't mean you can get uppity with me!'

'S-sorry,' Gambol finger-cringed, 'I, of course revere your ischial pleat, Dr Whatley,' and he presented low, but bided his time. Every lap pony has his day, he told himself for the fourth time that morning.

They ended up at the back of the joint, behind a waist-high display of fake vernality. The café was packed with chimps anyway. It was first-lunch time and secretaries and other staff from the hospital were entwined in yammer and tickle. No one paid them any mind – especially the bonobo waiter with the dreadlocked head fur.

'Well,' Whatley gestured when they were seated, 'so, an alliance, a move to unseat the old chimp. Ideas of taking over his domestic group as well, have you, Gambol "huu"? Busner females in oestrus, are they "huu"? Not getting the mating you deserve "huu"?'

'I resent that, Dr Whatley, really I do, sir –'

'"H'huu" so you have a more high-minded reason for turning on your alpha, do you? I must sign, you didn't show such support for me last year at Bournemouth when Busner was trotting out his latest exhibition of mesmerism.'

'Well, I couldn't, could I, but – but, things are different now. I have – I have certain information about Busner that would be more than detrimental to him. I'm also fed up with the way he parades these patients around, exhibits them, makes his reputation off the back of their suffering. I don't think I want to go to another bout of drinks parties with some poor, deluded chimp who thinks he's hum –'

'Let's see some of this info, Gambol, pull it out.' Whatley seemed to have put his recent humiliation at the feet of Zack Busner to one side. He was all eyes now, and as imperious as his weedy manner allowed.

'We-ell "chup-chup-chupp", he's got bad arthritis for a start –'

'"Huuu" how bad?'

'Very. I believe he's in a lot of pain, certainly when he has to practically enforce dominance. Obviously maintaining the domestic hierarchy takes it out of him – after all he's plenty of sub-adult males . . .'

Outside the bookie's the junior members of the Busner patrol were trying to ingratiate themselves with some older bonobos, the posse that always hung out there, beering and openly spliffing.

'Where y'at, chimp?' fingered one, as Erskine presented low to her, his quivering scut buffing the pavement. 'Out on y'fuckin' patrol an' stuff "huu"?'

'We are,' signed Erskine, 'and pretty fed up with it too.'

'The troof, innit,' the bonobo hand jived. 'Well, that's as – but this is our territory an' that, so "wraff"! fuck off, an' that –'

'"H'huuu"? We were just going to – your anal funkiness –'

'Ya "huu"?'

'Just going to ask if you knew anyone who had a smoke of weed to flog us . . . "h'huu"?'

'I – I just don't want them to t-touch me . . .' Simon was still bent over the absurd device, squinting from the screen – which he looked at for as long as he could bear – to the flanges of yellowing, rind-like flesh, that squidged between his furry feet and the lino. 'Please, don't let them touch me.'

'I won't "chup-chupp",' Busner's fingers caressed the air in front of the camera, his vocalisations were as soft as a female's first swelling, as wholesome as a ripe grape. 'What we'll do is, after we've signed, you get a really good rest "huu"? Then, tomorrow, Dr Bowen and I will set up an environment where it's possible to run some of these tests on you. We're going to do it so there's as little possibility of you catching sight of *us* as we can. We'll clear the ward of chimps between your room and where we're going to do the tests –'

'So, who's going to do them then "huu"?'

'We will, but if you'd prefer we could disguise ourselves.'

Simon looked at the fuzzy image of Busner on the tiny monitor. Why was it that if he squinted too much, he couldn't seem to understand what the chimp was signing? The vocalisations alone were insufficient to convey full meaning, they were merely accent, styling, feel. But, of course, if he looked too hard he saw the canines, the leathery muzzle, the almost prehensile lip, the green eyes, the black fur . . . 'Disguise? H-how "huu"? "Hoooo".'

'Masks maybe "huu"?' Busner waved, literally off the top of his head.

'Y-yes, that might be a good idea. And – and maybe some trousers. Trousers or skirts, or something that covers your legs. I find the sight of your legs – with the fur on them – very disturbing.'

Busner made a sign to Jane Bowen. 'What does he mean, trousers "huu"? D'you think he means a swelling-protector "huu"?'

'I've no idea. Just humour him, he could go catatonic at any time, I've seen it.'

'OK, Simon,' Busner resumed, 'we'll get some nether garments. Now "chup-chupp", thank you for gesticulating with me today. I want you to stop pushing yourself to think about these things any more for the moment. Get some rest, and tomorrow we'll really begin to find out what's wrong. "HooooGraaa".'

Busner broke the connection and turned to Bowen. 'Trousers! Nice touch that, trousers!'

'D'you think it's fetishism of some kind "huuu"?' Her muzzle puckered up somewhere between distaste and amusement. 'I'll have to go into Soho to get a pair, or somewhere where there's an Ann Summers shop . . . Unless, that is . . . ?'

' "Clak-clak-clak – H'hee-hee"! Well, I suppose one of my sub-adults might have a pair hidden somewhere around the house.' Busner was clearly amused by the image. 'I'll see what I can do. If I can't find any I'll send Gambol. I need you to set things up for the tests.'

The two chimps had slid from their seats at the Ward Sister's tiny desk and were now curled around one another on the floor. Fingers plucked and preened at fur as they inparted. 'I know it's far too early, Your Eminence –'

'Please, Jane "chup-chupp", we've known each other too long for such extreme deference. Please denote me Zack.'

'Zack, d'you have any ideas "h'huu"?'

'I don't know "gru-nnn", I don't know at all. Is it a morbidity of some kind "huu", these questions are so hard to answer? Despite the intense and disturbing nature of his delusion, it could well be that Simon's affliction is potentially productive. There's obviously some kind of doubling of consciousness here, a mental diplopia, but we'll know nothing until we have those scans. Nothing more "h'huu"?'

Bowen went on teasing some particles of what looked like Gentlemale's Relish from Busner's belly for some time before asking, 'Had you considered Ganser's, Zack?'

' "Chup-chupp" interesting idea. But then, his answers aren't strictly speaking *irrelevant* – which is the absolute hallmark of Ganser's, as you know – they're more oneiric, more dream-like. It's funny though, whatever the symptomatology of this – it is beautifully coherent. Perhaps the human delusion will turn out to be like Ganser's or Tourette's; and once it's recognised for the first time, become both easily and constantly identified.

' "Gru-aaa" anyway, it's past second-lunch time, and I have

this bloody tedious lecture to give at UCL this afternoon. I'll collect the lads and crawl on. D'you know where my epsilon got to?'

'He went off with Whatley – I'll help you find them.'

"HooooGraa!" Busner drummed against the electronic doors of the hospital, which, being broken, were jammed open with milk crates. The doors shuddered with the force of his valediction. He turned and slowly knuckle-walked to the Volvo, where Gambol was waiting at the wheel.

' "H'hooo" Zack! One more thing –' Bowen came scuttling after him. 'Simon Dykes, you know his opening is tonight, at George Levinson's gallery in Cork Street.'

'No tickling "huu"?'

'I thought I might drop by – his consort is coming to see me this afternoon, she'll be able to get me – or us – on the list.'

'Not a bad idea. I have tickets for *Turandot*, taking Charlotte, my alpha, she's having a fairly stressful oestrus, y'know. But I'm sure she won't mind me missing the first act ...'

' "Wraaa"! Where the hell have you been, Gambol,' Busner waved as the big car eased its way out from the crowded precincts of the hospital, 'and where the hell are the rest of the patrol "h'huu"?' Gambol chose to ignore the first part of his alpha's query, and focus whatever opprobrium was going on Erskine, Charles and Carlo.

'They're over there, Boss.' He pointed to where the sub-adults were slouching outside the bookie's. As their alpha watched, Erskine was footed a spliff by one of the bonobos and took a long pull on it. The Volvo squealed to a halt and Busner leant out the window.

' "Wraaa"! Come on, you apprentice delinquents, give these chimps back their marijuana and get in the car, we're late.'

They did so with utmost celerity, Erskine weeping with the effort involved in surreptitiously exhaling. Then the three of them huddled on the back seat, awaiting a lecture on the psychological effects of marijuana, or the woeful prejudice of bonoboism, or the depredations of London's public-transport system, or all three. But the Volvo motored back up the Fulham Palace Road, with signless and novocal reigning. Until, that is, they reached the Hammersmith roundabout, and Busner put the finger on Gambol once more. 'You didn't reply "grnnn", what were you signing with that creep Whatley about?'

Later that afternoon Jane Bowen was back at the nursing station, together with Sarah Peasenhulme. Sarah wore her best daytime swelling-protector, a neat little thing in silk chenille by Selena Blow. The capacious gusset was cool against the rawness of her perineum. She had come straight to the hospital from home – where she sometimes did some work – and Dr Bowen had been kind enough to 'phone her, show her about the planned 'phone link with Simon.

Perhaps, Sarah had thought as she dressed, Simon will be able to look at me, and maybe the sight of the swelling-protector will – she couldn't exactly manipulate the thought, although her fingers shaped the signs in the act of fastening the eyelets at either hip, and below – perhaps he'll fancy me. Perhaps his lust will bring him round, bring him out of this.

'Nice swelling-protector,' Jane Bowen signed. 'Selena Blow, is it "h'huu"?'

'Y-yes, I got it in the sale last year. Otherwise I wouldn't have been able to afford it.'

'So, Simon isn't in the habit of buying you other clothes then? Clothes, sign, for the nestroom?'

'Why do you ask "huu"?'

'Well, my dear, you musn't be shocked.' Jane Bowen moved closer and began to groom Sarah, smoothing the fur on the younger female's neck first one way and then the other, loosening grains of talcum powder. 'But as part of this "chup-chupp" human delusion your consort has ... Well, he finds the sight of legs covered with fur disturbing. I gather "gru-nn" that in the "human world" – as Simon describes it – the animals' bare legs are covered –'

'With trousers "huu"?'

'And skirts.'

'And skirts "huu"?'

'Quite so.'

Sarah was blushing, hardly aware of the older female's fingers in her fur. '"Hoo-chup-chupp" I don't know, well . . . yes, he has bought me some skirts. Nothing really *kinky*, you understand. No tweed or wool, but I do have some simple cotton skirts. I dunno – I'd feel awfully strange wearing them here.'

'Well, don't worry about that for now "grnnn", Dr Busner did suggesture that Simon rest – but all the same let's just see how he responds to you in your *nice* swelling-protector.'

Simon was curled up in nest, forcing himself to sleep, when the 'phone began ringing once again. Fucking hell! He jerked upright. Fucking hell! The 'phone brought with it the world of his madness, the world of his disgrace. Won't they fucking well leave me alone!

He sprang from the nest in a jumble of arms and legs, hurling himself on to the floor. Amazingly, he landed on all fours, knuckles either side of the instrument. He plucked up the receiver and pressed it to his ear. The screen resolved itself into a monkey's muzzle. ' "Clak-clak-clak" whaddya' want monkey "wraff" muzzle?' Simon signed and snarled, his big teeth clacking.

'It's Jane Bowen, Simon, your doctor, I have another chimp here who'd like to sign with you.'

'Who is it "huu"? "Wraaa!" I thought that old ape signed that I should be left in peace "hnnn"?'

'Dr Busner, you mean "huu"?'

Simon was taken aback – and fell back on to his arse. 'Busner – you mean the Quantity Theory chimp "huu"?'

'He was involved with it, yes, together with other chimps.'

Jane Bowen was intrigued. Could this – Simon's recognition of Busner, a chimp he didn't know personally – be some vitiation of his agnosia, some pinion between his delusory world and the real world?

'I've seen of him – and heard him. He used to go on stupid game shows in the seventies, didn't he "huu"? Bit of a charlatan, I always thought –'

'"Wraaaf"! What the hell d'you think you're signing "h'huu"? Zack Busner is an extremely eminent chimpanzee – a great ape, in fact!'

Simon was stilled by the outburst, although he would have liked to continue taunting the monkey. Indeed, the act of taunting had made him feel more alive, more lucid, more embodied than he had since arriving at the hospital. But he feared the monkey. Feared she would come in. Feared she would touch him. '"Hoooo." I'm sorry, Your Medical Eminence,' the madchimp cowered 'I didn't mean to disrespect your colleague.' And without knowing why he did so, Simon found himself presenting his arse to the 'phone.

'That's all right, Simonkins, I quite understand,' Jane Bowen countersigned, and asign to Sarah, 'he's comparatively lucid, I'll get him to gesticulate with you.'

'Simon, Sarah is here, she wants to sign to you, I'll put her in front.'

Sarah? Simon dared to squint a little more closely at the screen, dared to imagine that he would see her adored features on its pitiful plasticity, the diamond visage, the widow's peak. But instead, one monkey muzzle was replaced by another. 'Simon, darling,' Sarah signed. '"Grnnn" it's me, it's Sarah, how are you, my love "huuu"? How are you?' His muzzle was so gaunt, his fur so lustreless and lank, but he was still her male. She pulled back from the 'phone camera as much as the confined space of the nurses' station would allow, so that Simon could see her swelling-protector and imagine the delights it contained.

But what Simon saw was a chimpanzee wearing a blue T-shirt,

and some sort of legless underpants, fastened by straps to the animal's legs and furnished with a voluminous gusset; this had a great many ruffles and pleats that formed a whorl, like the petals of a rose, in the approximate region of the animal's genitals. The sight was both comic – and disturbing. ' "Hooo" whassthis "huuu"?'

'Simon,' she resigned, 'it's me, Sarah.'

' "Hoooo" whatever you are, I can't –' His free hand was up by his eyebrow ridges, shielding the sight, and yet he still signed, 'I can't look at you.'

' "Hoo" Simon, "hoo" Simon, my poor love, I came to show you –'

'What! "Hoooo" show me what, you – you *absurdity*!'

'Show you that George is going ahead with the opening.'

'The opening "huu"?'

'*Your* opening. He's had all the canvases stretched and framed himself. He's opening your new show tonight.'

Sarah stared at her consort's features. He seemed to be digesting the news, had she been right to tell him? Would this bring him back him into shore, back into her, or push him out further on to the turbulent, dark lake of his derangement? "Hooo'Graa"! he suddenly cried and then terminated the pant-hoot.

Chapter Eleven

Tony Figes had been squatting in Brown's Hotel all that hot afternoon. He often went into Brown's on dead midsummer afternoons such as these, when he had no copy to file, or no young male to range after. He liked the blend of chi-chi and old world about the hotel's décor, and he liked to watch the American chimps come and go, tugging their little suitcases behind them as they arrived, then tugging the same suitcases, engorged by purchasing, when they left.

The Americans were often obese – even the bonobos. Tony, who imagined himself – quite rightly – to be ugly, got a rush of corporeal *schadenfreude* every time he saw one of them, knuckle-waddling along in a bell tent of Burberry, or a garish, Hawaiian shirt. And fat bonobos! – there was progress. To have gone, in barely over a hundred years, from slavery on the plantation, to obesity in a classy London hotel. Well, if that didn't show the reality of the American Dream, what did?

He rustled and plumped his copy of the *Evening Standard* into a rough oblong, then dropped it on the coffee-table. Not much of a read for a newspaper, Tony thought, but then – *It's Not a Newspaper!* The advertising slogan tripped off his mental fingertips so easily, and so irritatingly. In the last few months the ubiquitous *Evening Standard* vans, with their rapido design of red and white chevrons, had begun to sport the slogan, as had billboards and hoardings all over the city. *The Evening Standard – It's Not a Newspaper!* That this had become the paper's unique selling point was, thought Tony, a peculiar kind of justice.

As he knuckle-walked through the lobby, Tony Figes absent-mindedly plumped the side pockets of his rough silk, tunic-style jacket, checking for another oblong, the invitation to Simon Dykes's private view. Tony had pant-hooted George Levinson at second-lunch time, suggesturing that he arrive early at the gallery, so that they could twine around tactics. Tony liked Simon well enough – but his real loyalty was to Sarah. He didn't want Sarah upset by the press – or the punters.

As Tony scampered up Dover Street and round the corner into Grafton he tried to picture what lay ahead of him. George Levinson had embargoed any reproductions of Dykes's new paintings, and now Simon was hospitalised with this terrible breakdown, there had been no possibility of the artist himself doing advance publicity. All that had arrived with the invitation was a detail of one. This was printed with the technique used for novelty 3-D postcards, and showed an infant in free-fall towards the viewer, its fur fringed with flame. Turn the postcard this way and that, and the fringe of fire around the hurtling body would flare.

Tony had received the invitation at his home, the flat in the block on Knatchbull Road that he had shared with his mother since birth. He avoided the slobber of her ancient lap pony, and her query, ' "H'huu" what've you got in the mail "huuu"? To-ony!', to escape down the corridor, with its depressing, old-female smells, to his room. The room was decidedly odd. One half was intact from his sub-adulthood; posters of glam-rock bands from the early seventies, Slade, T-Rex and the Sweet; a nestspread was patterned with Beatrix Potter animals; shelves lined with the Narnia books, old comics – mostly young female's titles, *Jackie*, *Bunty*, and so forth – and a few figurines of ballet dancers spun from glass.

But the other side of the room was distinctly male; dominated by a large knee-hole desk, covered with books, papers and a lightbox. Above the desk were shelves crammed with high-quality books of reproductions. There was a metal ashtray on the desk, full of the mutilated butts of Bactrian Lights, and by its side a piece of glass, smeared with fragments of cocaine. The miniature desktop set was caught in the spotlight of an Anglepoise lamp.

Tony chucked himself into the swivel chair by his desk, limbs bundled round his torso, like an infant in the prelude to a weaning tantrum. With one thick fingernail he slit the thick yellow envelope, engraved on the back, 'Levinson Gallery. Fine Art', and the 3-D burning infant tumbled on to the desk.

How often – Tony thought to himself – it was the case that the infant was alpha to the male. This burning infant – what could it betoken? In the last few weeks before his breakdown, Simon had given strong hints that the new paintings dealt with themes of corporeality, of the basic *physical* integrity of chimpness. Whenever Simon dropped these hints, Tony countersigned, tried to draw him out. But it wasn't until the burning mite dropped on to his desk that Tony began to realise quite how shocking Simon's paintings might be.

Now Tony swung around a lamp post from Grafton into Cork Street, and hung there for a while, observing the marvellously pink and effulgent arsehole of a cycle courier who was powering himself, up on the pedals of his racer, down towards Piccadilly. Tony shook his head. His head fur was moulting already – although he was barely thirty-five. For events such as this opening he felt he *had* to wear a toupee. He was as small and lithe as a bonobo – but that was a mixed blessing. Worse than any of this was that he knew he carried with him the taint of his mother's decay; that the smell of her despairing old age hung around him prematurely.

Tony Figes linked his sense of bodily disgust with what he had gleaned about Simon, and Simon's work. How germane, he thought, that this should be preoccupying him too, perhaps to the extent of driving him mad. Maybe Simon has lost the ability to suspend disbelief in mating – just as I have. Although no doubt for different reasons.

Tony may have felt physically cowardly – but he was brave enough to apply pressure to these digitations and speculate that this failure was linked to how chimps now lived, cut off from the natural world – housed in an essentially de-natured environment. Was it any wonder that the newspapers and magazines were full of cartoons that primatomorphised?

The *New Yorker*, which Tony took mostly to catch the photographic portraits of Mapplethorpe – and latterly Richard Avedon – was always full of cartoons that primatomorphised and often in the most ridiculous way; signing dogs, wisecracking moose, speculative bison, philosophic humans. There seemed no self-consciousness about this – or at any rate Tony had never seen anyone remark on the obvious species neuroticism that he detected lying behind them. The compulsion that must be prodding these wits to expose our rift from the rest of creation.

Only the previous week, the *New Yorker* had carried a cartoon depicting a typical Madison Avenue advertising male in gesticulation with a squirrel who was attached to a tree in Central Park. The squirrel was signing, 'Sure, he's as guilty as hell, now can we gesticulate about something else "huu"?', an obvious reference to the trial of O.J. Simpson, a media circus that was whipping up the poisonous hysteria of bonoboism all over the USA. The ironies of the cartoon went deeper though, far deeper, Tony reflected as he got bipedal and swaggered into the Levinson Gallery.

'"H'hoooo" I'm so glad you're here, Tony,' George Levinson pant-hooted as he came knuckle-walking from the back of the gallery. 'I'm a bundle of nerves – a bundle of nerves "eek-eek-eek"!'

'"H'hoooo" now, George, really, do try and get a grip on yourself . . .' Tony countersigned, his scar writhed with embarrassment, transforming his already puckered muzzle into something resembling a crushed football.

The two chimps sank to the floor by the reception desk and cradled each other's genitals for a while, then began to groom in an idle way. Tony managed to free globules of glue from between George's toes, bits that had been troubling the dealer from the day before. George's grooming was far more desultory – just an inattentive preening of the younger chimp's fur.

As they groomed Tony could hear the grunts of the receptionist on the 'phone, who was putting off a number of would-be latecomers to the opening. 'It's been like this all day,' George inparted Tony's belly. 'Yesterday as well "hoooo". I'm very anxious about openings at the best of times, but I think this one may well finish me off! I'll probably end up in that hideous hospital – along with poor Simon "hoooo"!'

' "Grun-nnn" now, George "chup-chupp" – George, please . . .' Tony broke off and grasping the edge of the desk pulled himself upright. The receptionist, seeing who it was, and being an ambitious young gallery female on the make – half presented to him, without ceasing her flutterings to the pant-hooter on the other end of the 'phone.

George got bipedal as well. He was wearing, Tony noted, one of those irritating faux swelling-protectors that some of the younger gay chimps were currently sporting. Tony thought the fashion frankly absurd, and on George Levinson a case of an old ram dressed as a lamb, but didn't have the heart to point it out – given the state George was in.

Tony Figes had been to the Levinson Gallery many times before. He approved of it, generally – if not always of what was within it. While the traditional exterior – full plate-glass window, discreet engraved sign – implied a complementary interior of oak panelling and brass picture hooks, George Levinson had, in fact, done his best to create a pure, negatively capable exhibition space. The walls were covered with a fine light-beige fabric; the overhead lights were sunken pin-pricks, faint and sidereal; the carpeting was so neutral in both colour and weave, as to be barely there at all. Following George Levinson's scut down the long room, Tony imagined his hands and feet were sinking into

174

a comfy voidlet. But this was not what impinged – the canvases impinged.

The gallery space was some forty hands high, twice as many wide, and a full two hundred hands long. Ranged along either wall were Simon Dykes's paintings of modern apocalypse. The booking hall of King's Cross tube station at the exact moment that the fire of 1987 erupted was the first canvas to engage Tony's attention. He zeroed in on the pitiful wraaaaing face of the infant who was hurtling to a painful death, recognising it as the original of the detail he had received along with the invitation. Tony stood upright in front of the painting. It was at least twenty hands square. The brushwork at the very centre, where the infant was suspended, was exact, nearly photoreal, but towards the edges it grew looser and looser, until near the frame there were thick layers of paint, worked into ridges and troughs.

'"H'hooooo" my God, George,' Tony signed. '"Hoo" my God! I see what you m –'

'You see what I mean "h'huu"?'

'I do – I do.' Tony moved on to the next canvas, which Simon had entitled simply *Aerial Chartres*. This portrayed the interior of a Boeing 747 at – he instantly realised – the exact moment that its fuselage was being crumpled by impact. Whole rows of seating were being tossed together with their occupants, into a heavy salad of death. As with the previous canvas there was at the centre a photoreal depiction of an infant. This one was oblivious of its fate, still strapped into its seat; its toes and fingers were fully employed in manipulating the toggles of a Sony Gamemale. Clearly visible on the screen was the paradoxically miniature, humanoid figure of Donkey Kong.

'My God!' resigned Tony Figes, then vocalised, "Hoooo."

'They're scary, aren't they "huu"?' George Levinson was gaining some sense of security from Tony's distress. George had, after all, been living with the paintings for weeks. And because of Simon's breakdown he had also been responsible for the stretching and framing – work the painter normally undertook himself. He continued gesturing. 'To put it crudely – with Simon in hospital and apparently mad, the urge the critics always have to conflate life and work will become ineluctable, wouldn't you sign "huu"?'

'I would, George. Let's go out back and have a drink and a line. I think we're both going to need them.'

When the two chimps emerged from George's office, some twenty minutes, two drinks, and three lines later, the gallery was already beginning to fill up. It was the usual sort of opening crowd – or at any rate the usual sort of crowd attracted to one of Simon Dykes's openings. The group of younger conceptual artists who were currently dominating the scene in London were among the first to arrive.

Tony knew them all – of course. He'd met them at the Sealink, or out with the Braithwaites, who were closer to them in both age and aesthetic. Tony found them – at least collectively – more than a little affected, if not absurd. They were now hanging about the place, all either dressed to the nines, or looking like dossers, ostentatiously not grooming one another. There were a couple of females among them – both attractive, both with magnificently pink, bulging swellings – and yet none of the males made any attempt to display to them – let alone mate.

This 'Like, chimp, we *don't* groom' act was constantly being undercut by the nervous and repetitive presenting they all indulged in. They'd try to restrain themselves, but when – as now – someone like Jay Jopling, the dealer and prestigious owner of the White Cube, swung into the room, they would all begin to grunt, and shuffle backwards towards him, arses frantically waggling.

They tried – Tony Figes reflected – to prevent themselves, but they couldn't. For all their vaunted membership of the avant-garde, whatever that was, they were just like everybody else, addicted to the pecking order and the superior's arse-lick – however cursory.

But neither Tony, nor more importantly George, was worried about the Conceptualists. They had a certain – albeit grudging – respect for Simon and his work. As for the mental breakdown, Tony supposed they would in their normal, perverse way regard it as being cool. No, the worrying chimps were those like Vanessa Agridge, the pushy hack from *Contemporanea* who had just knuckle-walked into the gallery. The glossy manipulators of the press were going to have free range when they got an eyeful of this stuff. Tony pulled himself together. The liquor had calmed his body, and the coke had honed his mind. He would try to poke some sense into the critics he knew, and when Sarah swung by, he'd look after her, keep her under his wing.

George Levinson was gesticulating with the art critic of *The Times*, a bigoted New Zealander denoted Gareth 'Grunt' Feltham. 'They are, of course "gru-nn" explorations of the chimp body, the essence of chimpness. Freud, after all, said that the ego is first and foremost a bodily ego "huuu"?'

'"Wraaf"! I'm not so sure about that, Levinson. It would seem to me "euch-euch" that the soul comes into all of this, and here we see paintings that exploit the bodies of chimps – and furthermore make a mockery of their souls. "HoooGraaa," he pant-hooted forcefully, while aiming a mock blow at George's head, then resumed his imperious signing.

'"Euch-euch" you know, I've always had my reservations about your chimp Dykes's work and I have to sign, Levinson, that this sort of thing confirms them.' He gestured with one of his large, hairy hands at the work in front of them, *Flat Pack Stops at Ebola*. '"Waaa" what does he mean by this – this cheap, essentially degrading vision "huu"?' Feltham was furiously agitated and he now proceeded to lift back his head and unleash from behind canines winnowed by decay and yellowed by tobacco, a series of spine-tingling hoots and barks: "HoooooGra! Wraaaf! HoooooGra! HoooooGra! Wraaaaf"!

Whereupon other critics, throughout the gallery, also put their rented glasses on the floor, braced themselves and began to vocalise, "HoooooGraa! HoooooGra!" The air was thick with their vinous exhalations, and George felt quite queasy, regretting the drinks and lines he'd had with Tony. Some of the critics even began drumming on the walls and floors, until solicitously requested not to by the gallery females. But amidst all the vocalising, George couldn't really tell if any kind of fusion was emerging.

There were now well over fifty chimps in the gallery. Critics, collectors, dealers, artists and their hangers-on. Thankfully, George noted, the ratio of females in oestrus was fairly high, and quite a lot of attention was taken up with displays of one kind and another, but unrelated to the show itself. Indeed, after the vocalising had died down Feltham stopped applying pressure to George and shamelessly thrust his index finger into the ischial scrag of a passing female. She slapped his hand away, and Feltham brought it to his nostrils. "Gru-nn Gr-unn," he sniffle-grunted, then signed, 'She can't be more than a week off, excuse me, will you, Levinson – not exactly your bag "huuu"?'

George shucked off the insult, he couldn't be bothered to fight with the burly critic over such crassness. Later though, he was thrilled to see the burly critic mating the female at the far end of the gallery, his corduroy jacket riding down over his scut as he panted and tooth-clacked, and judging by the weary expression of the female – whose muzzle was pressed hard into the carpeting – not managing to effect climax in either party.

George looked once more at *Flat Pack Stops at Ebola.* As with Simon's other paintings there was an infant at its centre. In this case the poor mite was haemorrhaging horribly from mouth and anus, the blood pouring down its coat and on to the flat pack in question, which was – according to the stencilled lettering on its side – for assembly into an attractive, freestanding wine rack. Simon had caught the feel of an aisle at the Swedish furniture supermarket, Ikea, perfectly. The bland irradiation of overhead lighting, the bays full of flat packs for assembly into tables, chairs, shelving units and stereo cabinets. In this environment, constructed, as it was, to determine a pre-fabricated choice, the imposition of violent, contingent death was obscene.

Particularly the form of death Simon had chosen to portray. Drawing on accounts of the outbreak at Ebola in Central Africa, he had envisioned the effects of the flesh-dissolving virus, massively speeded up, on a group of furniture shoppers. The figures of the adult chimps were distressing enough, the blood, excrement and bile had worked into their coats and they slumped here and there against the flat packs, cradling one another's heads. But the sight of the infant on the wine rack *was* revolting.

"Hooo," George cried quietly and turned to confront the gallery. He saw Sarah Peasenhulme swagger in through the door, flanked by the Braithwaites. Immediately all three were surrounded by yammering chimps, some of whom presented to Sarah, while others tried to display to her. She was still in the full flower of oestrus, her swelling massive and pinkly gleaming, as if a party balloon were rammed between her thighs.

Some of the crowd mobbing her were toting camcorders, clearly intending to get some signs from her on tape. George decided he'd better intervene. He bounded quickly up, hugging the wall so as to avoid the mêlée. When he was within a few hands of Sarah he drummed the reception desk and vocalised, "Wraaaaaf!" It was the most ferocious vocalisation anybody could ever remember him making, and his fierce expression and bared canines belied – for once – his ridiculous oval Oliver Peeples fashion eyewear, his shot-silk jacket by Alexander McQueen, and the faux swelling-protector Tony Figes had signlessly derided.

The group fissioned slightly and George was able to get inside the hackled huddle, grab Sarah's arm and bodily haul her out. ' "Hoooo" come on, Sarah,' he imparted, 'you don't want to be doing with these chimps.'

' "H'huuuu?" George, what is it? Why are they so aggressive?'

'Have you see Simon's canvases, Sarah? Did he show them to you "huu"?' George led her the length of the gallery, aiming for the back office.

'Some, George. He let me in the studio a couple of times. I recognise that one of the King Kong figure in Oxford Circus . . . and that one of the crashing plane. Is it the subject matter "huu"? Is that what they're worked up about "huu"?'

'Yes, that, and of course Simon's breakdown . . . And I imagine – given the utter prurience of the press and the rest of this bloody carnival – your being in oestrus doesn't help.'

It wasn't helping. Even in the short time it took them to knuckle-walk to the far end of the gallery, George and Sarah acquired more attention. A chimp denoted Pelham, a feature writer for the Sundays, was displaying to Sarah, waving a copy of the *Evening Standard* about. More impressively, Flixou, the sculptor, a massive, tough chimp of legendary strength and sexual prowess was blatantly importuning as well; panting, squealing and grabbing sheets of newspaper away from Pelham. It looked very much as if there was going to be a serious scrap between the two males.

' "Err-herr-herr" George, I don't want this, I don't want to be here . . . It's, it's . . .' Her fingers went up above her head to grasp and describe the scene; the agitated chimps grooming, drinking, gesticulating and mating. 'Like a bloody *zoo!*'

'Well "gru-nn", that could be seen as success of a kind. At least, I think Simon would be pleased to know he's caused such a stir. But Sarah, why don't you go on to the Sealink and I'll join you there as soon as I can "huu"? "HoooGraaa!" he pant-hooted to Tony Figes, who was nearby gesticulating with the Braithwaites. Figes flagged down and came to join them. 'Tony, if you've seen enough of this, would you take Sarah in hand, she's not happy.'

'You're right, George, let's get her out of here.'

The party of chimps moved back up the gallery, the two

bonobos once more taking the flanks and this time dealing viciously with anyone who attempted to solicit Sarah. They reached the door without incident and pushed through it on to the street. Ken Braithwaite went to the kerb and began pant-hooting to attract the attention of a taxi. One pulled up within seconds, without its hire sign lit, and disgorged two chimps. They were arriving for the private view, although they were not the sort of chimps who normally attended these things. One was a large, rather flabby, but well-preserved male, wearing an old fashioned, double-breasted dinner jacket. The other a slight brunette, who looked dowdy in a once fashionable Lurex top and matching swelling-protector.

"HoooGraa!" Sarah pant-hooted, then waved to her group, 'It's Dr Busner, the Quantity Theory chimp, he's taken on Simon's case, and that's Dr Bowen, the senior registrar at Charing Cross. "HooGraa" Dr Busner, "HooGraa".'

Busner finished paying the cabbie and crawled over to them. ' "HooGraa" it's Sarah,' he signed, 'isn't it "huuu", Simon Dykes's consort?'

'That's right and this is George Levinson, Simon's dealer.' Sarah made the other introductions. Bowen joined them and for a few seconds there was a confused round of presenting and partial grooming. The art chimps didn't really know what to make of the psychiatrists, where to fit them into the hierarchy. Something of a stand-off emerged from the confusion of quivering scuts and mock-grooming; Sarah ended up with her fingers in Dr Bowen's fur while George and Tony attempted to out-grovel one another in front of the distinguished psychiatric practitioner.

'Well, Mr Levinson,' Busner signed after a while, 'I'm looking forward to seeing these paintings. Do you imagine that they could give me any probings as to Mr Dykes's bizarre condition "huuu"?'

'I hardly know, Dr Busner, I hardly know . . . They are quite a departure for Simon, not at all like his earlier work. They're very . . . very *graphic* –'

'I see, and the subject matter "huu"?'

'Well, the body, Dr Busner, the body of the archetypal chimp constrained, crushed and distorted by the pressures of modern, urban life.' George was warming to his theme, his fingers gesturing with a smooth tempo. 'I think Simon has done something "chup-chupp" quite remarkable with these paintings, although whether the critics will be prepared to give a hand to it I cannot sign.'

'Well – well, we shall see. Jane, would you like to swing in "huu"?'

Dr Bowen broke from Sarah, giving the younger female a reassuring pat on her rump. 'But Dr Busner,' Sarah signed, 'how did you find Simon, do you think he's improving "huu"? What are you going to do for him "huu"?'

Busner came over to Sarah and bestowed some rather clumsy caresses on her head. 'Now, now, so many questions. I do "gru-nn" appreciate how upset you must be, Ms Peasenhulme, but it's far too early for me even to attempt a diagnosis. Your consort's condition is intense, but I have no reason to believe – as yet – that it isn't treatable. I adopt, as you may know, an holistic and psycho-physical approach to what are denoted <mental illnesses>. The whole chimp is what concerns me, hence my presence here. We hope to be able to complete some tests on him tomorrow; why not give Dr Bowen a pant-hoot after second lunch – we may have some news for you then.'

With that Busner gave a valedictory pant-hoot to the assembled chimps, drummed on a metal litter bin, gathered Bowen in his scut and entered the gallery.

Nothing had happened in the secure room for some hours now. Simon Dykes, the artist, lay in nest cradling his tousled head. Through that head raced a vile cavalcade of images. The material of his paintings; bodies thrown about, bodies burnt, bodies mashed and macerated, all confused and consorting with the unacceptable apes; the grinning, tooth-clacking visions who disputed with him as to their own reality. He moaned and rocked, moaned and rocked.

The beast-claiming-to-be-Sarah had signed that the private view for his show was taking place tonight. If I were insane, Simon plaited the musing with the moaning, I wouldn't care about this, I wouldn't be able to comprehend this – would I? But I do and can. I can imagine the shit they'll sling at me . . . the shit they'll sling at me. . . . like the shit *I* sling at the beasts.

Who are they? Simon framed a view of the Levinson Gallery filled with chimpanzees. A preposterous vision, the animals with their scraggy rumps, their bandy, old men's legs, their ears bracketed with field mushrooms. They all gesticulated at the paintings with their wiggling fingers, full of twisted import – and they all shoved their arses in each others muzzles, their digits in each other's fur. They formed a writhing, zoic rug, a pathetic travesty of the appreciation of art – or was it?

For the first time since his breakdown, it now occurred to Simon that perhaps the content of these hallucinations, these delusions of the bestial masking the human, were made up, constructed from the materials of his own mordant obsessions. What, after all, were the apes, if not distorted versions of the body? That they were all body – all *embodiment*, was the only certainty. For the rest of what they signed was clearly nonsensical – or inadmissible.

These thoughts seemed to Simon to possess the true assay of insight. They calmed him. A hidden observer, able to penetrate the gloom of the secure room, and sympathetic to the madchimp, might have noticed a relaxation of Simon's limbs at this point. He gave several long nest grunts, rearranged himself as comfortably as he could and waited for the monkeys to come with his sedative stab.

Supposing the opening *had* been tonight? Where would Sarah be now? George Levinson couldn't possibly have arranged a third dinner of any kind – not with his client sectioned on a mental ward. No, Simon guessed that Sarah would have attended, with Tony Figes and the Braithwaites, no doubt, and then probably gone on to the Sealink for a drink. The vision of Sarah in the Sealink, Sarah demure, Sarah touchable, coiled in Simon's gut, curdling whatever kind milk had been there. In its place he felt a tense spring of lustful jealousy. He remembered the particular look of Sarah's eyes when she was aroused, pupils dilating into astonished empowerment. He remembered the dispensation of her limbs when she moved over him, lowered herself on to him. He groaned and fretted. Where was she now? Was she thinking of him?

She was. Sarah was thinking of Simon, but as she was also thinking about Ken Braithwaite's cock, which was slamming into her with quite explosive energy, her thoughts were thus scattered, a little diffuse.

The two chimps had begun mating halfway down the stairs from the main bar to the toilets of the Sealink Club. Ken hadn't so much displayed to Sarah, as signed concerning the possibility of a fuck. Indeed, it was this off-handedness – the signs glibly flipping from his fingers – that decided her to accept. Mating with Ken would be – she felt – as neutrally reassuring as being covered by the Reverend Peter.

So it was. Sarah braced herself by the turn in the stairs. Ken entered her with consummate ease, her swelling so slack, so wet, that it sucked him in. Ken was transported. His slim body bucked and writhed over her, while his fingers inparted her blonde scruff, 'Your "gru-nn" swelling, your "gru-nn" swelling, your swe-ll-ing . . .' until the squeals and pants of copulation got going in earnest.

A number of chimps scampering up and down the stairs had to hand themselves over the jerking pair, but they made no remark. It was considered bad form to point to mating activities in the club and this was usually adhered to.

Ken came with great alacrity – withdrawing so rapidly from

Sarah that the hooked barb of his cock rasped her internally in just the fashion calculated to bring her off. She squealed, her teeth clacked. She felt the plash of Ken's spunk fall across her back fur. "EeeeWraaa!" she shrieked, then twisting herself round signed, '"Hooo" Ken, d'you think Simon's going to be all right "huu"?'

'Who can sign, Sarah, who can sign. But at least if he troubles to think about it he'll know that you're in good hands.'

Zack Busner felt dreadfully constricted in his old dinner jacket. The stalls at Covent Garden weren't really air-conditioned to anything like the right levels and as the day had turned out hot and muggy, the temperature was well up in the eighties. He tried to concentrate on the stage, but *Turandot* had never been an opera he liked and having come in only at the second act the action was confusing. Weren't the vocalisers meant to be Chinese? If so, why were they dressed in Ruritanian costumes? Really, thought Zack, modern opera productions often put the less into artlessness. Even Peter Wiltshire's stabs at shifting time, genre and *mise-en-scène* often appeared contrived to Busner.

At least if he ignored the sur-titles running across the screen above the stage, he could listen to the mellifluous pant-hooting and soaring screaming of the vocalisers; and Charlotte seemed to be enjoying herself, grunting contentedly and passing her fingers gently over the ragged bulge of her subsiding swelling.

Busner was free to muse, free to consider the strange case of Simon Dykes and his human delusion. Busner had been more impressed by Dykes's paintings than he expected. The idea of depicting, allegorically, the anti-naturalism of the condition of modern urban chimpunity appealed to him. What Dykes was doing with visual imagery was, he felt, similar to his own search for a psycho-physical approach to neurological and psychiatric disorders. The bodies of the chimps in Dykes's paintings were placed in destructive environments – a crashing plane, a burning escalator, a plague-struck furniture superstore – which could be seen as analogues of the distorted relation between chimps' minds and chimps' bodies.

Was it possible that Dykes's breakdown had been foretold in the paintings? That like an epileptic's furious flash of mystic lucidity prior to a fit, they were anticipations of the furious alienation from his own body, his own chimpunity, that he was now experiencing. And how did the human delusion itself fit into all of this? Busner ranged freely in his own mind over the associations that the human called up. The human was held to be the most bestial of the animals because it was the most chimp-like. This had been understood and incorporated into descriptions of all simian creatures, even before the discovery of the true anthropoid apes – the orang-utan, the gorilla and the human – in the sixteenth century.

The human thus had a ready-made niche of demonisation waiting for it to occupy. If the Barbary ape, the hamadryad and the baboon had been seen as offspring of Lucifer – and some patristic writers claimed that the devil was made in the image of the baboon – then how much more diabolic could the human be? The human with its ghastly exposed skin; its repugnantly bulging hind parts; its voracious, inappropriate licentiousness? Yet paradoxically, the imagery of humans retailed in contemporary culture was almost always benign, cuddly even. Infants often had stuffed humans as toys. Birthday cards with humans dressed up as chimps on them were available in almost every newsagent. There were also the notorious commercials for P.G. Tips tea, with their absurd use of humans mimicking chimp behaviour; special effects used to convey the impression that they were signing intelligently and enjoying the beverage.

Then there was the upsurge in the ethical preoccupation with animal rights. Some moral philosophers now advocated the extension of a limited form of chimpanzee rights to the human, on the grounds that given their genetic profile they were the closest living relative to the chimpanzee, as well as the most obviously intelligent.

What elements of all of these images and versions of the human could Dykes have drawn on to provide the furniture of his delusion? Was there evidence to be found elsewhere in his life, outside of his art? Or was it sadly the case that this delusional system, like so many others Busner had seen elaborated, would collapse on closer examination, into the confused, disjointed wavings of the paranoid schizophrenic?

One thing was certain, there could be no progress until they had managed to divine the extent – if any – of organic damage to Dykes's brain. Then, and only then, would Busner be able to move forward. As yet there was little to go on, but he Busner had a good feeling about his new patient. This was a case that might attract a considerable amount of public interest, something Busner had never been that averse to.

As if he had somehow deliberately timed his thoughts to coincide with the end of the performance, the audience chose this moment to derail Busner's train by all leaping to their feet and pant-hooting their approval. "HoooGraaa! HoooGraaa!" Busner got bipedal and politely pant-hooted as well. 'I hope there'll be an encore,' he inparted Charlotte. 'I've been picking over the nitty matter of this chimp Dykes so much that I missed <Nessun Dorma>.'

Chapter Twelve

The scraggy toe-tip tapped on the lino, "Tap-tap, tap-tap, tap-tap". It was notable how much harder the skin was than that of a human toe, for precisely this reason, that as the toe hit the lino it produced the noise "tap-tap, tap-tap, tap-tap". "Euch-euch," Simon Dykes coughed irritably.

The idiotic mask – made he assumed for infants to wear at Hallowe'en – turned to muzzle him, and from behind the rigid bow of vivid red lip came a soft grunt, ' "Gru-nnn" are you all right then, Simon – not feeling too anxious, or uncomfortable "huu"?'

Simon couldn't have signed how he did, but from the combination of familiar vocalisation and gesture, he *knew* that it was the psychiatrist called Bowen who was putting the finger on him. He had insisted that only she should accompany him while he knuckle-walked from the secure room, to the bowels of the hospital where the MRI and the CAT scans were done. But afterwards, as he slid from the great, hammering, steel gullet of the machine, he hadn't dared, or wished, to gesticulate with the creature awaiting him.

Busner had been as good as his sign, and done his best to clear the corridors and areas Simon traversed on his way down. The occasional simian figure scurried out of their path as he followed Jane Bowen's scut; and each time this happened Simon recoiled and pressed himself against the wall. And each time she had coaxed him back up on to all fours, then led him on. Bowen wanted desperately, seeing his distress, to give

Simon a good, sound grooming and reassure him in the most chimpmane fashion she knew, both as a doctor and a female. But she knew better than to attempt it.

There had been no shot of Valium that morning. Bowen had delineated over the 'phone that were he to be in any way sedated it would affect the validity of the testing. 'If you feel a bad attack coming on, you simply have to call to me and I'll take you straight back to the secure room. We are only trying to help you, Simon – please remember that.'

But besides catching sight of the odd chimpanzee, what had disturbed – and perversely reassured – Simon, was the interior of the hospital itself. Simon had been in Charing Cross Hospital before. How many times he could not have signed, but enough for it to seem familiar. The notices pinned up on bulletin boards along the walls; the glass doors with their graticule of mesh; the tawdry, squeaking linoleum floors; even the route they took, down an escalator, across an internal courtyard, down in another lift – all of it could be matched with memories of coming to the hospital to visit ill allies.

Perhaps it was the absence of the Valium, or simply being released from his confinement, but there was also something about the hospital that jarred with his expectations: the scale of it. Everything, the height of the ceilings, the width of the doors, the bulk of the furniture, was slightly diminished. It was so subtle as to be almost indiscernible, but Simon caught on. This was Charing Cross Hospital maddeningly rebuilt for beings just that bit smaller than humans. Redesigned for chimpanzees.

For the first few minutes after he emerged from the relative safety of his confinement, Simon was bewildered. Bowen's mask certainly concealed her ghastly, simian features, but the trousers she donned to cover her brutish, furry legs were made from some diaphanous material, and fur could still be seen through them. This, together with her down-at-heel white coat, made her a clownish figure.

I must keep seeing them as absurdities, figments, Simon

abjured himself. I must not give them too much credence – to do so is to accept that I really am mad. I must cling on to my humanity. So he huddled himself up like an old chimp with some chronic, wasting illness and shuffled along, head down, fur lank.

Bowen was dismayed by Simon's behaviour when she led him from the secure room. True, he wasn't lashing out or spraying at her. True, he seemed able – just about – to bear the occasional glimpse of another chimp, but his whole manner was so torpid, so lacking in affect, that she found herself making a damning – but signless – diagnosis. Dykes reminded her, she realised, of chimps in states of near-catatonic depression, or suffering from severe neurological dysfunctions. The human delusion, she began to think, might only have been the flamboyant onset of a condition, the chronic stage of which would be characterised by apathy, withdrawal and eventually complete mental collapse.

Now the two chimps were back up on Gough, waiting in the day room to do the perceptual tests – and waiting for Zack Busner. The day room was a bland space. There was a Melamine-topped table, some functional plastic-backed chairs, and a steel box of a dustbin in one corner. The vertical, textured louvres were blocking out the sharp, noonday brightness, and the strip-lighting hummed and flickered overhead. A 'phone squatted on the table, signlently. The basic odour of the place was – Bowen admitted – one of bleached despair.

'"HooGraa" Simon, I'm just going to go and get a cuppa from the machine, would you like one "huu"?'

He looked up at the sound of her vocalisation and counter-signed, 'Yeah, all right.'

'Tea, coffee "huu"? Milk, sugar "huu"?'

'Whatever.'

Bowen knuckle-walked to the door shaking her head, so that the ridiculous mask chafed her ears. Poor bastard, she thought, his gesturing just confirms my suspicions, the signs so fumbled, so lacking in emphasis or tempo.

In the corridor she encountered Busner, who was grinning broadly and bearing down on her fast. An old-fashioned leather briefcase was rammed up under one of his arms and he was bipedal, swaggering. In his scut came his research-assistant epsilon, Gambol. '"HoooGraa"! Well, hello there, Jane, recovered from your ranging into the art world "huu"? No, no, no need for that, please, please . . .' Busner began fending Jane Bowen off, for naturally on sighting him she had fallen to the floor, offered up her arse and was now insisting he kiss it. 'You'll just have to get used to some of my informalities, Jane, if we're working together again. Isn't that right Gambol "huu"?'

'"Hoo" absolutely,' Gambol countersigned, although his thoughts were knuckle-walking in an entirely different direction.

Would it be possible for him to get away this morning and have another gesticulation with Whatley? They had left things inconclusively the previous day. If an alliance was in the offing, it was time for Gambol to make good with his promise of some dirt on Busner, make good with his plans for advancement, conquest and eventual dominance.

'I'm just going to get Dykes a cup of tea, Zack,' Jane Bowen signed. 'I think you'll be "gru-nn" pleased to learn that the MRI and the CAT scan went off fine. I had them do a comprehensive set of X-rays as well; and I've asked them to try and hurry up with all of them so that we can correlate the results with whatever tests you intend doing.'

'"Chup-chupp" good "gru-nnn" good, we-ell I suppose now is as good a time as any for me to meet our patient muzzle-to-muzzle. Have you got one of those masks for me "huu"? As you can see I've brought my own trousers!' And with this Busner pulled from his briefcase a pair of harem pants not dissimilar to the ones Jane Bowen was wearing. The three chimps couldn't restrain themselves, the idea of donning these nestroom garments in a workaday environment was so absurd – it was positively kinky. '"H'hee-hee-hee",' Busner cackled. '"H'hee-hee-hee-hoo" my

God "clak-clak"! I know we shouldn't laugh about it, but this case is already throwing up some of the most ridiculous antics it's ever been my good fortune to indulge in as a medical practitioner. Here "h'hee-hee-hee" Gambol, hang on to my case while I put these on.'

The 'phone rang but for some seconds Simon didn't respond. He squatted, slumped at the table, his head cradled in his arms. I'm a lost soul, he thought, or no soul at all. I've lost it now – lost it for ever. As if looking down a long corridor, he could dimly discern some visions from his past; they were visions of lost bodies, human bodies. His first infant emerging in a splash of liquor from the womb – not just emerging but shooting out, a blue ball of life, hitting the rubber sheet, arms and legs flying out, larynx blurting an incontrovertibly human cry, a beautiful cry. "Wraaaa!" Simon screamed, "wraaaa!" and his fur shook with the emotion, the sadness, the loss.

The 'phone was still ringing. Simon answered it, and waited for the mist to clear on the screen. Another caricature mask of a human muzzle appeared, but this was different to the one Bowen was wearing. This 'human' sported a blond lick of plastic hair falling across its shiny, flesh-coloured brow and an absurd, blond handlebar moustache above its rigid bow of lip. Without quite knowing why, Simon guessed before the beast signed that it was Busner.

'"HoooGraaa" good day, Mr Dykes. I'd like to congratulate you on your show –'

'What "huu"?' Despite himself Simon was gripped. The fact of the mask and the gesticulating fingers didn't obtrude. He felt the same acute, skittering anxiety that always took hold of him when there was any evaluation of his work in the offing.

'At the Levinson Gallery, the show of your apocalyptic paintings – I am right in envisioning them apocalyptic paintings "huu"?'

'Ye-es, obviously "gru-nnn" I was positioning them in that overall context, although equally obviously I also intended them to subvert the religious tradition of depicting the apocalypse.'

'Obviously, obviously . . . "gru-nnn-euch-euch" I think the subversive nature of the work was what most impressed the critics who attended "huuu".'

Busner was trying to sign in what he imagined to be a 'human' way, while also maintaining an uncomfortably still posture. The performance was, however, ruined by his signing hands which kept going to the bi-focals hanging around his neck and fidgeting with them. Certainly Simon was unimpressed. The masks weren't working at all. He could see Busner's gnarled ears protruding either side and the meaning-conveying fingers that wiggled and tickled in front of the screen were as hairy and tough-looking as Jane Bowen's toes. "Euch-euch," he coughed, then signed, 'Look, Dr Busner, I don't think there's any real point to this charade with the mask, or the trousers, they're not helping – I still see you as a chimpanzee. Or rather, I still believe that you're a chimpanzee under that mask, so you may as well take it off.'

'"Huuu"? Really? You don't find them comforting? These were the best ones the shop had, almost up to the standard used for theatre and television. My infants were absolutely terrified by them. Don't you find them at all realistic "huu"?'

'Not at all "hooo".'

'"Hoo" well, in that case . . .' With a Mission Impossible flourish Busner removed his mask and at the same time asigned that Gambol should pull the harem pants off his legs. 'Bloody things are making me itch,' he inparted the epsilon's scruff.

Simon confronted the muzzle of the beast, steeling himself not to recoil. Whether to picture himself or the world gone mad was not the issue – it was important only that he try and *deal* with Busner. Accommodate the psychiatrist and maybe, just maybe, things would get better.

'Now "huuu" how's that?'

'All-all right,' Simon signed with fingers partially covering his eyes, 'just-just . . . well, please try not to move so suddenly –

especially if you come in here – I find the *speed* with which you all move quite terrifying. D'you understand me "huu"?'

'Well, of course I do, after all, chimpanzees do tend to move a lot faster than humans, don't we "huu"?'

'Do they "huu"?'

'Yes, a lot faster. It seems that you have quite a lot to learn concerning the world, Mr Dykes; perhaps if we regarded our sessions together as *educational* it would help you to find my physical appearance less disturbing "huuu"?'

'Maybe. I don't know.'

'"H'huuu" let's just proceed on that basis, shall we? Now, would you be prepared to accept my presence in the room with you – there are some perceptual and relational tests I need to do which really require that we be within grooming range –'

'What "huu"?!'

'I'm sorry, I misfingered, Dr Bowen shows me simian contact is disturbing to you. I simply mean that I need to be within . . . how can I put it . . . within *putative* grooming range.'

'Just as long as you don't touch me – or get too near.' Simon broke the connection, and leant back in the chair. His posture was, Bowen noted, as ever, curiously stiff and upright. He didn't grasp his toes, as most chimps did when arranging themselves in a chair, or make any perceptible nesting movements.

During this gesticulation Bowen had divested herself of her mask and trousers. She then shrank into the corner of the room, partially hiding herself behind a chair, so as not to appear at all threatening to Simon.

Busner came in upright, and moving with such exaggerated slowness that Bowen feared Simon might find it patronising, placed his stuffed briefcase on the table, pulled out a chair and squatted down, adopting a position not unlike Simon's, back straight, hands furled – when not signing – loosely in his lap.

'Now, Mr Dykes, I have some very simple tests I'd like you to do for me today, so simple I fear you may find them insulting to your intell –'

'Dr Busner "huuu"?'

'Yes, Mr Dykes.'

'You signed something before about the critics at the opening.'

'That's right.'

'You couldn't be a bit more forthcoming, could you "huu"?' There was no evidence of apathy now. Simon was bent forward, almost within reach of Busner, his muzzle puckered up with an intensity and concentration Bowen hadn't seen before.

'I took the liberty of getting my research assistant, Gambol, to photocopy the notices in this morning's papers – you'd like to see them "huuu"?' Busner withdrew the sheaf of paper from his briefcase and held it up for Simon to see. Simon lurched forward and tried to grab it, but Busner jerked it out of range signing, 'Not yet, Mr Dykes, you'll forgive me for this crude behaviourism, but I really feel we should do tests first, reviews later "huuu"?'

Simon fell back in his chair. 'All right,' he fluttered listlessly, 'but I'm buggered if I know what you expect to find out.'

The session lasted all morning. Busner and Bowen began with perceptual tests. The simplest of these were easy enough for an infant to do, matching shapes, fitting one figure inside another, arranging colours spectrographically and interpreting various symbolic congruences. On all of them Simon Dykes performed adequately, although by no means as well as you would expect of an adult chimp in good health.

The problems Simon had with the simple tests became clearer when they moved on to the harder exercises. His eye–hand coordination, his vision, his hearing, all were slightly impaired. There was no evidence of any actual cognitive dysfunction, but somewhere between Simon Dykes's brain and the rest of his body an attenuation, or diminution, was occurring. He would keep misplacing a digit, a letter, or a figure. When Busner or Bowen pointed these errors out to him, Simon could immediately see them, but when presented with a task to all intents and purposes the same, he would make the same mistake again.

Busner also gave Simon a very limited thirty-two-question Stanford-Binet test, devised for schizophrenics, and a similarly circumscribed MMPI, or Minnesota Multiphasic Personality Inventory. Simon sat, his shabby fur oozing with sweat as he worked his way through these sheets of questions with only one sane answer. He neither asked Busner what they were for, nor showed any animation, except when querying those parts of the tests that cut against the grain of his delusion. With the MMPI, for example, there was an entire section dealing with mating, a section Simon passed over save for ringing each instance of the sign 'mating', and placing a question mark next to it.

Busner and Jane Bowen looked on in novocal, using the opportunity for an extended grooming session. Busner slid gratefully from his chair to the floor and laid his head in Bowen's lap. She worked her way carefully over his head fur, his neck fur, and after removing his jacket and shirt all the way down his back fur, giving little smacks of her lips the while. She popped some of the gleanings – mucus, dried sweat twistles, crumbs, food particles – in her mouth; and made a small pile of others – paper bitlets, plastic filaments, lice eggs, staples, scabs and winnets – on the linoleum. When she was done, they reversed their positions and Busner got to work on her back. He snuffled and grunted as his lips palped and his fingers combed. Finding himself surprised by the quantities of medicaments mixed up in Bowen's sleek, dark fur, he inparted between her shoulders, 'I shall have to watch what I'm doing here, Jane, or I'll find myself sedated!', at which she heaved with soundless laughter.

Simon finished the last question and threw his pencil in the air. It fell to the floor with a minor beat. Busner heaved himself upright. ' "H'huuu" are you done then, Mr Dykes?' he signed, one hand cradling his testicles.

' "Hooo" yes, I am. I'm done, done-fucking-in. Show me I'm mad now, Doc-tor human-muzzle "euch-euch", show me . . .' The artist's fingers faltered – then fell signlent. There was shocked signless between the three apes that endured and endured, while Bowen expected an outburst from Busner, but none came. He merely regarded Simon quizzically, his eyebrow ridges deeply furrowed.

The 'phone rang, Bowen answered it. She employed a toe to smooth some fur Busner had set against the part, while watching the chimp on the other end of the camera, then broke the connection with the same digit. 'It's the biotechnician down in the bowels –'

'And "huu"?' Busner's ridges unfurrowed, rose.

'They're ready.'

'Good, good. Very "grnn" good. That *is* quick. Tell me, Jane, was this your influence alone, or did Whatley have a part in it "huuu"?'

'I've no image, Zack, I like to envision it was down to me.' She scratched her knees.

The patient, who during this exchange had remained squatting in novocal, now sparked up again and his fingers flew. 'So "euch-euch" what about these reviews then "huuu"? Didn't you sign I could look at them once I'd done your stupid tests "huu"? Now didn't you, human-muzzle. Human-muzzle! Human-muzzle!' Simon illustrated these insults by picking up one of the human masks and waving it in the muzzle concerned. Busner lost patience and swung on him, a roundhouse punch that sent Simon sprawling. The results were traumatic to observe. Simon crumpled up into a ball and began his odd, low-pitched keening, while his hands, half covering his anguished muzzle, shaped the signs, 'You fucking bastard! You hit me! You bastard. You aren't a fucking doctor – you're a monster, a fucking monster!' and then he began to scream in earnest, "Aaaaargh! Aaaaargh! Aaaaargh!"

Busner and Bowen exchanged wary looks. This was not the response to physical admonishment either would have expected from a psychotic patient – whatever the nature of his delusion. Busner had seen Simon's case notes, but he still found the lack of physicality in the chimp, of basic reflexes, difficult to handle. Even with his many years of clinical experience, the atypical behaviour wrongfooted his impulse to offer reassurance. It was left to Jane Bowen to squat down by Simon, grunting gently, ' "Grnnn-gru-nnn-hooo" Simon, I'm sorry, but you really shouldn't challenge Dr Busner's authority in this way, it can't help matters –'

'AllIwan, allIwan –' he fumbled.

'What's that "huuu"? Simon "huu"?'

'AllIwans t'see them. Thass all.'

'See what, Simon "huu"?'

'The reviews, the fucking reviews.'

'Simon, Simon "gr-unnn" Simon, please, "chup-chupp" I'm sorry. You're still my patient, you know – and a very interesting patient too. Here they are . . .' Busner crouched by Simon on the biffed and battered linoleum. He so wanted to take the chimp's head in his hands, to cradle it, to pressure it, to offer proper, chimpmane comfort, but Bowen's look warned him off. 'Please accept that what I "grnnn" did to you I would have done to any patient who behaved in this fashion. Now, Dr Bowen and I need to have a look at your test results. It's boring stuff for you – very technical. What I suggesture is that you go back to your room, have some third lunch, read your reviews – I think you'll find them entwining, if not altogether pleasing – and in the meantime we'll go over the results. We can reconvene in an hour or so . . . "huuu"? . . . What d'you sign?'

In the staff canteen Bowen grabbed a corner table. It meant they could go through the x-rays and scans without a light box. Busner brought the trays from the serving hatch, Bowen the buff envelopes and buffer folders. They spread out the sections of Simon Dykes on the table top and dived in. 'I don't want to do this systematically, Jane,' Busner gestured, while cramming an individual steak and kidney pie into his mouth. 'I just want to look at the things as rapidly as possible, form an impressionistic diagnosis. If you notice anything – sing out!'

Bowen rubbed her thighs together, feeling her fur comb

itself, hookless Velcro. Oh to be licking a pink, damp swelling at this moment, to feel deliciously hairy teats swell in her mouth like ripe – Enough! She shoved the image aside. Her nestmate, Rachel, wouldn't be in oestrus again for another, frustrating week, better to give the finger to the thought, rather than visualise fingering her.

'"Wraaa-hoo" my God! Look at this!' Busner was holding up one of the slide sheets with the MRI sections on it. 'Look! He's got a definite focal signal hyperintensity, here, here . . . and here! Several of them, right along the Sylvian fissure. "Hoo-hoo-hoo" I never really thought we'd turn up such obvious organic damage at all. And his frontal lobe doesn't look right either . . . No "hooo" it certainly doesn't –'

'It's swollen, isn't it "huu"?'

'Horribly swollen. If I didn't "grnnn'yum" know better "grnnn'yum" I'd sign this was hydrocephalus –'

'It would square with the other wet bits, "huu" wouldn't it?'

'*If* that's what they are – maybe they aren't. Pass me the PET scans, I want to try and correlate them.'

While the MRI scans were colourless, like ultrasound, pictures defining the shape of the brain in shades of grey, rendering it as massy and weirdly differentiated as a ball of fluff recovered from a blocked vacuum cleaner, the positive emission tomography produced fantastic coloured slides, more akin to heat-sensitive satellite imaging. Simon Dykes's brain, as revealed by PET, was a lurid collision of deep blues, dark purples and virulent greens. And as the cerebellum was palette-shaped in outline, the effect was as of observing some arty-facts, or analogies of colour sensitivity.

This is what Dykes himself might have thought on seeing the nuclear mapping of his mind, but Busner, despite his vaunted artistry, looked at the PET scan with technical eyes, noting the disjunction between the dark, depressed shades on the left-hand side of the brain, and the lurid flashes of red, yellow and orange on the right-hand side. "Grnnn-grnnn" he grunted as he perused them. ' "Grnn-grnnn" look at this,

Jane – this certainly correlates with Dykes's behaviour, even if it doesn't explain it. You did an EEG on him, didn't you "huu"?'

'Yes. The results are here in the folder.' She footed it over.

'"HooGraa" as I expected. There's this massive burst of electrical activity on the right-hand side of his brain – really quite universal – but the left is terribly depressed, terribly depressed. That explains why our chimp is so cack-handed; and *possibly* why he has these extraordinary delusions. It's by no mean inconsistent – although not altogether characteristic – of a multi-infarct dementia "hooo". As for these FSIs, well, they sort of *blanket* that central cortical region, don't they, but as the MRI shows, they must in fact be spread *throughout* the brain "h'huu"?'

'You don't think they're tumours of some kind, do you, Zack "huu"?'

'Good point "chup-chupp". They don't have the right tints for wet patches, but on the other foot they're by no means solid. No, I think they're some sort of shadowing, perhaps lesions or scarring. Foot me the MRIs again.'

While Busner pored over the slides, Jane Bowen turned her attention to the X-rays; and now it was her turn to exclaim "HoooGraa!" Every chimp in their section of the canteen turned to see who was pant-hooting.

'Keep it down! Keep it down!' Busner signed frantically. 'We don't want any fusion over these "wraaa"!' He warned off some of the more inquisitive chimps, who nearly had their muzzles on the table. 'What is it, Jane "huu"?'

'Here, look here on this transverse image of Dykes's head. Here, below the jaw.'

Busner, heedless of his own warning, took the X-ray and held it up to the sunlit window. A waggish surgeon some fifteen feet away from them could see the shape of the cranium, and reacted as excitedly as Jane Bowen. He burst into loud, tooth-clacking laughter. '"H'hee-hee-clak-clak" whatever next,

Busner! Got yourself a human to lead around on a chain now, have you!'

Busner didn't rise to this. He dropped the X-ray back on the table, and inparted his colleague's leg, 'He's got no simian shelf, has he, Jane "huu"?'

'No, Zack, he doesn't appear to.'

'Could it be the result of some kind of accident "huu"?'

'Unlikely – I'd sign.'

'A congenital defect then "huu"?'

'Maybe.'

'Or perhaps he is human after all!'

... why Dykes feels it necessary so crassly to manipulate the consciences – and even the stomachs – of his public is beyond the scope of this review, but there is something both crude and self-seeking about these paintings that takes them down a peg from being true examples of art, to mere caricature ...

... Dykes, whose *World of Bears* caused such a buzz of interest when it was bought for the Tate's permanent collection last year, disappoints mightily with this slipshod series of exploitative tableaux. Having abandoned the perverse formalism of his earlier, more sculptural work, he proffers in its place the formal perversity of his painting ...

"... an infant, burning in mid-air, is at the centre of a canvas that makes a mockery of the suffering of real chimpanzees, in the most horrific London transport disaster in recent history. Why Dykes feels he has a right to do this is beyond ...

... no sign of the artist himself, there was a great deal of screaming and mating among the assembled critics and art-world types. Dykes's consort, Sarah Peasenhulme, appeared briefly, but was hustled away by Tony Figes and his coterie ...

interest that perhaps wouldn't have been shown were it not for the disappearance of the artist, who is rumoured to have suffered a total mental collapse in the week preceding the opening . . .

. . . he's mad – and she's bad, chimp. Swelling bigger than her head and not averse to receiving some 'constructive advice' from prominent bonobo installation artist Ken Braithwaite. The two of them were seen after the private view, more down than up on the stairs of the Sealink Club . . .

The madchimp in question gathered together the leaves of photocopying paper that he had spread out on the institutional grey cover of his nest. He formed them into a loose ball, by scrunching one sheet up tightly and then wrapping the others round it. Even though he was distracted and enraged by what he had read, Simon still found himself appreciating how, when he willed them, his fingers responded with more exactness, more subtle dexterity, than he could remember from the time before his breakdown.

He regarded the fingers as they shaped and tucked. He'd never really noticed how hairy the backs of his hands were before – nor his thighs for that matter. Was it age, or some awful side-effect of the drugs they were giving him? The monkey denoted Bowen signed they'd taken him off the Prozac, but Simon couldn't believe this had had any impact on his mental state – unless it was to provoke these delusions of a topsy-turvy world. He tooth-clacked mirthlessly, tossed the balled reviews in the air and without bothering to see where they fell, curled himself up into a ball as well, and began to rock back and forth, back and forth.

Some things didn't change. The world might be ruled by apes – be a *planet* of apes, but a moiety of them were still odious, grubbing hacks. Odious, grubbing hacks. Simon didn't simply remember the resentments – he felt them corroding his gut, as if his gut were a slopping sump full of battery acid, and this anchored him to the perversities of now more than any shrink could have done – human or chimp.

He groaned, clutching his shins. Were the paintings now

of apes? Apes burning, apes falling, apes bleeding? Could this be true? And Sarah, what they'd written about Sarah and Ken Braithwaite, could that be true as well? Why don't I feel more jealous? When she was human I wanted her body to be exclusively mine. I wanted to have sole use of her smoothness, sole occupancy of her wetness, sole rights to her moans. And now the image of some oiled shaft sinking *inside* her . . .

. . . the dream. Me moving out of her. Being extruded from her. She was sitting in a tree. Hunched up. Biting at the cord that tied us. Biting with sharp canines. In the dream – she was a chimpanzee. She was.

Whatley and Gambol picked at salads in the Café Rouge across the road from the hospital. Given Gambol's acknowledged presence in the department, there no longer seemed any necessity for them to be secretive. He twined his fingers in leaves of rocket and *radicchio*, then signed from this thicket, 'I have something I think may "grnnn" interest you, Dr Whatley.'

' "H'huuu" yes?' the consultant countersigned around a wedge of avocado. 'You know, Gambol, that I have no intention of an alliance with you unless it proves productive – and quickly! "Aaaaa" –' He broke off to call the waiter.

' "H'huuu"? Everything all right here, gentlemales?' The waiter had a white apron tied tightly around his waist. His white shirt had bright red buttons. His head fur was teased and dyed into a red quiff. Whatley and Gambol looked at him with undisguised contempt. 'Fine, as far as it goes,' Whatley gestured, 'but I ordered some garlic bread "euch-euch-huu"?'

'Coming right up, sir.' The waiter bounded away towards the kitchen, and meeting one of his colleagues *en route* they tumbled over each other in a precisely coordinated mêlée of limbs. Whatley grunted, turned back to his salad, and found that it had acquired a covering in the form of a shiny folder, the kind used by corporate entities to port reports and other documents. 'What's this, Gambol "huuu"?' Whatley eyed the thing, then picking it up scratched his head fur with one of its sharp laminated corners.

'Please take a look,' Gambol countersigned. 'I think you'll find it *very* interesting – and entirely relevant.'

Jane Bowen took a pant-hoot from George Levinson in her office. ' "HoooH'Graa'" Dr Bowen, how are you today "huu"?' He was, even at this range, suffering from an obvious hangover. Sportive sunglasses teetered precariously on his high nasal bridge. His long, brown sideburns were dirty, still encrusted with bits of last night's fun. ' "HoooH'Graa" not too bad, Mr Levinson.'

'Did you enjoy the opening last night "huu"?'

'Well enough, well enough – not really my sort of thing.'

'I "euch-euch" wouldn't sign it was altogether representative of private views. I suppose you saw some of the fights that broke out "huuu"?'

'The beginning of one. Was fusion eventually reached?'

' "Euch-euch" well, not exactly. Show me, has Simon seen this morning's papers "huu"?' He worried his sideburn fur, twisting it this way and that between fiddling fingers, as if this cheekborne dangleberry were the artist himself.

'I believe he's reading them now. We've had a fairly successful morning. We got him out of the secure room and did the tests we wanted –'

'And "huu"?'

"Hoogrnn."

'Dr Bowen "huu"?'

' "Hoogru-nn" I'm afraid I'm not entirely at liberty to delineate them, Mr Levinson – as I'm sure you appreciate.'

Jane Bowen hoped Levinson would hold back – but knew full well he wouldn't. He goggled at her from behind the sunglasses for a while. Even though she couldn't see the dealer's eyes, Jane knew they would be bedded down in hammocks of enpurpled veins.

Eventually his fingers twitched. 'The thing is . . .'

'Yes,' she snapped back.

'The thing is, as you are aware his ex-alpha has no real inclination to take up cudgels strongly on Simon's behalf –'

' "Euch-euch" but you do "huu"?'

'I am his ally . . . I've gesticulated with his lawyer. If he's to be put on a full whatsit – section, we have the right to claim power of attorney – we are both executors and named in this further capacity –'

'Would you want to object to a section "huu"?'

' "Hooo" I don't know, Dr Bowen. Please, I don't wish to challenge your authority, I think of you as the wisest, most benign, most adorably perspicacious psychiatrist. Your ischial pleat entrances me . . . And now you've been joined by the *eminent* Dr Busner, well . . . I'm sure Simon is quite safe in your hands, but the point is, is he a risk to himself or others "huu"? Do you think further confinement will help him "huuu" – ?' He broke off, one finger up under the eye wear. It reappeared sporting some bit of grit – or grout – which he placed gingerly on his tongue.

Bowen visualised for a moment. Clearly it *was* time they made a decision about Simon Dykes. His condition was becoming more rather than less anomalous as they investigated it, and what with this evidence of organic damage – even deformity – could it really be argued that he was insane in any ordinary sense?

' "Grnnn" well, Mr Levinson, I must confess we are in a bit of a quandary as to what to do with Mr Dykes – I believe we shall convene a case conference sooner rather than later –'

'Meaning "h'huu"?'

'That it probably *would* be an idea for you and his lawyer to secure power of attorney. If Simon won't agree voluntarily to whatever course of treatment we decide on, it may be a question of persuading *you* to force *him*.'

'That looks rather ominous from where I'm sitting "euch-euch".'

'I think I can sign this without in any way prejudicing the situation, Mr Levinson. I don't think the chances for Simon Dykes's recovery are that good – whatever it is that ails him.'

After hanging up Bowen lifted the receiver again. She

pant-hooted Whatley, she pant-hooted Gambol on Busner's mobile, she called the psychiatric social workers' department, and finally – out of courtesy – she pant-hooted Sarah, in order to show her that there would be some sort of decision made about Simon in the near future. Then Dr Bowen lay back in her chair, put her feet on her desk, pushed her head forward, and gave herself a good, thorough licking out.

The chimps assembled singly some two hours later, in Whatley's office. Norris, the nominee from the social work department, swung himself up the outside of the building from balcony to balcony and in through the secretary's window. Zack Busner barrelled along the corridor that ran the length of the psychiatry department, shucking submissive chimps off as he came. Whatley showed up from his conspiratorial feed with Gambol. They staggered their entrances, Whatley manifesting himself like the Cheshire Cat in reverse – the first anyone was aware of him was his teeth nibbling furtively at their calluses; and Gambol turning up late, ostentatiously cleaning away the evidence of a recent mating with fingers and lips.

Bowen came in from her own office, knuckle-walking with her rump aloft, a sheaf of folders shoved up in her armpit.

Dr Bowen convened the meeting: "HoooGraaa!"

"HoooGraaa!" they echoed, some more vigorously than others – Gambol gave merely a token grunt and drummed the lino, whereas Busner roared while bashing a cushion so hard Whatley mewled, then signed, 'My daughter made that "hooo"!'

When there was novocal and signlence Bowen proceeded to flick over the particulars of Simon Dykes's case from the beginning, his collapse, his reaction to the crash team, his behaviour towards both the hospital staff and the chimps well known to him. Then she recapped the details of his medical history, reading where necessary from the records supplied by Anthony Bohm. Putting the notes to one side she digitated for a while on the possibility that Dykes's current condition represented some sort of hysterical symptomatic conversion from his essentially depressive state. She also palped and picked at the image that there was some maladaptive response to the Prozac Bohm had put him on; possibly catalysed by the MDMA he had taken the night of his breakdown. She then returned to the matter in hand – and teased out its various parts. Finally she presented some of the test results showing evidence of a bipolar disorder, and without going into it exhaustively, drew their attention to the organic neurological damage.

When she had finished she pant-hooted and squatted down, thrusting out a leg so that Norris, the social worker, could get to work on it. Whatley's fingers were the first to fly. 'So, what are you signing, Jane "huu"? It seems to me as if the probable, eventual diagnosis will centre on these FSIs, or areas of manifest organic damage in his brain. The prognosis must be, with this degree of "euch-euch" damage – whatever it turns out to be – pretty poor. Obviously Dykes's human delusion is besides the point; there's no way that understanding it can help us to help him "h'huuu"?'

Bowen wrinkled up her muzzle, scratched the thick fur beneath her jaw line, freed a bit of pasta lodged there since her third lunch and gestured, 'Well, yes, Dr Whatley, I really think you may be right there.'

Norris flicked in, 'Is he insured "huu"? Will his mating or natal group help out "huu"? Has anyone investigated whether they're prepared to fund private rather than NHS hospitalisation?'

'I'm afraid it's "euch-euch" no on all counts,' Bowen countersigned. 'His natal group has long since fissioned, same with his mating group. His consort tells me that there's no insurance – because of his history of mental illness "hoooo"; and his close ally and art dealer, Mr Levinson – who's in the process of getting power of attorney in case we deem a further section necessary – shows me there's nothing much in the way of assets until the proceeds from his current show come in – if "hooo" there turn out to be any.'

All the chimps appeared suitably grave about this information. Dykes might be an artist of some repute, but mental illness was a great leveller – that they all knew. It was quite possible to imagine Dykes a few months hence, drooling his days away in a dark corner of some long-stay institution; or doing the same in the frighteningly exposed surroundings currently offered by 'tree-covered accommodation'.

'I'd sign that there's some "grnnn" quality of life element to be considered in all of this.' Whatley chose his signs carefully, placing them so all could see. 'It does seem particularly cruel to leave this chimp – who's felt by many to be a fine, if unbalanced individual – to rot on the wards here, or elsewhere for that matter. Surely Levinson is prepared to do *something* for him "huuu"?'

There was a deep rumble of phlegm from the corner where Zack Busner lay, on his back, his feet softly bicycling against the walls so that the Artex deliciously abraded the itchy soles of his horny feet. "Grnn-grnn-HooGraa!" he vocalised – and when he had gained their attention signed, 'I do think there may be another course of action available to us.'

'Which is, Dr Busner "huu"?' Whatley smoothed down the signs, coated them with symbolic glycerine.

Busner hauled himself into squat, grunting, and directed Gambol to groom his back fur. 'Which is to allow me to take care of Mr Dykes. I've done as much in the past, with both psychiatric and neurological patients that exhibit unusual symptomatologies. I don't doubt that there is nothing *ultimately* mysterious about Mr Dykes's condition; and as for the prognosis – I've seen patients with far worse trauma achieve a form of recovery. The brain – as you all know – has a marvellous "aaaa" plasticity. Correctly channelled it can regain "chup-chupp" homeostasis. Furthermore ... "grnn" as he represents no danger, except to himself, I cannot see why he shouldn't be released into my care –'

'If he and Mr Levinson, or his lawyer, or whoever it is who wishes to take "huu" responsibility agrees – ?'

'Obviously.' Busner let the sign hang for a moment, his fingers circling and sweeping, before slapping Gambol's hands from the back of his neck and hauling himself bipedal.

'Well, Dr Busner "euch euch" where are you going to berth your human-deluded chimp "huuu"?' Norris couldn't keep the sarcasm out of sign or sound.

Zack Busner reared up, took two steps and bit the social worker on his eyebrow. Red blood trickled through black fur. Norris screamed, then hunkered round and presented. Zack patted the mewling member of the caring profession gingerly, as if he were an animate settle, then waved 'Why, at my group home, of course. Where else better, if he's to stand a chance of relearning his essential chimpunity "huuu"?'

There were grunts of assent from the others. Bowen adjourned the meeting.

In the corridor Gambol hung lazily from a section of architrave for a while. His feet – at waist level – footled with a coil of fire hose attached to the wall. Busner knuckle-walked past at speed, Bowen in his wake. 'I'm going to sign with Dykes right away, Gambol – you wait for me here.'

Gambol went on footling. Really, he thought, things couldn't have gone much better if they'd planned them that way. If Busner hadn't suggestured taking Dykes on fully – either Whatley or Gambol would have pointed it out themselves. For reasons of their own, there was nothing they hoped for more than that Busner would enfold Dykes in his ample furry bosom. Whatley knew why after their second lunch at Café Rouge, after reading the contents of the shiny folder. Whatley, emerging from his office, winked at the dangling, epsilon machiavel. The two chimps were visualising the same thing; Dykes was like a grenade that had been tossed to Busner. And Busner – the fool – had obligingly caught it, not realising that the pin had been pulled.

Chapter Thirteen

S imon Dykes, no longer an artist, merely a mental patient, squatted on the nest in secure room six and pondered the events of the morning. His madness – he felt – was beginning to take on a new texture, like a fog which, having appeared impenetrable, begins to boil then shreds to reveal tatters of landscape. Could his humanity be the delusion – and his chimpunity – preposterous sign! – the reality?

He yawned, scratched his armpit with one hand, his ischial scrag with the other. Then – without being conscious of it – fell to examining his body. His hands smoothed along his thighs, his fingertips splayed over his shins and then his feet. He didn't *feel* any different – or did he? True, he hadn't shaved for two weeks now and the stubble under his chin had acquired the pile of beard – he could smooth it this way and rough it the other. But his chest, his arms, his thighs, they were no more lanate than before.

Simon's questing fingers sought out a pit on his right kneecap. A pit that they knew should be there, a pit caused by a bad bicycle crash when he was six or seven. They failed to locate it and the former artist brought his eyes to bear. He stared at his knee. Perhaps the fur there *was* thicker. He couldn't remember it braiding together in this fashion, individual clumps flowing into mini-dreadlocks. Where was the pit? The old scar? Fingers scrabbled – yes, scrabbled – in the sparse fur until they found it, then

Simon sighed. Sighed to find himself still Simon, still human.

He rolled off the nest and knuckle-walked to the window. It felt comfortable to move quadrumanously, good to stretch and grab the thin bars across the slit of window. Simon pulled himself bipedal. There was nothing to see outside, the window looked on to an internal courtyard of the hospital, but a view no matter how limited was part of the outside world. Simon was, he realised, imagining going outside. More than that – he *wanted* to go outside, whatever he might find there.

What did the vile piece in the paper about Sarah mean? Was she fucking Ken Braithwaite? Did chimps fuck? And what of all the other people he knew? 'People'. The sign sounded odd to Simon – more like some garbled vocalisation than anything truly meaningful. And what of his infants, his three little males? Simon pictured them lined up, off-the-peg kids representing a series of standard sizes: small, medium, large. They were all identically clad in dark blue pullovers, with the name of their school emblazoned across their chests. They all had the same squeakily new, shit-coloured, leather satchels slung around their shoulders, and they all had the same expression puckering their muzzles, creasing up their sweet, green eyes. Then they fissioned and scampered towards him, clawed their way up on to him, one leaping for his shoulder, another grabbing an arm, the third – and littlest – shinning up his leg. The four Dykes males made a bundle of mock aggression, from which came the occasional hysterical giggle, clack of teeth, quavering grunt.

The judas on the door slid open with a dull click. Simon shook himself out of his reverie and glanced towards it to see a familiar eroded muzzle, familiar hooded eyes; their vertical irises flicking from side to side. "HoooGra!" Busner drummed on the outside of the door.

Simon felt his chest contract – involuntarily; and a gout of air suck inside with a rushing "Hoooo," then it splurged back out through the grate of his great teeth, "Graaa!" and he drummed a little on the side of the nest, producing a leaden timpani.

Busner was more than a little surprised by this. 'Simon,' he signed, 'that's the first time I've heard you pant-hoot –'

'What "huu"?'

'No matter. "H'huu" would you feel upset if I came in? I need to sign with you.' Busner's fingers moved awkwardly, feeling up the crack of the judas.

'N-no, if you "grnnn" must.'

The door swung open and the eminent natural philosopher – as he liked to style himself – swung in, landing heavily on his hirsute feet. He sat there for some moments and Simon regarded him warily. Busner was *all* ape. His chest a thick barrel, its depth emphasised by the way his tweed jacket rucked up. His bandy little legs supported this mound of muscle readily enough, but the contrast between their feral aspect, the exposed 'V' of white shirt and the coil of brown mohair tie, was quite simply – nauseating. Simon could feel a bubble of anxious revulsion building in him as he stared into the muzzle of the beast. Its crescent of hard lip which drooped to reveal canines the size of clothespegs; its bashed-in nose, the nostrils oval, black tunnels; and above them the eyes, the inhuman eyes with their green lambency, their mutant pupils.

' "Euch-euch" Simon, don't look at me that way – I can see that you *are* getting upset. Sign with me, gesticulate with me – that's the way to stop yourself overreacting. It doesn't matter whether I'm chimp – or human – the important thing is that *we* can sign.'

'Sign,' Simon signed bemusedly. 'What does that mean "huu"?' Busner's eyebrow ridges widened questioningly.

'Sign, Simon, sign, gesticulate with your hands – as I'm doing now "grnnn".'

Simon grimaced. A peculiar little grimace. 'But humans don't sign, Dr Busner, we "speak". That's how we communicate. I believe some chimpanzees and even gorillas have been taught to make a few signs – signs adapted from the sign languages deaf and dumb people use. But humans don't sign – we don't have to. We "speak".'

It was Busner's turn to look bemused. His mind whirred. Dykes's delusion was so beautifully symmetrical. Clearly he had retrieved – from some far bank of his memory – the information that wild humans gesticulated through a large repertoire of vocalisations. But this raw fact had been subjected to baroque embellishment with further suppositions. Dykes had coined an original vocalisation to express the image of that form of gesticulation. Busner hunkered forward, his splayed fingers agitated the air. 'Simon "gru-nnn", d'you think you could teach me this "eek", "huuu"?'

' "Speech", Dr Busner, "speech". And yes, I don't see why not. After all,' and here Simon paused and regarded his own fingers, fingers that now shaped with as much fluidity as those of any chimpanzee, 'I appear to be able to "speak" like you "grnnn".'

Busner nodded at this, rocked back and forth on his heels, rose, knuckle-walked to the window, handed his way up on to the bars. The former television personality swung there for a while. Simon stared at the ape's naked hindquarters. Busner's runtish buttocks and fleshy scut were both an intimate and an alien sight. The folds of brown and pink skin formed a virtual bill, poking out from the furred protuberance. Busner, as if sensing Simon's gaze, let go of one of the bars and made a sinistral exploration of his arsehole. He then brought his fingers to his prehensile lip and nonexistent nose, where they were subjected to a critical, multi-sensory analysis. The same hand then sped signs at Simon. 'My arsehole looking all right "huuu"?'

'Fine, Dr Busner – <top hole>, you might sign.'

Busner cackled and clacked at this. ' "H'hee-hee-clak-clak" oh dear, well, I suppose it's a little infantile, but *I* think your joke rather funny. Now, Simon, we have to decide what we should do with you –'

'Do with me "huu"?'

'Quite so.' Busner dropped back to the floor. 'I'll be frank, we've found structural abnormalities in your brain. We don't know whether they're evidence of some organic damage or part of a disease process, or even a congenital deformity, but they're there – and almost certainly implicated in your "euch-euch'" human delusion.'

'Can it be cured "huuu"?'

'I can't put my finger on that.'

'Then you're going to keep me in here! Keep me in this bin! Is that it "h'huu"? Is that what you're signing?' Simon was bipedal, pacing about in a peculiar, jerky way, like a bonobo sub-adult dancing to jungle music. He started making some of his strangulated, low-pitched vocalisations, which to Busner sounded like "Ohgodohgodohgodohgod . . ."

'"Waaa"! Simon, snap out of it, this isn't going to help. No, I don't think there's any point in keeping you here, or sending you to some long-term institution.'

'No "huu"?'

'"Wraaa"! No! If I am to impact upon this delusion in any way, I must help you to confront reality. I want you to come and live with me at my group home. To range with me, to see something of this planet of the apes you find yourself in – and at the same time –'

'"Hoo" yes! What, what at the same time? What! "Wraaa"!' Simon came to a halt in front of Busner, he was shaking with anger, with fear, with awful weariness. Busner was near to cracking – he felt his control going. Only long years of dealing with the most abusive and intractable of patients allowed him leeway, leeway not to punish this insolence.

'At the same time, Simon, you can "gru-nn" show me about your world – your view of the world.'

'"Wraaa"! I'd like that very much, really I would –'

'"Hooo" we can regard the exercise as educative – as much as therapeutic –'

'Of course, of course, why not. What a good idea "euch-euch"!' Simon's signing was, Busner noted, improving rapidly. This last semiotic string was shaped with oblique slashes of sarcasm. The anti-psychiatrist couldn't stand it; his arm lashed out and his nails raked across Simon's chest. For good measure Busner bit him on the eyebrow ridge   quite hard. Simon, naturally, turned tail and squeezed off a spray of liquid shit at his bestial soul doctor. The two of them then engaged in brief scrimmage – arms and legs flying, wraaing and screeching.

It was all over in seconds, Simon lay spreadeagled on the filthy linoleum, his shit-dashed shrink atop him. Simon mewled and whimpered pathetically. 'Now then, Simonkins darling.' Busner's fingers as they played upon Simon's body were tender, placatory. 'You get out the fear, get out the hurt, the anger. Attack me by all means – that's very chimp, very chimp indeed.'

And the former artist responded to the fingers that moved on his chest, responded to them as he hadn't before. He *felt* Busner's concern – and allowed himself to believe in it. Within minutes the two apes were squatting cross-legged, Simon behind Busner, and he was picking the fast-drying shit out of his doctor's fur. It was his first grooming session since the breakdown.

Dr Bowen did a pant-hoot round. She pant-hooted Jean Dykes and Anthony Bohm in Oxfordshire. She pant-hooted George Levinson in Cork Street, and Tony Figes at the newspaper. Finally, she pant-hooted Sarah Peasenhulme.

"HoooH'Graaa'."

'"HoooH'Graaa'". Have you any news for me, Dr Bowen "huu"?' Sarah's signing betrayed all kinds of anxiety – she was, Jane Bowen noted, wearing a very elaborate swelling-protector for a female who was squatting in an office.

'I have, Sarah, some good, some not so good. Dr Busner is – as it were – taking Simon in hand '

'"Huuu" meaning?'

'Well, he's done it with others of his patients before – usually those with neurological damage, or a condition that is "graaa" productive –'

'What do you mean "huu"?'

'"H'hoo" I mean that we fear Simon's condition may be fundamentally intractable – there is considerable damage to his brain.'

'"Wraa" but how "h'huu"? Why? Was it the drugs, or that bloody Prozac he was on? What "huuu"?'

'Sarah, we don't know, but believe me Dr Busner has had considerable success with this kind of case in the past. He takes what he ascripts a <psycho-physiological> approach to such disorders. He may not be able to cure Simon of his delusion that he's a human, but he could make it possible for Simon to come to terms with it – make use of it even, sign in his art.' Bowen furled and unfurled an ear as she gesticulated.

Sarah's small blonde head shook with disbelief and sorrow. She was tipped back in her seat, feet up on her work table, which was why Jane Bowen had an uninterrupted view of the silken rosette of her swelling-protector. A hand went now to a foot, grasped it, pulled it to a questing lip. Sarah signed back immaturely with toes and fingers intermingled, 'Can I – please, can I – will he see me "huu"?'

'I don't know if that's such a good idea, Sarah. He still finds any simian contact very difficult to cope with. Dr Busner is, I believe, just beginning to win some trust from Simon. There's been a limited grooming session today, and, of course, Simon has agreed to be discharged into his care.'

'But "hooo" we're consorts, nestmates, surely –'

'I'll show Simon you requested contact, Sarah – but really, the rest must be up to him. You must understand that given the nature of his condition it may be that a nestmate is the last chimp he wants to see.'

Tony Figes knuckle-walked along Ladbroke Terrace and swung into the Portobello Road. He wasn't really following

216

the cute young Italian chimps who scuttled in front of him down the road – he just happened to be behind them, and happened to be enjoying watching their pink little anuses bobbing about. One of the sub-adults was sporting a novelty knapsack, designed to resemble a human infant. The Italian chimp was bipedal, full of holiday swagger, and his anthropoid portmanteau wiggled and waggled as if it were alive and enjoying the ride.

The sight put Tony Figes in mind of his errand. He had acceded readily enough to Dr Bowen's request; yes, he could get the key to Simon's flat from George Levinson; no, he didn't mind going over there, packing a bag for Simon and then bringing it down to the hospital. It would be a pleasure – the least he could do. 'Kiss my arse!' he had signed respectfully – if a trifle ironically – to Dr Bowen before breaking the connection. 'Kiss mine!' she had countersigned with equal formality.

The market was in half-swing today – a Friday – and the costermongers were wraaing their wares to each other, as much as the tourists. From time to time one of them would let out a howl and do a little display, racing upright along the tarmac alleyway between the stalls, kicking rinds, cobs, husks and other vegetable detritus in front, while juggling two hands of bananas, or a dozen oranges.

Tony Figes paid this no heed; he kept his muzzle down and the knapsack-wearing Italian's scut in view. It was a muggy day and Tony could feel the sweat percolating through his fur. He paused, opened his jacket and allowed the slack breeze to play over his chest. By the time he readjusted his clothing the Italian chimps were gone. Tony grunted softly to himself. He considered stopping in at the Star to translate his brown loneliness into the sepia tones of the bar, into the inky heft of a pint of Guinness, but thought better of it and swung into Colville Terrace.

A gaggle of tough Bonobo sub-adults was hanging out on the corner, holding cans of Special Brew to their pink lips and signing to each other with the fluent gestures of patois.

Their body fur poked in tufts through the holes of their string vests; their head fur was either razored with lightning strikes or carved into squares and triangles. Tony hunched himself up protectively and scuttled along the inside of the pavement. He certainly wasn't frightened of bonobos in general – but these ones were so lithe, so gracile. Tony envied them their effortlessly upright posture, but all bonobos – and especially these ones – had a hint of the human about them, a hint of the bestial. Tony shook his head, internally admonishing himself – like any good liberal he considered bonoboism beneath him – and knuckle-walked on by.

The bonobos were listening to a ghetto blaster someone had plonked down on the pavement. It was pounding out that summer's ragga hit. The vocalisations were familiar to Tony and brought back memories of the night of Simon's breakdown. "HooGraaWraaHoo / HooGraaH'hoo / EeeWraa-EeeWraa . . ." He shook his head; Simon was in a place where no one could possibly want to mate.

The heavy door whooshed open. The stairwell smelt of cabbage and urine. Funny, Tony mused, how the separate waves of gentrification had backed up on one another in these terraces, to create a choppy sound of poverty and wealth, where the targets for health education, and the members of exclusive health clubs were quartered scut by pleat.

Tony rubbed his eyes in their sore sockets. He was shagged from the night before, a night that had ended with him picking up a rentmate at a club in Charing Cross, taking him home – a manoeuvre that involved considerable risk, given the radar ears of old Mrs Figes – and getting him so pissed and coked-up that the poor little thing's dick had telescoped into desuetude. Tony had paid him all the same.

Simon Dykes's flat was on the third floor of the house. With a conversion as raggle-taggle as this one, some of the flats were expansive, others were contracted into the interstitial spaces available, bits of half-landing, former bathrooms and servants' bedrooms. Simon's was the latter kind. It was, Tony knew, the first dwelling he had managed to organise after his group fissioned, but even so, for a chimp allegedly doing well in his career, his paintings and other art works selling for considerable sums, it seemed on the seedy side of humble.

Tony swung himself up and over the last set of banisters, had the door open before all four limbs had touched carpet, and knuckle-walked in. The long, airless corridor was rank with the odour of male chimp gone to seed. An overflowing wastepaper basket shedding fag butts, whisky bottles and worse caught his eye. There was a cotton trail of discarded clothing leading to a heavily shuttered, cubicular bedroom. In the front room, which Tony vaulted into, the venetian blinds strained the sun outside into the room's fetid stock of images, illusions and mortal tokens.

A large table set beneath the bay window carried a slew of sketch pads, picture books, pots of pens and pencils, photographs, ashtrays and empty glasses. In the corner, a dicky divan was piled with more filthy clothing. Tony paused, mewling. The atmosphere of dislocation – despair even – was far worse than he feared. This was the credible compost from which such a fearsome delusion as Simon Dykes's might sprout.

Still mewling Tony knuckle-walked to the table. Gathering himself on to a chair he tipped back and began to feetle his way through the mess of papers. There was, he registered, a lot of material relating to humans. All of Jane Goodall's books on working with the wild humans of Gombe, newspaper articles on research into humans, flyers put out by animal rights groups concerned with human welfare. Tony hoooed softly; there was more than enough fodder here to provide high-calorie nutrition for Simon's human delusion. But there was also more concrete evidence of the direction the artist's thoughts and fantasies had been travelling in the weeks before his breakdown, the weeks he had spent completing his series of apocalyptic paintings.

Sketch after sketch, executed using thick pencil on thick

card, showed the backdrops for his vast canvases of modern London, but in place of the chimpanzees who inhabited the finished works were the naked, zombie-like figures of humans. Humans running upright with their stiff-legged gait; humans walking in throngs, all separated by an arm's length; humans sitting with one another, not touching, not grooming, lost in the uncommunicative prison of their own meagre sentience, their own primitive cast of mind.

Tony Figes had begun sorting through these sketches out of curiosity, as an ally of the ally who was ill, but as he scrutinised these oddly satirical depictions of the city as an arboreal enclave, his critic's acumen came into play. They were really – he concluded – rather better than the canvases that had resulted. By making his focus the conceit of a world dominated by humans, Simon had managed to express far more, with a few pencil lines, about the condition of modern chimpunity, than he had achieved with barrels of oil paint.

Thinking about what an unscrupulous character might do with this material made Tony pant-grunt apprehensively. At the very least it could constitute the illustration for a devastating report of Simon's breakdown, and that would compromise not only the artist's reputation but the art itself. What to do? Tony, still hooing to himself, got up from the desk and patrolled the flat. He found a plastic bag in a kitchen drawer and filled it with several of the cleanest shirts and T-shirts he could find. He paused, seeing a pair of trousers at the bottom of a gaping cupboard, but the possibility of Simon engaging in such intimate mating practices was, he knew, a long way off.

The pitiful packing done, Tony readied himself to leave. But he found he couldn't turn his back on the sketches of the world-turned-human. He tried to, but each time he started for the door the sketches seemed to pant-hoot in his inner ear. He knuckle-walked backwards to the table and looked over his shoulder at them. His eye caught the dark socket of a cardboard tube propped by the dusty radiator, and before he had time to analyse what he was doing Tony was holding the tube with his feet, while his hands furled and inserted the sheaf of rolled-up card.

Revealed beneath where the sketches had lain was a little cache of prescription-pill pots, three in all. Tony picked them up one by one and examined the labels. They were Simon's home head-doctoring – Prozac 50mgs daily; Diazepam 20mgs whenever; and something called Calmpose which came in 5mg pink spangles. He opened the pots and swirled their confected contents in the powder of their own disintegration. He capped them again and pocketed the Prozac – a good prequel to dropping a white dove; and the Valium – a good antidote. Neither would be much good to Simon in his current condition.

The long, low Seven Series Volvo grumbled under the portico, at the entrance to Charing Cross Hospital. A thick burble of exhaust fumes boiled out from its scrag-end, soiling a patch of the sky that was too near the earth. Gambol was at the wheel, all four limbs grasping it in the recommended ten-to-three, twenty-past-eight position. There was a fixed grin on his foxy muzzle, a grin that was unusual in being both entirely sincere – *his* plans were coming to fruition – and utterly duplicitous.

There was something of a kerfuffle over Gambol's right shoulder, a kerfuffle he registered with one of his mobile ears. He didn't have to turn to know that Zack Busner, together with his new house guest, was leaving the hospital.

' "HoooGra'"! Well, Jane, Whatley, we're off then.' Busner was upright in the vestibule; one hand firmly grasped the shoulder of his new charge, the other was fending off some of the more persistent junior doctors who were, even at this late stage, attempting to give him a groom.

' "HoooGra'" Busner. I would wish you luck with Mr Dykes's condition – but I don't think "grnnn" luck will be enough –'

' "H'huuu" what do you mean by that exactly?' Busner's

signing was contained – but spiky. Whatley immediately backed off and turned arse-about.

'Nothing! "Hooo" really, nothing at all.'

'Good. Well, Jane, I will pant-hoot you in the morning. As we gesticulated, I consider your input to Mr Dykes's care has been invaluable for both clinical *and* research purposes.'

'"Chup-chupp" thank you, Your Effulgence, Your Radiant Arseholeness –'

'Jane, please. Let me kiss *your* arse –' Busner bestowed a valedictory kiss on the slim female's scut, drummed briefly on an orange plastic milk crate that was keeping the dysfunctional electric doors to the hospital open, then guided Simon – who was too bewildered by the daylight, the chimp activity and the prospect of queered liberty, to be anything but signless – to the car. Busner opened the back door, pushed Simon in, shut it, reared up, vaulted over the top of the Volvo, drummed again on the roof, pant-hooted once more to the assembled company, then leapt in through the open passenger window.

There was a chorus of loud, valedictory pant-hoots from the chimps on the kerb, and the Volvo pulled away. Only to become hopelessly entwined in the metallic weave of stalled traffic on the Fulham Palace Road. It was already four-thirty and the rush hour – which lasted for four and involved hardly any rushing on anyone's part – was underway. '"Euch-euch" anything you can do about this, Gambol "huu"?' asked the preeminent natural philosopher of the age. He was still spattered, despite their session, with some of Simon's shit, and as he signed he scratched a dried glob in his neck fur.

'"Euch-euch" nothing I can think of, Alpha – it's Hammersmith that's the problem. We could try and cut along the Lillie Road, but quite honestly we'll get just as jammed there.'

Busner swivelled round to see how his suitable case was dealing with the first few minutes of freedom; he even toyed with asking if Simon had any image of the route they should take – after all his consort lived nearby, he must be able to visualise the area. But Simon had his muzzle pressed against the glass, his hands cupped tight around his eye sockets and those hands rammed against the window. 'No, there's probably no point, we may as well take our time and let our passenger get a good look at the world he's rejoining "hooo".'

It was a world that Simon was finding utterly bewildering. He had walked, driven and been driven to distraction down this stretch of road many thousands of times. He knew every scabrous take-away joint, losers' bookie and extra-strength-lager-stocked off-licence in the crippled parade of shops that limped from the hospital to the Hammersmith Flyover.

While he occupied secure room six, Simon had tracked this tawdry topography many times in his mind's eye, confirming over and over the veridical nature of his memories. Now he was out it was as he remembered it, right down to the grottily stylised yellow rooster's head that adorned the Red Chicken Shack take-away; right down to the eroded lip of tarmac that leprously kissed the traffic islet, right down to the net curtains that smeared the windows of the flats above the shops like giant cobwebs. Everywhere Simon directed his gaze he saw something familiar, a shop sign, a petrol station decal, a peg-board menu in a café window. To be confronted with such a mundane, familiar scene only served to enhance the distortions which had been wrought upon it.

As with his trip to the hospital sub-basement for the tests there was a problem of scale. Simon had to hunch up to fit in the back seat of the Volvo, even though he knew it was a large car. This spatial incongruity infected everything around, buildings, other vehicles, the road itself – all were small. And roving over this two-thirds set were its dwarfish inhabitants.

They knuckle-walked the pavement, arseholes aloft for all to admire; they congregated in shaggy groups by bus stops; they swarmed up the outside of buildings, using spindly trees, narrow ledges, crumbling rendering and insecure television-aerial stanchions to haul themselves aloft. They moved with astonishing ease and insouciance. As the car advanced haltingly, Simon watched one of them who was level first knuckle-walk twenty yards, then leap-frog a series of bollards and dustbins, then strip-the-willow through a gaggle of oncoming conspecifics, then brachiate along the underside of a bus shelter, before dropping to the ground and resuming on all fours.

If Simon concentrated on one chimp's progress up the road, or up a building, he could almost admire the power and efficiency with which it moved; he could see the foresight and anticipation required to negotiate the crowded pavement, the packed road and the pocked escarpment of masonry. But if he allowed himself to view the mass of chimpunity as just that: a mass of chimpanzees, he saw nothing but a pack of animals, locomoting with as much awareness as a herd of sheep, or worse – a swarm of locusts.

It all got appreciably nastier as the Volvo finally reached the Hammersmith roundabout. Here the rivulets of bobbing, bouncing chimps flowed into a racing river of bobbing backs-for-breakers. The fact that all the chimpanzees Simon had seen wore only upper garments was vitiated when observing them in – as it were – captivity. But now, seeing the cataract of animals that poured into the brutal maw of the pedestrian underpass, Simon was struck anew by the absurd sight of furry little legs and fleshless arses poking out from the hems of pin-stripe jackets, denim jackets, flowery blouses, and T-shirts blazoned with slogans. When one turned, wrinkled its muzzle, then bagged out its cheeks with the beginning of a pant-hoot, Simon laughed out loud at the animal's expression. It was this deep-throated chuckle that provoked the first fiddling since they had departed from the hospital, the first real gesticulation since Simon had regained his liberty.

' "Gru-nnn"! Well then, Simon, what is it that you find so amusing "huuu"?' Busner leapt so that he was standing on his seat, then leapt again, swivelling in mid-air to muzzle his ward. He ended up grasping the thick headrest, his chin propped against it, his fingers titivating the car fug.

'It's the chimps "clak-clak", those chimps.' Simon gestured at the bobbing scuts going down the concrete stairs. 'They just "clak-clak-clak" look ridiculous – utterly ridiculous!'

' "Hoo" and why would that be "huuu"?'

'It's the way they're dressed, you see, dressed only on the top half of their bodies, exposing their "h'hee-hee" silly, scraggy, ugly bums.'

Busner followed Simon's gaze. It was a tribute to his skills as a highly empathetic therapist that he could partially work himself into his patient's perspective. He furrowed his eyebrow ridge and squinted. True enough, there was inevitably something absurd in the contemplation of the mass of chimpunity going about its business. What appeared purposive in the individual looked lemming-like in the multitude. It was, Busner reflected, manipulable that a twisted shard of clarity should lance through Simon Dykes's delusory state in this manner, and he signed as much.

' "Chup-chupp" I suppose you have a point there, Simon, but there's nothing ugly about the rear end of a chimpanzee; a chimp's ischial scrag is his or her most beautiful feature. Wasn't it the "chup-chupp" Immortal Bard who wrote <What's in a name? that which we denote an arsehole / By any other ascription would smell as sweet> –'

'Was it "huu"?'

'It was, and furthermore you can, so to sign, know a chimp by his arsehole, divine a chimp's soul.'

'Is that so "huu"?'

'It is.'

'So, presumably that's why you chimpanzees don't cover them up.' Simon was enjoying this fencing, it provoked a burgeoning hilarity that eclipsed the horror of the simian street.

'Cover them up "huuu"?'

'Yes, you know, like I wanted you to do.'

' "Hoo"! I see "chup-chupp" you mean wear *trousers*. Is that what humans do "huu"?'

It was Busner's turn to feel like giggling, but he retained his composure, sensing that this idiotic exchange might be the beginning of real gesticulation with the delusion. If he could correctly map this territory, might it not dissolve, leaving Simon Dykes a whole chimpanzee once more. 'Yes.' Simon chose his signs carefully. 'You see nudity is a taboo in most human cultures, to expose the lower half of the body is to reveal the genitals which arouse an inappropriate sexual interest.'

Busner was taken aback by this and fell to self-grooming. He'd long since dealt with Simon's shit, but there was another, tiresome, dried secretion that was bugging-up his chest fur. He dabbed his hands with saliva and smeared the tacky portion, then countersigned from within this slick bib, 'I do see, I do see, it does make sense, after all humans are – I assume – without much fur "huuu"?'

'None at all to sign of.'

'And humans, so I envisage it, mate whether or not the female is in oestrus "huuu"?'

'Mate "huu"?'

'Copulate, have sexual intercourse, make love . . . *fuck*, when the female isn't in an ovulating frenzy.'

' "Clak-clak-clak"! Absolutely! Why, most of the human males I know would go out of their way to *avoid* fucking a female human who was ovulating. After all, you don't want to make an infant every time you fuck, do you "huu"?'

'I see, I see, no, of course not.'

Busner flagged down at this point. He felt quite bewildered by the ramifications of Simon's delusion, they all made such perfect – if deranging – sense. If you had an intelligent animal with such mating practices, completely divorced from the paradigm of biological necessity; an animal without fur covering its genitals, then nether garments of some kind *would* be essential 'to cover up their sexual swellings, I imagine . . .'

"HooGraa!" It was Simon's turn to grasp the headrest, pull himself up on his hind legs and present an uncomprehending, wrinkled muzzle to his therapist, for Busner had signed visibly.

' "H'hooo" what I was imagining was that a female human would need to wear nether garments to avoid exposing her sexual swelling . . .' Busner's fingering turned once more into smearing the patch of lubricated fur. Simon goggled at him signlently. That was what was so disconcerting about these animals, they gesticulated with you, albeit in sign language, but obviously with great intelligence. Then, just when you thought you were getting somewhere, they started fidgeting with themselves like the most mangy, old dog imaginable. Like Sarah's retriever, Gracie, one rigid leg spasmodically raking her underbelly.

Sexual swellings – that's what they were, right enough. They were like grossly engorged pudenda No, they *were* grossly engorged pudenda. Simon turned the idea over in his mind, and remembered turning Sarah's body over. Her hairless, slim, body. Turning it over so that her legs, slight as a young girl's, fell open to reveal a brush of hair and gaping, stratified pinkness. The chimpanzee – the one claiming to be Sarah, the one who had visited him in the hospital, gesticulated with him on the 'phone – she had sported an engorged groin. What was this, if not the ultimate, incarnate crotch-shot? Was that the truth? That this ape world was a ghastly phantasmagoria, built out of odds and ends of obsession? His apocalyptic paintings, his uneasy relationship with Sarah's body, the dismal truncation of feeling that followed the loss of his children – all seemed implicated, all seemed incorporated in this ugly now. A now at once so ineffable and so mundane, with its current set – the Hammersmith roundabout; and its current props – a Volvo saloon; a hoarding advertising a soft drink; a chicken thigh, half-eaten, lying in a gutter; and next to it the ironic eschatological counterpoint – a turd.

Simon shuddered, hunched still lower in his chair, indicated to Busner that he didn't feel like signing any more for the moment. He placed his hands over his large ears, pushed his head down into his lap, and sat waiting for things to change.

Gambol carried on piloting the Volvo through the traffic. His alpha, giving up on Dykes for the moment, hunkered down in his seat, pulled out his briefcase and opened the latest issue of the *British Journal of Ephemera*. Neither the pant-hooting of chimpanzees, nor the growl of the traffic distracted him. For, of course, he was reading one of his own articles.

Simon came out of his funk as the Volvo came off the Marylebone Flyover and started up Gloucester Place towards Regent's Park. This was an area of London that Simon knew far better and he was intrigued to see how chimpification had changed it. The answer was – not a lot. London was, Simon reflected, at the best of times an unholy mish-mash of buildings. Something old, something new – borrowed architectural styles all over, and blue reflective glass everywhere, mirroring segments of the same.

By the Regent's Park Mosque Simon was amused to see Muslim chimpanzees. The males wearing skull caps and flicking inordinately long strings of worry beads; the females' purdah compromised by their cutaway chadors.

In the branches of the trees that filled the wide verge between the canal and the road, chimpanzee dossers reposed. Simon didn't notice them at first – so hidden were they by the foliage, but when first one leafy limb quivered, then a furry limb tossed out a crushed Special Brew, he saw the pongid piss artists and once more grinned to himself.

Then the Volvo was tilting up Hampstead High Street, past shops, wine bars and cafés that Simon had known, Simon had drunk in, flirted in, got drunker in. The chimps in this area were better dressed than those in the centre of town. Most of the females carried rigid paper bags, bearing the names of designer emporia. They also affected those garments that Simon now knew were swelling-protectors, rosettes of satin or silk, several hands in diameter, artfully pleated and ruched so as to resemble the engorged – or potentially engorged – folds of perineal and ischial skin that they hid from view. Simon heaved with soundless, bitter merriment. The correspondence was so neat, so exact and so *asinine.*

Gambol twirled the wheel at the lights. They turned left into Heath Street, then right down the bare Georgian terrace of Church Row. Simon stirred at last and resumed gesticulation with his hirsute hermetist. ' "H'huu" where exactly are we headed, Dr Busner?'

Busner raised a hand aloft. 'To my house, as I signed.'

'And where "huuu" might that be?'

'On Redington Road – d'you "huu" know it?'

' "Hoo" yes, I used to come here with my parents when I was an infant – to visit friends of theirs –'

' "Gru-nn" well, it will be something of a home from home for you, won't it "huuu"?' and Busner resumed reading the *Journal,* without so much as a backward glance.

Gambol brought the Volvo to a halt by the kerb and his passengers clambered out. 'I won't be needing you the rest of today,' Busner flicked at him, 'but please be sure to get here in good time tomorrow. I want to take Mr Dykes on an outing.' Busner pounded on the car roof by way of valediction, and Gambol peeled away. As soon as he'd rounded the corner the epsilon let out a great shriek of irritation. Then he shifted up five gears in as many seconds and the big car lurched back in the direction of central London.

The Busner group home was empty on this sultry afternoon. It was partly by design – Busner had pant-hooted ahead, to warn them to keep a low profile – and partly by accident; summer sales, jobs, patrolling, school, mating activities and twenty different, other reasons were keeping the bulk of them away from home.

Once Busner had unlocked the front door, and Simon had followed the skimpy derrière of his therapist inside, he found an environment so familiar, so reassuring, so homely after the antiseptic, sigmlent, screaming nightmare of the hospital, that he almost wept from relief.

Simon padded from room to room, examining everything, sniffing everything, rubbing the palms of his hands and the soles of his feet over carpeted, painted and upholstered surfaces. In the main living room there were high fitted shelves of dark wood, stacked with a multitude of volumes, without regard for subject or author classification. Simon recognised titles that he knew. Most of the classics – ancient and modern – were represented; there were also works of history, philosophy and, of course, medicine and psychology. Simon pulled the occasional Everychimp Library volume, or Penguin out, just to check the feel of the cover with his questing lip. Naturally he grinned and clacked to see a copy of Maugham's *Of Chimpanzee Bondage*.

There were paintings on the walls. Real paintings. In the hospital some of Simon's greatest mental anguish was provoked by the ghastly, washed-out reproductions that the administration had seen fit to place on the walls. Some of Busner's paintings were amateurish daubs – obviously by group members, but others were more impressive. There was a small Eric Gill drawing that with one pure line defined the silhouette of a chimpanzee. Simon sighed when he saw this. The articulation of the line was so elegant and necessary, it was like a graphic sedative for the disordered psyche of the former artist.

In the large, parquet-floored hall there was a ticking cabinet clock, a hat stand, some old mezzotints in heavy frames. Everywhere Simon roamed in the house the colour scheme was muted, dark, comforting. Walls were painted either in shades of plum and mulberry, or else blood reds and ochres. On the floors were thick rugs; some Persian, cluttered with curlicues; others old geometric Axminster.

Upstairs each of the nestrooms was decorated individually. One was oppressively female with a flounced, white-painted four-poster nest, adrift on a sea-blue carpet; another was equally masculine, full of footballs, ski sticks and other sporting equipment.

It could be, Simon fluttered to himself, just the sort of house my infants and I might have lived in – had things turned out differently. A substantial group home on a tree-lined road in a comfortable North London suburb. Only two things marked the Busner house as being unassimilable, different, other, as furnished by the delusion as by furnishing: there were all sorts of handholds attached to the walls at convenient heights for bustling apes, handholds that were obviously as old as the house itself – wooden, brass, or covered with anaglypta. There were these, and there was also the oppressive, rank smell of those animals, who although now absent, were bound – like the three bears – to return.

Chapter Fourteen

'He's in the sub-adult males' room,' Busner inparted Charlotte, his alpha female. 'They're out on night patrol and he seemed more comfortable in there for the moment than in the spare bedroom.'

' "Hoo" Zack.' Charlotte stirred in the nest. ' "Grnn-gr'" do you really think it's a good idea to have such a severely disturbed chimp staying with us "huu"?'

'Good idea for who "huuu"?' he replied absent-mindedly, the signs falling like the footfalls of some heavy insect between her shoulder blades.

'For him, for you "hooo", I don't know. It seems like only yesterday that you had that chimp with Tourette's here – don't you remember how his ticcing and involuntary vocalising began to drive you round the bend "huu"?' She rolled over to muzzle him and pressed her soft, liver-spotted cheek into his belly fur.

' "Chup-chupp" that's true enough, old thing, but remember what irritated me most about poor Nairn was how stereotypic his condition was. It was flamboyant, true enough, but there was nothing really there to get my fingers round. With Dykes I think the situation is rather different. His is a unique condition "gru-nn". I don't know, Charlotte, you could be right, but I have a hunch that Dykes's may well prove to be my last truly important case –'

'Zack, Zack, you shouldn't sign so.'

'Charlotte, "huh-huh" as my oldest nestmate, my adored alpha, I think I need to show you something.'

'What, Zack "huuu"?'

Charlotte struggled upright in the nest, pulling the sheets with her, and snapped on the nestside lamp. Dr Kenzaburo Yamuta, the Busner distal-zeta male, and Mary the theta female who were sharing the nest deprived of their covering stretched, groaned, rearranged their limbs and recommenced snoring.

In the sudden exposure Busner noted again how tired Charlotte looked. This oestrus had really taken it out of her. She was wearing a cotton nightgown that had rucked up over her belly. Her swelling was healing but still raw, there were gashes and nail marks around her neck. 'Charlotte "clak-clak", Charlotte old thing, neither of us is as young as we used to be "huh-huh". We've done well in the past few years, the group is better established than ever, all our offspring are doing well – at the end of this year I'll be able to retire on full pension.'

'Zack, do you really mean this "huuu"?'

'Not only do I mean it, but there's another, less voluntary factor. I believe that Gambol is making an alliance against me.'

' "Euch-euch" Zack! You can't be serious, the little swine! "Wraaa" after all that you've done for him!'

Her fur erected under the thin cotton, her fingers grasped his, her brown eyes stared deep into his green ones. Busner began to groom the backs of Charlotte's hands. This was a special, intimate act of grooming that was exclusive to them. Busner, ever so delicately, teased out the fur on the back of Charlotte's fingers using the thicker fur on the backs of his. It calmed her more or less instantly and she began to pant and smack her lips, while snuggling back down into the nest. 'Charlotte,' the former television personality inparted, 'your arsehole means more to me than anything, your "huh-huh" swelling is the whole world engulfing me –'

'"Chup chupp hoo" sweet scrag, you silly old fool "chup chupp" –'

'I mean it, Charlotte. But you know, if Gambol can topple me from the apex of the hierarchy, then so be it. I'm old – this is the chimpanzee way, always has been. No, the only thing that really troubles me is that he and Whatley – I know Whatley is in with him – will mount a coup before I can make any real progress with Dykes. I'm certain that they're going to leap from the branch soon – the only question is when.'

The two senior Busners went on grooming each other for a long time. Through the open windows of the bedroom came floating the faint valedictory pant-hoots of chimps departing from the bars and restaurants of Hampstead. The night air cooled, the house around them quietened. Eventually Charlotte began to snuffle and then when her snores oddly harmonised with those of her sleeping subordinates, Zack Busner was left alone with his thoughts.

As was Simon in the sub-adult males' room. It was true, he did find its ambience more comforting that the chintzy, emphatically spare room. But at the same time, the doubly scaled-down pine bunknests with their brightly patterned duvet covers; the posters of pop stars and football players stuck to the walls; the model aeroplanes dangling from threads pinned to the ceiling; and the pygmy bookcases overflowing with picture books – all of it dragged the memories of the Brown House, the memories of his infants, the memories of humanity, screaming back to him.

"Daddy". Nothing. "Daddy". Nothing. "Da-ddy!". Nothing. "Daddy-Daddy-Daddy!". "What? What is it?". "Daddy, you're pooh-pooh."

Lots of giggling about this. Three blond heads knocking together like nuts; and the squirrely fingers digging into his thighs.

"Daddy". Nothing. "Daddy". Nothing. "Da-ddy!". "What? What is it now?" "Da-da, Magnus is the sky and I'm the world. And the sky is more biggest than the world, isn't it?" "Bigger, darling, it's bigger than the world . . ."

He had thought his love for them was more biggest than the world, but perhaps it had been nothing of the sort. He had thought that the intense physical sympathy he felt for his infants would keep him anchored to that world, but he'd been wrong. How could this have been so? As he lay in nest, in Hampstead, in a world dominated by the physical, the bodily, Simon stared at the dark wall, stared at a poster tacked there that showed a chimpanzee with a pronounced eyebrow ridge screaming into a microphone. Underneath the muzzle was the legend 'Liam Gallagher, Oasis'. Some oasis, Simon mused, more like a mirage. A mirage that should dissolve.

Every scab, every graze, every knock and blow. The time the hernia swelled, hour-by-hour, in Magnus's little groin, until it was the size of a goose's egg and he and Jean cried with anxiety while Anthony Bohm probed it with certain fingers.

The time Henry ended up on the children's ward, at Charing Cross Hospital. His little muzzle trapped by the plastic mask of the nebuliser. The awful "ker-choof, ker-choof" as it pumped the gas into his failing lungs, puffed the life into his labouring body. And in the plastic-curtained booth next to him, Simon had watched as a well-fingered young doctor delineated carefully to uncomprehending Somali parents, that their little infant's colon would have to be removed. That her life would be, from this day on, a veritable crock of shit.

And the time Simon junior, the middle infant, the sensitive one, had been bullied at school. Come home crying, his snub-nasal bridge red, biffed about. And Simon had marched into the prissy head teacher's office; marched in with Simon in his arms, and while the infant male's body shivered against his, berated the woman, berated the school, berated the more biggest world that could harm his offspring.

Simon struggled round in the cramped nest to muzzle the wall. He pulled the diminutive duvet tightly around him, feeling the cotton prickle against his hairy shoulder. He tucked his head into the crook of his arm and willed himself to sleep. To sleep was to dream of a world where you weren't touched unbidden, where the tedium of gussets reigned, where his infants slickly snuggled against him. Simon willed the Valium Busner had administered to work, to drag him away from this ravening reality. He wanted to dig into the nest, to submerge himself in its familiar cotton confines. He yanked the duvet up, so that it covered his fluffy head with its bright pattern of dancing little humans.

Morning arrived like it always did at the Busner house – with pandemonium. The night-ranging, sub-adult males were back and racketing around in the kitchen. The older females were preparing first breakfasts for everyone who had to get off to work. Cressida was still in oestrus after three whole weeks, a fact that caused her pride and discomfort in equal measure, but mating activity was relatively subdued.

Taking one look at the large room with its leaping, bouncing, gyrating and overwhelmingly chimp inhabitants, Busner decided that it was too soon to subject Simon Dykes to the full force of normal life. "HooooGra!" he pant-hooted loudly and tom-tommed the top of a freestanding plastic bin. The noise died away. 'Right! "HooGrnn" you lot. I showed you that I would be having another patient staying with us, but I just want to drum this home a bit more . . .' He drummed on the bin some more. 'This poor chimp Simon Dykes has a genuine malaise that has afflicted him with the delusion that he's human –' Some of the younger Busners began giggling and tooth-clacking. ' "Wraaaf"! Can it, you lot, or you'll feel the clamp of my jaws on your miserable muzzles. "Waaaa"!' The giggling spluttered to a halt. 'Now, I want a reasonable amount of quiet and decorum in here. I'm going to take Simon out to the summer house to have his first breakfast – I think he may find the company of the lap ponies a little easier to bear than yours. "HooGraaa"!'

Busner leapt back out of the room and bounded up the stairs. He hesitated on the threshold of the sub-adult males' room and grunted interrogatively a few times before swinging in. Simon was just levering himself up, rubbing his eye sockets.

Busner was intrigued that he'd chosen to sleep on the bottom one of the bunknests. This was undoubtedly, he mused, another ramification of the human delusion. Human-like, Simon sought shelter wherever he could. '"HooGraa" good morning, Simon. Did you sleep well "huuu"?'

Simon could barely focus on the digitations. He massaged his head. For some seconds he knew where he was, he knew who he was signing with, but he couldn't have said which species he belonged to. Then the fug of sleep cleared and the former artist confronted the hell of another day among the apes. "HooGra," he vocalised feebly, then signed 'Good morning, Dr Busner. I'm sorry, Your Radiant Arseholiness, I was dreaming ... dreaming ... of being human –'

'And you're human on awaking "huu"?'

'Yes, yes, of course.'

'You have no fur "huu"? Your limbs are straight, the arms shorter than the legs "huu"?'

'Yes "hooo" yes! Of course –'

'Your buttocks are as rounded and smooth as two salad bowls "huuu"?'

'"Clak-clak-clak" well, if you sign so! Although it's not exactly the image I would have chosen!'

With this distinctly good-humoured outburst, the ape man grabbed the bottom of the top nest and swung himself out of the bunk. He swaggered around the room, ignoring Busner's presence, and picking up articles of clothing. He put on one of the T-shirts from the plastic bag Tony Figes had provided, and a denim jacket.

Simon refused to attempt the climb down the outside of the house, so the maverick anxiolytic drug researcher led him down the stairs and out the back door. Simon was still forcing himself to walk upright on the level – and he ignored the handholds.

Simon hung back as they traversed the terrace, and laughed on peering through the french windows. He'd yet to see so many chimps of different ages in a domestic setting, and the sight recalled parody; the films he'd seen as an infant of chimps' tea parties at the zoo. They all seemed to cram as much fruit or bread in their mouths as possible, and they all grabbed at the food in each other's mouths. They swung around the place using the very ordinary furniture – a set of pine chairs and matching table, a Welsh dresser and the formica-topped breakfast bar – as a species of jungle gym. Observing Simon's amusement, Busner merely fluttered something about 'Family, too noisy, bit much for your first day. Daughter still in oestrus . . .' and led him on to the octagonal gazebo at the end of the garden, which he'd ordered from a catalogue in a moment of bucolic aspiration.

Here Simon sat and chomped his way through a bowl of sloes – remarking that they were unpleasantly bitter, and a bowl of custard apples – remarking that they were nauseatingly sweet. Busner tried to interest him in a slice of durian, signing, 'Best there is. My gamma female gets them from some Sumatran deli in Belsize Park,' but the smell alone put Simon right off.

The things that seemed to calm Simon most and distract him from the more problematic aspects of his new home were the Busner lap ponies. As usual three or four of them were trotting around the garden, neighing reedily and depositing their small, hay-encrusted droppings neatly among the rose bushes. Simon found them captivating. 'They're so small,' he signed wonderingly to Busner, who was deep in the *Guardian*. 'Why are they so small "huuu"?'

'Small "huu"? Yes, they are. Of course, the original wild horse was considerably larger, but over the millennia that chimpanzees and horses have lived together they've been bred for size until the modern, domesticated horse has achieved this convenient stature – just right for fertilising gardens and crops without damaging them "chup-chupp".' Busner hoisted one of the little beasts aloft by its bridle and petted its caramel mane.

'But what about dogs? What's happened to dogs "huuu"? I suppose "clak-clak-clak" you're going to tell me that *they've* got larger!'

'That's right, Simon, they've got larger. The wild dog only stood about five hands at the shoulder. In fact, recent research shows that the ancestor of all modern canines must have been about the same size as the modern wolf. Well, obviously an animal of this stature would be impractical as a beast of burden. So, over the centuries chimps have selectively bred dogs for size. If you're interested I can take you to some kennels locally and show you dogs that are sixteen hands high.'

Simon met this intelligence in signlence. This reversal of domesticated species was like some surreal drogue, adding a further half-twist of weirdness to the reversal of the natural order he was already having to endure. He thought – inevitably – of Sarah, her canines bared in ecstasis as he plunged into her that final time, and he thought as well of Gracie, Sarah's retriever, and how that last morning she had worried at the door to the bedroom, snuffling and snarling to get in. Then he remembered the diminutive horse that was racketing around when he awoke in this no-fun house world of hirsute persecutors. How many more such role reversals could the world encompass? Flying rabbits? Viviparous fish? He curled his limbs around him on the garden chair and began rocking back and forth on his scut, like a caged primate, or an autistic child.

Busner caught the shift in Simon's mood. Better to keep him distracted, he thought, push on with my programme of integration, of psychically outward-bound activities. ' "Grnnn" Simon.'

'Yes, what is it "huu"?'

'I thought we might carry on with your reinduction to the world today. Keep – as it were – the pressure up.'

'What did you have in mind exactly "huu"?'

'Why, a trip to the zoo – naturally.'

Gambol pant-hooted through the window of the Volvo as he pulled up by the kerb outside the Busner house. Then he sat and waited. As if on cue, Simon Dykes emerged from the passageway that ran down the side of the house. He was, Gambol noted, still walking upright with a bonobo-like, stiff-legged gait. And like a bonobo, the posture pushed into prominence his pink penis. Gambol blanched; there was an offensive as well as an unsettling quality about Dykes. He held himself too still, he didn't fidget like a chimp – and those guttural vocalisations, that warped signing. Still, he was Gambol's meal ticket and the epsilon male knew it.

He vaulted through the open window of the car and met Dykes halfway up the garden path. ' "HoooH'Graa" good morning, Mr Dykes, how are you today "huu"?' Simon squinted down at the chimpanzee who addressed him. He was beginning to notice subtle differences by which he could distinguish the animals. This one's ears were unusually small and neat. Its muzzle was almost hairless and its skin whiter than that of Busner or Bowen – let alone the apes who inhabited the hospital, most of whom had been much slimmer, with blacker muzzles and pinker lips.

' "Hooo" yeah "HooGraaa".' Without understanding why, Simon found himself drumming on the trunk of a nearby tree and whooshing air through his parted teeth. Then he advanced down the path with the small chimp walking backwards in front of him. Simon was struck by the ease with which the ape moved in this fashion, never hesitating as it placed one heel behind the other. When it reached the gate, it unlatched it with sure, unobserved hands and slid – still backwards – through the gap. Then it knelt down, swivelled and pushed its scraggy rump in Simon's direction.

Simon had seen so many animals do this to Busner that he knew what was required. He bent down and pressed his hand on the proffered arse. As ever he was struck by quite how human the feel of the thing's body was, once

240

the awful furriness was factored out. ' "Grnnn" there-there "chup-chupp", it's Gambol, isn't it "huu"?'

'That's right. I admire your delusion, I revere your looniness –'

'All right, all right Gambol, there-there "chup-chupp.' Simon bestowed a few more patronal pats.

Busner joined them, carrying his briefcase and with a couple of squealing infants dangling around his neck. There was also a bunch of sub-adult males trailing him in a sinuous coiling of grooming hands and smarming arms. The first of these was at Busner's neck fur, the next in the fur of the first, and so on. They all bristled, they all growled. It was quite a procession of excitable chimp-flesh, and accordingly Simon was intimidated. He shrank back against the hedge. Busner rounded on the sub-adults. ' "Wraaaf" no patrol for you lot today, I don't want you annoying Mr Dykes ... and as for *you* "wraaa"!' He unceremoniously pulled the infants from his neck and dropped them, squealing, in a flowerbed.

Left alone, the three apes swung into the Volvo. Gambol started the engine and pulled away fast, changing up through six gears in as many seconds. The big saloon bucketed down the steep incline towards Frognal, turned right and disappeared in the direction of Primrose Hill.

London may have appeared comparatively breezy, clear and spacious to those occupants of the car who could acknowledge their chimpunity, but for Simon Dykes it was a cramped, dismal place. From the red-brick detached houses at the crest of Hampstead, down past the long chipped terraces of Belsize Park, to the sandwich-stacked ones around Primrose Hill, everywhere Simon directed his gaze he saw a cityscape cluttered by its own jumble; a lumber room of the ages with buildings dumped against one another like so many discarded chattels, wreathed in cobwebs, dusted with smut. Never had London been as claustrophobic, as dwarfish as this. And everywhere he saw the gnome-like, unshaven inhabitants, their hard toes snapping against

241

the pavement, their hard hands grasping and grappling, ceaselessly in motion.

Simon hunched in the back, feeling like Alice in Apathyland, half wanting to ask the ape denoted Gambol to open the sun roof so that he could poke his giraffe neck through it. To diminish as far as possible the disjunction between his sense of his own body and his apprehension of the world it inhabited Simon spent the journey with his eyes, once more, pressed against the window, and one hand loosely cradling his cock and balls. Funny how being half-naked doesn't seem to discomfit me, he thought, or perhaps only thought he thought.

The Volvo pulled into Regent's Park and accelerated towards the zoo. Then, as they drew level with the main gates, Gambol swung the car into a wide arc, whilst expertly changing down through eight or so gears. He brought the vehicle to a halt right next to a chimpanzee clutching a great bunch of helium-filled novelty balloons.

Busner piled out the front door and gathered Simon from the back. Simon found Busner's touch much easier to cope with since he himself had picked dry shit from the radical psychoanalyst's fur. Busner's body had acquired an odd penumbra of acceptability, somewhere between that enjoyed by one's own arsehole – by virtue of being touchable while most others are not – and a familiar, if stinky, old dog – like Sarah's Gracie.

Busner paused by the balloon seller, and signed 'You must have been here with your infants, Simon "huu"?'

'Yes, that's right, many times. Magnus, the eldest, is particularly keen on animals, wildlife, that sort of thing. The others would tag along . . .' Simon's fingers fluttered to a halt. He was staring at the metallic painted surfaces of the novelty balloons jostling overhead. In amongst the Mickeys, Minnies and Mr Blobbys, were other, stranger caricatures, pale-muzzled, with exaggeratedly large proboscises.

Busner, seeing what had transfixed Simon, exchanged signs and coins with the hawker, gained possession of one and thrust the string into Simon's hand signing, 'It's a human, Simon, the infants love them ...' He drew Simon on by the arm, towards the gift shop. 'And look here "grnnn".' Together with the Lifewatch mugs, the pennants and stickers, were a number of plastic masks affixed to a pegboard, lions, giraffes, tigers, and also paler muzzles, more Fagin proboscises. 'See! Human masks.'

The two apes moved on. Simon trailed behind, keeping his muzzle level with Busner's scrag, observing closely the way the eminent psychiatrist's grey-skinned testicles swung lazily this way and that; first appearing, then disappearing, beneath the hem of his tweed jacket.

Busner bought the tickets from a bonobo in a booth, they knuckle-walked down a curving ramp and into the zoo. It was all as Simon remembered it from the last trip he'd taken there with the infants. When would that have been? It was now – or so Busner had shown him – nearly a month since his breakdown; and what with the preparations for the show and the long nights at the Sealink, Simon hadn't seen the infants in the month before that. But the last time they had taken any kind of excursion together, it was here, to the zoo.

The furry animals, in their farcical, bum-freezing half-garb, knuckle-walking here, swaggering there, hauling hand-over-hand up there – all wavered, then dissolved into a Kodachrome vision of pink-to-red-to-orange, inhumanly human flesh tones. His infants, with their fair hair and blue eyes, the irises so round – like boiled sweets: suckable humanity. The three of them licking on ice-cream cones as they scampered hand in hand in hand, towards the gorilla enclosure.

'"H'hooo" Simon!' Busner was bipedal now, in lecturing, hectoring mode. 'Now, as you are aware, in your therapy we intend to take a didactic and explanatory approach. We will confront you with the reality of your chimpunity, to try and dissolve the content of your delusion. Remember, if at any stage you find the sight of these beasts too disturbing, you simply have to pant-hoot and we'll beat a retreat.'

Simon goggled at the ape who stood in front of him with wiggling fingers. An ape half-dressed in tweed jacket, Viyella shirt, and hank-of-mohair tie; an ape who had bifocals hanging on a chain around his thick neck. He couldn't prevent himself from guffawing, clacking his big canines together. What could possibly be more disturbing than *this?*

Sensing the see-sawing of Simon's mood between hilarity and horror, Busner decided to move him on. They rounded a raised bed full of suburban verdancy and came muzzle-to-muzzle with the large statue of Guy the gorilla, for many years the zoo's primary primate attraction. As ever, the larger-than-life-size bronze had its mini-mahouts in the form of chimpanzee infants clambering between the blades of its broad back, cachinnating, chattering, and being wraaed at. Their parents showing them to stay still, keep novocal, so they could take the shot.

Busner drew Simon up to the privet fringe edging the safety barrier. Beyond this there was a two-foot gap and then the close steel bars that constituted the gorillas' enclosure. The enclosure – which was about forty by eighty hands and thirty high – was upholstered with great drifts of straw. An enormous, bottomless plastic dustbin lay on one side with a tuft of straw escaping from it. There was also a rope net set up between four thick posts, and half a bale of straw lay in this hessian depression, providing the means – or so Simon assumed – for the gorillas to make day nests.

Busner crooked one finger in the direction of a near-pyramidical thing covered in silvery-black fur that was crouched in the embankment of straw towards the middle of the enclosure. ' "H'hooo" look, Simon! There he is, a big silverback – your first, live human!'

If Busner had expected any particular reaction, laughter wasn't it, but laughter was what he got. Full-throated, high-pitched, gnashing, clacking laughter. Simon's fingers articulated his incredulity, while his cackling was loud enough to attract the attention of the chimps in the vicinity: ' "H'hee-hee-clak-clak" that's not a human! That's a gorilla!'

'Yes, yes "chup-chupp" – please – it is a gorilla, but it belongs within the human family, along – I believe, although I'm no zoologist – with the orang-utan; all three species being tailless "huuu"?' And Busner grabbed Simon by the scruff at this point, so as to calm him down, because the poor chimp was whimpering, his hilarity flooding with despair.

'Of course, Dr Busner, of course, how stupid of me "u-h'-u-h'-u-h'" you see, naturally, that as far as *I* am concerned the gorilla, the chimpanzee and the orang-utan belong in the same family – the human being distinct, unique, imbued with both self-consciousness, and of course "u-h', u-h'" made in the image of his creator.'

It was Busner's turn to fall signless, as once more he apprehended the perfect symmetry of Dykes's delusion. Busner was aware that some radical philosophers and anthropologists were currently attempting to redraw the species boundaries; in the process dubbing chimpanzees as 'the second human'. There must be, Busner reasoned, a part of Dykes's psyche that has absorbed this information and flipped it round, a comi-tragic reversal.

But no matter how deluded Dykes was, he responded well enough to being out of the hospital. His signing was becoming more fluent and articulate by the hour. And although he still tensed up whenever another chimp got too close to him – a reaction that left dismayed vocalisations in his wake – he no longer lapsed into uncontrollable hysteria. Busner judged that now was as good a time as any to force the pace. So, he took the still giggling chimp by his brown scruff and led him on, towards the humans' enclosure.

This was part of the same complex as the gorillas'. At its core were four internal rooms – two each for the humans and the gorillas. These were painted a serviceable orangey-yellow and equipped with niches and sleeping platforms. The gorillas' were far smaller, as the zoo only had the one pair, whereas there was an entire party of humans. Both accommodations featured the adventure playground appurtenances deemed necessary for captive humans, thick hessian ropes, strategic arrangements of telegraph poles and handholds set at different heights.

Knuckle-walking to the left of the complex, Busner and Simon came first to the smaller of the two glassed-in rooms that housed the humans. There was a group of chimps assembled here, muzzles pressed against the thick plate glass, so as to cheat its bold reflection. The chimps were signing and vocalising to each other excitedly. ' "HoooGraa" look at that one, it's peeling a banana!'; ' "H'huuu" is that a male?' ' "Grnnn" what's that one trying to do, is it "huuu" playing?'

Simon, unwilling to get close enough to see what was behind the glass, hung back and studied these animals-looking-at-animals. Did they have any idea how ridiculous, how stupid they appeared? "Wraaa" a thick-set male called, and then gestured to his female companion – was her head fur arranged, ever so slightly in travesty of a human hairstyle, feather-cut and bleached at the edge of the temples? It certainly seemed that way to Simon. 'Look at the stumpy teeth on that fucker "wraaa"!' And she giggled, clutched the thick fur on his anguiform arm, smarmed herself against him and rearranged her bandy legs around her straggly swelling.

There were other chimps, chimps with oddly slitty eyes who held camcorders and filmed each other adopting what they imagined to be human-like postures in front of the enclosure. This spectacle brought the bile buckets coursing up Simon's gullet. He tugged Busner's sleeve, then inparted his therapist's palm, 'Why do those chimps have such peculiar eyes "huu"? They're slitty, and their head fur is far darker and sleeker than that of the others.'

Busner looked at Simon, his eyebrow ridges arched with incredulity, before replying, 'They're *Japanese*, Simon, and please keep your fingering discreet, they may sign ES for all we know.'

But Simon wasn't paying any attention, his curiosity was getting the better of him. There were grey, blobby shapes moving behind the glass, coming into the light and then retreating. He pushed forward between the press of lanate limbs until he was able to shield his eyes against the glass. Busner was by his shoulder, keeping a firm hand on him, ready to provide restraint if he reacted adversely. There they were, the first human forms that Simon had seen since Sarah's body had bucked in orgasm beneath his ramming pelvis. The first human features he had set eyes on since those loved ones had furred-over.

There was one standing with its back to Simon, some seven feet away. Two more lay on the sleeping platform by the right-hand wall, back to back. Another was supine in the straw, an infant jumping on its billowing belly. The first thing Simon noticed about the humans was their buttocks. They were obscenely null and ludicrously curvaceous, more like blanched beach balls than body parts. The animals' buttocks were all the more exposed-looking because of the relative furriness of the rest of their bodies. Simon couldn't tell which were male and which female, but all saving the infant had large crops of pubic fur, and some had sparse fur on their chests, arms and legs as well.

Then the one at the back of the room turned and ambled, upright, towards the chimpanzee spectators. There were "aaas" and "wraaas" from the chimps as the human emerged from the shadows into full visibility. Simon gazed at the human – if that's what it was. He'd never seen anything quite like it. For a start it was very fat, but fat in an unusual way, the flesh falling in distinct dewlaps from all its limbs, and in a great distended bib from its belly and chest. There were also warty-looking wattles of flesh on its neck, a neck that to Simon seemed quite oddly elongated, as did the rest of the body.

But the body, strangely steatopygic as it was, was nothing like as impactful as the thing's blunt muzzle. Simon concentrated, trying to discern the physiognomy of a man, but couldn't really perceive it. It certainly had something that might be a nasal bridge – at any rate a fleshy proboscis; and also a flat area above its eye sockets, rather than a pronounced ridge. This either made the beast's eyes appear more prominent – or else they were in reality; at any rate they blearied at Simon, blue, protuberant, and utterly without the least flicker of rationality, or self-awareness. Simon tugged Busner's sleeve and inparted his palm, 'D'you know, is that a male or a female "huu"?'

Busner stared at his patient, quite taken aback, before fluttering, 'It's a male, Simon, look at the beast's great sausage of a prick.' Simon was aghast that he hadn't noticed the fire-hose-thick, ten-inch length of penis lodged in its bushy groin. As if remarking on this error, the human grabbed hold of his limp organ and began yanking it hard and mechanically.

This brought forth a chorus of delighted pant-hoots from the assembled chimps. "HoooGra!" they all cried and then signed excitedly among themselves, 'Look! It's wanking! It's wanking!' Some of the chimps became so aroused by this display of animal sexuality that they started mock-mating with one another, but this soon died down again.

Simon remained, eye sockets rammed against the glass, focusing intently on the vacant muzzle of the masturbating human. After a while it stopped, let go of its still flaccid member and shambled back to the tenebrous rear of the room. As it turned, the chimps became agitated once more, tremendously taken by just that feature that had so surprised and revolted Simon. 'Look at its bum, Mummy,' signed an infant who was near to Simon 'it's all horrible and smooth!'

' "Wraaf" still!' the mother snapped back.

But the human lying on its back with the infants playing around it was the one who had most of the chimps' attention. They were charmed by the antics of a roly-poly mite, who time after time struggled up the slick-skinned belly of the prone adult, attempted to stand, then fell in a windmill of truncated arms and lengthy legs, back into the straw.

Each time this happened the chimp infants gave voice, their

shrill, piercing screams bouncing off the glass. Then they would all sign the same – to Simon's eyes, stereotypic – response: '"Aaaa" look, Mummy – they're playing!' whereupon the attending adult female would also "aaa" and remark, 'They're *so* cute,' as if this cuteness, this apparently chimp-like behaviour were entirely novel and unsuspected.

The two prone humans on the sleeping platform now stirred, then sat upright. One was clearly female, with even bigger distensions of flesh on its chest than the male – and possessed also of long brown teats. As for the other, it was extremely difficult to establish its gender as it kept all its limbs hunched up in a tight bundle, and rocked back and forth on its buttocks-for-runners. Neither of these animals acknowledged the presence of the other, and like the masturbating male their porcine muzzles were devoid of feeling or expression.

Busner caressed the side of Simon's neck and gently teased some signs into his fur. 'Notice "chup-chupp" how the humans don't groom one another. Indeed, "chup-chupp" hardly touch.'

Simon, becoming aware of what Busner was signing about as he became aware of the fact of the signing itself, was struck for the first time by the potential for poetry that such a signage might have. Signing of touch – while touching; a dance and play of the fingers, one on another – one *to* another. Simon reached out an exploratory hand, found the powerful thigh of the psychiatrist and inparted, 'I find them very peculiar to look at "u-h'-u-h'", not quite what I expected.'

'Well, I believe that humans reared in captivity do have some significant differences from those in the wild.'

'Which are "huu" – ?'

Simon didn't get a countersign because there were loud noises, as of various metal objects being moved, bolts shot, gates opened, chains rattled. Simon had noticed the exaggerated languor with which the humans moved, reminiscent of mental patients sedated with Largactil, but this racket jerked them into attention. All save the swaying, genderless individual on the sleeping platform got bipedal and with their peculiar, stilted gait moved to the doorway at the left of the room

One of the supine adults was male, although not nearly as large a specimen as the masturbator. It was shorter, stockier and had a sparser, lighter pubic pelt. This individual jostled with the big male for precedence in the queue, nudging him shoulder to shoulder. The big male then opened its slack mouth to reveal a mouthful of stunted, rotten teeth. If Simon had been expecting an intelligible vocalisation, some of what he had denoted "speech", then he was to be gravely disappointed, for all that emerged was a low, throaty roar. A roar so bass that it made the toughened glass vibrate.

The big human male roared and gave the other male a hefty barge which sent it staggering a couple of paces. It fetched up against the glass and Simon looked deep into its empty eyes. 'You see,' Busner tickled Simon's scruff, 'the beginnings – albeit crude – of a dominance hierarchy.'

The other humans were filing out of the doorway, ducking as they passed under the lintel. The putatively beta male picked itself up and followed in their scut. "Aaaah", vocalised an infant who was grabbing Simon's leg, then signed, 'Poor thing, he's been left behind!' Simon was surprised – he didn't find the infant chimpanzee's touch difficult to endure. The trailing human moved towards the doorway, but failed to duck in time. Lintel met unprotected head with an audible crack and the human fell back, smack on its cushioning arse. A peal of unrestrained, joyfully effervescent laughter splurged from the chimps.

Simon felt anger rise up in him. White rage. He turned to muzzle Busner, ' "Wraaa"! That's horrible, so callous. Can't chimps show any sympathy for these poor creatures!'

' "Hooo" now, Simon, I agree with you, of course, but let's not attract too much attention to ourselves.' He drew his unorthodox patient away from the other chimps, who were still heaving and clutching their sides. 'You must realise that the sight of the human banging its head is an archetypal form of slapstick "huuu"?'

'Whaddya mean "huu"?'

'Well, the human is markedly less spatially aware than the chimpanzee. Its capacity for extroception – intuitive awareness of the dispensation of surrounding objects – is diminished, barely there at all. Chimpanzees have thus always used the human as a clownish paradigm. Circus acts often incorporate chimps dressed up as humans, running around bashing into one another, d'you see "huuu"?'

Simon saw a lot. Over the top of the gibbons' cages he saw the trees of Regent's Park wavering in the distance. He saw the Lifewatch badges that some of the surrounding chimps sported, and he also saw his three infants, laughing as they scampered between the Coca-Cola machine next to the panda cage, the Lifewatch badge dispenser which played its inane, five-note jingle over and over, and the chimpanzee enclosure. Running easily, fluently, with that ungoverned feel so redolent of childhood, so redolent of a time before energy must be husbanded, conserved. The boys' bodies, so gracile, so fleet, so unlike those of the lumpen animals whose forms were smeared behind the toughened glass. Simon was riven by contrary, oppositional views, like an infant who places one eye on each side of a door, affording it different perspectives that are simultaneously unassimilable. He saw down the corridor of his life. Simon was a tall man. He had bashed his head against a thousand lintels, bulwarks, undersides of tables and horizontal poles. Was this wherein his humanity resided? These biffs and bonks, each of which – he remembered this too – had encoded within itself the knowledge that it could have been avoided, as if effect had preceded cause.

The corridor of Simon's life tipped up. It was a shaft now, a shaft tricked out to appear like a corridor, with items of furniture attached to its sides, against which his plummeting body crashed. Back and back, hip-on-corner, elbow-against-knob, jaw-slaps-door . . . until reaching what?

Some primary, definitive bang? And now Simon thought he apprehended it – that big bang. Felt its hard thwack running from occiput to nape, nape to shoulder, shoulder to coccyx. One hand went to his arse. His fingers fiddled in the ischial pleats. Then emerged, rose, spread. He turned to Busner, who was still touching him, still at his side, and signed, 'D'you know, when I was a child I was hit by a bus. It was on the Fortis Green Road . . .' He was fluttering. 'Coming back from a film . . . but what film "huu"?'

' "H'hooo" really.' Busner was distracted, perhaps caught in the same corridor as Simon, or one parallel to it. 'Well, that's duff extroception for you "huuu"? Now, shall we see what the humans are up to "huuu"? I think it's their feeding time.'

After dropping his titular alpha and the deluded chimp he was seeking to capitalise on at the zoo, Gambol sat for a moment, toying with the controls of the Volvo. Gambol may have been treated like a cab driver by Busner, but he was far from being just an intellectual grease human, running errands, placing pant-hoots, arranging for research to be done. Gambol had a first-class degree in psychology from Edinburgh, and won a Morton-McLintock Grant for a Master's in clinical psychology.

After obtaining this second degree he came under the influence of Zack Busner. Naturally Gambol had been aware of Busner for years; his distinctive pant-hoot was one of the sonic icons of the early seventies – now endlessly repeated on the reruns of game shows and gesture shows that disgraced the cable stations – but it was Gambol's reading of Harold Ford's definitive monograph on the Quantity Theory of Insanity that made Busner his hero. Gambol proceeded to read everything by Busner he could find, from his woefully misguided doctoral thesis *Some Implications of Implication*[1], through his accounts

---

[1] Abstracts are available from the Concept House Archive. Send £7.99, and allow twenty-one days for delivery.

of his ill-starred Concept House, to his later works on the existential, phenomenological ramifications of extreme neurological disorders.

Gambol became an acolyte. His own doctoral thesis was to have been a survey of Busner's much vaunted psycho-physical approach to his unusual patients. Was to have been, until the shiny folder that Gambol passed across the table to Whatley in the Café Rouge first came into his hackled hands.

The folder's source was a chimp called Phillips, who worked in a menial research capacity for a multinational drug company, Cryborg Pharmaceuticals. Gambol had knuckle-walked into Phillips a number of times at the seminars Cryborg ran on psycho-pharmacology for professionals. Learning that Gambol was Busner's epsilon and research assistant, Phillips blazoned it that he had a marked antipathy towards the great ape, indeed, that the resuscitation of Busner's career and reputation struck him as a gross travesty.

However when Gambol pressed Phillips about this, the chimp grew circumspect; his signing reduced to little more than fingernail clicking. Was Gambol aware, he snapped, of the odd lacuna in Busner's career that transpired in the early nineties? Did Gambol know that during this period Busner had resigned his consultancy at Heath Hospital and gone to work for Cryborg? Had Gambol any prinkling of the nature of that work?

The answers were, of course, all negative. Gambol pressed Phillips, arranging to meet him for drinks in various pubs around Hampstead. Gradually, over the course of months, the elements of the story had emerged. First was the revelation that Busner had, according to Phillips, been employed by Cryborg to conduct an anxiolytic drug trial; next came the implication – although not the direct demarcation – that the trial had been illegal.

And there Phillips stalled. It was an odd alliance, because both subordinates retained affection for Busner as they probed the possibility of undermining his reputation and destroying his career.

Then came Dykes – and the situation changed rapidly. Phillips was staggered when Gambol showed him about the artist and his peculiar delusion that he was human. He asked Gambol to keep in touch with any further developments and gave Gambol the folder that was passed on to Whatley, who then became – with Phillips's assent – the other angle of their conspiratorial triangle.

The folder was a dummy of an advertising brochure for a drug ascripted – provisionally – Inclusion. The facts, as set out in the brochure, made Inclusion a potential panacea for all modern neurotic and depressive ills. How exactly the drug worked was left vague – the brochure was aimed at not-so-sedulous general practitioners, without much time on their hands – but that Cryborg believed it to be a major breakthrough in psycho-pharmacology was written between every line of the medicalese.

Phillips inparted Gambol that the relationship between Busner and the chimp who thought he was human was more enduring than Simon Dykes knew. He promised to enlighten Gambol on these matters, but only on condition that he supplied regular updates on Dykes's progress. It was one of these that Gambol was contemplating as the Volvo, exhaust burbling, stood beside the zoo gates. He hated having to go to call boxes and hunch there, furtively signing, as if he were some low-rent industrial spy. But using the car 'phone was out of the question. Busner was absolutely correct about outgoings. Every paper clip, every pant-hoot, every cup of tea was accounted for on a weekly basis.

Gambol sighed and engaged gear. He'd drive down to Camden Town to make the pant-hoot. And he'd better make his gesturing snappy – Busner had intimated that the trip to the zoo might not last very long, and he wanted Gambol there when they were ready to leave.

Simon felt like leaving now. They had ambled in the wake of the other chimps, around the barred, open part of the human enclosure, to the room which lay on the other side. It was here that feeding time was going on.

Simon wasn't exactly expecting tables laid with white cloths, set with a silver service and crystal wine glasses, but even so the scene that confronted them was pitiful as well as disturbing. A large heap of food had been dumped on top of the layer of rank straw covering the floor. And what food it was, apples, oranges, bananas and bread. That was it. Simon looked in vain for anything else, any garnishes, side dishes, or meat, but there was none, just apples, oranges, bananas and white bread, the processed variety, so soft and gungy that slices remained cemented together even within the jumble of fruit.

It was obviously this bounty that had sparked off the spat between the two human males. For now, the biggest of the males – 'the Wanker' as Simon had mentally denoted him – sat by the heap, his long legs loosely crossed and a mound of the foodstuffs hiding his repellent lap. He was eating a quintuple-decker sandwich, constructed in the best cordon bleu fashion, by grabbing five stacked slices of bread.

All the humans were in this room for the feeding session. Simon forced himself to view his conspecifics with some kind of objectivity, to look for physical characteristics, identify ages and genders. Besides the Wanker, there were three other mature males. The one who'd been barged now stood knock-kneed, his head leaning against a sleeping platform, apparently waiting for the alpha male to finish scoffing. But another mature male was clearly in favour with the Wanker and, judging by his warty flesh, he might have been a blood relation.

This one stood slack-jawed, grasping a metal handhold, looking for all the world like some maladapted rail commuter, abandoned in a terminal rail siding by the passage of evolution. The Wanker would pass an occasional titbit to this individual, and the Commuter – as Simon now dubbed the putative relation to the Wanker – would take the apple or banana and scrunch it between his stubby teeth, pulp, pips and juice squirting over his chin.

The scene, which had at first merely bewildered Simon, then despite his revulsion, intrigued him, now engaged him fully. The longer he looked at the humans the more he felt akin to them. They, like him, preferred to be bipedal or to recline. They, like him, moved sluggishly, their actions cushioned by inertia jibing with the hard, material reality of their enclosure. Their hunched and dejected manner as they picked over the food, fiddled with the strewn swatches of straw, or moved about their unadventurous no-playground, was a cruel portrayal of Simon's own halting progress through the topsy-turvy hideousness of chimp world.

' "U-h'-u-h'" why have they painted the walls in there with that stupid shrubbery motif "huu"?' Simon grasped Busner's thick arm, inparted the fur between watch strap and cuff.

'What's that "h'huu" why? So as to resemble their equatorial habitat, I suppose. Here, look at this plaque – it'll fill you in on some of the key facts.'

The plaque showed Simon that humans were distributed throughout a steadily narrowing band of African rainforest and savannah. That their numbers were in severe decline as bonobos encroached further and further on their range; and that their Latin name was *Homo sapiens troglodytes*. ' "Huuu" and what does that mean?'

' "Gru-nnn" well.' Busner scratched his generous ear. 'I'm not altogether certain, <wise cave dweller> perhaps "huu"?'

'But Dr Busner, the sign <human> itself – what does that mean "huu"?'

' "Euch-euch" well, Simon, you've got me there. Must be a native sign of some kind; possibly a transliteration of the human's vocalisation, like this: "huuum'a". That's plausible, isn't it "huu"?'

Simon looked at his mentor, his guide, his one conceivable route back to any semblance of sanity. ' "U-h'-u-h'" you don't really know – do you "huu"?' he fingered, his signing anxious, jagged.

'You're right, Simon, I don't know – but I'd like to find out. We're embarked on a journey together, a picaresque search for knowledge. I must find out more about humanity – you about chimpunity "huu"?'

While the two chimps were chopping the air, a zoo volunteer arrived at the humans' enclosure. He was a mangy, ineffectual-looking male, even to Simon's indiscriminating eyes. Overweight, wearing a white jacket with a Lifewatch badge dangling from the lapel, the volunteer waved to the chimps gathered along the railing and attempted to put his fingers on their more pressing queries. Why were the humans – according to the notice affixed to the wire – 'Dangerous Animals'? Why was there so little mating activity? How was it possible to differentiate between the males and the females? And so on.

'"H'hoo" believe me,' the volunteer almost wrung his hands over this, 'your human is an extremely dangerous animal. Don't be deceived by all those films and advertisements you've seen, in which humans are dressed up as chimpanzees and taught to do clever things. All of the individuals used for this work are under five years old. Around five the human gets too clever to be safely handled and has to be retired. The next batch of four-year-old humans will take their place. Either that, or some older humans are "euch-euch" drugged, so that exploitative chimps can use them as novelty models, trailing them around Mediterranean resorts where chimps can pose for photographs with the beasts.'

Simon watched this conducting intently and then felt moved to ask the volunteer something himself. '"H'huu" but aren't humans weaker than chimpanzees? "Huu" physically ineffectual? How can such stupid, febrile creatures be a real threat to chimpanzees "huu"?' Busner beamed at Simon, delighted that his patient was interjecting with other chimps. However the volunteer looked askance. To him, as to the majority of chimps Simon had been in contact with, the former artist's spastic signing, his odd posture and lank fur, betokened mental instability, whether acquired or innate.

The volunteer gave Simon that particular look with which chimps mark down the mentally ill, pity and fear mixed so as to be patronising, then signed, 'Well "euch-euch", you are right there. But although weaker, the human is considerably larger than a chimpanzee. And although by no means intelligent in chimpanzee terms – human intelligence is really anything intelligent that humans actually do – a human has a raw, native cunning and an ability to make destructive use of its environment. Put "euch-euch" bluntly, they fashion weapons and given half a chance will use them –'

"H'H'H'Hee-hee-hee-hee!" Simon's scimitar teeth opened and squeals of laughter poured from their enamel grating. He was thinking, of course, of the kind of weapons he would like to fashion – and make destructive use of.

The volunteer clenched his fists. The other chimps were put out as well. It was, Busner judged, time for them to get going. Obviously Simon had had enough exposure for one day, best not to push things. Busner grasped him firmly by the shoulder and drew him away from the humans' bogus living room. Behind Simon's back he flicked some clipped signs: 'So sorry. Patient of mine. Not too well. Do excuse us – I'm his doctor.'

And into Simon's nape fur the existential phenomenologist ran on, 'Now, Simon, "gru-nn" Gambol will be waiting for us at the main entrance. We've had enough of an outing for today and I think you've done "chup-chupp" very well.'

Simon wasn't feeling much of this. Knuckle-walking away from the human enclosure under the covered walkway, the two chimps came muzzle-to-muzzle with a sign on a brick wall next to the lion tamarinds' cage. 'The Primate Tree' depicted the evolutionary relation that all primates stood in to one another.

Busner assumed it was this that had caught Simon's eye –

the line drawings of gorillas, humans and monkeys. Chimps and humans were grouped together. Indeed, the human was upright, loosely arm-in-arm with a gorilla, while off to one side the chimpanzee sat in splendid genetic isolation. They were on the uppermost branch of the tree, with Old World monkeys alongside. Two lower and more widely spaced branches supported the slack fraternities of New World monkeys; to the left – marmosets, tamarinds, douroucoulis and capuchins; and to the right the prosimians – lemurs, bush babies and tarsiers.

Busner tried mentally to realign this schema so as to match his patient's warped view of the natural world, but gave up because the poor, sad chimp was half laughing and half crying now, grabbing at the sleeve of Busner's jacket with both hands, forcing his attention towards another, smaller sign.

' "Euch-euch" what is it, Simon "huu"? What do you want?'

'It's this "hee-hee-hee", this thing here "clak-clak-clak", does it symbolise what I think it does "huuu"?' Simon tittered, titivated and whimpered.

Busner read the sign: 'The Michael Sobell Pavilions were opened by the Duke of Edinburgh on May 4th 1972.' 'Well, it seems straightforward enough to me –'

'So it's "hee-hee-hee" true then "huu"?'

'What's true "huuu"?"

'That the Duke of Edinburgh's *really* a monkey! "Hee-h'hee-hee-hee-clak-clak-clak".' The formerly renowned artist doubled up altogether.

'Not a monkey,' Busner admonished him, signs confused with clouts, 'an *ape*, Simon – an *ape*. Although arguably not that great a one.'

Simon, raising his arm to ward off Busner's blows, let go of the balloon string he had been holding throughout the zoo visit. Busner ceased dominating and for several minutes they squatted, watching the shiny, orbicular human caricature float gently up and away into the deep blue sky.

Chapter Fifteen

In the following week there were two quite bad episodes at the Busner group home. The first involved Simon and the postchimp; the second, Simon and a group of sub-adult Busner males. In each case there was no provocation, but he had either reacted to a perceived threat, or else wilfully and maliciously attempted to wound several chimps.

The postchimp was surprised, knuckle-walking up the front path at about eight in the morning, by a tall male who made a series of low, incoherent vocalisations before dropping an empty plastic dustbin over the poor chimp's shoulders, then kicked his groin region unmercifully.

It was broken up by Nick and William, a couple of older Busner sub-adult males. They were accustomed to dealing with those of their alpha's unusual resident patients that got out of hand. They chimphandled Simon to his room, left him there, woke their alpha, then went back to mollify the postchimp and prevent him from calling the police. Even when Busner himself got there, it took considerable persuasion to calm the chimp down.

The second episode involved a number of vases that Simon had taken from around the house. The Busners had so many ornaments that their absence wasn't noticed, until one morning when they came raining down on to the sub-adult males who were mock-displaying on the back patio. "Waaaa-Wraaaaf!" Simon screamed, hurling blue-glass flute after tubby porcelain pot. No one was hit directly, but several chimps were cut by flying glass, including Charlotte.

This was too much for the old ape. He'd swung himself up to the guest room, which Simon had fled to, and administered a sharp, salutary beating to the madchimp. Charlotte had been fairly calm, but Busner felt beholden to offer to have Simon taken back into hospital. ' "Euch-euch" I have to admit it looks as if you were right, my dear, and this fellow really is too disturbed to cope with any semblance of ordinary life –'

'But Zack, darling scragg, do you think that you're actually "huuu" getting anywhere with him?'

'Well, I did . . .'

'In that case he must stay – it's our duty.'

'Yes, it's our duty "gru-nnn"!' Mary and Nicola – respectively theta and iota females – added. They were sharing their alpha's nest that night.

It was true that there had been further progress. Simon was prepared to go out and encounter the world, but each trip left him obviously debilitated and morose. Dr Jane Bowen came to Redington Road as frequently as her schedule allowed. Simon found her the most sympathetic of his keepers – she was gentler and less inclined to physical admonishment than the great ape.

Bowen took Simon – usually in the early morning or late evening – out for knuckle-walks on the Heath. Here she encouraged him to try a little brachiating and to get more quadrumanous. Sometimes these outings were successful – but other times they ended in hysteria, as when Simon witnessed – without realising what it was – the end of one of the astonishingly long conga-lines of buggery, that gay chimps formed in the dense thickets of trees below Jack Straw's Castle.

Bowen always toted a camcorder on these trips and observed her unusual ward with all the techniques of objectivity that an anthropologist might have used, following wild humans in the African bush. She was becoming convinced that Simon's human delusion had a definable symptomatology – the possibility of an important academic paper beckoned.

Simon also moved into the spare room – under some duress. When Busner pressed him as to why he found the room so disturbing, Simon stabbed at the charming Pre-Raphaelite painting of a beautiful young female, half-submerged in aqueous morbidity, her William Morris swelling-protector garlanded with deathly lilies, and signed contemptuously, 'This fucking travesty.'

Busner got the point and had it replaced with an abstract.

After their trip to the zoo, Busner also instructed Gambol to trawl up as much material as possible on the human, and the other anthropoids. 'I want everything you can lay your hands on,' he showed the treacherous epsilon, 'works of theoretical anthropology, field studies, fictional works –'

' "Huuu" and films as well, Boss?'

'Naturally, films, television documentaries, still photographs as well. You can get a proper computer in here as well – link us up to that web thingy "euch-euch"; the most up-to-date human research will have been computerised. I want to see all the material available and delineate it. I also think that this odd study project will bring Dykes and me more fusion.'

So it was that Gambol, cursing inwardly at this abuse of his intellect, physically trawled through the libraries and archives of London – and virtually trawled through electronic space. But even he was surprised by the rich morass of human references there were to be uncovered.

He brought back Robert Yerkes' classic 1927 study, titled simply *Humans*, the first field study of the wild human. He bought all of Jane Goodall's books on the wild humans of Gombe. He went to Videocity in Notting Hill Gate and bought the *Planet of the Humans* videos – all four of them – and set up a video and television in Simon's room, so that the artist and his therapist could watch them while resting.

Gambol also obtained more recondite texts. A facsimile

edition of Edward Tyson's classic anatomical study – published in 1699 – of an immature human specimen brought from Angola: *Orang-utang, sive Pongid sylvestris. Or, THE ANATOMY OF A PYGMIE Compared With That of a Monkey, an Ape, and a Man.* This text had a most interesting effect on Simon Dykes. It sparked something deep inside the artist – or so Busner hypothesised. A forgotten, but originally conscious memory of the first meaningful encounters between the humans and Western civilization; or perhaps even a buried, phyletic memory, riven from the artist's waking mind in the same way that the great riving of the Rift Valley itself separated human from chimpanzee, leaving the former in the evolutionary cul-de-sac of the jungle; and the latter ranging free over the patchwork of ecosystems that cranked up the accelerating process of allopatric speciation.

Simon's acute interest was all the more interesting because Tyson's text marked the formal entry of the anthropoid human into Western consciousness. Some commentators believed that Tyson should be put on the same pedestal as Vesalius and Darwin[1]. But his classification of the human – he placed it within the chain of being somewhere above the Hottentot, according the species effective chimpunity – had a slow-burning impact. It took fifty years and the *mythos* of the Noble Savage, for the anthropoid humans to become material evidence in the great eighteenth-century trials between the anatomists and the Augustinians.

Busner, observing the zest with which Simon fell upon the Tyson facsimile, began to keep pace with his patient. He had given notice to the Trust that he was working on a most interesting case. 'Confidentially,' he had inparted Archer, the senior administrator at Heath Hospital, as they picked over each others ischial rats' tails in the canteen, 'this

---

[1] Darwin of course foresaw everything with his remark, 'If chimp had not been his own classifier, he would never have thought of founding a separate order for his own reception.'

patient I've "chup-chupp" acquired from Whatley at Charing Cross is something of a coup. His human delusion may have an organic basis that will reveal more about the relation between chimp consciousness and chimp physiology than a busload of ordinary neurological patients.'

It would have been stretching a point to sign that Archer had seen it all before where Busner was concerned, but this wasn't the first time the former television personality had flagged a Significant Breakthrough, and Archer knew it wouldn't be the last. Wouldn't be while Busner retained the network of alliances that had enabled his return to favour. But then alliances are always only provisional – and what goes up can come down again.

So, Busner delegated his teaching responsibilities, and handed over his nominal caseload to a pushy work theta, an SR who was on the make. Apart from the occasional trip out to attend unavoidable meetings and untouchable grooming sessions, he remained at Redington Road during the day.

Gambol had set up the large first-floor back room Busner used as a study so that Simon would feel as comfortable as possible there. All the pictures and photographs that gibed with Simon's delusional state – the ones depicting chimpan- zees in what Simon regarded as irreducibly human contexts – were removed. Even Busner's collection of appalling clay sculptures, executed by coprophiliac patients, were tidied away. Strict instructions were posted on the kitchen bulletin board that no group member could enter the study while the patient was there. Displaying and mating activities were to be confined to the kitchen and the sub-adults' ground-floor rumpus room. Lap ponies had to be severely reined in.

Gambol also cleared the desk so that Simon could have his own side: position his papers and effects – such as they were – to create a notion of his own space. At Busner's suggestion, Gambol even obtained some sketch pads, pencils and charcoals, and laid them out in case the artist decided to resume his work.

'You can never know,' Busner had gestured to Simon, the signs falling in among the carefully arranged art supplies, 'when the muse might feel called upon to visit you.'

'"Hoo-euch-euch" yeah,' Simon snapped back 'and what should I "euch-euch" do if she does "huuu"? Give her a really thorough grooming?'

Busner, sensing that physical admonition would only provoke more insolence, let this lie.

Thus the two of them sat, ape trying to imagine the mind of man, man labouring to accommodate the body of the ape. They would leaf through the books, study the photographs, and hunch in front of the new computer, taking it in turns to click their way around the virtual world of anthropology.

They garnered information from the directory of human research colonies at American universities. They visited the web site for the Uganda Six Day Human Safari; the Extant Animal Skulls, Human and Chimpanzee; the Human Zone – limited editions of human art, where Simon was able to see examples of humans' paintings, titled by the animals themselves.

They browsed through the on-line files of the Human and Chimpanzee Gesticulation Institute, checking out the biographies of Washoe and the other famous humans who had been taught to sign by the Fouts[2]. And of course they dropped into Dr Jane Goodall's Institute web site, where Simon tooth-clacked to discover the existence of a 'Human Ambassador Learning Kit'.

There was so much human information on the web it was bewildering. You could get a job working with humans via the net – as long as you had a negative hepatitis B, surface antigen test. And naturally you could contact human rights

[2] **'Favourite Activities:** Washoe loves to be outside. She also likes looking at catalogs (especially swelling-protector catalogs) or books by herself or signing about pictures with allies. Brushing teeth, painting, coffee and tea parties and playing tag through the window are also favourites.'

activists. Simply plugging the sign 'human' into the search engine produced over four thousand different links to sites.

As this was both Busner's and Simon's first experience of the web, they both began to conceive of the global electronic gesticulation system as being entirely occupied by humans; a jungle of bytes. More than ever, observing the preoccupation of chimpunity with their soon-to-be-extinct closest living relative, Busner wondered whether in his patient's condition the *Zeitgeist* had been fused with psychosis.

From time to time they would adjourn, crawling to Simon's cramped quarters to watch videos. But Simon could never stay with it for that long. It was as if each day he arose, determined to make something of his predicament, but as the morning wore on, it wore him down. Usually, after second lunch, just like some pathetic, captive human, Simon would get up and come round to Busner's side of the desk, proferring his crooked, lank-furred arm. Busner would know what the ape man wanted; would lead him back to his room, push him down on to the nest, prepare the syringe full of Valium and push needle into Simon, plunger slowly into barrel, so that the neuroleptic infused, and pushed Simon down into dream.

For if on the one hand the artist was making believably insightful – albeit obsessional – attempts to understand his psychic condition, so his physical being credibly failed to fit in. He still walked, like a travesty of a minstrel bonobo, quiveringly erect. His gait – even to a quinquagenarian like Busner – was gnawingly slow. What had appeared, initially, to both Busner and Jane Bowen, as a physical hypertrophy or hysterical paralysis was worsening. Simon seemed to be unable to get to grips with things. His feet never grasped. His extroception remained focused resolutely forward, in a tight conical beam, rendering his perception of the external world – or so Busner hazarded – like that of a car driver deprived of rearview and wing mirrors and unable to turn round.

The patient's reporting of his own physical state remained

puzzlingly incoherent. At times he accepted the testimony of his own senses; that he was possessed of fur, devoid of proboscis, and big on ears. But at other times the strange, bodily agnosia – or even diplopia – was fully in play. Simon saw himself as taller than everyone around him, smoother, and like some chimp who has fallen to earth – unutterably beautiful.

'It has occurred to me,' Zack Busner signed one evening to Peter Wiltshire, with whom at last he had managed to arrange a proper grooming session, 'that this "gru-nnn" acute impression Dykes has of inhabiting a human body might be some sort of phantom evolutionary memory. After all, if the chimpanzee foetus undergoes a series of morphological changes that parallel phylogenesis, then why not the psyche "huuu"?'

'It's an interesting notion, Zack. D'you "huuu" mind – ?' Wiltshire gestured in the direction of the drinks cabinet.

'Of course, of course . . .' Busner took the glass and swaggered across the room, his fulsome scrotum jiggling. Wiltshire got down from his chair and joined him, cradling his old ally's balls gently with one hand while Busner poured them both a generous measure of Laphroaig and added water.

'But what do you intend to do with Dykes now, Zack "huuu"? Will this particular psycho-physical approach go on indefinitely? And if so what do you expect to find out "huu"? Surely not just neurological data, because if that's what you wanted there's really no need for all of this . . . I don't know how to be tactful about it . . . but this chopping of the air –' Wiltshire signed, chopping the air to illustrate the point.

'I know, I know. I'm not convinced that there is anything to find out necessarily, it's just that the more time that I spend with him, the more interesting and unusual perspectives on chimpunity he throws up.'

'And what of *his* feelings, Zack? "Huuu" what about his infants – he must want to see them "huuu"? And his consort?'

Busner took a long pull on his drink, and let the brackish douche sluice around his teeth before countersigning, 'Yes, what of them, that is a problem. If it's a true psychosis then contact with his offspring isn't going to help matters at all – might even impede any progress. But if it's an organic problem –'

'You should let him go –'

'But go where "huuu"? Into a long-term institution? You forget, Peter, this is a gifted chimp, someone worth saving. Let me put my finger on it for you, either we have to help him to recover his submerged – but still present – sense of his own chimpunity, or else we have to make it possible for him to adjust to the world, despite perceiving it through the lens of this perverse delusion.'

'And how do you propose to do that "huuu"?'

'"Hoo", the usual way. The same as I would with any of my Touretics or more conventional agnosic patients. I'm going to take him on tour. But, whereas in the past I have had to get my patients to learn to cope with social, emotional and physical situations anew, in Dykes's case I'm going to have to assist him at more profound levels –' Busner broke off. Frances, a sub-adult female, had entered the drawing room carrying a tray of fruit.

"Grnn'yum," she vocalised, then signed, 'Mother thought you and Dr Wiltshire might need something to chew on, Alpha – where shall I put this "huuu"?'

'Pop it down here on the floor, my dear, then Peter and I can both get our toes on it.'

Frances set the tray on the carpet, then went over to where her alpha was squatting. Busner put an affectionate paternal hand on her lower belly and began gently to part the fur around her vagina, so that he could slide a couple of digits into her cleft. Peter Wiltshire thought how tender and affecting the scene was – his old ally had certainly mellowed. Busner gestured from within his daughter's crotch, so that the young female groaned and giggled, 'The first stop will be Oxford. I thought

I'd take Dykes to see Grebe, the philosopher, and possibly out to visit Hamble in Eynsham.'

' "Huuu"? Hamble – are you sure that's a good idea?'

'Why not, he's a naturalist, an ethologist and an historian. If I'm to give Dykes as much of an insight into the interface between his delusion and reality, he must have some knowledge of all these things –'

' "H'h'h'hoooo"! Alphy, it tickles!' Frances fingered.

Busner looked down at his agitated hand. 'Sorry my dear, quite forgot what I was signing on – you can go now "chup-chuppchupp".' He released the sub-adult and she knuckle-walked out, closing the door carefully behind her scut.

At the same time, in Chelsea, in a restaurant near the bottom of Tite Street, the three chimpanzees who were conspiring to bring about Busner's fall were meeting for first dinner. Phillips, the Cryborg chimp, had suggestured the venue – 'It's a nice little place. They've got a tree in the middle of the dining room, so if anyone feels like a clamber between courses they can just swing themselves up' – and he was waiting for Whatley and Gambol when they arrived.

There was something of a kerfuffle while a provisional hierarchy was established, Gambol presenting in a blur to both senior chimps, his arse poking first one way and then the other. Phillips half presented to Whatley – and Whatley did the same. Then all three settled down to a preliminary, huddled groom.

'So "chup-chupp",' Phillips signed after some minutes, 'what news have we of the esteemed natural philosopher and his latest patient "huuu"?'

'Well,' Gambol countersigned 'he's taken Dykes back to his group home in Hampstead, and they're studying together –'

'Studying "huu"?'

'That's right "clak-clak", Busner seems to feel that he can

educate Dykes out of the delusion. If he learns as much as possible about anthropology, he can relearn his chimpunity, or at any rate achieve a functional state.'

'It looks like an absurd idea – "chup-chupp" that's good "clak", just there – to me. I've heard of all sorts of atrophied, or even destroyed organic functions being relearnt, but an individual's basic chimpunity – that's simply bizarre.'

Whatley leant into Phillips at this point and commenced signing with great seriousness. 'That's as "chup-chupp" may be, Phillips, but if you – as Gambol and I have – had seen Dykes you would understand. The delusion is amazingly sustained, it's furniture firmly in place. But demarcate for me, Phillips "chup-chupp", what it is that you know about all of this "huuu"? Gambol has shown me the material relating to Inclusion. Is it really true that Busner was involved in an illegal trial of a new anxiolytic compound "huu"?'

'"Hoo" yes, yes indeed. He most certainly *was* involved in it. And there's something else, you see, something Busner himself may be unaware of.'

'And what's that "huuu" – ?'

'Excuse me,' a waiter flicked at them, 'are you gentlechimps ready to order just yet "huuu"?' Gambol held up three fingers and the waiter knuckle-walked away, swung himself round the ornamental tree and headed off to the kitchen.

'The pigeon looks tasty,' Gambol signed. 'Have either of your rear-end magnificences made a decision "huuu"?'

'Oh shut up, Gambol "wraff"!' Whatley administered a smack to Gambol, and Phillips did so as well, so that the poor epsilon chimp's head oscillated, cartoon-like, between their heavy hands. 'Let Phillips finish what he was going to sign – can't you. Phillips "huuu"?'

'Well, as I was signing, before being so rudely grasped, Busner was engaged by Cryborg to manage a double-blind trial of this compound Inclusion. A corruptible GP was found in the region of Thame, Oxfordshire, who would be prepared to administer both compound and placebo to numbers of his patients diagnosed with clinical depressions – or at any rate depressions that might be amenable to psychopharmacology –'

'What-what was the name of this GP "huu"?' Whatley's fingers almost plaited with Phillips's as he chopped in. Gambol was also standing on his chair, arms out, horripilating, teeth bared.

' "HoooGra" his name? Well, there's a thing, the name of this little country doctor, who was prepared to place his own advantage beyond that of his patients, was Dr Anthony Bohm.'

' "H'hoooo" well, I'll be buggered – Bohm, you sign.' Whatley slumped back down in his chair and began picking at the linen tablecloth in a distracted way, as if it were animate and in need of grooming. 'Well, this does put an odd complexion on things. Do you mean to sign that Dykes may be a victim of this compound Inclusion "huu"? I mean – what were the results of the trial? What's happened to the "huuu" drug?'

But the waiter had reappeared by now, and Phillips took his time, asked what specials were on offer, gave pointers as to how his cut of meat should be prepared, and then spent some minutes passing feet and hands over the wine list before he could be persuaded to make a decision. Eventually he turned back to his companions, whose avidity was unblunted. 'The drug "grnnn" has been withdrawn from any kind of testing – illegal or otherwise. Busner's trial did go perfectly well for a number of months, and without the results even being calibrated it was clear that the drug was having the desired effects. But then, one of the patients being unknowingly prescribed Inclusion, had a flamboyant mental breakdown.'

'Was it "huuu" Dykes, Your Anal Eminence?'

'Yes, Gambol, it was.'

The three chimps sat motionless for a moment, identical strings of drool looping from all three open mouths. The waiter reappeared, bipedal, walking backwards between the tables, their starters cradled between his shoulder blades.

He set two bowls of soup and a plate of pâté down on the table, then without so much as a frontwards glance, signed 'Bon appetit!' and knuckle-walked off. Whatley disentangled his watch chain from his neck fur with one foot, picked up his spoon with the other, and then gestured what all three were thinking: 'Does Dykes know any of this "huu"?'

' "Hoo" no, I don't think so. I mean, Dykes would hardly put himself in Busner's care if he knew that this was the psychiatrist who had irresponsibly precipitated him into a bad, psychotic interlude – now would he "huuu"? More interesting though, is the possibility that Inclusion is in some way responsible for Dykes's current delusory state.'

'Yes, yes, that is an interesting speculation – although perhaps ultimately unknowable. I reverence your bum bits, Dr Phillips, I revere your perspicacity, but highlight for me, why is it "grnnn" that you're prepared to point out all of this to Gambol and myself – what is your "huuu" motivation?'

'That, Dr Whatley, is a relatively simple question to answer. I've given the best years of my life to Cryborg Pharmaceuticals – nearly fifteen of them in all. Last year I was diagnosed with a terminal illness – I won't trouble you with the details. The Personnel Department has informed me that I am not eligible for either the company medical plan, nor my full pension, unless I manage to keep working for another year. This, I'm afraid, will not be possible. I "waaaa"! gave everything to Cryborg – now I'd like to take away as much as possible with me when I leave.

'As for Busner, well, I've nothing personal against him, but I find his latest reincarnation as psychic pundit nothing short of nauseating, given the zig-zag progress of his career, his showchimpship, his posturing. For me he is the absolute incarnation of hypocrisy, of hubris. The idea that he is currently being groomed for a position in the pantheon of great apes is fist-clenching. I have resolved to bring Cryborg down – if Busner is torn from the tree as well, then so be it. I won't "h'hooo" whimper about it.'

Whatley and Gambol stared at the impassioned dying research chemist for some time in signlence and novocal. Then Gambol, tentatively, asked him if he would like the salt.

Simon Dykes and Zack Busner were squatting in their shared study, perusing a copy of the *Essay of the Learned Martin Scriblerus, Concerning the Origin of Sciences*. This, one of the earliest satires to use the human as a 'motionless philosopher', was composed in all probability by Pope and Arbuthnot – among others. Drawing heavily on Tyson's work of comparative anatomy, the *Essay* was the precursor of the grand line of eighteenth-century satires, pitting evolved humans against primitive apes. A line that culminated in Swift's Yahoos.

Anti-psychiatrist and patient read in signlence and novocal, their mutual concentration broken only by the occasional rasp of horny fingertip against ischial pleat, the occasional grunt and attendant belch.

Busner was enjoying the research. He had never imagined the relationship between the chimpanzee and the human to have so many submerged implications. Western civilization, it was true, had projected itself towards divinity on the up-escalator of the Chain of Being. And, like Disraeli, everyone had wanted to be on the side of the angels. For white-muzzled chimpanzees to be approaching perfection, bogeychimps were needed, distressed versions of the other. It was easy to see how the bonobo, with its disturbing grace and upright gait, had fulfilled this role; but Busner now realised that in the shadow of the bonobo was a more unsettling, more bestial 'other' – the human.

Busner's seeming-human broke in on his thoughts at just this juncture: "H'hooo!" he vocalised, then signed 'Dr Busner, I want to see my infants now – really, I want to see them. I miss them "u-h'-u-h'" so much. Can't I – can't I see them, please "huuu"?'

Busner looked up at his patient. Simon's brown, bouffant head fur was lank, sweat-smeared – as usual – on his eyebrow ridge. His protuberant, grey-green eyes were dulled and unfocused. It was only when gesticulating those matters related to the content of his delusion that Simon achieved anything like full affect. For the rest of the time he was torpid, yet easily moved to weird and irrational outbursts.

Busner got up on the desk and stretched an arm out to grasp Simon by the shoulder. He now knew certain ways of touching his patient that produced the desired results. Simon had to be braced before his fur could be directly signed into, otherwise he complained about ticklishness, or even lashed out. Busner vocalised, "Chup-chupp," and inparted the matted dampness, 'Simon, I appreciate your feelings, but you have to consider theirs as well.'

'Meaning "euch-euch" what, "huu" exactly?'

'Meaning that it might not be such a good idea for them to see you in this state – to see what you demarcate of your inner life.'

'About being human, you mean "huu"?'

'That's "chup-chupp" right, my little patient.'

'If I'm your little patient I'm "euch-euch" mad, right?'

'I never signed that Simon, I don't like to gesture in such terms.'

'I want my world back. I want my "hoooo" smooth body back. I want my infants' bodies back. I want them "hoooo"!'

Busner, still grasping Simon's arm, came right across the desk. He knew exactly when the mounting rhythm of Simon's hysteria was about to twist into the parabola of abandon. The important thing was to contain him – as one might an autistic infant. Only using the full language of the body could any gesticulation really be achieved. "Huh-huh-huh," Busner soothed and then inparted the chimp's lower back, 'Do you miss them, Simon "huuu"?'

' "Er-herr-er" you know I do! I want to see them all, Henry, little Magnus *and* Simon –'

'But Simon "chup-chupp", had you considered "huuu" what they might be like?'

'What do you mean "huuu"?'

'Well, they'll look like chimpanzees to you – do you think you could stand that? Your children looking like *animals*. What if you were to react to them the way you do to other chimps "huuu"?'

Simon relaxed in the older chimp's arms. He sniffed in the odour of Busner, its lanate tang oddly comforting. He pictured his infants again, but concretely this time, not simply as outgrowths of his own misery, but as they would appear fixed, fixated, imprisoned behind the plastic sides of a photographic cube, on a coffee-table at their mother's house. Could he stand it? To see instead of blond heads, brown fur? To see sharp canines in place of crumbling milk teeth? To hear the squeak, chirrup, growl and jabber of infant apes, rather than the piping chatter he remembered?

But perhaps, Simon thought, feeling Busner's fingers soothe his back fur this way and that. Perhaps this vision of the boys I'm holding on to is not sanity, not memory, but the absolute keystone of my breakdown. Yank it out and sanity would reerect itself, like a film of a demolition played backwards. 'No,' he signed into Busner's thick scruff, 'no, I have to see them – will you try to arrange it with my ex-alpha – she'll watch what you sign. Please "huuu"?'

Sarah Peasenhulme was absolutely doing her best to remember Simon, and to arrange to see him, but the sad fact of the matter was that her memories of him were already becoming indistinct and blurred. In the days immediately following the artist's breakdown her recollections of his digging, coked-up penetrations of her were fresh and unsullied. She was still tangled up in his belly fur, blazoned with his nest gestures. But since the reassuring covering by Ken Braithwaite, Simon's body was wavering in her memory, and mirage-like dissolving.

Since seeing him for herself and witnessing his madness, psychosis, delusion – whatever it was – persist, Sarah had begun to lose faith that he would return, come back to her.

Confronted with the madchimp in the hospital, his scattered fingering, his nonsensical screeching, had run back into her recollections of the Simon she had known. Hadn't he always been scattered? And much of what he signed also nonsensical. He might have been the fastest lover she had ever had, but perhaps his speed was a little pimp-like, a little controlling, a little inchimp.

Sarah had had hopes. Simon was still young – barely thirty. He was successful. He earned some money. Was it too much to imagine that he might have begun another group with her? On the one hand the thought of having an infant's greedy little fingers twined in her fur, an infant's ravenous mouth pulling on her nipple, was awful, stultifying, disempowering. But on the other hand there was the lure of fixity, of status, of the way that having infants made it impossible to wish you were anyone other than who you were. Made your life determined – rather than contingent. There was that – and the good, solid mating you got when there were at least four healthy males sharing your nest.

So Sarah went back to work. Went back to flipping through portfolios with her toes, while tossing slides on to the light box with her hands. She shuffled the imagery of the artists she represented, and in so doing attempted to cut the pack, placing Simon's joker countenance near the bottom.

Nights she still found herself knuckle-walking from her office in Woburn Square, into Soho, in order to meet the glossy happy chimps at the Sealink for drinks and drugs and fulfilling hugs.

In the week immediately following the opening of Simon Dykes' show at the Levinson Gallery there had been a certain amount of kerfuffle. Fiddle columnists pant-hooting at work and home. On a couple of occasions Sarah had even been doorknuckled – but this died down as well. From time to time, at the club, or elsewhere, Sarah turned abruptly, conscious of someone signing behind her back, and saw fingers flick the

276

fact that there was that artist's ex-consort. But she wouldn't – or couldn't – let it bother her.

One evening, about a week after Simon had left the hospital, Sarah met Tony Figes for a drink at the club. Figes was – along with the Reverend Peter Davis – the mainstay of Sarah's emotional life. A cross between counsellor and helpmeet. When in gesticulation with him Sarah forgot about her swelling, forgot about her oestrus, forgot about the pink, penile spillikins that lingered in the pressed fur around the bar.

Tony had brought with him the cardboard tube he'd taken from Simon's flat. As he came in the swing doors to the bar area, he banged against one of the walls with the thing, producing a "thwok-thwok-thwok" noise. "HoooGraa!" Tony pant-hooted and scampered across to where Sarah squatted, a bundle of blonde fur and black satin.

"HoooGraa!" she backbarked – then signed, 'What's that, Tony, something you're working on "huuu"?'

'Not exactly, my dear, come down to the car-deck room where we can have some privacy and I'll show you.'

'Have you got a Bactrian on you "huu"?' Sarah asked as soon as they were squatting in the downstairs room.

'Here,' Tony proffered the familiar pack, 'I'm afraid they're Lights.'

'No matter,' Sarah countersigned, sparking the cigarette, 'nowadays I like to keep things light.'

'Sarah.' Tony eased out the sheaf of drawings. 'I found these at Simon's place when I went to get his things. They're by no means light – in fact they're distinctly heavy.'

Sarah took the loose bundle of thick art paper from Tony's outstretched foot, and began to sort her way through them with practised, professional ease. She registered what the subject of the drawings was, examined the quality of line, the use of shading. She judged them as she might the work of an artist unknown to her, blocking out the instant emotional charge she had aways received when looking at her former consort's work.

When she'd worked her way through all of them, she laid the drawings down on the carpet and stubbed out her Bactrian. '"Hooo" well, they certainly *aren't* light. Do you think Dr Busner should be shown about this "huuu"?'

'I don't know –'

'Clearly this "hooo" delusion of Simon's was more deepseated than we – or he – realised.'

'It looks that way. Simon was obsessing about humans for longer than we knew. What do you imagine the human represents for him, Sarah "huuu"?'

'I dunno. What it represents for the rest of us, I suppose, the dark side of our nature as chimpanzees "huu"? To be watered down by making the human a cute accessory, or expelled by making the human a brute, terrifying animal "huu"?'

'But in these drawings the humans are inhabiting *our* world, aren't they "huuu"?'

Sarah sighed heavily, levered herself up from her chair and swaggered over to the fake window. She leant her head against the pane, and felt pain. She remembered the last night she had been in this room – the night of Simon's breakdown. She remembered the rasp of cocaine in her nostrils, and the rasp of his cock as he had taken her, pressing her head into the corner.

She turned to muzzle Tony. 'Well, Tony "u'h-u'h-u'h" I think Simon was fucked up. Pure and simple. Fucked up. He was fucked up about mating. He used to sign that he'd lost his suspension of disbelief – in mating. That he could no longer *believe* in mating. He could "hoo" see the boom microphone pushing into the corner of the frame, like a bill dipping for intimate vocalisations. He could see the camerachimp leaping around behind the lights, trying to get us in hard focus. He could "hoo" –'

'"Gru-nnn" Sarah, my dear, calm yourself.'

Tony knuckle-walked over to her, took her in his skinny arms. Held her. She nuzzled her muzzle into his scruff. There was signlence for a while, and just the quiet lip-smacking of old allies in touch with one another. Then Tony inparted Sarah's back, 'I think you should keep these drawings, Sarah "chup-chupp". You see, I don't think Simon is going to be coming back to us. And –'

'And what "huuu"?'

'And you should have something to remember him by. Something of worth to you, and' – the gay – in denotion only – chimp, pulled away from her, Sarah could see the scar writhing in his chin fur – 'of potential worth to many others. Sarah, these may be the last drawings that Simon ever does. If he was still in his right mind I'm sure he would want you to have them, to make use of them as you see fit.'

At last Sarah grasped Figes's fingering. He wanted her to use Simon's drawings of distressed humans wandering a destructing cityscape as some kind of nest egg. To set herself up. To free herself. But while she kissed Tony warmly on his nasal bridge, she could only envision what the drawings might look like haloed with cold fire, for all she could visualise doing was burning the things.

Zack Busner pant-hooted Jean Dykes from the 'phone in the hall. Simon was in his sedated slough upstairs, but Busner didn't want to take the chance of the artist waking, coming on him unawares, seeing what was being gesticulated with his ex-alpha. "HoooGra'," he vocalised and drummed on the 'phone table, 'Mrs Dykes, I'm Dr Zack Busner, I believe George Levinson may have signalled my involvement with your ex-alpha "huu"?'

'Yes, George has, Dr Busner, how may I help you "huuu"?'

'It's about your infants, Mrs Dykes, sign me, has Simon had much involvement with them since you fissioned?'

Jean Dykes took her time in countersigning. So long, in fact, that Busner almost repeated the question. He had time to study the artist's former alpha, and even to grasp at elements of their life together, from what he could make out on the screen. Could this dowdy, weightily serious female have been closely involved with Dykes, have nurtured infants with such a volatile, irreverent chimp? Judging by the worn beads of the rosary, which poked out from her signing fingers like subsidiary knuckles, this was a female who took belief seriously.

Eventually she deigned to countersign, 'Dr Busner. In our society males have – as you know – very little to do with their offspring. The so-called mating revolution of the sixties may have made it possible for males to indulge in more and more unsuitable copulations, but it hardly seems to have affected their sense of responsibility. Simon, however, has always been an attentive alpha, and he has made an effort to keep in touch with Henry and Magnus.'

'And Simon "huuu"?'

'Simon "huuu"?'

'The middle infant – Simon. I suppose I should sign Simon junior.'

'Dr Busner "hooo", there is no Simon junior. There were only two infants in our natal group. Only two.'

Busner took a while to absorb this new information. Here was another peculiar twist to Dykes's delusion, another kink in already warped reality. Eventually his fingers stirred. 'Mrs Dykes, I realise this must be distressing for you – but have you any idea why Simon might think that he has three male infants, rather than two "huuu"?'

'Dr Busner.' The fogeyish female pressed the hank of beads to her forehead. 'I don't "euch-euch" have a great deal of respect for your profession. If you are a soul doctor – you would do well to doctor my ex-principal's soul, rather than heading down the blind alleys of his psyche.'

'By which you "huuu" mean?'

'I mean precisely this, that I'm not "euch-euch" really entwined by such digitations.'

The eminent natural philosopher – as he liked to style himself – took his time absorbing this rebuff. He picked abstractedly at some egg in the fur of his lower abdomen and stared out through the front door to where, in a patch of sunlight, two infants were mock-mating. So, Dykes's delusory state was still more ramified than he had suspected. What conceivable organic dysfunction could account for such a quirk? All diseases – organic, or psychic – could be ebullient and productive; this Busner believed. But productive of an infant that didn't really exist? Preposterous.

'"Gru-nnnn" Mrs Dykes, I had thought I would be pant-hooting you to manipulate the possibility of Simon seeing the infants –'

'"Hoo", really "huuu"?'

'That's right – although in most cases it's not a good idea for psychotics to have contact with those to whom they have close emotional ties.'

'I would have no objection to Simon getting in touch with Magnus and Henry – if that's what he wants.'

'That's very "gru-nnn" good of you, Mrs Dykes, but I don't really think it's a good idea at present, given this new development. If you'll allow me to point out any improvement in his condition, for the moment we'll leave things as they are.'

'As you wish, Dr Busner. "HoooGraa".'

'"HoooGraa."

Some hours later when Simon awoke, levered himself from nest, tripped upright to the study and found the soul doctor absorbed in his reading, he was muzzled with another gross singularity, another warp in the world. Busner looked up from his copy of *Melincourt*. "Gru-nnn," he vocalised, then signed, 'Simon, I trust you feel refreshed after your rest. I've been absorbed by the progress of your cousin Sir Oran Haut-ton. In Peacock's novel he is tutored by a Mr Forrester, who believes that all great apes, including humans, are part of the chimpanzee family. Not something I'd agree with myself "grnnn".'

Simon paid little attention to these amicable gestures. He presented to Busner – as he had learnt to do – pushing his scraggy arse in the general direction of the old ape; and when he had received a reassuring pat, reared up so that he could place his signs right in the shrink's flabby muzzle. 'Did you gesticulate with Jean – my ex "huuu"?'

'Yes, Simon, I did.'

'And "huu"?'

'Simon "grnnn", what I have to point out may upset you –'

'She won't let me see them "huu"?'

'No, Simon – it's not that. Simon –' Busner dropped off his chair and knuckle-walked to where the sad, mad chimp squatted. 'Jean showed me that you only have two male infants – not three, two.'

' "Hooo" really "huuu"? And which two are left to me, then "hooo"?' Sarcasm welled from each of these vocalisations – Busner chose to ignore it.

'Simon, there is no Simon junior. Do you understand what I'm signing "huuu"?'

'Yes, yes, perfectly – you're simply wiping out all of those memories, the bloody push-me pull-you of birth, the first embrace, the first this, the first that; and not forgetting a personality. This isn't *nothing* you're gesticulating about "euch-euch"! This isn't *nothing*! It's a fucking "boy", that's what. A real, human "boy"!'

With these last, guttural vocalisations – a reversion to the earliest days after his breakdown – the former artist slumped to the floor, rolled into a foetal pod, and commenced spraying. It was all Zack Busner could do to get a tourniquet on, shoot the solution home, haul the bag of misery back to its room, put it to nest.

In drugged repose Simon Dykes revelled in a transposed world. A marvellous realm inhabited by beautiful, courtly beings, their smooth bodies clad in weightless white shifts. A giant space, a hall of some kind, the walls of transparent rock worked into soaring arches and buttresses, the floor a grassy undulation. Around the pleasure dome the beings moved slowly and diffidently, with such natural grace. Their hands remained side-swaying, or if they sat, loosely folded in their laps, fingers as still as those of stone effigies, awaiting the apocalypse in quiet country churches. And when they parted their red red lips, mellifluous, sonorous, beautifully intelligible vocalisations emerged and soared up into the luminous vaulting.

Simon wandered among these aliens, not feeling the need to touch or be touched. As with so many dreams since the fateful night when chimpunity overwhelmed him, Simon was disconcertingly lucid in this measured gavotte of anthropoid forms. Is this what I've left behind? he wondered, as they floated past. Is this what I thought was Simon – little Simon "huuu"?' He identified the lost infant as himself – or to be more precise his lost body. He saw his infant's body, standing, shivering, naked of its protective coat. Little Simon, as gracile as a young bonobo; head fur blond and cropped at the back, features refined and serious, tiny cock and balls like the stamen of some superior orchid. Simon turned towards the lost infant, wafted across the grassy floor to get him. But as he drew nearer the infant's blue eyes widened, and his red red lips parted, and the sapling body bent in an afflatus of anguish. Then Simon heard the awful, meaningful vocalisations; so guttural – but so just "Get away! Get away, Beelzebub! Foul beast! Ape man!"

Simon Dykes awoke, in nest, in his psychiatrist's Hampstead home, screaming his way into his second month of chimpunity.

Chapter Sixteen

Despite this regression, Zack Busner didn't waver in his determination to, as he put it, take Simon on tour. 'It may look absurd to you, my dear old bum hole,' he inparted Charlotte's scrag as the two of them lay in nest, along with five others, 'but "clak-clak" Grebe is the ideal chimp to have a gesticulation with Simon about the philosophic ramifications of his delusion "chup-chupp".'

' "Huh-huh-huh" and why's that, dear "huu"?'

'Because the young fart's a coprophiliac – that's why. Simon's spraying won't put him off in the least "h'h'hee-heehee"!'

Busner was so invigorated by this slapstick image that he leapt from the nest, grabbed a handhold, swung to the door and disappeared in the direction of the bathroom still cackling.

Autumn had come to London, stripping the leaves from the trees with damp, chilly fingers. In the mornings Redington Road flowed with white rivulets of ground mist and the tarmac gleamed, dark and wet. With the sudden leaf fall, the bodies of chimpanzees out for matitudinal brachiation were now visible, browner blobs outlined against the greyer skies. In the sharp air the pant-hooting of chimps in the environs of Hampstead sounded far louder, and the copulation screams of natal groups indulging in a round of mating before work were clearly audible above the background hubbub of the city.

At the Busner home, however, things were quieter. Charlotte and Cressida's oestruses were long since over and although Antonia and Louise – respectively gamma and zeta – had come on, their swellings were never as impressive, and the numbers of suitors they attracted correspondingly fewer. From time to time, Busner would come upon a forlorn male specimen, romping up and down the drive, or banging on the gate, his penis and fur erect. But these were second-rate scut-chasers, dismissible by the Busner females with a mere wave of a dishcloth, or spurt of furniture polish.

Many of the sub-adults had drifted off, either to work or to university. The infants were back at school – save for afternoon patrolling expeditions. Some days Zack Busner and his strange patient were the only adult males in the house, remaining in tight reclusion, ministered to by a scuttling, squeaking, but mostly invisible group of females.

Zack Busner finished his toilet with a quick check of his rear end in the mirror, and went to see how his patient was preparing for his longest outing to date. He found Simon Dykes lying in nest, undressed, the television screen flickering in the darkened room. The smell of rank, distressed adult male chimp was quite overpowering – even for Busner. He knuckle-walked in quietly and propped himself on the edge of the nest. Simon had frozen the video he was watching so that a single frame stretched and twanged on the screen.

It was, Busner infurred, a frame from *Planet of the Humans*. He had watched all four films in the science fiction series with Simon already, observing the chimp's reaction to this inverted world, that must by rights conform to his fantastic recollections. But they'd hardly made any impression. Simon signed only that the make-up used to create the 'humans' was risibly inauthentic. 'Humans have mobile, "euch-euch" expressive muzzles – these travesties are stiff and rigid, you can see where they've used a prosthesis. And anyway, as I keep "euch-euch" pointing out to you, Dr Busner – humans gesticulate with their voices, not their hands. Why wasn't the writer of this beta feature more imaginative "huuu"?'

Simon was also, naturally, discomfited by the fact that the humans in the film weren't exclusive rulers of the planet, joint suzerainty being granted to orang-utans and gorillas. He was grateful that the humans were pacifists and intellectuals, but Roddy McDowell's portrayal of the human scientist Cornelius infuriated Simon. '"Euch-euch" he's ridiculous, the way he struts about like that, as if he were being dangled from a wire! Why "wraaa" didn't he take the trouble to observe some real humans so he'd get the bipedal swagger right.'

Perversely, Simon had far more sympathy for the three chimpanzee astronauts, whose ill-fated interstellar mission brings them after three thousand light years, to the distant future of earth itself. He particularly admired Charlton Heston's performance. Something chimed between his character Taylor's world-weary, embittered attitude and Simon's fervid despair. 'I have to delineate this though,' he signed to Busner as they sat watching Heston fingering. 'In my world Charlton Heston was the very acme of smooth-chested virility. The idea that this shaggy thing and he are one and the same is . . . is . . . "clak-clak-clak" preposterous!'

It was Heston's firm features that were now smeared across the screen, the top of his head flapping as if he were mutating to a steady beat. The frozen scene came from early on in the film, just after the astronauts have crash-landed, and are struggling to accept that 'Haslein's Hypothesis' means they are now two thousand years in the future. Taylor confronts his more idealistic, more emotional companion, Landon, signing, 'It's a fact, "euch-euch" accept it – you'll sleep better.'

It was the last sign, the 'better' that Heston's splayed fingers were forming. Busner stared at the fiddled comparative for some minutes, while musing on what the day's outing would bring. Then he leant back and inparted Simon's leg fur, '"Gru-nnn" good morning, Simon, are you ready for your "huuu" outing?'

Simon stirred and propped himself up on his elbow. Busner noted – as ever – the apparent atrophy of the chimp's lower limbs. His toes didn't flex, so he was unable to sign with them; perhaps Grebe would have something interesting to impart on this when they saw him. ' "HoooGra'" Good morning, Dr Busner. I'm sorry. I was just dozing. I don't know about this outing – I'm, I'm feeling a bit like Landon there –'

' "Grnnn" really? In what way "huuu"?'

' "Hoo" two thousand light years from home, I suppose. Yes, that about sums it up.'

Busner wasn't about to allow his patient to fall into some perverse reverie, some finial fugue atop the mansion of his delusion. He gave Simon a quick clip round the ear, and when the chimp began to whimper and keen, Busner was able to take him in his arms, give him a proper groom and a firm fingering. 'Now "chup-chupp" poor Simonkins, I'm "chup-chupp" only admonishing you for your own good. I believe – in all sincerity – that it's only by getting out, and finding out more about the nature of your own chimpunity that you will be able to recover. You're like anyone else who's had brain damage – if you properly encourage them, new neural pathways will replace the functions of those that have been destroyed.'

Simon obliterated this and pressed on. 'But who is this chimp we're going to see "huuu"?'

'David Grebe is a fascinating chimp. He's a bit of an allrounder. His main range is semiotic philosophy, so I thought it would be interesting for the two of you to gesticulate about your notions concerning human signage – this thing "speech". But more than that, I'm sure Grebe is the right chimp to pull together certain strands of thought, form – as it were – a hank.

'Then.' Busner got up from the nest and began to revolve around the room upright. 'We'll have a bit of light relief. I'd like to go out to Fynsham and visit Hamble.'

' "Huuu" Hamble the naturalist?'

'That's right.'

'I've read his books – they're very good. Very funny.'

'Yes, yes. Well, as you'll be aware, Hamble has encountered humans in the wild. He's also more knowledgeable about more aspects of the natural world than anyone I know. I'm sure you'll find it interesting gesticulating with him – he's rather eccentric.'

Busner decided against driving up to Oxford. For one thing Gambol was unavailable. He was spending less and less time around the Busner group home. He had indicated to Busner that there was some outstanding work to be done on a longitudinal study they had initiated the preceding year; and without bothering to check with him exactly what this might be – and such was the pace of Busnerian innovation, it could be anything from compulsive brachiating to nest wetting – Busner had given him a leave of absence.

And Busner himself didn't like driving. Once, when his first batch of infants was still young, he had even gone so far as to buy an automatic car, claiming that the constant shifting of gears interfered with his thought patterns. He always preferred to travel by train, and on this occasion it was advisable to get Simon into the world a bit more. He might become distressed, but Busner would bring the sedatives. He felt quite able to handle Simon – if that's what it took.

They left on feet and hands. 'We'll knuckle-walk down to Baker Street and get a cab – if that's all right with you "huuu"?' Busner waved as they quit the house. Simon acquiesced with a grunt, but the truth was the prospect of the knuckle-walk appealed strongly. He swaggered upright for a few steps, then without giving the posture any thought, dropped down on his knuckles. With his therapist's nonexistent buttocks, and marvellously refulgent anal scrag on a direct eye line, Simon took up the rear and the patrol commenced.

The first halt occurred when they reached the junction of Fitzjohn's Avenue and the Finchley Road at Swiss Cottage. It

288

was mid-morning by now, and the ground mist had cleared, but it was still going to be an undistinguished day. Here in the very crook of urbanity, where car on car seemed bent on coldly welding, the contrast between grainy buildings, grainy atmosphere and the scurrying grains of chimpunity was no contrast at all. Busner kept his muzzle to the pavement and went on, down towards the concrete packaging of the library-cum-swimming pool. He had gained the arboreal precinct that islanded this building – not unlike a petrified Rotadex in outward appearance, or some other piece of desk-top giganticism – when he sensed that the rear end of his patrol had become detached.

He looked back to see that Simon had halted by the entrance to the tube station. Busner hustled back. ' "HoooGra'" what's the problem, Simon "huuu"?'. Simon signed nothing, just reaching out a hand with one finger crooked in the direction of the dirty descending stairs, where some desultory mating activity was going on, and on, and on.

Busner understood, without the need for further pres-digitation, what the problem was. Simon had been isolated at the hospital, and apart from the short forays with Jane Bowen and the carefully circumscribed trip to the zoo, he'd barely been out. As a consequence he hadn't seen much mating activity at all. With his psychosis so bound up with matters bodily, it was unsurprising that he maintained his 'human world' to be a mating-free zone; or at any rate as somewhere where copulation took place mostly between two individuals, and – Busner thought this a particularly clever, and most artistic flourish – in the dark.

"H'h'hee-hee-hee!" Simon tittered, then signed, 'Look at this! I realise that you "euch-euch" chimps fuck like it was going out of style – but this!'

In fact there was nothing much to this particular round of mating. A middle-aged female – a bank worker judging by her plain grey jacket and plainer white blouse – had, Busner judged, come on that morning. She'd decided to advertise the fact by wearing a not unattractive swelling-protector, which now lay, a heap of pleats, some steps below where its owner bucked and yawped.

She must, Busner concluded, have accepted the first suitor when she reached the tube, and having presented her delicous pink bowl for an initial stirring, she was now receiving other cooks that had arrived at the kitchen. There was now a loose line of these males, all with erect, slimy cocks poking from their erect, slimy fur, ranging up the stairs. While further down on a half-landing, two males who had already coupled were licking and picking sperm and mucus from each other's groins.

'Actually, Simon,' Busner inparted Simon's leg fur, 'this is far from being a particularly libidinous spectacle – certainly by London standards. You wait until you see some of the mating chains there are in town when chimps get out from work and begin drinking. You may have a young female in full oestrus, trailing a line of twenty males as she scampers through a gauntlet of chimps who are lounging outside the pub.

'And if one of those males launches a successful suit on *another* female, while he's still importuning the first, you can get a cross chain of mating. I've seen the whole of Oxford Circus positively garlanded with these conga-lines of buggery. Sometimes the police have to cordon areas of the city off and give the rutting chimps there a dousing from a water cannon before they come to their senses. So, as you can see, this isn't much of a show. But one information sign, Simon –'

'"Huu" what's that?'

'Please be discreet when remarking upon mating practices. While it is in no sense taboo to observe, to comment can be regarded as distinctly rude "wraaa"! Watch out, Simon, that one's coming for us!'

It was true. The male who had just, with a hissed squeal, pulled himself from the oozing swelling of the bank worker was swaggering up the stairs towards them, horripilating and uttering a series of loud waa-barks. He was a big specimen, and the spectacle of his exposed canines, still encrusted with some wheaten breakfast food, and his exiguous tumescence, which metronomically beat from side to side, counterpointing his advance, would for Simon have been comic, were it not at the same time incredibly frightening.

Simon felt the fur at the nape of his neck stiffen and bristle – a sensation which he had never consciously experienced before. He too began to utter a series of aggressive barks, while drawing himself up to his full height. The angry male continued to mount the stairs, picking up handfuls of leaves, discarded tickets and other detritus as he came, and hurling these in the direction of the renowned anti-psychiatrist and his patient.

For a few, tumultuous moments it looked as if they would be able to intimidate the big male. But then the two other, post-coital males – who meanwhile had been leaping up and down, yammering, and slapping their attaché cases against the tile walls of the staircase – decided that they would like to get involved. With this shift in the odds, Busner decided it was time to leave. He grabbed Simon by the scruff. ' "Waaaa"! Come on, they'll be on us in a second!'

Simon behaved most peculiarly in response to this impulsion. Without waiting to be further galvanised, he dropped to his hands and moved away on all fours at speed – Busner followed on behind. As he gained the edge of the arboreal precinct, the former artist leapt for the lowest bough of the first plane tree, grabbed it, swung himself aloft, and continued, brachiating as a chimp to the canopy born.

Busner didn't have time to be taken aback by this; he could almost feel on the back of his neck the Ready Brek breath of the big chimp chasing him. He gained the tree some seconds after his protégé, and dragged himself painfully aloft, arthritis sparking in his fingers like neural electricity.

The pursuing chimps didn't even bother to ascend. Instead they halted at the base of the first tree, uttered some final, furious waa-barks, then disappeared back in the direction of the tube. Presumably, Busner thought, observing their pin-stripe-suited backs, off to work in some estate agency or insurance office.

It transpired that for Simon the whole episode had been a revelation of chimpunity. 'I just "chup-chupp" swarmed up into these trees. I didn't stop to think. It was astonishing the sense of fluidity, of ease – and of power. I haven't climbed a tree "h'h'h'hee-hee" since I was a sub-adult!' Simon's whole sense of embodiment was affected. He hung casually by one arm from an insecure bough, whilst prinking his therapist's lower belly fur.

Busner wondered – although not visibly – whether the transformation might be due to the rush of adrenalin Simon had experienced during the mock attack. That, and the fact that flight response would make use of the more primitive, more truly essential parts of his patient's brain. Confirmation came soon enough, for, as Simon's horripilation subsided, and his fur drooped to its accustomed lankness, he found himself unable to get down from the tree, or to continue above ground. He was also scared of falling. Busner had to disembark, go and find the janitor in the library, and return with him and a disabled chimps' ladder. Only then could Simon be coaxed down.

As they knuckle-walked on towards Regent's Park they encountered several more mating rounds, and each time Simon fell back to observe, although he didn't make the mistake again of wringing his hands over it. By the electronic gates of a large villa, an attractive young female with blonde head fur was dangling halfway out of a large black BMW. Her head thwacked the inside of the door and her copulation squeals were accompanied by the flashing of the headlights. Inside, artfully taking her from the driver's seat, was a wiry bonobo, his teeth tearing at the back of her dress.

By some garages recessed from the road, Simon paused to gawp while a tough-looking party of sub-adults, obviously down on patrol from somewhere up north, took a dark-muzzled female almost as big as they were, with quite blinding speed.

None of them needing more than fifteen seconds from the first screeching penetration, to the final tooth clack, pant and withdrawal.

When they reached the park, and plunged across the Outer Circle, they came through the fringe of trees and on to a broad expanse of grass where just the kind of conga-line of copulation Busner had described was in full swing. Busner, practised at disentangling such scenes, grasped at once what had happened; some culturally marauding phalanx of Benelux language students and attendant teachers had become mixed up with three distinct groups of patrolling cockney males. The resulting queues and counter-queues of displaying males and accepting – or rejecting – sub-adult females now formed interlocking and quite intricate arrangements of runtish buttocks and receptive swellings. The sub-adults had colonised the trees as well. From where Busner and Dykes squatted they could make out brown bodies swirling about in the branches, some even turning full circles while dangling by their arms, like gymnasts. The ragged symphony of vocalisations echoed over the park.

'Delineate for me more about all of this, Dr Busner – please.' Simon signed, his fingers tense, but his tempo even enough. He reached into the side pocket of his black jacket and pulled out a pack of unfiltered Bactrians, lit one and relaxed on to his haunches.

"Grnn," Busner grunted, then signed, 'Well, what you see here is the absolute core – some might point out – of chimpunity itself. Throughout the ages artists have depicted such mass matings. In the early Renaissance these reels of rutting would have been set amongst flora and fauna, framed by proscenium hills. Titian painted great aerial mating scenes, in which angelic chimps copulated amidst swirls and garlands of cloud –'

'But, Dr Busner, I don't understand it. Surely the connotation of such sexual practices is a fearful "uh-uh", unloving world, in which mating is anonymous and meaningless "huuu"?'

Busner regarded his patient quizzically, eyebrow ridges raised, bifocals lowered. Simon Dykes was, he thought, reaching towards an elegance of gesture. It made the artist peculiarly likeable. Busner nuzzled Simon's muzzle and inparted, 'Well, indicate for me once more what it's like in *your* world. Humans are, of course, monogamous "huuu"?'

'Well, no, not exactly. It's the prevailing cultural norm in most Western and Western-influenced societies, but elsewhere polyandry and polygamy are still practised –'

'I see. So do Western humans view such sexual arrangements as – in some sense – more primitive "huu"?

'That's right.'

Busner, observing the way the smoke from Simon's Bactrian curled and snagged in his neck fur, reflected wryly on the elegant reversals and mirrorings of this persistent delusion. Monogamy as an end rather than a beginning, a state of rarefied intimacy, rather than a crude, animal pairing. Which is, of course, what it was.

'But, Simon "gru-unnn", do all human consortships last a lifetime "huu"?

'By no means, no, no. Humans will bond with one another for all sorts of periods of time. There are unions that may last many years and consortships which are over in days or weeks.'

'And the organising principle of these couples remains "huh-huh" fidelity "huuu"? Exclusive mating rights?"

'Yes.'

'And is it adhered to "huu"?'

'Not exactly.'

"Huuu?"

'Well, obviously both males and females find themselves mating outside the relationship . . . it happens all the time.'

'And these exogamous matings – are they all intentional "huu"?'

Simon took another pull on the Bactrian, pinched the glowing tip between his calloused fingers and jettisoned it. 'I should "h'h'hee-hee" sign not. In many cases they're involuntary – driven even. The human impulse towards inconstancy seems as strong as the drive to consort.'

At this point a young female in full oestrus scampered past the two gesticulators. Her swelling – as big as a three-pint bowl – nearly coming into contact with Busner's muzzle. The great ape inhaled noisily, savouring the whiff of musk. 'Look at that!' he flourished. 'If we didn't have a train to catch I'd have a crack at her myself, she's delicious! Look at that pink flower dangling off her "h'hoooo"!

'But, Simon,' the eminent natural philosopher continued as they resumed their knuckle-walk, 'you sign of numerous consortships, and of consistent exogamous mating despite their existence. Mark me if I'm wrong, but it looks to me much the same as what chimpanzees get up to "huuu"?'

Simon looked at the grey testicles swinging in front of him, marking out procreative time like the pendulum of a biological clock. He had to admit it – the old ape did have a point.

Chapter Seventeen

Sniffing and snuffling, his muzzle pressed against the diamond-patterned mullions of his study, Dr David Grebe peered myopically down into the back quad of Exeter College. Cackfootedness made contact lenses a problem for Grebe; vanity – and a more than averagely deep recession in his nasal bridge – put spectacles out. Zack Busner and his latest pathological protégé should have been here by now – it was nearly time for third luncheon. Grebe hadn't bothered to make any particular arrangements for the repast – a restaurant reservation, whatever – and he had no image whether the ape man would be sufficiently held in Busner's captivity to be presentable in hall, let alone at high table.

He checked his watch again, pulling away the thick hanks of ankle fur that covered its face. Nearly one-thirty, where could they be? The Paddington train got in at five to one, surely they would have taken a cab from the station? Grebe scratched his ischial scrag meditatively. Would the ape man be worth it? That was the question. The notion of a delusion that played upon basic concepts of signage acquisition was – to a philosopher such as Grebe – an intriguing one. Busner had indicated on the 'phone that Simon Dykes was sensitive, intelligent and – despite his ataxia – elegantly gestural. If this was the case, Grebe might learn something.

Learning things was what Grebe craved. A bent little Welsh chimp in his early thirties, yet with only a few grey hairs fringing his bald pate, Grebe had bounded up the steep stairs and the wide treads of the university hierarchy, grabbing easefully the awkward handholds of influence. He had obtained his fellowship at Exeter not through the conventional methods of alliance and intrigue; nor by currying favour with a clique of graduate students and junior academics, but simply through his dogged capacity for absorbing more and more information – and then manipulating it into credible theories.

From where he now crouched, atop a twenty-shelf escarpment of a bookcase, he could turn and take in with one sweep of his eyes five other repositories of the Sign – each as geologic. Grebe's study, which occupied the body of an arch over the back gate to the college, also had ample room for four filing cabinets, two large work tables and an impressive computer system to boot. This was in addition to the usual Oxfordian clutter of occasional tables, over-stuffed tutorial armchairs, teetering piles of papers, journals and still more books.

For, while Grebe was an inveterate hoarder, holding fast to a single byte if he thought it might become useful, he was no anal retentive, amassing philosophical information with no regard for its dissemination. In fact and this explains why Zack Busner had chosen him as an interjector for his perverse patient – Grebe was a theoretician of great flair.

It was Grebe who first proposed that signing developed as a means of gesticulation for chimpanzees directly from the practice of grooming. Grooming, Grebe posited, while effective in the small groups chimpanzees must have originally lived in, when they – like humans – roamed the tropical zones of Central Africa, would have been insufficiently visible to allow for cohesion and progress in larger social units. Hence signing.

Hence also – and this explains why Grebe's name was known beyond the narrow precincts of academia – the magnificent efflorescence of the female chimpanzee's sexual swelling. However peculiar and repugnant it might seem to contemporary chimpunity, Grebe – in association with a primatologist colleague – firmly believed that the perineal regions of primitive female chimpanzees were in all probability small to the point of being discreet – not unlike those of modern human females.

By the same token, the human ability to generate as many as fifty different phonemes, and – it was believed – interpret them, must, Grebe had argued, be an example of how human neural development had become maladaptive. So much of the vast human brain capacity must be taken up with the business of interpreting these confusing sounds that there was no possibility of the 'Big Bang' that had occurred in pongid evolution.

Unlike the chimpanzee, whose signage competence had evolved over two million years of continuous selection, determined by brain–sign interaction, the human had become bogged down in a perverse and clamorous sound garden; its capacity for effective gesticulation as stunted and atrophied as its stunted and atrophied fingers and toes.

Such arguments placed Grebe firmly within the range of Noam Chomsky, and the other psychosemioticians who held that signage was a unique attribute of the chimpanzee's compact brain. Given the incredible plasticity of the primate brain, was it any wonder that a neural over-sufficiency resulted in natural selection being unable to work on cognitive capacities? Thus, the human's ability to process information and hence learn tasks was ironically circumscribed by a lack of circumscription. Put simply: the human was lost inside her own head. Unable to create an esemplastic mind; doomed for ever to obey the useless dictates of phyletic memory, and the ghastly gargles of her own purposelessly promiscuous vocalisations.

But Grebe wasn't fiddling with this as he stared down at the quad – noting the pert anal scrags of the undergraduates poking out from the hems of their commoners' gowns – he was palpating that part of himself that wanted the decanter, wanted it very badly.

The decanter sat on a small octagonal table positioned strategically by his favourite armchair. It never moved. When necessary Grebe, or Grebe's scout, would recharge it and check the seal on the stopper – but it was never ever moved. Was it too early in the day for a snifter? Grebe fumbled. Should I wait and see whether Busner and his ape man would like one? It would hardly be polite for them to arrive and find me already at it.

As is so often the way with habit Grebe's body made the decision for him. He arched backwards on the high bookcase, turned an inelegant – but not inefficient – back-flip, and landed on all fours right next to the table with its precious load. "Aaaaa'," the distinguished fellow cried out appreciatively. He unstoppered the decanter and gave its neck a judicious lip-curling sniff.

In point of fact Zack Busner and Simon Dykes were in plenty of time for the Oxford train. As they knuckle-walked up the platform at Paddington, alongside the hammering bulk of the engine, Simon looked up at the barrel vaulting of the Victorian station and signed to his doctor, 'Some things really don't change.'

'"Hoo", really "huuu"?'

'This station,' Simon gestured. 'It's got exactly the same light quality it always had, as if the entire structure were sunk beneath a dirty green sea – like the English Channel.'

Busner regarded his psychic ward with undisguised pleasure. It was the first metaphoric representation he could remember Dykes making and the first painterly remark. Could it imply some further slackening, or dilution of the delusory state?

The journey was uneventful. Busner bought first-class tickets, anticipating there would be fewer chimps and less stress for Simon. But in the event it was Busner himself who was discomfited. The constant tapping of horny fingertips on the keyboards of laptop computers; and the incessant yammer of businesschimps using mobile 'phones irritated him to such an extent that shortly before they reached Reading he was compelled to launch a display.

Busner grabbed an armful of the Intercity customer magazines from their wall-mounted dispenser, and charged up and down the aisle tossing them in the muzzles of his fellow passengers. For good measure he gave a couple of the more noisome individuals a smack on the head. Although this exhibition of dominance had the desired effect – novocal reigned for the rest of the journey – it was at the cost of a very English kind of frozen collective embarrassment. Just like Paddington Station, Simon realised, some things don't change. Ever.

Quitting the station at Oxford, Simon caught up with Busner, whose scut was moving purposefully towards the taxi rank, and presenting low signed, 'Would you mind if we knuckle-walked to this chimp's college "huuu"? You know I used to live outside Oxford, I'd like to see something of the town again.'

'That's all right Simonkins,' Busner replied, laying on reassuring hands 'but "gru-nnn" remember, try to give me some warning if you feel a panic attack coming on.'

Simon didn't feel anxious as they proceeded up past Worcester and along Bartholemew Street to St Giles, he felt something between amusement and disgust. His memory of Oxford was of a graceful, Renaissance city of elegant, immemorial architecture; not this tacky warren of aged buildings swarming with chimpanzees.

In London the tri-dimensional character of chimpanzee urban life had been apparent to Simon, but not to this extent. On top of the Randolph Hotel, swinging from the Martyrs' Memorial, scampering over the roofs of Balliol and St John's – everywhere Simon looked were chimp students, scrapping, mating and brachiating. The fact that so many of them wore the short gowns of commoners – it was the first week of Michaelmas term – cut strategically so as to expose their anal scrags, only served to tickle Simon more.

As they rounded the corner of Balliol – bipedal such was the press of tourists coming in the other direction – Simon witnessed a scene that made him break out into great peals of merriment. "H'h'hee-hee-heee," he cackled. Busner stopped and turned back towards his patient, worried lest this presage an attack, but Simon held out a hand to his therapist. "Gru-nnn," he cried, then signed, 'Look, there!' Busner followed Simon's finger. On the other side of Broad Street there was a tourist attraction denoted 'The Oxford Experience'. Simon remembered it from before his breakdown, from his years at the Brown House. Around the entrance to this gimmickry milled a crowd of American tourists – even Simon could tell they were American by the cut of their shortie Burberry mackintoshes – who had become tangled up with a group of undergraduates returning from their matriculation ceremony at the Sheldonian Theatre.

A couple of the female undergraduates were in full, magnificent oestrus, their sexual swellings marvellous pink beacons lighting up the grimy esplanade. Naturally a mating chain had got going, with the male tourists scuttling up and down the pavement waving expensive cameras and video equipment about their be-hatted heads. The combination of signboard and scene was cartoonish. *This* was the Oxford experience, rutting, scrapping beasts.

Simon chopped the air. 'The thing that gets me about this' – he indicated the mêlée on the other side of the road – 'is that contrary to what one expects of Oxford students "hee-hee-hee", they're all so lowbrow!' and with this he collapsed into a serious episode of giggling.

Busner took him in hand, pressed him on past the gate to Balliol; they crossed Broad Street, skipping between the parked cars, and Simon gave way to another small cackle attack when he saw the stone heads of chimpanzee philosophers, on top of the pillars that bounded the Sheldonian enclave. Socrates with outsize canines, Plato with a nasal bridge, Heraclitus supporting a lithic laurel wreath on his nonexistent forehead.

Outside the panelled door of Grebe's study Busner called, "HoooH'Graaa!" and when there was a pant-hoot from within the two chimps entered. Simon found himself moving across the Persian carpet in a low crawl, turning and pushing his scrag into the muzzle of a wizened chimp who was tenanting a large armchair and sipping a crystal sherry glass filled with thick brown fluid. As ever Simon was taken aback – literally – by the way his body automatically understood which apes he should present to.

Grebe put his glass of shit down on the octagonal table and bestowed a welcoming caress on the long back of the chimp who was presenting to him. Grebe had observed Simon's progress from the door carefully and noted the odd atrophy of the chimp's legs, also the air of automatism about his deference. When Busner approached and the two senior chimps presented to one another, Grebe gave shape to his immediate impressions. "Euch-euch," he vocalised, then signed, 'So, Busner, is there heautomorphism of some kind here "huuu"?'

Busner, amused by the accuracy of this probing, leapt up beside Grebe and gave the academic a cuddle, inparting as he did so, 'No, actually that's not the case "chup-chupp". He appears to see us as we are; and although the furniture of the delusion remains, as it were, in place, "huh-huh-huh" his perception of his own body as human is undoubtedly vitiated. Observe him now . . .'

Having presented, and grasping that his subordinate position in the hierarchy released him from the obligation of an extended groom, Simon was now ranging along Grebe's bookcases pulling a volume half out with a hand here and a foot there. 'The trip appears to have done him good, my little Grebeling "chup-chupp". That's some of the first footling I've seen him do and just now he produced a ticklecism – of sorts. Furthermore, while we were getting on the train in London he pushed a metaphoric representation at me – the first piece of allusion he's signed "gru-nnn".'

Grebe, his right hand cradling Busner's scrotal sack, gestured with the other, 'I hate "chup-chupp" to be so precipitate, Busnerkins, but I'm more than a little peckish, this' – he indicated the glass – 'may refresh, but it doesn't sustain. Do you "chup-chupp" feel that Mr Dykes will be able to cope with hall "huuu"?'

'I don't see why not "grnnn", he's coped thus far.'

'Good, in that case why don't we adjourn for third luncheon, then come back here and gesticulate later "huuu"?' Grebe checked his watch again. 'I can give you until about three-thirty, then it's back to the quadrumanous querulousness of my undergraduates.'

Simon was subdued during lunch. The dark immensity of the Exeter College hall was clamorous with the pant-hooting of the undergraduates, who weren't so much squatted as clustered along the long tables. From the dark oak panelling the painted eyes of noblemales, scholars and prelates bleared into the gloom. Simon stared at these portraits of robed apes, apes in armour, apes whose scruffs were ruffed up under ruffs, and marvelled at the accuracy with which each curl and lock of fur had been rendered. He longed to quit his position – at the very corner of the podium-sited high table – and swing up on the ancient handholds that studded the walls, so as to see whether the quality of the brush strokes would be as good on closer examination.

Other brush strokes bothered Simon as well. Grebe had given no delineation to his fellow dons as to why Simon should be present – although he had presented Busner, who was, of course, known by reputation to all. Despite this they had enfolded him in their hairy bosom. His immediate neighbour – a physicist denoted Kreutzer – continually turned to Simon and inparted some observation about the college, or the weather.

The dons also passed a decanter of claret on an apparently interminable round. As soon as it was emptied a servitor would bound on to the podium, retrieve it and bound off; returning from the cellars in a matter of seconds with it refilled. After the decanter appeared by his elbow for the fourth time, Simon declined it for the fourth time as best he could, gesturing to

Kreutzer, 'I haven't been "u-h'-u-h'" well, I'm afraid, I'm not sure wine at third luncheon will "hooo" agree with me.'

Kreutzer, eyebrow ridges raised so precipitately they threatened to fall off his head, peered at Simon quizzically. 'Really "huuu"? I'm not sure it altogether *agrees* with me, but surely the dispute is "hee-hee" the thing.'

The bibulous chimp then lifted his full glass to his drooling mouth and downed half of it in one pull, the fluid gushing out from between canines stained with previous indulgence. His muzzle still sopping, his fingers walked on, 'In the old days "grnnn", you would be asked as a matter of course when you squatted at high table, are you a two-bottle chimp, or a three-bottle chimp "huuu"?' For some reason he seemed to find this very funny and went off into a great clacking and gnashing fit of laughter.

The other dons must have been watching this throwaway sign, because they too broke into laughter. In the dimness of the hall their gaping mouths dangled in the gloom, their outsize teeth lanced from their furry muzzles. For the first time that day Simon felt utterly remote and disembodied. He longed to leap up, swagger from the hall, leave the college, go to the Cornmarket and get a bus out to Tiddington, then knuckle-walk to the Brown House. But could he bear encountering his infants? Infants whose muzzles might well be unrecognisable without a shave?

But this fugue of hysteria – its notes of corporeal dis-ease already beginning to mount the scale – was shut off abruptly. Despite the clamour at high table, a greater row was erupting in the body of the hall. The undergraduates, whose demeanour throughout third luncheon had been rambunctious, were becoming violently restive. They got upright on the benches and pant-hooted so loudly that their lips funnelled. They drummed on the tables vigorously, so that the china and cutlery crashed and rattled.

Simon; observing Kreutzer's gnarled and mighty ears vibrating with the cacophony, expected him and the other dons to respond to this riot with an enforcement of dominance. And knowing chimpanzee society, Simon foresaw violence. But to his surprise the dons only added to the clamour, mounting the high table and proceeding to charge up and down it, their gowns flared, their ischial scrags refulgent.

So horripilated were the distinguished academics that they swelled to almost twice their actual size. But what amazed Simon – as ever – was their incredible fleetness of foot. By God, these apes are snappy movers! he thought. Not one glass was overturned, nor plate disturbed, as horny, scholarly foot after naked horny, scholarly foot planted itself neatly on the damask.

The undergraduate chimps' brouhaha subsided when one of their number, having been passed a large glass vessel, swaggered upright to the end of the central table opposite the dons' podium and stood there uttering loud, discordant pant-hoots, "HooooGra! HooooGra! HooooGra!" Novocal filled the hall. Simon took the opportunity to gain Kreutzer's attention, "HooGra,'" he cried, then signed, 'What on earth is going on, Dr Kreutzer "huu"?'

'You really *aren't* an Oxford chimp, are you "huuu"?' the don countersigned.

'No, no, I studied fine art at the Slade.' The physicist squinted at Simon, his muzzle wrinkled with distaste. It was, Simon reflected to Busner later, as if I'd told him I was a ballet dancer.

'Well "aaaaaa", this is, my artistic friend, a sconcing. There are certain rather archaic traditions that we like to preserve here at Exeter, and one of them is that a forfeit must be paid if any undergraduate shows signs of particular subjects while in hall. "HooooRaaaarg"!' This last, roaring pant-hoot coincided with the undergraduate chimp's giant beaker being filled by a servitor with a draught of dark ale. Meanwhile, the other undergraduates had formed a hispid huddle around the swaggering young ape.

'"Huuu" what subjects exactly?' Simon enquired of his companion.

Kreutzer again gifted his disdainful muzzle. 'The usual, politics, religion, any kind of shop whatsoever –'

'Shop,' Simon countersigned, 'meaning academic subjects "huu"?'

'Of course "wraff".'

'But that would cover just about anything it's possible to gesture –'

'No, no,' Kreutzer's fingers fiddled sarcastically, 'There's still sport – or the weather!'

This fingering was cramped by the undergraduates, who commenced beating loudly and with a mounting rhythm on the table tops. The student who was being sconced began pouring the ale into his mouth. Simon, his curiosity piqued, could not forbear from inparting Kreutzer, 'Is this "huuu" the penalty? Drinking a draught of ale?'

'It's three pints – and if you think it's easy, give it a go yourself "aaaaa"!'

Even from where he sat some twenty feet away, Simon could see the chimp's scruff rise and fall as he ingurgitated the beer. He was an impressive specimen and the contents of the beaker were disappearing rapidly. 'Good sconce!' several of the dons blazoned, then cried, "HoooGraaa!" to urge the chimp on. All looked to be going well for the penalised undergraduate – he was down to the last half-pint or so – when Simon saw that his scut was quivering, elongating. Then, without further warning, the chimp started spraying uncontrollably and spinning at the same time. First his spluttering scut, then his guttering pink penis appeared, as he whirled and twirled. Piss and liquid shit splattered the other undergraduates in wider and wider arcs. Finally, the incontinent dervish fell off the table and was borne out of the hall by his fellows.

The dons, far from being disgusted, were positively buoyed up by this perverse ceremonial. Their excited cries and exaggerated gesturing took minutes to die down. Eventually, when he could discern anything in the blur of bristling hands, Simon saw that Kreutzer was putting the finger on him. 'You're visiting Grebe, aren't you "huuu"?' the physicist pointed out.

'That's right,' Simon countersigned.

'Well, this'll put the pervert in a good mood – he's partial to some shit at third luncheon "hee-hee-hee"!'

Simon didn't have time to take in this mark, because Busner appeared next to him and made it clear that it was time to leave. Simon presented to his third-luncheon companion, but Kreutzer bestowed the most cursory of caresses on his proffered rump. The three-bottle chimp was intent on the port, which was coming rapidly down the high table towards him.

The day, grey until now, was wavering into insipid sunlight as the three chimps knuckle-walked back across the front quad and into the back. Grebe bounded ahead and when Busner and Simon reentered his study after handing themselves up the spiral stone stairs, he was squatting in his armchair, the dun decanter already aloft. 'Shit "huuu"?' the philosopher enquired.

'I won't, thanks,' Busner countersigned. 'Simon "huu"?'

'I'm sorry – what was that "huu"?' Simon's muzzle was uncomprehending.

'Would you like some shit "huu"?' The decanter was waggled so that its viscous contents slowly sloshed.

'"HoooGrnnn" if it's all the same to you, Dr Grebe, I don't think I will.'

Busner expected some kind of outburst from Simon when he was confronted with Grebe's coprophilia. Busner himself was partial to the occasional glass of shit, but Grebe was an *aficionado*, who he knew for a fact kept an extensive personal midden in the college cellars. Surely Simon, with his conviction that he was human, would find this aspect of chimpanzee behaviour insupportable?

The answer came soon enough, because Grebe had done his own research. Sipping his shit judiciously, his upper lip questing, prehensile, he lifted his feet and toed Simon a line.

'Mr Dykes, I would have thought you, as a human, would have found my coprophilia disturbing – if not repulsive. I understand that your conspecifics, both in the wild and in captivity, show a marked aversion for their own excreta, often travelling some distance from their nesting sites to perform their bodily functions and then "euch-euch" burying the result.'

Simon turned from the bookcase to muzzle the philosopher. The journey from the Busner group home, the bizarre scenes in the hall at third luncheon and now Grebe with his coprophilia – it was a day of contrariness. For Simon, although more present in the world of chimpanzees, more at ease, nonetheless felt his humanity as strongly as ever. It was convenient – he reasoned – to walk on all fours as they did. So diminished was the scale of this realm, that to have done otherwise would have been to court a skull-drubbing. Likewise, it was a matter of mere conformity not to wear nether garments or shoes and to pick at one's ischial scrag from time to time, freeing troublesome winnets and dag-tails. Signing came easily enough to Simon – but then why shouldn't that be the case; human signage – "speech" – was as much gestural as vocalised. But eating shit? No. Never. This, like the chimps' high-speed multi-rutting, was the stuff of true bestiality. Furthermore, Simon realised that his lack of aversion to Grebe and his diarrhoeic decanter was a function of just this fact: it was animal ordure – not human crap. Despite being liquidised, imprisoned in crystal and placed on a table, it was no more repugnant than the brown shot of rabbit shit, scattered across a hillside.

So, Simon gave Grebe a knuckle sandwich: 'That's right. *We* only "euch-euch" shit where we should shit – to do otherwise would be unhygienic. Human coprophiliacs are regarded as perverts. But, if I'm not misdirected, Dr Grebe, I gathered from one of your colleagues at high table that you are seen in that light yourself "huuu"?'

Busner kept hand in glove at this juncture – if Simon was

due for a thrashing it might as well come from Grebe as anyone else. But Grebe, instead of punishing this impertinence with violence, chose to do so gesturally. He tipped his muzzle back so as to stare at the ceiling, and apparently concentrating on the mouldings, proceeded to unleash a flurry of dexterity.

'*Mr* Dykes, you would do well to remember how we view "euch-euch" the spectacle of humanity. To quote the *Cauda Caudex,* one of the earliest treatises to deal with the animals: <Humans are so denoted because of the humorous way they ape the behaviour of rational chimpanzees. They are very conscious of the elements, and are cheerful when the moon is new and sad when it wanes. Humans have no tails. The devil has the same form, with a head but no tail. If the whole of the human is hateful, his backside is even more horrible and disgusting ... > Some theological stuff follows here "euch-euch"; then, more relevant to your peculiar semantic arrogance, the *Caudex* continues: < 'Simia', the Latin sign for human comes from the Greek and means 'with nostrils pressed together'. Their > – or should I sign *your* – < nostrils are indeed pressed together, and their muzzles are horrible, with folds like a disgusting pair of bellows – >'

"HoooGrnn," Simon pant-hooted apprehensively, then signed, 'Dr Grebe, I take your point, but surely the <humans> referred to here aren't wild, African humans. This text must date from before their discovery – or at any rate their full apprehension by chimpunity "huuu"? And anyway,' Simon continued conducting, 'if you are intent on nit-picking semantics, what does <human> *really* mean "huu"? Delineate that for me, if you can.'

Grebe took another slug of shit before answering. Busner saw he was enjoying the gesticulation – that he was learning things and had more to inpart. Busner was also impressed by his protégé – Simon's passionate defence of his own delusion was in and of itself a most fascinating ramification.

Grebe vaulted from his armchair and swung to his work table, where he snatched up a piece of paper. This he passed to

Simon, signing, 'I think you may find this interesting, Mr Dykes "h'huuu"? You see, I anticipated your question and e-mailed an ally in London regarding this very matter, knowing that Busner was bringing you here – a Dr Phelps at the School of Oriental and African Studies. Perhaps it would "grnnn" interest you to see his reply "huu"?'

Simon took the print-out and read the following:

HooH'Graaa. Dear David,
About humans. I asked the acknowledged expert on English signs with African origins and he wrote:

The earliest attestations of 'human' indicate that this is the 'native name in Angola'.

In Kimbundu (an Angolan signage) it is _ki-humanze_, in Fiot (a signage of Cabinda) it is _ki-hpumanze_, and in the Kikongo signage as gestured in Zaire it is _ki-hpumanzi_ (the _ki-_ is a noun-prefix).

When I asked if these signs meant anything, he wrote: All these signs are glossed simply as 'human', with no other meaning given.

Hope this helps. H'Hoooo, Nigel.

Simon remained signlent after reading this missive. There was tenable *froideur* coming from Phelps's note, an apprehensive icicle that poked into Simon's state of conviction. Seeing it written down like this, in dry academic signage, Simon could almost believe it; put on acknowledgement like a hat – then take it off. Put it on – take it off. But if he put it on and took it off too often, like a real hat it would leave behind a phantom sensation; and then he'd really have lost all vestige of humanity.

Simon roused himself, scratched his ischial scrag. He was wearing a jacket borrowed from Busner today, a tweed thing – all Busner's jackets were tweed, saving his human suit for black-tie engagements. It itched Simon's ischial scrag if he didn't tuck it up a little, expose what he had begun to think of – purely as a matter of habit – as his beautiful, effulgent arsehole. Better, Simon reasoned, to have one's arsehole shining out when engaged in a debate such as this.

He got upright, swaggered a little, and waved Phillips's note in the air. "HoooGrnn," he vocalised, then signed, 'Dr Grebe, you wanted to gesticulate with me concerning my notions of human signage – shall we proceed "huuu"?' Grebe, taking yet another gulp of his crapulent cocktail, sprang bipedal. The few remaining hairs traversing his scalp were erect, forming a peculiar, saggital crest.

'"Euch-euch" I congratulate you,' he logic-chopped, 'on your poise, Mr Dykes. For a chimp afflicted with such a peculiar belief system, you have acquitted yourself well. I assumed from your doctor's description of your condition that you were subject to an aphasia; rendering you incapable of understanding signs *per se* although capable of comprehending signing through a preternatural sensitivity to tempo "grnnn".'

Warming to his lecture, Grebe next employed a technique he found useful for holding at bay his undergraduates. He jumped up so that his feet were on either projecting wing of the chair's headrest, then leapt and grabbed the light fitment. Throughout what followed he signed elegantly and arrogantly, employing only his toes. "H'huuu?" he resumed from his inverted, pendulous podium. 'Either that, or I had assumed the – as it were – opposite condition, a loss of what psychosemioticians term <feeling-tempo>, and Frege denoted *Klangenfarben*, or <tempo-colour>. In other signs an agnosia of tempo – or atempia. You follow my scut "huuu"?'

Tracking the puckered scrag of the don, Simon countersigned, 'I do, Dr Grebe – indeed I do.'

'Good "grnnn". Well, as you are no doubt aware, gesture does not consist of signs alone; it consists of blazoning – blazoning forth one's whole being, not mere sign recognition. Now, do you mean to direct me that you have within your consciousness an entirely different method of gesticulation based on vocalised phonemes "huuu"?'

'That's exactly right, Dr Grebe. We humans vocalise beautifully, we can, of course, interpret gesture as well, indeed human signage comprises manipulable signs – expressed as sounds; and visual indicators – provided by gesture. Signage is the "grnnn" totality, and the interaction between the two semiotic systems.'

Simon squatted down on the Persian carpet after this finger flurry, pleased with his own elegance of gesture. Busner too was impressed and crawled over to administer a tender tickle to Simon's groin fur. Grebe, however, was not so easily handled. Still dangling from the light bracket, he put the proverbial boot in. 'It looks to me,' he signed sententiously, 'as if there's nothing much to choose between these two signages. Unless "gru-unnn" you are marking out a signage in which all gesture is only manipulable by one individual – and that, as we know from Wittgenstein, is an impossibility. I take it that that *isn't* what you delineate with this call "speech" "huuu", Mr Dykes?'[1]

Simon, despite the reassuring tweaks the eminent natural philosopher – as he liked to style himself – was administering to his testicular fur, found these patronising directions more than difficult to take. Grebe was trying to mine his sense of conviction from within, collapsing the distinction between Simon's memories of humanity and this – hideously didactic – planet of the apes.

Clenched up inside of Simon was a hard ball of recollection. It constituted all the things he revered most about the human voice: the ineffable beauty of Jessye Norman singing Strauss's *Four Last Songs*; the richness and vitality of Shakespeare

---

[1] In fact Dr Grebe was showing his true colours here, and would undoubtedly have accepted the contention of John B. Watson, the founder of modern behaviourism: 'I should like to throw out imagery altogether and attempt to show that practically all natural thought goes on in terms of sensory-motor processes in the fingers and toes.' Author's note.

declaimed; the lowering coloratura of Mandelstam's poetry, rolled out in the Russian; or a scratchy recording of Bernard Shaw setting the world to rights. The sound of African tribespeople chanting up a storm came to Simon's inner ear; as did that of Aboriginal elders singing up their endless, oneiric country. What about Billie Holiday hitting a high note of pure sucrose; and the sweet burble of a infant – one of his infants? And there was more, much more; a lover's tender endearments, breath like a caress in his ear; or a lover's more strident exhortations – Sarah's exhortations to fuck me . . . fuck me . . . fuck me! All gone? All never have been?

The former artist, his perspective banished, looked up at the foreshortened prospect of the dangling ape above his head. His eyes followed the furry runnel between ischial scrag and scrotal sack. Simon raised himself up, drummed on the seat of Grebe's chair. Busner, taken aback, noted that Simon's horripilation was entire, the fur bulging up from beneath the collar of the borrowed jacket, the head fur as spiky as that of a punk.

Then Simon let out the most astonishing vocalisation that either Grebe or Busner had ever heard before; an utterly convincing imitation of an enraged wild human, and yet suffused with a weirdly visible, essentially chimp meaningfulness. "You-fucking-shit-eating-monkey!" he screamed, "I-ought-to-tear-you-a-new-fucking-arsehole!" Next, having judged the philospoher's trajectory with a decidedly chimp accuracy, Simon leapt up, grabbed Grebe's testicles and ripped him from the ceiling.

The don fell to the floor with a heavy crash, knocking over the precious decanter on the way down, so that the vile contents browned the carpet. Allowing Grebe no quarter, Simon commenced to lay about the expert on psychosemiotics and human sign acquisition with great openhanded blows, the reports from which resounded around the study.

It was, quite simply, no kind of a contest; and within seconds Grebe's pale rump was aloft and his paler muzzle

313

buried in the tipple tarnish. One hand was waving frantically, "Eeeek!" Grebe vocalised, and, "Aaaaargh!" whilst signing 'Please, please, Mr Dykes – sir! I revere your artistic vision! I worship your "hooowraaa" ischial scrag! I bow before the magnificent effulgence of your arsehole! I acknowledge your suzerainty now – and "hooo" for ever!'

Simon, naturally, stopped hitting Grebe and administered the necessary, reassuring groom beholden to a hierarchical superior. Although, in truth, he wouldn't have minded doing what he'd vocalised that he was going to – if only he could remember what that was.

Later, as Simon and Busner knuckle-walked through the covered market, Busner couldn't help but express his admiration for his patient's spunk with a spontaneous pant-hoot. 'Did you,' he signed to Simon, who was lighting his 'nth Bactrian of the day, 'enjoy that display of dominance at all "huu"? I know you aren't so inchimp as to have been indifferent.'

Simon squinted at the maverick anxiolytic drug researcher through his nicotine miasma, and gestured with his four-for-a-pound disposable lighter, 'I'll point out what's been troubling me, Dr Busner. If as Grebe there delineated – and the testimony of my own senses appears to confirm – we inhabit a world in which visual gesticulation is primary, and aural secondary, then surely the invention of a television must have preceded the invention of radio "huuu"?'

'That's right,' Busner countersigned, eyebrow ridges creased, 'it did. I don't believe there was radio much before the Second War. It was invented by a chimp called Logie Baird, you know – Scotschimp, I suppose "grnnn".'

'And how did he invent radio then "huu"?'

'By accident, completely by accident. One day he went into his laboratory and his research assistant had left a television on inside a cupboard. All Baird did was shut the door. Shall we crawl on "huuu"?'

Chapter Eighteen

In London, a distinctly less helpful – if twistedly reverent – research assistant was convening an extraordinary meeting of the alliance against Busner. In attendance were his co-conspirators: Whatley, looking drawn and tired; and Phillips, who was obviously ill. Whatley had a pretty good idea now of what was wrong with Phillips – he could see the lesions of Karposi's Sarcoma beneath the chimp's scruff, despite the cravat he was wearing. The consultant psychiatrist wondered how Phillips had contracted CIV, but was uncharacteristically tactful enough not to ask.

'So "grnnn" Gambol, an amusing choice of venue for our meeting "huuu"? Just as well since we were all in touch so recently.' Phillips pointed at the walls of the restaurant, on which a mural had been executed. It was a garish jungle scene, done in the style of Le Douanier Rousseau. Emerging from between two broad tessellated leaves was the brutishly blunt muzzle of an adult male human. Deeper in the undergrowth were the equally bestial visages of females with infants on their backs. The bare teats of the human females bored out from this two-dimensional undergrowth like the barrels of lactifluous guns.

The human motif recurred *ad tedium* elsewhere. On the menus were line drawings of cavorting humans; on the ceiling there was a large – and rare – photograph of humans rutting muzzle-to-muzzle, the female's hind legs grasped tightly around the male's waist, her senseless toes splayed. Even the waiters at Human Zoo – for that was the name of this themed restaurant – were dressed in human costumes made from a synthetic fabric, the weave of which approximated to the rubbery texture of the animals' skin.

Whatley indicated out one of these waiters. 'Why's that one got black skin, Gambol "huuu"? I didn't know that humans had black skin.'

Gambol looked up from a sheet of paper he'd been scanning. 'I'm sorry, did you sign something "huu"?'

'The black human "euch-euch",' Whatley repointed irritably.

'No, no, they can be black. That waiter's meant to be a specimen of Western human, the Latin ascription is *Homo sapiens troglodytes verus*. There are also central and eastern sub-species –'

'Like separate races "huuu"?' Whatley broke in. 'As if this human were a bonobo "huu"?'

'That sort of thing.'

'Are the black humans different from other humans, the way that bonobos are different from Caucasian chimps "huu"?' This gesture came from Phillips, who was also fascinated by the waiter in his black body stocking.

'I've no idea,' Gambol countersigned. 'I'm a clinical psychologist – not an anthropologist "euch-euch".'

Despite registering the jagged, angry nature of Gambol's signing, Phillips continued, 'I mean to sign, are they good at dancing and entertaining like bonobos "huuu"? Good at sport – that sort of thing "huu"?'

'"Wraaaf!" Gambol barked – with Phillips so ill he had no fear of him. 'Why don't you shut down, Phillips, that waiter is coming to take our order and he *is* a bonobo. Remember, we're all the same under the fur.'

Of course, it was precisely because he didn't believe this that the Cryborg chimp had got himself into such deathly trouble. Bisexual and partial to a bit of bonobo rough, Phillips had been one of those Western European males who thought it amusing and stimulating to visit Central African countries and mate with the natives. The result was the disease which was killing him in front of his allies' eyes. All three were plangently aware of the irony that the bonobo who infected Phillips with CIV might possibly have contracted the virus from the bite of a wild human.

"HooGra'," the bonobo in black body stocking vocalised, then signed 'Can I take your order, gentlechimps "huu"?'

' "Huu" what's this thing Just Bananas?' Gambol tapped at the menu. The bonobo waiter scratched his false crotch before countersigning, 'It's a dish named after our other branch in Wardour Street – a crostini of squirrel brains on a bed of banana mush. It's very popular "grnnn'yum".'

' "HooGra'" well, I'll have that then and the soup to start.'

The other chimps ordered, the waiter – despite his ridiculous and clumsy costume – noting their requests with great sinistrality. He then bounded away and the conspirators were left to wring their hands over the situation with Busner. "Euch-euch" Whatley coughed, then signed, 'Well, I think it's time we took the leap of pointing out to the GMC Busner's gross misconduct. He's not only patrolling this severely disturbed chimp around the place "euch-euch", it's also virtually certain that Dykes's delusion, psychosis, whatever, is a function of Busner's own misguided involvement in an illegal drug trial "wraff"!'

'I agree,' Phillips flicked. 'Whatever the respect due to Busner for his achievements in the past – and even that's moot – his conduct now is "euch-euch" incontestably malpractice. We must do something!'

Whatley, signing into Gambol's upper arm, applied further pressure. 'Gambol, "huu" do you think Busner knows Dykes may be a victim of Inclusion, and that his human delusion is more than likely drug-induced?'

'Gentlechimps, there seems little doubt that he must have a prinkling. He knows that Dykes's GP was Anthony Bohm.

He knows that Bohm was the conduit for the illegal Inclusion trial. Whether or not he's delineated any of this for Dykes is anyone's guess –'

'Well,' Phillips chopped in again, 'surely the point is, kneads must – kneads do "huu"?'

'Quite so, which is why I've prepared this letter to the GMC detailing Busner's misconduct. I've two copies here, perhaps you'd like to twine them around a bit; then, if fusion is achieved, we can push the thing forward "huuu"?'

Naturally, as Gambol suspected, the practitioner of the psycho-physical approach to mental pathologies and organic dysfunctions had more than a prinkling of his own potential involvement in his patient's drastic condition. But, Busner reasoned, such a liana of twisted causality hardly implied *blame* of any kind. He and Dykes had been thrown together – so be it. Dykes might well have actual neurological damage – whether innate or acquired; or he might be in the grip of a more than believably baroque psychosis. Neither possibility cancelled out the validity of what they were doing. Every day Busner could see changes wrought in Simon. He was, the psychiatrist concluded, adapting to his peculiar phenomenological interface much the way that any severely perceptually impaired chimp would adapt, whether to blindness and signlence, or to deafness and novocal.

Busner was also aware that it couldn't be long before awkward questions would be asked about his relationship with Dykes. Gambol's absence from both domestic and occupational ranges betokened the fomenting of a new alliance. Well, Busner thought to himself as he followed Simon Dykes's scut through the crowded passageways and caterwauling cacophony of the covered market, if my entanglement with this poor chimp's psyche results in my being struck off as a medical practitioner – then so be it. My entire philosophy and career has been based on a repudiation of dry functionalist categories; this will be a fitting end to my reign as alpha.

But these digitations – felt and examined in Busner's habitual way, as if they were termites of thought being prised from a mound of cogitation – were abruptly curtailed as Busner's muzzle rammed into Simon's scut. "Chup-chupp," the radical psychoanalyst's great rim of lip curled up appreciatively as he savoured the odours of Simon's ischial pleat.

"Huh-huh-huh," Simon panted – then began to cough. He had stopped to light another of his interminable Bactrians. Busner made no objection to the smoking – although a lack of dextrality meant Simon's chest fur was pitted and scoured with burns – but worried that it represented a return to a destructive cycle of intoxication.

This wasn't what was bothering Simon. He was squatting, puffing on the Bactrian and peering at the packet with eyebrow ridges creased. 'These cigarettes,' he signed. 'There's something not quite right about them.'

'Too strong perhaps "huuu"?'

'No, no, it's not that. It's just that the animal on the packet has two humps –'

'That's because it's a Bactrian, Simon.' Busner tweaked his protégé's fur.

'I know – I realise that. But in my memory' . . . an inexpressive flutter . . . 'in my memory of being human I always smoked Camels.'

'Camels "huuu". You mean to sign that Bactrians are denoted camels on your "gru-nnn" planet of the humans?'

'That's right "h'hee-hee-hee" how absurd and trivial a reversal – almost comic "huu"?'

'There's nothing that "clak-clak" comic about the mess you're making of your chest fur with those Bactrians,' Busner countersigned, gently applying saliva to a particularly raw patch below Simon's left teat, 'and now we must get on, Hamble will be waiting for us – I know what he's like.'

Indeed, Hamble, the second of Busner's delusional dissolutives *was* waiting for them as the cab – driven by an annoyingly fiddly bonobo – came skittering up the stony track from Eynsham and skidded to a halt in front of the house.

Hamble was on all fours, staring at the arrivals over the top of a hawthorn hedge that bordered his garden – but such was the size of his chest, and his ferocious shagginess, that to Simon he presented a most animalian aspect. All the more so because he wore nothing save for an old army camouflage jacket – which was unbuttoned. With his great shoulders and his vigorous breath smoking the autumnal air, Hamble looked all chimp. Looked – Simon thought, taking in the bucolic setting of Hamble's house, with its apple orchard to one side and rolling stubble fields to the other – exactly like a creature that's escaped from a zoo.

Hamble's muzzle was pale for an adult male, but he sported particularly curly, gingerish sideburns of an almost muttonchop aspect. These, together with his exposed canines, were more than enough to unsettle Simon, who, leaving Busner to pay the driver, felt obliged to pant-hoot with utmost deference, then drag himself backwards across the yard, arse aloft, ischial scrag nervously puckered.

But Hamble was as eccentric as Busner had intimated. He gave the most cursory – and necessarily soundless – drum on the top of the hedge, pant-hooted as faintly as Simon, "HoooH'Gra," vaulted over the hedge and began gently to groom him, inparting as he did so, 'Please, Mr Dykes, may I call you Simon "huu"? Don't put yourself down with such deference. I acknowledge your submissiveness joyfully, but really "chup-chupp" don't trouble yourself!'

Simon got tit about arse and regarded his gesticulator. Hamble's mouth was wide open, but his top lip covered his teeth, giving him an unthreatening mien. "H'huuu?" Simon pant-hooted.

'Of course,' Hamble replied. 'After all, remember what Coleridge wrote in his Epigram: <He saw a cottage with a double coach-house / A cottage of gentility; / And the Devil did grin, for his darling sin / Is pride that apes humility> "huuu"?'

Simon took in the big chimp's grinning muzzle, the eyes creased with good humour, and without troubling to consider what he was doing, pulled himself upright and embraced Hamble. It felt more than good to have those serpentine arms encircling him, and to feel Hamble's reassuring knead. After some seconds they broke the embrace and Simon signed, ' "Hoo" Dr Hamble "chup-chupp", I can't blazon how much it means to see you sign that inscription. Coleridge remains one of my favourite poets. Why, only the day before my breakdown I was dwelling on his image of the mind as a roiling flock of swallows, fusing and fissioning –'

'Just like a chimpanzee group,' Hamble flagged Simon down.

'"Huuu"? Well, yes, I suppose so, just like a chimpanzee group. But I was thinking of the *human* mind – do you find that absurd "huu"?'

Hamble maintained his playful expression and turned to Busner who was gingerly picking his way across the muddy yard on some-threes, his briefcase tucked under one arm. The two senior males met and presented to one another in the cursory fashion of old – but not close – allies. "HoooH'Gra," Busner pant-hooted and Hamble echoed him, then signed, 'Well, well, Zack Busner, you look in good shape. I haven't felt you in . . . how long is it "huuu"?'

'It must be a couple of years, Raymond,' Busner countersigned, 'since we went on that disastrous pub crawl together with McElvoy, after his lecture at the Royal Society "grnnn".'

'Disastrous,' Hamble fleetly fingered, 'only because of the poor Tourettic you had with you. It was his inappropriate vocalising – if you recall – that got us into that fight. Honestly, Zack – all of that pant-screaming!'

'Well, Raymond, that's what they do – Tourettics – pant-scream inappropriately. But anyway,' Busner continued, gently dabbing the thick fur in Hamble's groin, 'we're "chup-chupp" in touch now and that's all that matters "huuu"?'

Hamble bared his canines and let out a loud tooth-clacking chuckle. ' "Clak-clak-clak" well, Zack, you've certainly made your point. Now, if I'm not entirely misdirected, my hump is that Simon here might benefit from some fissioning as far as your party is concerned. Why don't you leave us to gesticulate alone and take a knuckle-walk "huuu"? It's shaping up to be a beautiful afternoon.'

Busner took these signs in the manner they were posted. Why not? he thought. Hamble is as kind-hearted as any chimpanzee, and his eccentricity may make it far easier for him to reach out to Simon. Busner broke off the intromissive grooming and got upright. 'Which way should I scuttle, Raymond, over there "huuu"?'

'Yes, that's as good a way as any, you can get down to the river, but watch out for the bottom paddock, the farmer keeps dogs there and they can be frisky.'

Busner bestowed a sloppy kiss on Simon's muzzle and commended him to Hamble's care, along with his briefcase. The last the two remaining chimps saw of the eminent natural philosopher – as he liked to style himself – was his prominent perineum, like a pink-and-yellow flower, appearing first here and then there between the rows of hardy perennials at the bottom of the garden.

Hamble grunted, took Simon by the hand and led him inside the house.

The next couple of hours were the most stimulating, engaged, and embodied Simon had spent since his breakdown; and also the most disconcerting. Busner's estimation of Hamble's influence was correct in one sense, because the naturalist's knowledge of all things connected to anthropology was so playfully tweaked and caressed that Simon found himself finangled by the foreplay into more acceptance of his chimpunity than heretofore.

But at the same time Hamble's obvious eccentricity, his peculiar house and his decidedly chimp behaviour enhanced

Simon's sense of his receding humanity. There was that – and there was the fact that before his breakdown Simon had read Hamble's books and retained a mental picture of the chimp as a man, of his seeming sideburns as real whiskers. Hamble didn't help matters by encouraging Simon to smoke a joint.

But that came later. First they entered the Set, which is what Hamble denoted his house. This was blazoned by the bas-relief of a vixen suckling its young which formed the lintel of the old, oaken door; by the curving corridor, carpeted in an earthen colour that led from it; and by the further curving corridors that branched from this, each one ending in another burrow-like room. On their way down the main corridor they encountered three of Hamble's large brood of infants, and both adult males stopped to tickle them and applaud their playful displays.

Besides the infants, knuckle-walking around the Set was difficult. Everywhere Simon placed his feet or hands there was another thing. The Set was heavy on things – full of them in fact. There were animal skeletons, stuffed birds, chimpanzee skulls and collections of butterflies, either hanging on the sagging walls or stacked against them. There were shelves groaning with tomes of all sorts, and a bewildering variety of tables and chairs. Some of these surfaces also suppported smaller collections of sea shells and crustacea, dried flowers and plants, rock samples and semi-precious stones, all arranged with amazing precision. Any remaining wall space was filled with water-colours of flora and fauna, pen-and-ink drawings of the same, African tribal masks, and the Hamble infants' clumsy poster-paint daubs.

Not only were there the daubs, there were also the infants themselves, and their toys: lead and plastic soldiers, doll's-house furniture, Lego bricks, model trains, teddy bears – and, naturally, some stuffed humans – all arranged with the same lavish attention as the adult artefacts, and mingled with them so as to make the most peculiar palimpsest of reification.

Hamble moved about this domestic museum with utter

assurance, and after squatting Simon in a comfortable leather armchair and commencing gesticulation, it became clear to him that there was an internal order supplied to this intermural moraine, an order supplied by Hamble himself.

In the squatting-room-cum-study, with its small windows set high in the walls and its cheerfully crackling fire, the jumble was overwhelming. Hamble, as he fingered, would from time to time leap and pluck up an object or a book to illustrate his remarks. He always, Simon was amazed to see, selected the right thing, whether it was in front of, or behind him. This extreme extroception, Simon knew, was not unusual for a chimpanzee, but more peculiar was the way it was expressed by the arrangement of artefacts. It was as if they were an analogue or simulacrum of the contents of his own mind. After only a few minutes of flicking, Simon had the sensation that he was signing with the big chimp inside Hamble's own – admittedly capacious – head.

"Gru-unnn," the naturalist happily vocalised as soon as they were squatted, then signed, 'In answer to your question, Mr Dykes –'

'Please,' Simon flagged him down, 'denote me Simon.'

'Simon then. Well, while in no way wishing to lend my support to the activities of extremist animal rights campaigners "euch-euch", I have a more inclusive view of the nature of consciousness than most of the scientific community. Drink "huuu"?'

'Yes, thank you.'

'Beer, wine, something stronger "huuu"?'

'Beer would be fine "grnn".'

Hamble bounced up, reached hands behind his head and without looking took a bottle from the drinks tray, uncapped it, poured out a glass of beer, then passed the full glass to Simon without spilling a drop, while continuing to footle on the subject. 'Even though he wrote at the beginning of the century, and had more than a fondness for morphine, I think

Eugène Marais' delineation of mind is still worth manipulating. You've read, I suppose, his *Soul of the Human* "huuu"?'

'I'm afraid not, Dr Hamble.'

'Please, denote me Raymond. Well "grnn", it was Marais who first made the distinction between individual and phyletic memory in animal minds. His theory was that the ratio between the two determines the degree of consciousness, sentience, what you will. He might have agreed with' – and here the naturalist lunged unerringly for a book, opened it, and passed it to Simon while continuing – 'Linnaeus himself who maintained, <It is remarkable that the smartest human differs so little from the wisest person.> See, here is his original *Systemae Naturae*, which classifies the human as a species of chimpanzee, and assigns it the name of *Pongis sylvestris* or *Pongis nocturnus*. Although I doubt that Marais would have gone quite this far "huuu"? Beer all right "huu"?'

Simon knew better than to express irritation at this representation of reading he had already done. Instead, he got down off his chair, crawled across the room and presented low, whilst gesturing, 'Please "HoooGrnn", Dr Hamble, Raymond, I revere your books and despite our short acquaintance find your anal scrag most affecting ... I am familiar already with most of the historical literature concerning the primatoids, and in particular the human. Everything I learn merely increases my "HoooGrnn" sense of the world having been subject to a complete reversal – human for chimpanzee, chimpanzee for human.'

Seeing that Hamble was still holding out a hand to him, Simon continued signing as he backed to his chair. 'What I'm intrigued by, and what I think will help me most with my "euch-euch" bizarre impression that I am "hooo" human, is information about *wild* humans. I couldn't see myself in the humans at the zoo at all. I'm missing one of my infants, you see – and wonder if he may be with wild humans ...' And with this distinctly strange revelation Simon Dykes's fingers fell still.

It was an idea the former artist had been harbouring for some time. While the unorthodox therapy Busner was applying to him had been effective to this extent – Simon's impressions of his own chimpunity becoming less problematic, as he adapted his unfamiliar body to the world – still the former artist was plagued by incontinent nostalgia. Memories of his own very human sexuality, of Sarah's body, and dragging behind these images of Simon junior, his infant, clear and irrefutable. In this arsy-versy world he found himself in, Simon battened on to this one fact, that he had *three* infants. If he could locate the missing infant then perhaps that would act as a rip cord, opening a parachute that would then deposit him safely back in a smooth, hairless world.

Hamble's eyebrow ridges creased when he saw this. Busner had outlined Dykes's condition when he 'phoned to make the appointment. Hamble had expected the partial atrophy of the chimp's limbs, and the amazing coherence and insistence on alienation from chimpunity, but this was something else. He steepled his fingers, then flicked, 'As you wish, Simon. Well "gru-nnn", it's true that I've encountered humans in the wild.' Again he reached unerringly for some illustrative material, this time an unmistakably human skull. This he passed to Simon, who cradled it throughout what followed. 'And as you correctly surmise they are considerably different to those in captivity. But let me mark out a quid pro quo, I'll show you about my encounter with wild humans – and in return you show me something of your understanding of humanity. What I would most like "grnnn" to know is more about human sexuality "huu"?'

This touched Simon's painful core of recollection, and despite paying close attention to what Hamble signed next, he remained haunted by a bare expanse of fleshly imaginings.

'I have,' Hamble let his fingers do the walking, 'been in the Congo for six months of the past year, and while not ostensibly researching wild humanity, I did "gru-nnn" encounter them. I was out ranging with some of the local bonobos. We weren't actually in the heart of the equatorial forest, rather on the "h'hooo" fringes, with sparse tree cover. Some of the bonobos were brachiating ahead, but I found it easier to knuckle-walk. We came down into a broad, shallow river valley and saw on the opposite ridge a vast patrol of the creatures "hooo".'

'It was frightening then "huuu"?' Simon flagged down.

' "Wraaa"! Absolutely, there were well over a hundred of them, thronging in the trees like ghosts or zombies. That's the reason they're so feared by the indigenes; the humans always patrol in large numbers and if they find an isolated group of bonobos they can overpower them through sheer weight of numbers.

'Anyway "grnnn" on this occasion our patrol came to a halt and formed a tight huddle, waiting to see what the humans would do. Even at this range – and we must have been five hundred and eighty-three metres away – we could distinctly hear them gesticulating with their odd, low-pitched vocalisations, and even making crude signs. It must have been their night nesting site, because we could make out some of their crude shelters among the trees –'

'They construct shelters "huuu"?'

'Indeed they do "grnnn". Your wild human suffers from agoraphobia and cannot bear to be entirely unconfined. Anyway, after a while the human patrol reached some sort of consensus. I could see a large, alpha-type male – frightening specimen with a great mane of head fur – indicating that they should split into two groups, and execute a pincer movement encircling me and the bonobos. What about the river "huuu"? Well, the harsh truth is that humans have absolutely no fear of water – some can even swim! So you can imagine how "hooo" frightened we were.'

Simon wasn't concentrating too well on Hamble's conducting, his eyes were turned in on his own, infernal shadowplay. There were also the distracting pant-hoots of the Hamble infants coming from the recesses of the house, pant-hoots that insistently reminded Simon of his own infants. But now, seeing that Hamble had fallen motionless, Simon snapped a stock sign. 'What did you do "huuu"?'

'Well, we all advanced down towards the river waa-barking and pant-hooting for all we were worth. A couple of the bonobos had guns with them – incredibly old-fashioned pieces, virtual blunderbusses – but they primed and discharged them, over and over and over. This had the "grnnn" desired effect and the human patrol retreated – as did our own. It was something in the manner of a Mexican stand-off.'

'H'huuu?" Simon jerked himself upright on his armchair and into attention. 'Do you mean to sign, Raymond, that you consider wild humans to have manifest consciousness "huuu"?'

'Of some kind – certainly, although not what these maverick anthropologists ascribe to them.'

'Meaning "huuu"?'

'Meaning, that if you take these films that chimps like Savage-Rimbaud have made of captive humans being taught signing and slow them down, you can see that the humans are in fact gesturing millimetrically after their chimp instructors. In other signs, they're clever enough to pick up on what's being signed and countersign using it, without necessarily being able to manipulate "grnnn". The point being, as Stephen Jay Gould has remarked, that it's uninteresting teaching any animal to behave like another one; and by the same token, human intelligence is by definition what humans naturally do "huuu"?'

While conducting this dissertation Hamble had footed a bag of grass from an inside pocket of his camouflage jacket. He now flipped it in the air, caught it, waggled it and waved, 'How about a smoke "huuu"? From what old Zack signed you're no stranger to crossing the herbaceous border.' His playful grin stretched his broad lip across his canescent muzzle.

'I don't know "hooo" . . .'

'Come on, chuck me a Bactrian and I'll roll one, while you

mark out for me something of human sexuality. You know, of course, that in the anthropological community interspecific sex is a common – if unremarked on phenomenon "huu"?'

'Are you serious "huuu"?'

Hamble deftly caught the Bactrian with one hand, whilst continuing with the other. 'Absolutely. It was suspected – although never confirmed – that Dian Fossey, the female Louis Leakey, sent to study the Rwandan mountain gorillas, had an "euch-euch" affair – if you can ascript it that – with a young male gorilla denoted "clak-clak-clak" Digit. Most suitable "huu"? It was after "huh-huh" Digit was killed by poachers that Fossey went humanshit and embarked on the anti-poaching campaign that led to her death. Either that, or the local bonobos had something of an aversion to the idea of a chimp mating a gorilla.

'And "grnnn" that chimp Aspinall is another example.'

'Aspinall "huu" the casino chimp?'

'That's the one. Well, as you probably know "grnnn" he has a zoo in Kent where he allows his keepers to have a rather more "chup-chupp" proximate relationship with the animals than is usually the case. Aspinall has often intimated that he "grnnn" enjoys a *very* close relationship with his gorillas. Perhaps that's why one recently ripped an arm off its keeper – it was just looking for a "clak-clak" cuddle!' A lighter had appeared in Hamble's foot and he lit the fat joint he had rolled with a flourish, then squatted back down in his chair wuffling with enjoyment.

A gush of smoke spilled from his slack mouth, the blue hooks and curlicues airily entwining with the naturalist's flocculent chest. His signing was partially obscured by this local thunderhead, so that Simon only caught flicks of what followed. 'But you must satisfy my curiosity, Simon, "huuu" you say that you have experience of a reality in which humans are the dominant primate species. A reality much the same as this at the, as it were, macro level, with industrialisation, the Japanese television game shows and "euch-euch" – this stuff tickles – hydroponic skunk; but at the micro level, the level of physicality, of sexuality, everything is different, mating practices and so forth "huuu"?'

There was signlence and novocal for a while; Hamble footed Simon the joint, and without considering what he was doing, Simon footed it from him. It was his first non-anxiolytic drug since his breakdown, and it was also the first time he had used feet-for-hands. Simon raised his leg to his muzzle, marvelling at its suppleness, its accuracy of movement and position. He took a great pull on the joint and honked up the distinctive flowery aroma of the weed. The first hit was so delicious that he took another, then another, exhaling and inhaling simultaneously like a saxophonist playing an extended riff.

'What's it like "huuu"?' Simon's signing was loose and expressive, the hallucinogen was doing its work. 'Well, Raymond, we mate – as you know – muzzling one another. And our skins have a gorgeous softness and silkiness to the touch. There's not a lot of touching in our world, so mating is our opportunity to feel one another all over. I've seen chimps "euch-euch" mating, and in comparison to human mating it seems a frenzied, unsatisfying experience. *Our* mating can last for ages and involves the most tender "gru-unnn" and orchestrated of palping "chup-chupp", prodding "chup-chupp", caressing "huh-huh-huh" and stroking –'

'It looks rather like a grooming session to me,' Hamble cut in.

'No, no "euch-euch", not at all. *We* muzzle one another, we stare into one another's eyes without fear of reprisal; and we kiss – our teeth you know are so much smaller than yours – for minutes at a time. And furthermore, Raymond, we only mate love with exogamous partners. The idea of mating love with close group members is anathema to humans. Utterly taboo. Where can there be romance when you mate any female whose swelling attracts you "huuu"? Where can there be any tenderness "huuu"? And how can you feel any real distinction between adults and sub-adults

330

when you so promiscuously mate with your own offspring "huuu"?'

Hamble, not exactly put out, but confused by this symmetrical paradox, fluttered to himself: How can there be any romance or adulthood when you *don't?*

Simon was high now, and the images of his past, his caressing human past, were coming back to him with hateful acuity. How could he have thought that he had lost his ability to suspend disbelief in human sexuality? Or perhaps – and this made his hackles rise – perhaps it was precisely his failure to apprehend what was most sacred, most important, most inherently human in life – the physical expression of love, that had precipitated Simon into this nightmarish realm, with its dope-smoking apes and doctoring chimpanzees.

The doctor in question reappeared at this point, and Busner was none too pleased to see that Hamble was sharing a joint with Simon. He clenched his fist as he knuckle-walked into the room. "HoooH'Graa," he greeted them, then signed, 'Really, Raymond, I don't think hypomania and marijuana consort happily, do you "huuu"?'

'I don't know about that "euch euch".' He footed the joint from Simon's outstretched toes. 'I thought it might help to unpack more of this poor chimp's delusion, and fumigate our gesticulation, which really has been most representative for me. Anyway,' he dropped off his chair and crawled over to Busner, *'we're* too long in the tooth to fission over such a thing "huuu" Zackiekins?' The two alpha males commenced grooming one another with rare artistry, while Simon slumbered in his chair, a rhodomontade of defiantly human rutting cries resounding in his tortured brow.

They left the Set soon afterwards. Hamble inscribed a copy of his book about travelling in Amazonia – *In Deep Shit* – to Simon, who fluttered that he had a copy already, albeit under another title and in a parallel world.

The cab was waiting for them, and as they pulled away down the rutted track, the last thing Simon saw was Hamble, in exactly the same pose he'd been when they arrived; behind the hawthorn hedge in his garden, his big muzzle creased with good humour, his gingerish sideburns catching the rays of the setting sun.

For the whole journey back to London Simon was plunged in a torment of recollection. Sarah's small blonde head tilted back. His hand smoothing over her head fur. Her sharp little canines bared in ecstasis. Her small hands tugging softly on his engorged cock. And those peculiar human vocalisations, uttered in the heat of mating. "There-there, there-there ... There. There."

When they got back to Redington Road Simon shut himself up in his room and put on the video of *Battle for the Planet of the Humans*. It was the one of the film cycle that amused him most; and paradoxically allowed him to capture the tenor of his lost identity, hold it fast for a few seconds. He liked the risible setting of the film, the battle for the planet taking place in what looked like a Milton Keynes shopping mall. There was that ticklishness and there were the zombie-like humans themselves – massing on aerial knuckle-walkways to overwhelm their chimpanzee masters – and all so implausibly portrayed. The film's designer hadn't troubled concretely to imagine intelligent, domesticated humans. So, like chimpanzees, they were naked from the waist down and shoeless.

Some of the lines in the film – the last of the cycle – sent Simon into tooth-clacking fits of laughter. In particular, when the beastly chimps have cornered the super-intelligent offspring of the humans who escaped from the future in the penultimate film (*Escape from the Planet of the Humans*), the head badchimp – as Simon couldn't help ascripting him – wrung his hands. 'Seeing him is like watching some awful bacillus and knowing you've got it trapped "wraaaa"!'

Then, at the very end, when the hordes of humans are overknuckling the entire complex – *so* seventies that – the same character blazons the immortal signs: 'This will be the end of chimpanzee civilization, and the world will become a planet of the humans "wraaaa"!'

If only, thought Simon, staring at the screen while moodily puffing a Bactrian. If only. The effects of Hamble's weed – which was very strong – had faded, leaving behind solely a hardened conviction that he must meet with his ex-alpha Jean, that he had to come muzzle-to-muzzle with his infants. If there was a full correspondence between this world and the world as it had been before the disastrous night at the Sealink, then the only chimps who could help him were from his fissioned group.

Busner broke Simon's reverie. He pant-hooted outside the door and receiving no recall, entered. "HoooH'Graa", he vocalised, then signed, 'Well, Simon what did you think of your day out, instructive "huuu"?'

'Definitely, Dr Busner. It did me a power of good administering a thrashing to that creature, and as for Hamble, well, I liked him "grnnn". He seemed utterly unconcerned about the notion that I consider myself human and the world I perceive a ludicrous delusion –'

' – Well, yes,' Busner chopped in, 'but do remember Hamble is *very* eccentric.'

'Other than that it's been "hooo" the same.'

'The same "huuu"?'

'Sometimes I feel half-able to acknowledge the reality of things as they are – but then the past comes flooding back "hooo" – it's incredibly disturbing. But one thing I signed at Hamble's house I'm convinced is the truth. I have such a clear and unmistakable memory of my middle infant "hooo". I *must* meet with my ex-alpha, only she can help me to discover the truth. Please Dr Busner, it's been over two months now, can't I see my infants "huuu", please?'

Simon crawled to where Busner squatted and presented to him with utmost, grovelling deference. The radical psychoanalyst – as he liked to denote himself – laid a hortatory hand on the lanky chimp's ischial scrag and

inparted the bewhiskered rump, 'There – there "chup-chupp",
Simonkins, don't worry, my poor fellow, I was impressed with
your conduct – and your conducting – today. I think that some
good may be served by having a session with your old group.
Your ex-alpha is amenable, so I'll "huh-huh-huh" see what I
can do to arrange it as soon as possible. But there's something
else I want to put to you –'

'What's that "huuu"?'

'I was pant-hooted just now by your old consort's ally Tony
Figes. He signs that there's an opening tonight at the Saatchi
Gallery. He seemed to think it was an exhibition that would
particularly entwine you.'

Simon broke from the grooming and turned to muzzle
Busner. 'Are you suggesturing that we should go "huuu"?'

'Well "euch-euch", certainly not if you don't feel able to deal
with it. There will, no doubt, be a lot of chimps you know there,
but on the other hand ...' Busner went on signing sinistrally
'... it's only down the road, within knuckle-walking distance,
and as always, if you feel an episode or seizure coming on we
can leave. I think it might be a good idea. After all, it's another
handhold back up the tree to recovery "h'huuu"?'

Chapter Nineteen

T he evening was cold and blustery. But Simon and Busner
did knuckle-walk down Fitzjohn's Avenue and through
Swiss Cottage to Boundary Road; although in contrast to
that morning there was little mating activity for them to
observe. However, things were considerably different when
they reached the vicinity of the gallery. From two hundred
and twenty-four metres away, despite the gloom, Busner could
see that the junction of Abbey Road and Boundary Road was
packed with the art crowd of chimps, rutting, screeching,
grooming, networking and queuing to get into the Saatchi
Gallery.

Busner pulled upright and turned to muzzle Simon.
'"Huuu" are you sure you'll be able to cope with this?
There will be a lot of chimps there you know –'

"Hooo", Simon recalled, then countersigned, 'Surely I won't
be able to recognise them, there's such a big crowd, and they're
chimpanzees "clak-clak-clak"!'

'Yes, Simon, but remember they will certainly recognise
you. You haven't been seen in public since your show *and*
your breakdown has been reported in the press. I think you
can safely "euch-euch" assume that we will attract attention.'

What Busner was really counting on was that Sarah
Peasenhulme, Simon's ex-consort, would turn up for the
opening as well. Certainly that had been the gist of the
gesticulation between Busner and Figes. 'She's having a sort

of consortship with Ken Braithwaite, the performance artist,' Figes signed on the 'phone, 'but she'd love to mate with Simon again and feel his ischial scrag. Do you think he's prepared to get it "huuu" up for her, Dr Busner?'

Busner countersigned he had no way of knowing, but that Simon seemed more and more accepting of his chimpunity. It wasn't an overhead sign, for on the knuckle-walk down from Hampstead Simon moved with greater fluidity than Busner could remember. The atrophy in his feet and legs was slackening and he'd left his jacket undone despite the cold wind, surely an acknowledgement of his own preference for real as against fake fur?

The two chimps were dominant enough to push their way through the outer eddies of the crowd and penetrate the large, spike-topped grey steel doors at the entrance to the gallery compound. From there a smooth ramp horse-legged away to the entrance of the gallery proper. Set in the crook of the ramp was a full-size model of a fire engine. Simon, his scut moving ahead of Busner's muzzle through the shaggy mêlée, ignored it. From his purposeful manner Busner deduced that coming to this familiar place was reassuring him.

Not so reassuring were the enquiring pant-hoots that floated to Busner's ears from the fusing art chimps. Simon had been recognised and the Chinese caresses were doing the rounds.

Busner gave their invitations to the gallery female on the door, who seeing Simon presented her scrag, then asked them both to autograph the book. Despite the no-smoking sign above her head, she didn't show the former artist to stub out his Bactrian. Simon marked his name with a flourish, erect at the desk, proud and disdainful. A few chimps clustered there and a couple of them presented to him, and he automatically bestowed reassuring pats on their vibrating scuts. "H'huuu," Busner vocalised when they had moved on. 'Did you know those chimps, Simon?'

'I don't think so,' he countersigned. 'Perhaps they're art students.'

336

Busner had been to the Saatchi Gallery before, but the sheer size of the place took him aback anew. The vestibule was large enough to contain the entirety of Levinson's Cork Street haunt. Crawling to the right down a broad, short flight of stairs, they entered a room with an area as big as an aircraft hangar – and almost as high. The floor was painted with the same thick grey emulsion as the ramp outside and the walls were blanched. The lighting was so comprehensive and monotonous that its source was irrelevant. There were some sculptures placed here and there on the aestheticised bled, and a few canvases hung from the voided walls. But it wasn't these that struck Busner and Simon – it was the bombinating mob of chimpunity.

For, if the entrance to the gallery had been crowded, the interior was absolutely packed. One might have signed that all of chimpanzee life was here, were it not so manifestly untrue. Rather, all of trendy, arty London was here. They were all wearing their best threads, they were all drinking the champagne on offer, they were all gesturing wildly, preening, posing and displaying.

The females wore shortie dresses, bustiers, blouses and swelling-protectors in a bewildering number of styles – all absolutely *à la mode*, and the males were just as fashionably garbed. The jackets and shirts of both genders were mostly open to reveal their chest fur, and in many instances a pierced teat, or even two. There were chimps garbed in leather, in vinyl, in what looked like gold leaf, in PVC, in chiffon and in black serge; which was – Busner's delta, Isabel, had recently inparted him – *this* season's black serge.

Observing this over-caparisoned horde, Busner was driven to put his finger on what bothered him. "H'huuu?" he vocalised.

Simon turned tail, 'Why are they all *so* dressed up?' The former artist looked at his therapist. The poor old ape, he thought, he's really a fish out of water at this sort of gig. For the first time since he had come under Busner's care, Simon felt their relationship was definitely pivoting. He was so accustomed to Busner helping him, grooming him, inparting, and providing a constant massage, that the novelty of being in a situation where *he* could bestow some hortatory grooming and informative prodding brought him out.

' "Euch-euch" Dr Busner, you have to appreciate this scene,' Simon flourished, 'as an expression of the – how can I put it "huu"? – of the dominance order operating amongst the disparate elements of the art world. They are all *so* over-dressed, because that's one of the few ways they can gain any attention, any preening, from their "euch-euch" hierarchical superiors – or subordinates, or peers –'

'That's what I assumed.' Busner chopped the air and the two chimps squatted, cradling one another's scrotal sacks, whilst the seraglio of simians whirled past.

'After all,' Simon continued, placing the signs carefully in Busner's groin fur, 'they can't very well carry their reputations around with them on their "h'hee-hee" backs – now can they, Busnerkins "huu"?'

'Please,' Busner gently kneaded, 'as our grooming has become so mutual, won't you denote me Zack "huu"?'

'Of course, Zackiekins "chup-chupp", I am honoured that you acknowledge my ascent up the hierarchy. Now, as I was signing, the reputations of these artists – if that's what they are – are also so arguable, that they require continual interpretation and "gru-nnn" adjustment by a large party of critics "grnn". The critics have their own hierarchy, and the hierarchy that exists between them and the artists' party is also highly fluid – subject to continual flux. That's why "chup-chupp" they're all dressed up, and displaying and presenting and grooming and mating, for all the buggers are worth "h'hee-hee-hee"!'

Busner giggled as well, when Simon inparted this last ticklecism. Then, finding themselves by the drinks table, both chimps took a rented glass of champagne and continued knuckle-walking around the edge of the exaggerated room. This main part of the gallery was hung with a series of large, garish canvases. These depicted scenes of ordinary life in

Middle America – car washing, barbecueing, frisbee playing and the like – but all skewed to one side, as if the viewer – or painter – were astigmatic. There was this distortion, which produced a sense of Lynchian unease, and there were also the hyperreal colours and jagged brush strokes, squaring the effect.

'Not bad,' Simon gestured, 'not bad at all, what did you sign this was ascripted "huu"?'

'It's a show of young American artists, Simon,' Busner replied.

They had circumnavigated and scooped up another rented glass of champagne when Simon, who was taking the lead on this patrol, halted, his scut quivering, the fur on his rump erect. Busner rushed to get soothing fingers in his protégé's fur. '"Huuu" Simon, what is it?'

"HoooGrnnn," Simon called apprehensively, then signed, 'I may be wrong, Zack, but I think I *recognise* those two chimps at the top of the stairs.'

Busner followed Simon's gaze, and saw two non-identical twin bonobos. 'The two bonobos there "huu", is that who you mean?'

'Yes, that's right, *those* are bonobos, are they "huu"? I've seen signs of them, but no one's shown me exactly what they are.'

'Who do you think those bonobos are, Simon "huu"?' Busner's signing was the lightest of caresses.

'I think "h'hooo" that they're two friends of Sarah, denoted the Braithwaites. Ken and Steve. One of those notices on my show, that you gave to me in the hospital, implied that Ken had been mating Sarah. It's weird . . .' Simon fell motionless. Busner tweaked him 'What "huu"?'

'I imagine I *ought* to feel jealous seeing Ken – if it is Ken, but for some reason I don't, I'd just like to muzzle him and see who presents to who "huu"?'

Busner regarded Simon sceptically. He understood, of course, what Simon was aiming at. Given the perverse human practice of monogamy, presumably the mating of a longstanding alpha, beta, gamma; or even a consort, or even – and Busner clacked internally at this absurdity – a temporary nestmate, would be cause for emotional distress. But while this entwined the anti-psychiatrist – as he liked to style himself – all the more inveigling was Simon's recognition of the bonobos.

The two chimps continued to observe the Braithwaites. The bonobos were bipedal at the top of the stairs, and a procession of chimps was presenting to them in a most unusual and cursory fashion, hardly dipping their rumps, barely bestowing a touch, certainly not bothering to groom. 'What are bonobos "huu"?' Simon inparted after a while.

'They're simply the race of chimpanzees who inhabit Africa, Simon.' Busner countersigned.

'You mean to sign they're *blacks* "huu"?'

Busner's knowledge of human sub-species was now good enough for him to be unfazed. 'That's right, Simon,' he countersigned. 'They're "grnn" analogous to the black human sub-species.'

'So, presumably there's such a thing as bonoboism "h'hee-h'huu"?'

'Indeed.'

'Well "h'hee-hee",' the former artist bared his lower teeth with merriment, 'that certainly explains a lot.'

'Like what "huu"?' Busner was perplexed.

'Like why there aren't a lot of them at this opening. Some things – as I've had reason to sign before – just don't change.'

With this finger flourish, Simon got bipedal and swaggered up the stairs to where the Braithwaites were. Busner hurried after his scut. However, in the few seconds that had elapsed as they mounted the stairs, the Braithwaites had vanished into the crowd of openeers. Simon leapt in the air, but all he could see was a setose sea of chimpanzee heads, bobbing up and down towards the vanishing point of artifice. 'They've regained the safety of the crowd.' Simon waved to Busner – then he froze. '"Hooo" this is peculiar . . .'

This part of the gallery was as null and void as the other – although not as great a waste. Scattered around its uncoloured inexistence were various chimpikins. They weren't exactly statues – being constructed so far as Simon could see from plastic or latex – but nor were they conventional chimpikins. The lifesize figure nearest to them was arrested in mid-stride, attempting to depart its own plinth. White-coated, and brandishing a test tube, its scruff gave way not to a simian countenance, but an enormous, mutant, massy head. 'That,' Simon gestured facetiously to Busner, 'is how I often "h'hee-hee" imagine you!'

The other chimpikins were equally aberrant – a potato headed figure, a Bugs Bunny mutant and a dodo. But strangest of all was the forlorn little figure of an infant human. This creature had also been transmuted by its creator. It was covered with a most inhuman coat of patchy fur, and had hind paws with prehensile digits, one of which it was using to give itself an interminable mainline fix with a two-millilitre disposable insulin syringe.

Simon and Busner knuckle-walked around all of them huuing softly as they went, until, gaining the far end of the gallery, they paused by the cross-breed junior junky to apply pressure to an exegesis. '"H'hoo" most suitable material, Simon, wouldn't you agree "h'huu"?'

'"Gru-nnn" I suppose you're right about that, Zack. These are all obvious remarks on the queering – as it were – of the natural pitch; the distortion of our bodily sense in response to the anti-natural way we, as chimpanzees, now live.' Busner, although surprised by his protégé's admission of conspecifity, nonetheless held his hands, only flourishing, 'Not dissimilar to your own recent work "h'huuu"?'

'True enough,' Simon countersigned, 'like my apocalyptic paintings these chimpikins are alluding to some crucial loss of perspective, occasioned by the enforcement of a hard dividing line between chimp and beast.'

While this gesticulation had been going on, unnoticed by either Simon or Busner, a bent little freckle-faced chimp, wearing an obvious toupee and a white linen jacket, carefully hoicked to expose his scrag, had come up beside them. Seeing Simon fall signlent, this chimp presented his arse to them, flicking, '"HoooH'Graaa" Dr Busner, I'm honoured to abase myself before you, Simon, it does me good to see you out and about again, please allow me the pleasure of cradling your pendulous scrotum.' This, the chimp duly did.

Feeling an oddly familiar palmar sensation, Simon stared straight into the muzzle of this joyful subordinate, a muzzle on which two mouths gaped, one with teeth, the other sealed up with scarring. It was, Simon acknowledged, Tony Figes. ' "HoooH'Graa" Tony! Dr Busner inparted you might be here, what do you think of these "huu"?'

Tony Figes, looking up at Simon's guileless muzzle, decided to play it the way he visibly wanted for the moment, and not finger to the fact that the last time they had been in touch was at the shebeen off Cambridge Circus, only hours before Simon's breakdown. He calmly countersigned, 'They're not uninteresting. I saw what you were showing Dr Busner here, and I agree with you. These chimpikins – and it's particularly remarkable that the artist has seized on the human in this context – are, as it were "grnnn" modern therianthropes, chimeras constructed from chimpanzees, animals and aliens – the fauna of the future. Like the therianthropes of traditional chimpanzee cultures, it's not so preposterous to imagine them fulfilling some sacredotal purpose "huu"?'

Simon, Busner noted, was far from being put out by Figes' manipulation. On the contrary, eyebrow ridges raised, fur pleasingly erect, the sometime ape man let out a spontaneous pant-hoot, "H'hooo," then applied more pressure. 'What sort of sacredotal purpose, Tony "huuu"?'

'Well, our hunting activities may be circumscribed by the way we, as chimps, now live; but I think Lévi-Strauss's observations on the subject "gru-nnn" remain as true today as when neolithic artists first applied ochre to the walls of Lascaux. You will "chup-chupp" recall that he pointed out that the beginnings of all chimpanzee art are in the impersonation – and depiction – of animals "huuu"?'

Simon had become distracted. With the reference to Lévi-Strauss a circuit was completed in the former artist's brain, his delusion had traversed the three-minute memory loop; what had been around had never gone away. And without in any way accepting his furry limbs; his slim, pink cock; his blackened face and bony brows; his protuberant green eyes and bouffant head fur, Simon Dykes found himself able to work a room for the first time in months.

Over there, swaggering, waving a brace of catalogues in the air and gesticulating with his inimitable arrogance, was a large, white-bearded male with thinning head fur and a pronounced goitre on his neck. It was – Simon knew with certainty – Gareth 'Grunt' Feltham, the opinonated art critic of *The Times*. And with him was his occasional sidekick – a truth Feltham underlined as Simon watched, by kicking him – Pelham, the feature writer. Pelham was as scrawny in his simian incarnation as he had been in his human one. As scrawny – and gifted now with physical rather than psychic mange.

And there, that huge chimp – who was starting to move on a squatting female, shoving aside her plain black Bella Freud swelling-protector to effect panting insertion – was Flixou the sculptor, Simon's sometime professional rival.

The recognition of Flixou pushed Simon up on to another platform of this absurd game. The arrival of several females in the vicinity, several females in oestrus, was provoking the mating activities. A couple of them were resplendent, protectorless and flaunting engorged perineal areas the size and dazzle of plastic washing-up bowls. A couple more had hardly come on, their slickening flesh only on the turn, bulging from behind their groin fur. And there was one

343

more female, a female with blonde-tinged head fur; a young, delicate female wearing a Selena Blow swelling-protector over her withering pink flower. Simon flared his nostrils – even from twenty feet away he could tell that this one, although nearly at the end of her oestrus, was still recepetive.

Looking full into her muzzle, her heart-shaped muzzle, and seeing her flawlessly thin yet floppy lips curl back to reveal canine teeth that were oddly pointed – even for a chimpanzee – Simon knew it was Sarah. He let out a great, roaring pant-hoot, "HooooRaaargh!" Both Busner and Figes jerked to attention. Simon was on the verge of bounding over to Sarah to do he knew not what, when he saw that others were there already.

The Braithwaites, to be precise. Both Ken and Steve were displaying to Sarah in a decidedly unorthodox way. Skittering bipedally between the chimpikin art works, revolving, dancing, turning back-flips, the bonobos were entrancing to watch. Other males, scenting that a popular female still in oestrus – although late on – had arrived at the opening, were keen to encounter *her* opening. There were males in Shandong silk jackets; males in Paul Smith jackets; males in Levi's denim jackets; and all of them had erect, quivering pink cocks; and all of them had erect, quivering ischial pleats. And they all paraded around her, importuning her, desperate to cover her; screaming, waa-barking and drumming on the floor.

As Simon watched a loose dominance hierarchy was arrived at, with Ken Braithwaite at the head of the queue. Sarah, peering back at Simon over her shoulder, squatted down. Ken Braithwaite twitched aside her swelling-protector and commenced mating her with characteristic chimpanzee nonchalance. Not even bothering to put down his rented champagne glass the ape thrusted, panted and eventually tooth-clacked. Reaching climax in a matter of seconds, he withdrew, flourished, 'Thank's for the "huh-huh" fuck, Sarah,' and swaggered away. Steve Braithwaite followed him, snuffling at the fresh come in his fur.

Without waiting for the next male in line to cover his former consort, his adorable nestmate, Simon let out a second roaring pant-hoot, "HooooRaaargh!" and sprang towards the copulatory conga-line. Tony Figes waved to Busner, 'Do you think he'll "hooo" be all right "huu"?' and the former television personality went some way to snapping one of his infrequent jokes, when he countersigned, 'In this case it's probably mate – or break "h'hee-hee"!'

They watched as Simon skidded to a halt on the lack-of-industry floor-covering. Flixou, the sculptor, had managed to break into the chain of would-be copulators and was preparing to mount Sarah. Simon grasped the situation and went straight for him. "Aaaaieee!" he screamed and delivered a swingeing blow to the back of Flixou's neck. The sculptor – whose most celebrated work, to date, had been an enormous block of ice, sited on the South Bank and denoted simply *A Waste of Ice* – reeled back. Before he could recover himself Simon had delivered a raking smack across his muzzle. This drew blood, and rather than stain his Jasper Conran jacket, Flixou accepted defeat. He presented to the ape man, who bestowed a reassuring pat on his rump, as simultaneously he smoothly entered Sarah.

"EeeeWraa!" she squealed, as his familiar cock lunged into her.

"Huh-huh-huh" Simon panted as he thrust, while inparting her back fur, ' "Hoo" Sarah, Sarah, this is so "chup-chupp" strange!' He smoothed the ruff of blonde fur from the apex of her round head down to the bunched muscle of her back. He reached one hand beneath their gyrating hips and grabbed hold of the front of her swelling, feeling the engorged flesh, with its cocktail of lubricants, scrunge between his fingers. "Huh-huh-huh!" Another three plunges and they both started clacking to a climax: "Huh-huh-clak-huh-clak-huh-clak-" then, as one soul, tortured by pleasure, they achieved an orgasm the like of which hadn't been heard at the Saatchi Gallery for some days. "EeeeeeeWraaaa!" they squealed. Chimps as far off as the next room fell signlent and turned to see what the rumpus was all about.

Zack Busner was delighted by this turn of events, and reasoning that Simon, having covered Sarah *so* successfully, would certainly take time for a proper post-coital grooming session, moved off on some-threes, his rented glass aloft, to see if there was any champagne left.

By the drinks table there was a gaggle of chimps who were paying no attention to the mating chains getting underway in the upper gallery. Busner recognised one of their number, a tall individual with light-brown head fur and rather feminine hips. Busner, adjusting his own bifocals on his nasal bridge, identified the chimp by his ridiculously trendy oval Oliver Peeples eyewear and even more absurd faux swelling-protector. It was, of course, George Levinson.

George was conducting the group, his large hands chopping the air. As he broke in Busner caught the signs 'Of course Jews are like other chimps – only more so –' then Levinson saw him and presented low. ' "H'hooo" Dr Busner, what a pleasure to see your revered scrag at this event. Tony Figes showed me that Simon might be with you "h'huu"?'

Busner bestowed a pat on Levinson's large rump. ' "H'hooo" Mr Levinson, you must have been absorbed in your conducting – didn't you hear that marvellous copulation squeal "huu"? That was Simon mating his old consort –'

'Sarah "huu"? What excellent news, what excellent news. I suppose this means he's on the mend "huu"? That your rather unorthodox methods, Dr Busner, have borne fruit.'

One of the huddle gathered around Levinson had been watching intently, and he now presented to Busner as well. ' "H'hooo" Dr Busner, isn't it "huu"?'

'That's right.'

'I admire your beautifully effulgent ischial scrag, your rump is like the morning star, and your maverick philosophy is a beacon of intrigue in a dull world. I am, sir, your most obedient subordinate.'

Busner, delighted by this abject grovelling, bestowed several pats on the proffered rump and also kissed it. 'Thank you for kissing my arse,' the chimp gestured, getting bipedal, 'you probably don't remember me but we groomed briefly at the Cassell Clinic last year.'

Busner took a closer look at the chimp, who was young – only in his early twenties – with very black fur, a very white muzzle, and extravagantly permed head fur which didn't really suit him. '"H'huuu"? No, I can't altogether sign I do,' he countersigned. 'What's your name "huu"?'

'Alex Knight,' the chimp demarcated. 'I'm a television producer. I was making a documentary on gesticulating cures – hence my presence at the Cassell –'

' "Gru-nnn" I do resign you now, yes, Bernard Paulson highlighted you, indeed he did. What can I do for you "huuu"?'

The television producer abased himself a little more, conscious that what he was going to sign might constitute overstepping the mark. ' "HooGrnn" I understand, Dr Busner, that you're treating the artist, Simon Dykes "huu"?'

'That's correct.'

'And that since his breakdown he's been suffering from the distressing delusion that he's "huuu" human?'

'Yes, yes, that's also the case, although only this evening he's been showing remarkable evidence of recovery, breaking into mating chains, very much back in the swing –'

'But he still visualises himself as human "huu"?'

'Yes, I'm afraid that the core of his delusion remains "euch-euch" intact. But show me, Knight, why is this of interest to you "huu"?'

'Purely speculatively, Dr Busner, *purely* speculatively, I wondered whether you – and Mr Dykes, naturally – would be interested in gesticulating the possibility of making a television documentary "huu"?'

'A documentary "huu"?'

'That's right. Obviously dealing with the therapeutic

relationship you've developed with him – and by extension with your entire existential-phenomenological philosophy of mental disorders "gru-nnn".'

Busner looked intently at the chimp's muzzle. The television producer seemed guileless enough and he'd been highlighted by Paulson, whom Busner trusted. But the factor that really nipped at him was Knight's casually displayed knowledge of his philosophy. Perhaps this was a chimp Busner could do business with. ' "H'hooo" Mr Knight, I don't as a rule hold much of a brief for television. In my experience, all too often it bowdlerises as much as popularises. However "hooo" certain circumstances have arisen which mean that I might be interested in such delineations. Have you a card "huuu"?'

Knight didn't have a card, and had to prod others in the group for pen and paper to scrawl down his numbers. Busner took the slip, footed him, signing, 'I think you may confidently expect to have a pant-hoot from me in the near future, Mr Knight . . . ' He was going to wave through, worried he might have had his hand on the matter, when there came a series of loud pant-screams from the upper gallery: "HoooWraaa! HoooWraaa! HoooWraaa!" pant-screams that unmistakably belonged to Simon.

It had only been a few minutes since they fissioned, but it was time enough for Simon to get himself into trouble. After covering Sarah the two of them had squatted together and Simon received the most satisfying, most soothing groom since his breakdown. His ex-consort's little fingers expertly palped, tweaked and kneaded his groin fur, teasing out the drying semen and. vaginal secretions, stroking his still-jolting cock. ' "Gru-unnn" Simon, it's so good to be in touch with you, my love,' she inparted, 'and you seem so much better "chup-chupp". I've been so worried about you –'

' "Grnnn" I am better, Sarah "chup-chupp", it's true. I can't show you how or why, but the world doesn't seem so strange any more. Why, even the sight of Ken

Braithwaite covering you just now didn't seem to disturb me –'

'But, but, why should it, Simon "huu"? Your position in the hierarchy remains secure.'

Simon looked into her green, vertically slit eyes, they were animal – true enough – but quite devoid of malice or fecklessness. He combed the blonde scruff and reparted, 'It would be difficult to manipulate all of this for you – but anyway, it didn't bother me "grnnn".'

The bonobo in question knuckle-walked up at this point, and with him were the rest of the posse, the glossy happy chimps, Steve, Tony Figes and Julius, the barchimp from the Sealink Club. A slim female – but bigger than Sarah, with longer tufts of blonde head fur – scampered up as well, screeching over her shoulder at two males displaying in her scut. "H'hooo," Simon vocalised, then gestured, 'Hello, Tabitha, still being chased by the males "huuu"?!'

' "H'hooo" Simon!' She planted a sloppy kiss on his muzzle, 'How good to touch you!' Julius gave him a kiss as well and held Simon's scrotal sack for a while.

' "H'hooo" my chimp,' Simon signed.

' "H'hooo" my chimp,' Julius countersigned, 'can I assist you to a refreshing beverage "huu"?' The two old allies heaved with signless laughter.

Julius had, Simon noted, shaved himself a new inverse goatee, more extensive and more sharply angled than the one he'd had before. '"H'huu" new inverse goatee, Julius?'

'Yes "hee-hee",' the barchimp giggled, 'courtesy of Gillette – it's the best a chimp can get! "H'hee-hee-hee"!'

With such high spirits all round and such fervid grooming underway as the glossy happy chimps effected their refusion as a group, it was little wonder that Simon didn't demur when Steve Braithwaite gestured, 'Fancy a line, Simon "huu"?' They all crawled off to the toilets.

The stall was high enough for the seven of them to squeeze inside. Steve put the seat down and squatted atop it chopping lines out on the cistern lid. Simon squatted below together with Tony, and Sarah, while the Braithwaites and Tabitha dangled happily from the ceiling, occasionally feetling the head fur of those below and provoking much lip-smacking. Simon took the rolled-up note he was offered and thrust it into his nostril. He snuffled up the line and immediately tasted the chemical bitterness at the top of his throat; turning to muzzle Steve he signed, 'Where did this stuff come from, Steve "huu"?'

'I got it off that chimp Tarquin who hangs out at the club,' the bonobo countersigned. 'It's basically crap – although it delivers quite a boot up the scrag.'

Simon sniffed copiously and felt the stream of crap cocaine and mucus trickle down his larynx. 'You've put your finger on it there, Steve,' he signed. 'This stuff is certainly crap. Thank God some things *really* don't change "h'hooo"!'

But the peculiar warm cheer that the crap cocaine inparted didn't last that long – and just as in his deluded recollections of being human, cocaine had always tipped Simon on to the brink of acute anxiety, so it did this time. Back in the gallery, when he lit his umpteenth Bactrian of the day. Julius, knuckle-walking beside him waved, '"Hooo" I shouldn't smoke if I were you, Simon – not after a line.'

'What on earth are you gesturing about, Julius . . .' Simon countersigned, but when he tried to vocalise the interrogative he began spluttering, "Huuueurh –" then coughing, "Eurgh-euch-euch!" for, of course, the poor madchimp's somatic delusion had kicked in, and he no longer knew that chimpanzees cannot breathe and vocalise at the same time. The crap cocaine had anaesthetised Simon in more ways than one.

Now, bipedal against the unwall of the gallery, Simon Dykes's heart rate accelerated and his protuberant green eyes darted about, taking in the nightmare vision of a world gone bestial. All around him the chimpanzees scampered and scuttled, bristling, bewhiskered, horripilating. And when he looked into their slit irises Simon could see nothing but alien intelligence.

Even the glossy happy chimps were becoming strange to him as the crap cocaine infused his disordered mind. The set of the Saatchi Gallery, with its cast of half-dressed chimps holding rented champagne glasses aloft as they moved about on some-threes, reminded Simon of a gigantic circus act, put on for the benefit of human infants.

Simon laughed and cried as memories and impressions were cut, then shuffled before his eyes. The glossy happy chimps did their best to administer an emergency grooming, but Simon's giggling and coughing soon became hysterical and he commenced pant-screaming.

Busner swaggered over at this point. The clique fissioned from around Simon and Busner administered some calming blows to the former artist's muzzle. Then, without bothering to pick over the detail of what had happened, he gave a valedictory pant-hoot to the assembled chimps: "HoooGraaa!", drummed on the base of a plinth – suitably enough, the one occupied by the mulish human infant – and led Simon away.

As he turned the last thing that Simon saw through his tears was Sarah's darling muzzle. On it was an expression of almost insane bewilderment, but despite that she was taking comfort – as apes do – by mating again with Ken Braithwaite.

Busner managed to pant-hoot a cab in the street and they were back at Redington Road within minutes. He took Simon straight up to his room, and administered the customary intravenous shot of Valium. Simon goggled woozily at Busner as the former anti-psychiatrist searched for a vein beneath his elbow fur. ' "Huu" what it is, Simon?' the old ape asked.

' "Hooo" I don't know, Zack, I don't know . . .' Busner had found the vein and, releasing the tourniquet, was easing home the plunger. Jane Bowen had insisted on Simon's medication being administered this way because of Simon's extreme febrility and Busner considered it wise to continue. The intravenous method allowed the dosage to be effectively titrated.

Simon's eyes rolled back in their sockets; Busner sensed

the muscles in the arm he was grasping relax. The fingers of Simon's hand sketched the air, 'When you give me these shots . . . When I look at my arm when you're giving me these shots . . . I almost see it as a chimpanzee arm – really, I do. I see it with fur, really I do . . .' and with this further revelation of his burgeoning chimpness, Simon Dykes fell back into the nest, curled up foetally and slept. Busner hauled himself up with difficulty – it was a damp night, always bad for the arthritis – and peered down at his patient.

Professional dispassion had never been at the core of Busner's therapeutic philosophy. Looking now at Simon's muzzle, drugged into provisional repose, and at the chimp's sorry chest fur, pitted with Bactrian burns, Busner allowed himself to accept that their relationship had gone beyond the bounds of treatment. That they were – in some sense – allies now, united against a hostile world, whether of apes or men. Busner shivered in the stuffy spare room, then checked his ischial pleat for winnets, before going in search of a third supper.

As he slept Simon dreamed. In the dreams he was human again. He was walking upright, easefully, feeling the long length of his back support a forward-pointing cone of quintessentially human extroception. In and out of this cone there skipped his infants, his three little males. They were all laughing, they all had tow heads and cuddlesome pink skin. But the most cuddlesome of all, the apple of his father's eye, was Simon junior. Simon ran to him, lifted him up, felt little Simon's knees grasp his trunk. He sank his muzzle in the soft flesh of his infant's scruff and whimpered, inhaling the human essence of him, the beautiful sensuality of him.

Later that night Simon passed from this Erewhon into one more nightmarish, one in which he and Sarah were mating as humans mate. He lay on top of her feeling her bald body gyrate beneath him. Her hairlessness was nauseating, rubbing against his own. They were like two shaven muzzles, slippery with sweat, slicking and slopping.

Sarah's eyes were also disturbing, blue, feral, they stabbed up at Simon; and her horrible little mouth with its miniature teeth, opened to emit low-pitched grunts and garbled vocalisations, "Gru-nnnfuckme! Gru-nnnfuckme!" Simon thrust into her as best he could, but he could feel nothing in the region of his groin, no homecoming mush of sexual swelling, merely an absence, a local void. "Gru-nnnfuckme! Gru-nnnfuckme!" Still she vocalised and still he laboured, but neither of them could come, it was taking *ages*, this mating – *minutes*. It was – Simon realised with an access of dream logic – some awful presaging of impotence, of old age, of death.

In sleep the sometime artist's muzzle creased with anxieties. His mouth opened and from behind his big teeth came yawps and keening noises.

Busner was up early the following morning, well in time for a first breakfast with the infants who were heading off to school, and the sub-adults who were going out on patrol. He played with the former and mock-fought with the latter. He petted the ubiquitous Busner lap ponies and covered a couple of his younger daughters who were within weeks of their first oestrus. All in all it was a happy, very group morning. Into this innocent arcadia came a missive that was a missile; a bombshell of a brown envelope.

Mary, the Busner iota female, came in from the hall on some-threes, bearing the envelope aloft to where Zack squatted at the kitchen table, reading the *Guardian*, while Dr Kenzaburo Yamuta, the distal-zeta male, groomed his back fur. Looking at the envelope was enough – and getting bipedal on his chair, the old alpha addressed his group. ' "HoooGraa!" There's something important I need to gesticulate about. I want group adults – both male and female – beta through to epsilon, in my study in three minutes. The rest of you are to keep the noise down. Colin' – he waved at the theta male – 'in a while, check and see if Simon's all right. We had quite a night and he may need something for a hangover "h'hooo".'

353

By the time the chimps he had summoned swung into the study, Busner had read the letter and absorbed its contents. "HoooH'Graa," he welcomed them, and gesturing to the letter which lay on the desk signed, 'I gesticulated with Charlotte concerning this business when we were in nest some weeks ago, shortly after poor Simon came to stay with us . . .' He paused, and looked up at nine pairs of intent green eyes. 'At that time I suspected that our quondam gamma male – and my former research assistant Gambol – was fomenting an alliance against me –'

This revelation provoked a flurry of disconcerted signing and an eruption of distressed whimpering from the assembled Busner chimps. '"Gru-nnn" now calm down, all of you! As I sign, this was not unexpected. You all know that I've had more than my fair share of enemies in the medical and psychiatric hierarchies "chup-chupp". Furthermore, you are also aware that I've never knuckle-walked out of my way to present to these individuals, or show the requisite deference, I've simply done what I've thought necessary to assist those chimpunity chooses to denote "euch-euch" mentally ill.

' "Hooo" now all of these pigeons have come home to roost. Gambol – I don't know how – has obtained information that compromises me severely. Information concerning a rather inadvisable trial for a new anxiolytic drug I stupidly got entwined with. I won't "euch-euch" burden you with the details, but suffice to sign, my putative *mis*conduct in this matter also involves Simon Dykes. Gambol has seen fit to show all of this to the ethical committee of the General Medical Council. There is to be a probe "euch-euch" and this letter,' he waved the hateful thing aloft, 'informs me that my licence to practise medicine is temporarily suspended pending that probe "waaaa"!'

For some seconds there was pandemonium in the study. The Busner chimps all leapt about bouncing off the walls, horripilating and waa-barking furiously. Busner braced himself behind his desk – if there was going to be a coup against his

354

reign as alpha – now was the time. But no fusion was emerging, nor was the fur whirl resolving into any spontaneous alliances, so after a minute or so he beat on the desk and vocalised to regain their attention. "HooooGraaa!" Signless fell and novocal filled the study.

'Now, I'm not inclined to kowtow to these chimps, indeed I've resolved not to challenge the investigation in any way –' Another chorus of distressed hoooing from the assembled chimps. ' "Euch-euch" I feel it would compromise the whole of my career to do so. No, I am climbing down from the professional tree. I will continue to care for Simon Dykes, who I've come to respect as a chimp and an ally. I already have a vision of how I might continue to treat him.

'I should like to stay on here in the group home, but I "hooo" appreciate that my reign as group alpha may well be over as we –'

Pandemonium again. They all leapt up, they all yammered, they all drummed on the available surfaces, horizontal and vertical. There was some scrapping between Henry, the stolid Busner beta male, and David, the rather more excitable delta male, but it didn't amount to a fight and fusion quickly emerged, the chimps gesturing to Dr Kenzaburo Yamuta that he should sign on their behalf.

The distal-zeta chimp got bipedal. "HoooGraaa!" he vocalised, then signed, 'Zack, I wring my hands for all of us when I sign that the picture of us no longer bowing low before your radiant and effulgent arsehole is a very sad picture indeed. Zack, we adore your ischial pleat, we wish only to reverently caress your scrag, your maverick position on mental health issues is a fundament of great pride to us all "h'hooo". We wish you to continue as our alpha, and to be assured that whatever manipulations you choose to undertake, we will keep our fingers in the pie alongside yours.'

During this conducting Busner, despite himself, felt his eye sockets brimming over with tears. He had known that his home group respected him, but never been entirely certain how much this rested on fear and how much on love. Openly weeping, he now leapt over the desk and squatting at Kenzaburo's neat little feet began grooming his groin fur, making soft grunts and lip-smacks. The other Busners joined in and there was a spontaneous and deeply satisfying group groom.

After a decent interval Zack got bipedal, administered a final tweak of encouragement to Kenzaburo and a kiss on his flat muzzle. "HoooGraaa!" Busner recalled, then signed to the company, 'Well, that's settled then. Kenzaburo, take down those useless bits of paper' – he gestured to the framed medical degrees, his certificate of fellowship of the Royal College of Psychiatrists, his certificate of membership of the Institute of Psychoanalysis, his BAFTA award, and his Variety Club of Great Britain honorarium – 'while I check up on Simon. His ex-group and his infants will be at the house for first lunch. I have high hopes of their grooming session.'

Simon was hung over, and worse, haunted by the night's clandestine commerce of visions. But despite this he was delighted to learn that members of his ex-group were coming to the house. Busner squatted on his nest and gently inparted the news. 'I pant-hooted your ex yesterday and she agreed to bring the infants along today "gru-nnn". Obviously she'll have some other group members with her, do you think you'll be able to "chup-chupp" handle them "huu"?'

'I don't see why not,' Simon countersigned. 'After all "grnn" I handled that opening last night, up until I was fool enough to light-up.'

'And fool enough to "euch-euch" take that cocaine –'

'The cocaine was crap "hooo"!' Simon chopped in. 'Total crap!'

'That's as may be, Simon – and far be it from me to be censorious about using drugs . . . ' Busner's fingers, usually so adroit, faltered and he realised that he would have to sign something to Simon of his own predicament. This he did, although he made a significant omission – there was no representation of the débâcle surrounding the Inclusion trial. Rather, Busner concentrated on those sections of the letter from the GMC that were critical of his unusual therapeutic methods.

'You mean to sign,' Simon gestured when he had taken this in, 'that you may well be *struck off* because of the way you've tried to help me "huuu"?'

'That's about the size of it.' Busner countersigned ingenuously.

'But that's "euch-euch" preposterous! You've saved my sanity – perhaps even my life!'

Busner twisted the appropriate expression of humility on to his muzzle, but he was thinking to himself – and placed your sanity in peril to begin with, possibly even damaged your brain.

'Look, Simon,' Busner resumed gesturing, 'the fact of the matter is that we aren't through yet. There's this business of your missing infant to resolve. You're still convinced that there is one, aren't you "huu?' Simon mutely nodded. 'And with this missing infant come all the rest of the disturbing human fantasies, am I right "huu"?'

' "Hooo" yes.' Simon's muzzle blanched as he remembered the night before, the dreams of bestial mating, human copulation. For, from the perspective of the waking world, with its lap ponies, Bactrians and *Planet of the Humans* video cases, the dreams were no longer nightmarish, but erotically charged.

' "Gru-nn" Simon, until we've picked apart this negative cathexis surrounding the human, it won't be possible for you to resume ordinary life. Therefore it's necessary for us to gain some sort of funding in order to continue with our work –'

'I'll pay you, Zack,' Simon flourished, 'if that's what you need – or want "huu"?'

'No, Simon "grnn".' Busner was gentle but firm. 'I don't see that as being the right way to proceed. What I'd like to outline is more of a proper alliance . . .' And he waved on, showing Simon about his meeting with Knight, the television producer.

"Gru-nnn" Simon vocalised after a while – he manifestly wasn't disgruntled. 'Are you proposing that we co-operate in making a documentary with this chimp "huu"?'

'That's right. I have it on good authority that he can be trusted and I've seen his work before – it's good. I can only envision that Gambol's betrayal and the investigation by the GMC will add spice to the cake as far as the television chimps are concerned "chup-chupp". Simon, I know it seems odd, but just think, these chimps have so much money, if we should need to range far afield in order to continue our work – they'll pay for it.'

After an hour or so of careful, considered mutual grooming and accompanying gesticulation, Busner left Simon to prepare for the session with his ex-group. They parted with a clear understanding between them. Busner would pant-hoot Knight and show him the basis on which they were prepared to do the documentary. Knight could have absolute freedom to film as he saw fit, and would shoulder all expenses incurred, but the Busner–Dykes alliance would retain an absolute veto over the material.

Busner duly placed the pant-hoot. Knight was more than willing to accede to the demands. He was an ambitious young male, making his way up the hierarchy at speed, and because he worked with a pared-down unit – one assistant and a sound recordist, while he operated the camera himself – he was willing to take the risk. 'If you agree with what I'm suggesturing,' Busner signed, 'then it might be an idea for you to come to my group home in Hampstead around second-lunch time – I have a hump there will may be imminent developments in Mr Dykes's condition. Bring the requisite paperwork as well – if you can get it drafted in such a short time "huu"?'

Knight gestured that this was easily done, and after taking down directions, they finished the pant-hoot with some satisfaction on both sides.

Busner's hump was well rounded.

Chapter Twenty

The Dykes group – they still retailed the old ascription – arrived at Redington Road in good time. This despite the fact that Jean Dykes, although nearing thirty, still flaunted the long-lasting swellings that had attracted Simon to her in the first place. These went on for weeks and Jean liked to make the best of them – being a devout Catholic – by indulging in as much mating as possible. She had allowed herself to be covered several times in the train on the way from Thame, twice on the tube ride from Marylebone to Hampstead, and there had been four more couplings as the patrol knuckle-walked to Redington Road, only one of which was endogamous.

Together with Jean were the three new male members of the Dykes hierarchy. The alpha, Derek, was the garagechimp from Tiddington. Simon, peering out from behind the curtains in the sub-adult males' bedroom, recognised his heavily freckled muzzle, thick thighs and hefty rump. The other two weren't known to him and he didn't much like the look of them, especially the round-muzzled individual with the great ruff of white fur under his chin. As Simon watched, this male covered his ex right by the front gate, taking Jean with such rapid insouciance, that had Simon not known better he would have imagined the two chimps to be merely bumping into one another.

But it wasn't the adults that concerned him, whether mating or not, it was his own beloved infants. Where were they? First one little head, then another, emerged from behind the hedge. Simon had been desperately worried that he wouldn't be able to identify them – but he needn't have. He would've been able to pick out Magnus in a pullulating group, so distinctive was the lick of blond fur that flipped over his brow. And as for Henry, the infant, he was as chubby-muzzled and cuddly in his simian incarnation as he had been in his human.

As Simon watched, his two infant males barged past the mating adults, barrelled though the gate and came tumbling up the path to the front door, where they were met by a gaggle of Busner infants. The two parties fused into a typically chimpanzee ruckus, all leaping about, screeching, chasing and tickling. How unlike the standoffishness of human infants, Simon thought to himself as he came down the stairs hand over hand and skidded to a halt by the coat rack in the hall.

Busner emerged, and knuckle-walked ponderously from the direction of his study, with a chimp Simon recognised as Colin Weeks, the rather ineffectual Busner distal-gamma male. "HoooGraa," Busner vocalised. 'Are you prepared, Simon "huu"?'

'I'm as "hooo" ready as I'll ever be, Zack.' The front-door bell chimed its ordinary dissonance and Colin Weeks opened it. The Dykes infants came rolling in; a bundle of light-brown body fur exactly the same shade as Simon's halted in the middle of the floor. Disentangling themselves the two little males sprang up and came scampering towards their alpha crying, "HoooH'Graaa! HoooH'Graa! HoooH'Graaa!"

They leapt into Simon's outstretched arms, Magnus grabbing him around the neck, Henry around his upper arm, both began inparting at once so that the signs felt mixed up, spliced together: 'Alphy! Alphy! "Gru-nnn" where have you been "huuu"? Did you bring us a present "huu"? What have you got for us "huu"? Alphy! Alphy!'

'"Huh-huh-huh-gru-nnn" now calm down, you two, calm down . . .' Simon bestowed kiss after kiss on their muzzles. He ran his fingers through their head fur, he kissed their outsize ears and smelt the furry essence of them, the commingled odour of him-and-them – the very smell of consanguinity.

In those few moments that the infants dangled off him, their fingers and toes tightly entwined in his fur, Simon Dykes, who had once had pretensions, dared to ape his own ideal, felt nothing but love for his offspring, regardless of their species. ' "Gru-nnn" it's so good to touch you, my darlings,' he fingered, 'you look fantastic. Have you been good with your mother "huuu"? Looking after her "h'huu", obeying her?'

' "Grnn" ye-es, Alph.' Magnus prodded his alpha's muzzle, the signs beading Simon's brow like meaningful sweat. 'We've both got really good reports this term, and I got two gold stars from Mrs Greely –'

'Well *done*, Magnus "h'hoooo". What a bright young male you're turning out to be.'

They were oblivious to the rest of the chimps who crowded into the hall, but now Simon broke off, hearing a familiar pant-hoot. "HoooGraa"! Jean Dykes vocalised, then, when she had his attention, signed to Simon, 'Well, old Alpha, here we are!' Simon had been most worried about meeting his ex again. There was so much baggage, so many misunderstandings, fights and falling-outs. There had been disagreements on matters of principle, precedent, hierarchy and fact. There had been fusions, fissions, alliances and coups within their group – too many to recall.

Simon feared that the sight of Jean's muzzle alone might plunge him into his psychosis. And even if that didn't happen, he had no image of how he should behave with her, of who should present to whom. 'Don't worry "grnn".' Zack Busner had held him in check. 'When the time comes – you'll know what to do.'

Simon did – instinctively. He knuckle-walked to where Jean squatted, noting that she was unchanged, the same exact fringing of dark fur around her low brow, the same religious fervour flickering in her hooded eyes. "HoooH'Graa," Simon vocalised, then, presenting very low, he swivelled and pushed his trembling scut towards her muzzle. Jean bestowed a sloppy kiss on Simon's ischial scrag, then they reversed positions and Simon found himself kissing her arse. For a while after that, ignoring the other chimps who were establishing a provisional hierarchy around them, the two former nestmates gently and tenderly groomed one another – for old times' sake.

Zack Busner looked on at this emotional refusal of old group members with a mixture of feelings. He wanted Simon to be well, naturally, and this scene couldn't help but betoken a further alleviation of his ally's morbid condition. Yet Busner also felt a certain sadness. Simon was his last patient, his final case; with his full recovery would come the end of Busner's therapeutic career. The old ape might as well – metaphorically – crawl off into the underbrush and build his final nest.

Pushing these disturbing images to one side, Busner got bipedal, drummed the wall and vocalised loudly, "H'hoooo!" When the hubbub had died down a little, he flourished, 'I would like to welcome adult and infant members of Simon's ex-group to our home, and sign what a pleasure it is to see all your magnificently effulgent arseholes. Now "gru-nn", there is a purpose to this fusion – Simon, Jean and I need to have an important gesticulation. I think it would be a good image if you infants went off and played together in the nursery – I don't know whether you, Magnus, and your brother have the new play trees yet, I imagine you'll find brachiating in them a hoot – while you visiting adult males have some first lunch "h'huu"?'

The big male who covered Jean Dykes by the front gate had been tardy, but he now knuckle-walked through the door with all the pedestrian pomp of a provincial professional chimp. Seeing this familiar gait, Simon suddenly knew who he was. It was Anthony Bohm, his doctor and old ally. So, that's who Jean had taken on board, along with Derek the garagechimp and the thin beardless male with the dark-brown sideburns. "HooH'Graa," Bohm vocalised, then knuckle-walking quickly

over to Simon he presented low, gesturing, 'Simon, how good
to see your scrag, please kiss my arse "huu"?' which Simon
duly did.

Busner came over and gently separated the two chimps,
signing, 'Dr Bohm, please be so good as to have some first
luncheon, there's fresh durian on offer "chup-chupp". After
my gesticulation with these old nestmates, I'd like to finger
with you in private for a while – if you're amenable "huu"?'

Bohm presented low to Busner, signing, 'Of course, Dr
Busner, I am your guest, beholden to your beautiful ischial
pleat, dependent on your divine dominance. I shall look
forward to "gru-nn" holding forth anon.' Colin Weeks came
up beside Bohm and got his fingers in the GP's fur along with
Busner's. The two Busner chimps tickled the doctor's fancy
with more titbits, and in due course all the chimps fissioned
into other rooms.

Once they had arranged themselves around the large oak
desk in Busner's study – Jean and Simon curled up in the
chair, Zack squatting on the blotter – the three chimps got
on with the matter in hand. ' "H'huu" Mrs Dykes –'

'Please.' Jean waved him down. 'Do ascript me Jean, Dr
Busner. I acknowledge your temporary, temporal suzerainty,
and while initially I had not envisioned your "euch-euch"
soul doctoring doing any real good for my poor, benighted
ex-alpha, I see now from the expression of humility on his
muzzle that you have managed to drag him back some way
towards the path of righteousness "h'hooo".'

Busner was somewhat put out by this blazoning of belief, but
he had been warned by both Jane Bowen and Simon himself
about Jean Dykes's consuming piety, so he let the signs stand
uncontested, merely fluttering, 'You're too subservient, Mrs
Dykes, too subservient.'

Simon, who had been signlent since breaking from the
infant hurly-burly, was grooming Jean's groin fur with
great gentleness and – which explained the expression

363

on his muzzle – great humility. Of all the chimps he had encountered, apart from his own infants, Jean's body was the most familar to him. Her fur, her figure, her eyebrow ridges, even the peculiar dappling on her elongated teats – all of it reminded him of the past, of their group life together when he lived at the Brown House.

Now, teasing some of Dr Anthony Bohm's fast-congealing semen out of her groin fur, he inparted – with utmost deference, 'Show me "chup-chupp", Jean, did we always have other adult males in residence when I fused with you "huu"?'

Jean goggled at Simon – such a nonsensical question was unsettling. '"Hooo" my dear old cock, what are you gesturing about "huu"? Derek was your beta, and Anthony a rather distal-gamma. Of course Christobel used to live with us as well, but you never covered her as much as she would have liked. She fissioned well before we did "gru-nn".'

This palping of the past provoked Simon's most pressing concern. While the refusion with his infants had, thus far, gone well – there had been mutual recognition and satisfying grooming – nonetheless it was at some cost to the former artist. As much as the refusion drew him further into the bristling embrace of chimpunity, it also insistently presented to his mind's eye those visions of lost humanity, that he increasingly viewed as psychotic, mad, humanshit.

Shadowing his two male infants Simon still saw a third, human one. He could remember Simon junior's bare little visage, his undershot jaw and slightly goofy teeth, as well – if not better – than the muzzles of these unshaven offspring. With this memory came crepuscular images of a human past. Of making oven chips and fish fingers; of snapping *underwear* into place; of cross-peeing, the green streams plashing and spluttering over the bathroom floor. All of them involved *three* male infants. Where was that third?

Simon withdrew his fingers from Jean's swelling and squatted up. He gestured, including Busner in his digitations, 'I know this may be "hooo" disturbing for you, Jean, my adored ex-alpha. God knows, it's disturbing enough for me, but part of this "hooo" illness of mine, this breakdown, has been the absolute conviction that we had three infants together – not two. Jean, can you "h'huuu" think of any reason why this should be the case?'

Initially Jean Dykes seemed to have ignored this odd question, the only sign that she winced at was Simon's blasphemy. She now retaliated by poking her ex-alpha hard in the eye. "Eeeek"! Simon squeaked.

"Wraaa"! Jean vocalised, then gestured, 'You should know better that to take the Lord's sign in vain, Simon. Remember the Gospels: In the beginning was the sign and the sign was made flesh "h'huu"?'

Simon wasn't foolhardy enough to challenge this attack; he presented to Jean and fluttered, 'I'm so sorry "hooo", I didn't mean any disrespect, but, Jean, this missing infant "huu"? Why would I have such an odd memory "huu"?'

Jean Dykes was flummoxed. ' "Hooo" I really have no such image, Simon. Of course, *I* always wanted a third infant after Henry was weaned, but you "euch-euch" were insistent that you *had* to concentrate on your "euch-euch" art –'

'Jean "gru-nn", I'm sorry to flag you down, but the infant I have in mind would be between Magnus and Henry in age, perhaps around seven years old now. And Jean, I'm thinking of a "hooo" human infant.'

Busner was playing a subtle game of coochy-coo with Jean Dykes, signing with his toes on her volar region, 'Please, Mrs Dykes, I know what he's gesturing about must seem absurd, but try to humour him – he's been making such progress recently . . .'

Jean arched her ridges. 'A human infant "huu"? Of around seven years in age . . .' Her fingers faltered, a light suddenly went on behind her green eyes. 'A human infant "h'hee-hee". Simon, you must "h'hee-hee" forgive me, there was – there *was* a human infant –'

'What! "H'hoooo"! What, Jean "huuu"?' The former artist shot bipedal, he was horripilating, everything about him signed feral intent.

'Simon, please "hoogrnn" calm yourself. Yes, there was a human infant that we adopted –'

'Adopted "huuu"?'

'Yes "hee-hee" that's right, in the zoo, in London Zoo. You arranged an adoption for our infants. It was part of that conservation programme, *Lifewatch*, I think that's what it's denoted. You know how keen the infants are on animals and you thought it would be good for them to have an "gru-nnn" individual animal which they could fuse with. It was one of your more paternal acts. You arranged to sponsor this animal and it was an infant male of around seven years –'

'Did I "huuu",' Simon chopped in again, 'did I give this human a name, Jean? Did I denote it anything "huu"?'

'Well, you left that to Magnus, Simon, it was after all meant to be *his* project. As I recall he did denote it – I'm surprised you don't –'

'Why "huu"?'

'Because it was a group joke, you and the infants used to cackle about it the whole time. You see, when you went to the zoo to see the human infant, his head fur was rather like yours, my ex-alpha, and his eyes, so Magnus denoted him . . . Simon.'

When Alex Knight, the documentary maker, arrived at Redington Road a couple of hours later, Simon's ex-group were just leaving. Knuckle-walking up the front path he was confronted by the spectacle of approximately twenty adults and infants engaged in a vast valedictory grooming session. Without even bothering to present to any of them – they were so entwined with each other they wouldn't notice anyway – he set his camcorder going and began taping. He wasn't to stop for many days, so entertaining was the spectacle of Dr Busner and his unusual patient.

"HoooGraaa," Simon vocalised for the last time as the two little scuts disappeared in the direction of Frognal. Magnus and Henry stopped knuckle-walking, turned back and gave valedictory pant-hoots, "HoooGraa." Their falsetto cries shrilled in the afternoon gloom of an English day in late autumn.

Simon turned to Busner who squatted by him on the doorstep. 'I will see them soon "huu", won't I, Zack?'

'Of course you will, Simon, that "chup-chupp" refusion went exceptionally well. See how co-operative your ex was and how pleased your infants were to get a grooming from their alpha. Anthony Bohm, Derek and that gamma – what was he denoted "huu"?'

'I don't know.'

'Well, anyway, the other male too. They all signed to me that they wouldn't mind you coming to stay at the group home whenever you wanted to see the infants. Now, that's not so bad, is it "huuu"?'

'No, I suppose "gru-nnn" not.'

Busner saw Alex Knight and called him over, ' "Hooo-H'Graa" Mr Knight, please be good enough to present yourself.' The young chimp scuttled over, arse first, camcorder aloft. 'You're just in time,' Busner fingered on, after Knight had properly abased himself, 'for a trip to the zoo.'

'The zoo "huu"?'

'You saw me, the zoo. My friend Mr Dykes has an adoptive human infant at London Zoo, a human infant that may represent the very keystone of his unfortunate delusion. We think that if he comes muzzle-to-muzzle with this animal, the negative cathexis he has constructed around the notion of humanity may well be dissolved.' Naturally, the television chimp didn't really comprehend these signs, but he nodded sagely all the same and kept the camcorder rolling.

Simon was more agitated by this information. 'What do you mean "huuu"? Are we going to the zoo right now "huu"?'

'There's no time like the present,' the maverick anti-psychiatrist – as he liked to style himself – countersigned. 'While you were "gru-nnn" having a valedictory groom with your ex-group, I pant-hooted Hamble in Eynsham. As I suspected, he knows the head primate keeper at London Zoo, a chimp called Mick Carchimp. Hamble pant-hooted Carchimp in turn and he's agreed to show us round, see if he can assist us. "H'huu" I wonder if he's part of the same group.'

'Who "huu"?'

'Carchimp – part of the same group as that libel lawyer.'

They went in the television crew's van. Simon offered to drive the Volvo, showing Zack, 'Go on, let me, I used to really enjoy driving.' But when he saw how many gears the car had – twenty forward and fifteen reverse, all requiring double declutching – he backed down.

Together with Alex Knight was his sound recordist, Janet Higson, and a research assistant-cum-gofer denoted Bob. Bob drove the van, Alex Knight squatted in the front seat and kept the camcorder trained on the two chimps in the back. Poor Higson struggled to catch their vocalisations with a boom mike that she pushed out from where she squatted in the van's back compartment.

Mick Carchimp met them at the main gates together with the zoo's director, a cheery fellow who insisted on them denoting him simply Jo. He presented low to both Zack and Simon, fluttering, 'We are honoured, such an unusual patrol to visit us and both of you with such splendid ischial pleats, please be so good "gru-nnn" as to kiss my arse.' This they duly did, then the whole group of chimpanzees knuckle-walked down through the zoo to the humans' enclosure, Alex Knight filming the while.

The zoo was fairly empty on this weekday afternoon. A few tourists squatted here and there, eating peanuts and grooming in a desultory fashion. The animals were also torpid. In the herons' cage the birds stood, one legged, as static as garden ornaments. In the gorillas' enclosure, the only sign of life was a heaving pile of straw, hiding from view the silvery back fur of the giant male.

As for the humans, they were as zombie-like and uninspiring as the first time Simon had seen them. '"H'huuu" you've seen our human group before, I believe, Mr Dykes?' Mick Carchimp gestured as they came up to the glass which fronted the enclosure.

'Yes, that's right,' Simon countersigned. 'I remember that one in particular "euch-euch".' It was the human Simon had dubbed the Wanker who had caught his attention. The Wanker was making good his moniker, standing in a daze, his slack hand yanking his great wiener of a member; his vacant, white-pigmented eyes rolled back in his head. A silvery thread of drool was strung from his mouth to his chest, and this twirled in synchrony with his pleasureless onanism.

'That's our alpha male,' Carchimp signed. 'He's been with us the longest of any of our humans.'

'Was he born here "huu"?' Busner asked.

'No, he was born at Twycross – they have a very big human group there. But some of our other humans were captured in the wild – that one, for example.' Carchimp was pointing at the other sorry specimen Simon had denoted the Commuter. The Commuter was also living up to his title, standing motionless, one truncated arm hooked loosely around a shoulder-height handhold, the other dangling by his side, a slice of white bread clutched between his grey fingers.

'That human actually came originally from Tanzania, but we got him from a pharmaceutical company's laboratory, after they'd finished with him –'

'What do they do with the humans "huuu"?' Simon flagged Carchimp down.

'"Hooo" all sorts of things, Mr Dykes – none of them, I'm afraid, particularly nice. I believe this specimen was kept in a large compound – you know how humans *hate* being unconfined – and together with other adult males was shot at with hypodermic darts full of cocaine.'

'Cocaine "huuu"? What's the point of that then?'

'Good question, something to do with studying drug dependency, I suppose. It's the human species' great misfortune to be our closest living relative, so all sorts of research gets done on the beasts. Even here at the zoo we do some experiments – although as chimpmanely as possible.'

'What sort of experiments "huuu"?'

Simon's muzzle was a picture of anxiety. He hadn't exactly expected to see Simon junior in the humans' enclosure, but nonetheless an insistent image of his missing human infant kept coming to him. He peered through the thick glass into the dim recesses of the humans' room. It would be demonic, evilly bad to see the familiar muzzle, the undershot jaw and slightly goofy teeth in amongst these naked brutes. All of Simon's pictures were of a clothed infant, an infant in school uniform. If these humans were to be clothed, they'd look altogether subversive, like humans got up for a travesty of a tea party, or a P.G. Tips commercial.

Even more unsettling was the image of Simon junior naked, strapped down, electrodes wired to his shaven head, or hypodermic syringes shot into his furless flesh. Simon junior infected with CIV, or poisoned with anthrax, or with his eyelids pinned back so that perfumed fursprays could be tested on his exposed eyeballs.

' "Hooo" well, we don't do anything that involves harming our humans. We're more interested in attempting to get genetic profiles of human sub-species. One of our biggest problems with captive humans is that all the sub-species have interbred in captivity, so most of these humans are hybrids. You see, it wasn't known that there were human sub-species until recently –'

' "H'huuu" what, may I ask, distinguishes them?' Busner flicked in.

'It's difficult for laychimps to spot the difference without training, I think because the sight of humans is so unsettling to begin with – but, put simply, they have different "euch-cuch" skin colourings, and also different casts to their muzzles. Once you're trained in identifying them, it's quite easy to tell them apart. Not that that would help you much with our group – apart from that one,' he stabbed at the Commuter, 'they're all hybrids.'

The chimps squatted in silence for some minutes observing the lack of activity in the human enclosure. Most of the animals were gathered on the sleeping platform, but unlike chimpanzees they had no interest in touching one another. Instead they sat side-by-side in a long row, their dumb rigid feet sticking up like bony bookends, their bald muzzles devoid of expression or intelligence. The only movement came from a group of infants who were playing in the area underneath the platform. These mites were far more chimp-like. They rolled in the straw, they dangled from the handholds, they tickled and sported with one another.

Naturally it was these infants who were attracting the attention of what few visitors there were to the zoo. The chimps were, as ever, entranced by the human infants, and kept on fingering how like chimpanzee infants they were. Simon grasped Busner's thick thigh and inparted, 'If I see another chimp sign that they're cute, I think I'm going to scream.'

'Calm down "gru-unn",' Busner inparted in turn. 'It's only civil to allow Carchimp to hold forth for a bit before we get down to business.'

There were two adult humans who were attracting the chimps' attention. A pair at the very back of the enclosure almost completely concealed behind a bale of straw. All that could be seen of them was the buttocks of one individual rising up and down, up and down; and clutched around the obscenely smooth bulges the feet of another. The chimps were pointing at this and fluttering about it, but none of them seemed to have any idea of what was going on. 'Most unusual,' Mick Carchimp gestured, seeing that Simon was fixated, 'to see them mating during the day.'

' "H'huuu" mating?'

'That's right, you know, of course, that humans normally seek privacy for mating. I imagine that's why this pair have attempted to conceal themselves behind the bale. The male will be the one on top, and those are the female's feet grasped around his rump. It's not exactly a pretty sight –'

'They've been at it for ages!' Busner chopped the air.

'That's right. As you may be aware, humans can take anything up to half an hour to achieve a full mating – there are even some reports of them taking far longer in the wild, although no one is quite sure why.'

Simon thought he might be sure why. He watched the buttocks rise and fall, rise and fall, and the jerking animals pulled back a vision of Sarah from the deep recesses of his mind. A vision of Sarah as a beautiful human moaning beneath him, *her* feet clutched around his plunging buttocks. 'Please "huu", I hate to be precipitate, Mr Carchimp –'

'Please, denote me Mick,' the primate keeper counter-signed.

'Mick, I don't know whether Dr Hamble signed anything to you about the reason for our visit "huu"?'

'He delineated that it was something to do with an individual human that you had an interest in.'

Simon lit a Bactrian and inhaled deeply, before continuing, ' "Hooo" that's right. You see, I believe you have a programme where chimps can "euch-euch" adopt an animal, sort of sponsor its upkeep "huu"?'

'That's right, it's part of the Lifewatch 2000 scheme. Is the human you're interested in one of the adoptions "huu"?'

'We believe so,' Busner signed. 'My ally Mr Dykes sponsored the animal on behalf of his infants. A male infant of about seven – it might be one of that group there.' He indicated the sporting human offspring.

'We don't have any infants of that precise age at the moment, but why not come to my office "huuu"? I have the stud book there and the Lifewatch register; between the two we should be able to find out what's happened to your adoptive human.'

Carchimp's office was at the back of the main administration building, but while removed from the immediate vicinity of the enclosures, there were still strong animal odours fugging it up. The office had little in the way of furniture, only a couple of battered filing cabinets and a small kneehole desk. Posters of phyletic trees were tacked on to the walls, together with flyers advertising veterinary drugs.

Knight's crew crammed into the small room, along with Carchimp, Busner and Simon. The Director had scuttled off somewhere, signing about another television crew coming to film him.

They all indulged in a grooming session for five minutes, solidifying as chimps must the provisional hierarchy. Then Carchimp broke from the hispid huddle and swaggered over to a bookcase. He footed out a large ring binder from the bottom shelf and pulled a much thinner, glossier binder from the top shelf. These he brought back to the group on the floor. 'This,' he signed, 'is the Lifewatch register. Can you recall, Mr Dykes, what the serial number of your adoptive human was "huu"?'

Simon looked nonplussed. 'Serial number "huu"? No, you see, I adopted the human for my oldest male infant Magnus, and he denoted it . . . he denoted it Simon.'

'Simon "huu"? We don't really give our humans names for recording purposes, it's veering rather too far in the direction of primatomorphising them, although naturally the keepers denote them for reasons of day-to-day convenience. And some of our Lifewatch literature certainly "euch-euch" primatomorphises.' He held up a leaflet which invited readers to consider 'Groomin' a Human'.

'However, we can find your name in the register and get

373

the animal's serial number. Let me see ...' He began to leaf through the Lifewatch binder, 'Dykes, Dykes, yes – here we are. Simon Dykes. You sponsored this individual, serial number 9234, to the tune of some five hundred pounds – a very generous donation.

'Now, if I look in the stud book I can find out what's happened to 9234. He could have been transferred to another zoo, or even somewhere else –'

'He wouldn't "hooo"' – Simon chopped the air – 'have been given over to some awful research project, would he "huu"?'

'I can reassure you on that score Mr Dykes,' signed Carchimp, and he came over to Simon and laid on soothing fingers, inparting, 'We don't like to do that with any of our humans, and this one having been sponsored it would look rather "euch-euch" bad if he ended up in a laboratory. Picture what the animal rights activists could do if they got hold of such information.'

Carchimp finished this massage of meaning with an iterative tweak and went back to the stud book. 'Now, here we go, 9234. Simple when you see how, yes, he's no longer with us, I'm afraid, he has been transferred –'

'Where "hooo", where to "huu"?' Simon's fingers scratched, his anxiety visible as well as palpable.

'In a manner of signing, Mr Dykes, 9234 appears to have gone home.'

'Home "huu"?'

'That's right, he's one of the few humans to return from the developed world to Africa. 9234 has been included in a rather controversial programme to reintroduce humans to the wild. If you want to see him again, you'll have to track him down.'

Simon squatted, stunned by this information. It was left to Busner to continue. 'Show me, Mr Carchimp,' he signed, 'when you sign that 9234 has gone home, do you mean that he was actually born in Africa "huu"? That he's a wild human?'

'That would be extremely unlikely, Dr Busner. There are

now so many humans in captivity in the West that there's seldom any need for new specimens. Why, we have more than enough humans here and in common with many other zoos now have to castrate males when they reach puberty.'

Simon, who was watching this exchange of signs, shivered when he heard this. His sallow muzzle grew paler and he clutched his own genitals with an anguished, signless hand.

Busner pressed, 'And why, may I ask, Mr Carchimp –'

'Please, Your Ischial Refulgence, I would betoken it an honour if you too would ascript me Mick.'

' "Gru-nnn" Mick, then – why is it that you sign this programme is controversial "huu"?'

'Well, as you may know' – Carchimp adopted a relaxed posture – clearly he was going to conduct for a while – 'the original programme to observe humans in the wild was set up by Dr Louis Leakey. He sent "gru-nn" Jane Goodall to the Gombe Stream Reservation in Tanzania to study humans; Dian Fossey to Rwanda to study the mountain gorilla; and Birute Galdikas to Sumatra to study the orang-utan. While there has been controversy surrounding the work of all three females, they have also made undoubted and lasting contributions to anthropology.

'Goodall has herself been involved in reintroduction programmes, but this particular one is "hooo" rather different. One of the field researchers she employed was a German female, Ludmilla Rauhschutz. Rauhschutz is extremely wealthy, and has distinctly eccentric notions about the relationship between humans and chimpanzees. Having split from Goodall, she has managed to bribe the Tanzanian government to allow her her own research station in the Gombe region. Here she both introduces chimpanzee tourists to wild humans, and attempts to reintroduce captive humans to the wild –'

'Mick.' Simon roused himself and flagged the head keeper down. ' "H'hooo" can you show me why it should be that Leakey chose only females to study the humans "huu"?'

'A good question, Simon. Leakey thought that human males in particular would find female chimps less disturbing. Humans, as you know, have no appreciable sexual swelling, so a male chimpanzee might attract unnecessary mating interest.'

'I see.'

'We don't, as a rule, send humans to Rauhschutz, but occasionally, as in the case of this pubescent male, it seems worth a try. After all – it's either that or castration.' And with this final remark Carchimp fell signless.

Later that evening Simon was curled up in nest, in the Busners' spare room, watching an episode of *Sub-Adult Dominant Chef.* A male Simon recognised as the television presenter Lloyd Grosschimp was gesticulating with his guest, the equally media-friendly chef, Anton Mosichimp. The little muzzles of the aspirant sub-adult dominant chefs were crinkled up with anxiety as they watched the two big males begin to tussle. '"Euch-euch" Anton,' Grosschimp signed in his affected Bostonian tempo, 'it doesn't suprise me that you weren't enamoured of this young female's soufflé, I don't "hooo" believe that you have much affection for young females – or their soufflés – at all.'

'What on earth are you "euch-euch" implying "huu"?' countersigned the French chimp.

'Nothing "h'hoo" nothing at all – you have three female infants, I believe "huuu" – ?'

But Simon didn't get to see Mosichimp's reply, because the nestroom door swung open and the former psychiatrist knuckle-walked in. Seeing the chimps on screen he flicked, 'Mosichimp "h'hooo". Know someone who knows him slightly. It's rumoured he abuses his daughters – doesn't mate them enough – or at all!'

'Really.' Simon's signing was as without expression as the Queen waving from her carriage on a state occasion.

'What's the matter, Simon "huuu"? Were you disturbed by the trip to the zoo "huu"?'

'Of course I was.'

'You still think that this human infant, 9234 –'

'Not bloody 9234 "wraaa"! He's denoted Simon "wraaa"!'

Busner retaliated instantly to this insubordination. Springing on to the nest he delivered a number of hard blows to Simon's muzzle, his long arms windmilling. It took seconds to subdue the former artist, who yowled for mercy, struggling round in the nest to present to his alpha. Busner smoothed Simon's ruffled fur and inparted, 'That's all right, "gru-nnn" I understand you're upset, Simonkins, but I still can't allow such insolence, I'm sure you appreciate that –'

'I do, I do, I'm "chup chupp" sorry, your ischial pleat means more to me than I can sign.'

'I know, but the point is, do you still believe this human to be *your* missing infant, your Simon "huuu"?'

'I don't know why – but I do.'

'Well.' The eminent natural philosopher – as he still styled himself – settled back on his haunches. 'In that case I have some news that may "grnn" please you.'

'What's that "huuu"?'

'I've gesticulated with Alex Knight on this matter, and he signs that his company is fascinated by your case and prepared to put up the money.'

'The money for what "huu"?'

'For us to go to track down this human, for us to go to Africa.'

'To Africa "huu"? But when?'

'As soon as it can chimply be arranged.'

Chapter Twenty-One

The battered Toyota Landcruiser bucketed over the uneven, churned-up surface of the track, sending flobs and globs of liquidised mud high in the air. This sludge rained down on the bodies of the six chimps who were huddling together in the vehicle, necessitating ongoing and exhaustive grooming activities. Simon Dykes, once an artist, then a mental patient and now a chimp with a most unusual quest, was wedged in between the sound recordist, Janet Higson, and Bob the gofer.

Since the night when Busner had knuckle-walked in on *Sub-Adult Dominant Chef*, Simon's days had been a whirl of preparation for the journey back to Africa. Visas had to be arranged, vaccinations obtained, clothing and other equipment purchased. And everywhere that Busner and Simon went – Alex Knight's camcorder followed them.

'It's a question of background,' the documentary maker signed. 'I want to have plenty of footage that leads the viewer in to Simon's first encounter with humans in the wild, and hopefully his meeting with 9234, the infant male he believes to be his missing offspring.'

To begin with the constant presence of the television crew unsettled and irritated Simon. There were four or five quite bad confrontations between him and Knight, three of them ending in violent incidents, incidents which Simon came out of better. Better in his relationship with Knight and better and more confident in himself. It was, Busner imagined privately, only to be predicted that what would bring the former artist most forcefully back to his physical being would be those most chimpmane activities, sex and violence.

So, Simon weathered the crew and even became blasé to the extent of being unaware of their presence, taking a light from Bob for one of his interminable Bactrians, without so much as a glance or sign.

For Busner, the trip to Africa was the final watershed, the gutter at the back end of his career. Upon his return he had no idea what he might find himself doing – if anything. On the day Simon's ex-group had visited Redington Road, Busner had a brief private gesticulation with Anthony Bohm that confirmed all of his suspicions. Bohm had, of course, been targeted by the GMC as well, now that Phillips had blown the whistle on the activities of Cryborg Pharmaceuticals. 'I have no image,' his signing was fluttered, anxious, 'what Jean's reaction will be to this, I may be only a distal member of her group, but even that "hooo" status will undoubtedly be affected – you *know* how high-minded she is.'

Busner calmed Bohm down, soothed, smarmed and prinked him. 'Dr Bohm, you mustn't worry yourself, get so tangled up in this. I have resolved to take the blame for the unfortunate incident entirely on my own shoulders. If you stick to the line that you were unaware of the covert prescribing of Inclusion, which I asked you to do – then I will "chup-chupp" support that delineation. It is the least I can do – the least recompense I can make to all concerned. I hope that you'll get off with a caution.'

'And what "huuu" about Simon?'

'What indeed. He has many different images of what's responsible for his breakdown. Sometimes he attributes it to being hit by a bus as an infant, sometimes to the drugs he used to take. As he is now recovering I feel no special need to show him what may, after all, not be the truth.'

That was how they had left it – dropped from the hands

379

that held it. Busner informed the GMC that he would give evidence on his return from Africa, and that until such time he would give his sign that he would not gesture publicly on the matter.

As for Gambol, Phillips and Whatley, the three chimps whose alliance had toppled Busner from the tree and irrevocably undermined his status as a great ape, theirs was an altogether Pyrrhic victory. Phillips succumbed to an opportunistic chest infection within weeks of the grooming session at Human Zoo. This was lucky for him, for had he lived long enough, he would have seen Cryborg Pharmaceuticals throw the full weight of their corporate power on to the scales of justice, with predictable results – a full acquittal.

Whatley, on learning of the GMC's letter to Busner, went straight to the Trust and applied for the vacant senior consultancy at Heath Hospital. This, he duly won, once Archer – the senior administrator – had confirmed that Busner was to take early retirement. But Whatley's reign as psychiatric department alpha was a troubled one. The staff were used to a hierarchy both elastic and rigorous, whereas Whatley was a martinet as well as ineffectual. The patients were as aware of this as the medical and auxiliary staff, so it was little surprise to anybody when Whatley was badly savaged by a manic chimp whom he was attempting to thrash. The bite wounds took six months to heal and he was never the same chimp again. When last seen, Dr Kevin Whatley, MD, FRC Psych., was running stop-smoking seminars with Allen Carr.

He was succeeded as consultant at Heath Hospital by Dr Jane Bowen, whose sympathetic observation of Simon Dykes's deluded state resulted in an elegantly written paper[1]. Her careful delineation of the symptomatology, pathology and aetiology of the condition, led – as Busner had prophesied – to many more cases being diagnosed. Fittingly, the human delusion became identified and known as 'Bowen's Disease'.

[1] 'Dreams of Humanity' (*British Journal of Ephemera* March 1995).

Gambol, hooo Gambol! The scrawny, pale-muzzled epsilon who had managed to pull Zack Busner from the bough of celebrity and cast him to the forest floor. Gambol, once a fervent admirer, then a skulking Iago, naturally enough decided to quit psychology and do the next worst thing – write a novel about it. *The Far Side of the Mind*, a *roman-à-clef* based tightly on his experiences with Busner, and featuring a protagonist by the ascription of 'Jack Sumner' was a rogue hit and the toast of the autumn lists the following year. Gambol found himself taken up by the literary world and spinning from party, to reading, to fourth dinner, in a dizzy dance of celebrity. He began to get first instead of fiftieth crack at a fresh swelling and joined the Sealink Club.

Needless to sign, this phase didn't last for long. His material exhausted – Busner was the only interesting thing that had ever happened to him – Gambol was unable to complete his second, contracted book. He'd spent the advance on high living, and could no longer find any sort of employment in his old field, such was the long shadow that the Cryborg affair cast.

Within months Gambol was a pathetic, broken male. The literary types dropped him as speedily as they'd picked him up. They might all have pretended that they found nothing more romantic, or honourable than the idea of the writer as a selfless artist labouring away in a poorly heated tree house, with no hope of readers or remuneration, but the truth was that they had as little time for failure as the rest of chimpunity.

The only chimpanzee, besides Jane Bowen, to come out of the sorry affair of Simon Dykes's breakdown with any semblance of an improvement in her life was Sarah Peasenhulme. The final, joyous mating with her former nestmate at the Saatchi Gallery completely released Sarah from the oppressive vice of her consortship. She found herself curiously relieved to be rid of the responsibility of caring for the highly strung male. When at the end of her longest oestrus ever she discovered that she was pregnant despite a barrier contraceptive the size of a sink plunger, she decided to ask the Braithwaites if they would form a natal group with her.

Steve and Ken were delighted. They brought on board Earl – an old, old ally – as gamma, their uncle, Marcus, as distal-delta, a friend denoted Cuthbert as epsilon, and two other brothers, Paul and Delroy, as respectively zeta and theta.

Sarah got all the mating she needed – all the firm, fast penetration that she'd so missed out on as a sub-adult. And years later, when her daughters were only just beginning their own small swellings, Sarah rejoiced in the sight of them getting a good solid fucking from all their loving male parents. If she ever chanced to visualise the artist at all, it was with a wistful expression playing on her muzzle, but she wasn't remembering his speed and athleticism as a coverer, only the drawings which Tony Figes had taken from Simon's flat. They'd secured a handsome five-figure nest egg when sold to a private collector.

This was particularly useful to Sarah, because, of course, given the nature of her new group – she could never go back to Surrey again.

' "H'huu" do you think we should be grooming the driver?' Bob, the swaggerer, inparted Simon's shoulder as they lurched and bucked together.

'I don't know,' he replied. 'It could be a mistake – you know all of this region is riddled with AIDS "hooo".'

"Euch-euch," Busner coughed in the front seat, then gestured, 'I hardly think you can get CIV from grooming – let me "chup-chupp" see if I can help the fellow out.' The eminent natural philosopher – as he still styled himself – put his fingers in the bonobo's muddy chest fur, and was instantly rewarded with a great clack of teeth and a sloppy kiss on the muzzle. This Busner received only just without wincing.

The flight from London had been long and bumpy. Busner had no idea why it should be that Air Lanka had the only scheduled service to Dar es Salaam, unless it was on the bizarre assumption that chimps in one crisis-torn part of the world might want to check out what it was like in another.

The Busner–Dykes group then got stuck in the city for three days while permission for internal travel was secured, together with a guide-cum-driver who could get them the eight hundred miles from the coast to Lake Tanganyika, where Camp Rauhschutz squatted on the shore. They were three days of getting to grips with a country in more than its usual disarray. The hideous massacres in Rwanda were still going on and even as far away as Dar es Salaam refugees were everywhere. If they had money, taking up whatever accommodation was available, and if they didn't whatever trees were still standing. The Busner–Dykes group had to put up in a brothel, where they were asked to pay by the half-hour.

This gave Busner an opportunity to lecture them all on curtailing mating activities while they were in Africa. 'It may not be the case that heterosexual mating is the most efficient means of transmitting the virus, but the females here have often been subject to "euch-euch" infibulation – and even swellingectomies. Not only that "hooo", but as far as we know the virus itself is still mutating. We are in the tropics – where the greatest "chup-chupp" biodiversity on the planet is to be found; there are more species here than anywhere else, species of virus as much as any other organism. And with this "hooo" dreadful business in Rwanda and Burundi, you can be certain that all kinds of "euch-euch" infections are on the move.

'Nonetheless.' He continued to wave his long arms about. 'I'm not too worried about any of you, because apart from these "euch-euch" working females, I don't think you'll find that much in the way of mating opportunities. The bonobos, as you are – with the possible exception of Simon – no doubt aware, are rather "euch-euch" perversely non-penetrative, preferring frottage to a good, sound insertion. A fact which helps to explain their woeful fecundity – with no alien sperm roaming around inside their uteruses the females conceive with ridiculous alacrity.'

Simon found the reality of chimpanzee-dominated Africa far too overwhelming even to consider mating. It was as much as he could do to pick out an individual female from the bustling black multitudes swarming over the crumbling concrete buildings of Dar es Salaam, let alone see whether she had a swelling on her. He kept his head down and followed his alpha's scut.

The driver-cum-guide recommended to Busner was trusty enough, but signed nothing but pidgin ES, making gesticula-tion difficult. As the group headed north the downpours grew worse and the country wilder. The road dwindled first from a pot-holed warped multi-lane highway, to a pot-holed warped strip of blacktop, and then eventually to the pot-holed warped track which ran from Kigoma, north to Nyarabanda, a mere five miles short of the Burundian border.

Refugees were thick on the ground here, and in the palm trees as well. They brachiated beside the road, limply hauling themselves from frond to trunk, or they knuckle-walked in the morass that constituted the verge, risking a mud bath every time a vehicle slewed by. Simon wondered how the humans could possibly be faring in this world turned upside-down – with chimpanzee life so cheap, who would care about a few miserable animals?

Simon's anxiety over the fate of humankind was only compounded by the suave bonobo he'd had a brief grooming session with in Kigoma. A bonobo who, judging by his neat tunic and designer sunglasses, must have been a party cadre. He showed Simon that human meat was more in demand than ever. 'It don't matter what they sign about protected species here, chimp,' he fingered, 'those humans still try and get our infants – so we go out and get "grrn'yum" theirs. And with this business' – he waved northwards – 'there's even a market for bush meat.'

But Busner – who'd seen this, reassured Simon. 'Don't

384

pay any "chup-chupp" attention. The truth of the matter is that the human reserve is better protected than anywhere else in this benighted country – although I'm afraid the same can't be signed for the Virungas Mountains reserves on the Rwandan–Ugandan border where Dian Fossey set up the Karisoke Research Centre to study gorillas. But here it's an "h'-h'" irony, which I'm sure hasn't escaped the locals, that while chimp is killing chimp with such relentlessness, humans go about their business undisturbed.'

Busner had sent sign to Ludmilla Rauhschutz that they were coming. As with almost any chimp he needed assistance from, Busner had discovered a useful connection. Rauhschutz's alpha, it transpired, was the opera impresario Hans Rauhschutz, whom Peter Wiltshire had directed several productions for in the past. Wiltshire pant-hooted Rauhschutz and he gave them a letter of introduction to his offspring, which was duly faxed on.

Ludmilla Rauhschutz was, even by the standards of anthropology – a branch of zoology which had always attracted zealotry – extreme in her belief that wild humans were both sentient and intelligent. In her book *Among the Humans* she had written that her fieldwork with wild humans led her '. . . as close as I will ever come as a chimpanzee to understanding the mind of God'.

While her work with the Gombe humans had been recognised initially as being of profound importance, both for anthropology itself and for the understanding of chimpanzee origins, as she continued to insist on their abilities and their claim to some form of chimpunity, she was sidelined by the scholarly hierarchy.

There were flutterings that the reintroductions of captive humans she was undertaking were little more than a pretext for getting more tourists to visit Camp Rauhschutz. Tourists wanted to see humans, and the formerly captive humans, unable to fend for themselves in the wild and often meeting with considerable aggression from their feral conspecifics, tended to stay close to camp for feeding and photographing. One anthropologist, who had visited the camp, gesticulated with Busner before they left for Africa signing, 'It looks more like a petting centre than a place where animals are rehabilitated.'

Busner had also seen worse things about the female herself. It was signed that she was 'a horrible fat female who treats her pet human as if he were a chimpanzee'. Other flutterings included a similar slur to the one fingered on Fossey and many other female anthropologists. Namely that Rauhschutz, whose swellings were so small as to be insignificant, sought out humans as nestmates because of her inability to get chimpanzee suitors. The further – and obvious – bit of tickle-slapple, was that the only reason Rauhschutz had achieved any position in the hierarchy, let alone research alpha, was *because* she was sterile. But this was what males always signed about successful career females.

Busner registered all this, but resolved to keep an open mind. After all, he mused, it would ill behove a chimp as vilified by the academic hierarchy as I am to believe seesign against another similarly vilified.

Now, within hours of their destination, Busner recalled all of these digitations and wondered what lay in store for them. In his own mind he remained absolutely undecided as to whether Simon's conviction that the human numbered 9234 was his missing infant was merely the appendix to the former artist's psychosis, or the very linchpin. Whether encountering humans in the wild would free him – or condemn him. Busner was, he decided, operating on the same principle as Alex Knight and his crew: point the recording device at what was happening and see what it looked like.

What the country around them looked like was highly telegenic. As they gained the border of the game reserve, and had their papers checked by the Kalashnikov-toting bonobo at the checkpoint, a vista of steeply rolling verdancy stretched away from them towards the blue immensities of the great lake beyond. As if Mother Nature herself were pant-hooting their arrival, the heavy rain faltered and then died away altogether. The Landcruiser bucked and slithered between thirty-hand-high banks of grass, which were wreathed with steamy evaporation. There were coconut palms in profusion and candelabra trees aglow with brilliant red blossoms.

Alex Knight kept his camera panning about the place, turning three hundred and sixty degrees in his seat every minute or so. ' "Aaaa" it'll be dark soon,' he delineated for Simon, 'and I want to be absolutely certain that I have enough establishing shots.'

They gained the final ridge of hills and below them was the lake. The dagaa fisherchimps' outriggers were coming into shore, their outboards cutting grey-white grooves across the rumpled azure. And there was Camp Rauhschutz, a mean little huddle of corrugated iron shacks, their galvanised roofs glowing orange with the rays of the setting sun, which like some stellar swelling bulged as it was penetrated by the horizon.

Simon saw it all and registered it all, but his thoughts and imaginings were entirely taken up with the human business in hand. How quickly would he be able to find Simon junior? He hadn't dared fully to form the image that lurked in the recesses of his mind, an image so in keeping with the other furniture of his human delusion that it might have been purpose-built by the same psychic carpenter who had converted his frontal lobes, installing the focal hyperintensities and manipulating the view. It was an image of Simon junior's bare little visage, his undershot jaw and slightly goofy teeth. It was an image that like a hardy tug drew behind it an entire freight of change. For, when Simon met Simon, the whole ghastly planet of the apes, would – or so he almost dared to hope – waver and dissolve. Busner would put on trousers and get a shave. They'd fly back to an England where the politicians brown-nosed metaphorically – rather than literally.

"HoooH'Graa!" The six chimps in the Landcruiser sent up a great pant-hoot of arrival as the vehicle lurched to a halt in the muddy compound. There to meet them was Ludmilla Rauhschutz, together with her bonobo assistants. Rauhschutz was a striking figure, so obese as to be almost a ball of dark-brown fur. Her muzzle was disturbingly flat and animal for a German chimp, and her close-cropped head fur didn't help matters. Nor did the hideously patterned shortie mumu that flared around her shoulders like a perverse material garnish on an unappetising dish. The mumu unobscured the non-object of desire that lay between her lanate legs. It was easy to see why Rauhschutz eschewed a swelling-protector – she had no need of one. When in full oestrus her swelling must have been a paltry affair, for now, in a fallow period, her perineal region was barely noticeable.

Even Simon found this off-putting to the point of being unsettling, inparting Bob's shoulder, ' "Euch-euch" it's revolting, she's got hardly any scrag at all!' Busner signlenced him with a low bark, because Rauhschutz was knuckle-walking over to the Landcruiser, while the useful-looking bonobos were drumming on the metal sides of the nearest hut to clamorous effect.

"HoooGraa!" she called, then gestured grandly, 'Welcome to my humble camp, Dr Busner. I have watched all day for the burst of light that would mean your radiant, refulgent scrag was drawing near. I have longed for many "gru-nn" years to get my fingers in your eminent fur, and to grope over with you the sorry state of chimpunity.' As was his way, Busner was not in the least put out by this nauseating display of sycophancy. He leapt from the Landcruiser, as fleet of hand as a sub-adult out hunting and presented low to the fat female, signing as he did, ' "H'hooo" I am honoured, madam, to make your acquaintance. The entire scientific community is in awe of your ischial pleat – the scientific community that matters, that is – and I too reverence your dangly bits. I would accord it an honour if you would kiss my arse.'

Simon, watching this exchange, wondered whether Rauhschutz would suspect Busner of any irony when he flicked the customary honorifics, but her flat muzzle betrayed no suspicion of anger as she bestowed the required kiss, then requested an arse lick from Busner in turn.

The rest of the English chimps swung out of the Landcruiser and knuckle-walked over, pant-hooting. They were joined by the bonobos, and for some minutes there was a round of presenting, counter-presenting and group grooming. As the hispid huddle began to fission slightly, Busner put the finger on Simon and tweaked him in Rauhschutz's direction. ' "H'hoo" Madam Rauhschutz, may I present the main reason for our visit, this is "chup-chupp" Simon Dykes the artist.

Simon presented low, pressing his muzzle into the mud; his scut trembled under the hortatory pat of the anthropologist. He looked up into eye sockets of an uncommon depth, and irises of uncompromising verticality. If he expected to see any trace of humanity in those eyes, engendered by the female's lunatic creed, then he was cruelly disappointed. For Rauhschutz's expression was chimpanzee through and through, acquisitive, curious, nakedly intent.

' "Hooo" Mr Dykes,' the alpha female signed, her fingers jagged, her styling heavily accented, 'Dr Busner wrote to me concerning your "hooo" disturbing complaint. Forgive me,' she crouched down again to run her fingers over Simon's ischial pleat, and tweaked his scrotum for good measure, 'but apart from a certain stiffness in your gait, I see nothing that is inchimp about you – let alone human "grnnn".'

'Madam Rauhschutz, your swelling is the tropical verdancy that surrounds us, your pleat is as the Rift Valley itself – a fount of speciation. It's true that I don't "gru-nnn" appear to be human, and it's also true that since my "euch-euch" devastating breakdown, with the assistance of Dr Busner here, I have manged to "hooo" come to terms with aspects of my chimpunity, but there's still one thing that troubles me. The thing that's brought us –'

'I know.' The maverick German anthropologist waved him

down; her plump fingers scrabbled his rump as she inparted, 'Dr Busner told me of your interest in Biggles –'

'Biggles "huuu"?!' It was Simon's turn to chop the air.

' "Hooo" I suppose you know him by some other ascription, but I've denoted this infant human Biggles – you'll see why when you meet him. But now, I'm neglecting my duties as host, Joshua here will show you to your sleeping quarters.' She turned to conduct the whole group, 'We first – and last – mess together in an hour's time, at dusk. You'll find that we've adapted ourselves pretty much to a human diurnal pattern here, lady and gentlechimps. We rise at dawn, and get to nest an hour after dusk. If it doesn't suit you, I can cordially sign – cunt off!'

With this challenging, if not abusive gesture, Rauhschutz gave a spontaneous pant-hoot of stentorian proportions, drummed on a water butt that was to hand, and knuckle-marched away. All of the bonobos save for one – clearly Joshua – followed in her scut. Simon was unnerved to see that two of them were carrying Kalashnikovs.

The sleeping quarters assigned to the English chimps were, of course, one of the huts. The floor was concrete and the corrugated iron walls stopped about a foot before meeting this foundation. When Simon gestured at this, Joshua merely signed, 'Wa' comes in, y'know – they's got to "hooo" get out again.' Simon considered pointing out to him that if the walls were better constructed nothing *would* get in, but seeing the bonobo's bared canines and funnelled lips, he thought better of it.

At least they had their own mosquito nets and inflatable mattresses. The camp nests provided were the size of infant baths. There was plenty of invertebrate life in the hut already – mosquitoes whined about the shadows, huge moths batted against the hissing gas lamp Joshua had lit before leaving them. There were also more sinister, more vertebrate noises, scuttlings and clickings, unmistakably rodentine in origin. Janet Higson and Bob the gofer were so agitated by the hut's atmosphere that they began mock-mating, even though she was weeks away from showing.

Zack Busner was the only one who wasn't put out by their reception. He'd travelled extensively in the tropics as a young chimp, when doing research on the perverse, hysterical Malaysian condition known as *latah*, and the descent to the lakeside, the makeshift camp and the beauty of the surrounding forest had pushed him into a nostalgic reverie. Seeing the distress of his group, Busner crawled across to where the two television chimps were whimpering and panting, and took them both in both hands, inparting, ' "Chup-chupp" come now! Madam Rauhschutz may be a bit strange, but I dare say we'll rub along well enough. As for these quarters, I have a few tips I picked up as a young chimp that should make things a little "gru-nnn" more salubrious.'

He showed them all how to rig up the mosquito nets and how to stash their gear where the rats couldn't get at it. He also produced a number of paper dishes, which he filled from a bottle of paraffin and set the feet of the camp nests in. 'It'll stop any six-legged friends we might have from getting too intimate "hee-hee".' Simon was most gratified to see this, because in the few days he'd been in Africa, despite rigorous applications of the plethora of repellents and unguents they'd brought with them, he was finding it difficult to keep all the tics, chiggers and worse that wanted to infest his coat from taking up residence.

It was this, as much as anything else, that was drawing Simon into a tighter relation to that preposterous concept – chimpunity. It was difficult, after all, to deny that you had fur, when mosquito bites were invisible beneath hanks of hair, but for all that damnably itchy.

The Busner–Dykes group groomed itself as best it could, then gingerly quit their hut. Gingerly, because night had fallen as it always does in the tropics, with a suddenness and totality that made it like the unconsciousness of Earth itself. The ancient forest sighed and groaned in the onshore wind.

The clicking of bats and the humming of insects infiltrated the cooling air. In the mid-distance there was the noise of larger animals brushing and crashing through the undergrowth, but although he strained his capacious ears, Simon failed to register the distinctive guttural calls of the wild human.

A long trestle table had been set up for their repast on the open veranda of the largest hut. This muzzled out over the midnight blue of the lake and as they chomped their meal – which consisted largely of the dagaa they'd seen being landed earlier and copious amounts of fresh figs – they could, if they chose to, watch the lamps of the night fisherchimps flashing over the water.

If they chose to, or if they were able to, for first-and-last mess at Camp Rauhschutz turned out to be a stimulating affair. To begin with they discovered that they were not the sole visitors. As they vaulted over the railing and thumped on to the deck of the veranda, waiting there for them was another party of chimps. There were three males and five or possibly six females. They were all Caucasians – their pale muzzles bright in the lamplight – and they were all wearing the most absurd new tropical kit, all made from Gore-Tex and other synthetics, all in bright pastel shades, and all furnished with more Velcro tabs, poppers and straps than were remotely necessary.

It transpired with aching predictability that they were Dutch. "H'hooo," Rauhschutz wheezily vocalised, levering herself up to join them, then signed, 'I see you've met my current guests, the Van Grijn group from the Netherlands –'

'We haven't,' Busner signed for them all, 'but we are delighted to do so, their scuts are so marvellously surmounted by their brand-new, high-tech raiments.' They all presented to one another. If Rauhschutz had seen the irony in Busner's gestures, she made no mark about it.

The Dutch chimps presented to the English. Their alpha, a hard-muzzled male ascripted Oskar, indicated that they were there in their capacity as members of the Dutch arm of a pressure group denoted 'The Human Project', the aim of which was to secure limited chimpanzee rights for wild and captive humans. 'We are coming to see Madam Rauhschutz,' he signed with irritating little swoops of his fingers, 'because she is, "huu" how you sign? She is the "hooo" most important female alive today –'

'Because of her work rehabilitating captive humans "huu"?' Busner chopped the air.

'Of course "gru-nn", but more that that, we think she is, you know, maybe a little bit better spiritually than other anthropologists. She is, like a very holy kind of chimp, but not religious.'

Busner remembered what Rauhschutz had written in *Among the Humans* and decided to hold his hands. However, the anthropologist herself was not so contained. From her position at the head of the table, which she had assumed with much shuffling pomp, she held forth to the assembled company while the bowls of figs made the rounds. 'I am grateful "chup-chupp" to Oskar here for bringing up the issue of spirituality. For me the human is no mere, brute animal, far from it. Rather, when I commune with wild humans I feel they are teaching me in their stillness, in their untouchability, in their apparent isolation, more about what it means to be chimp than any chimpanzee could.'

As she conducted, Rauhschutz smoked a little black cheroot, which was clamped between her yellow fangs. She also took periodic swigs from a tin mug on the table, a mug that was full of peach schnapps. Simon knew this, because whatever the other faults and drawbacks of Camp Rauhschutz, being dry – in any sense of the sign – was not one of them. The schnapps bottles had been produced shortly after they squatted down and throughout the meal they circled the table.

Simon, for the first time since his breakdown, felt relaxed enough to drink strong liquor. There was something about the maverick anthropologist that he found peculiarly reassuring. It was as if, confronted by a female chimpanzee who *really* believed in the sentience of humanity, Simon was able clearly to apprehend what it might be like for him to abandon such a conviction.

There was that, and there was the anachronistic ambience of Camp Rauhschutz as well. Despite her vaunted spirituality, Rauhschutz ran the place along the lines of an old colonial district commissioner. The bonobos who waited on them at table made no signs to the white chimps save to ask if they were finished, or if they would like more. Otherwise they skulked in the shadows. When they addressed Rauhschutz, they denoted her 'Baas'. When she addressed them, she used either their first names – as if they were sub-adults – or simply summoned them with a curt, imperious pant-hoot.

'We are on the cusp,' she went on conducting as they worked their way through the fish, 'of a catastrophe of enormous dimensions, a catastrophe that we, as chimpanzees, will live to regret fervently –'

'And that is "h'huu"?' Simon couldn't prevent himself from snapping.

'That is, my "grnn" human friend, the extinction of your psychic conspecifics in the wild. Yes "HoooGraa" within fifty years there will almost certainly be no humans left in the wild, and gone with them will be our chances of redeeming ourselves spiritually. We would do well to remember what Schumacher gestured: If chimpunity wins the battle against nature – we will find ourselves on the losing side!'

As Rauhschutz fingered, it became apparent to all the English chimps that she didn't altogether *mind* the prospect of chimpunity being on the losing side, that she had gone so far in her drive to identify with the mind of the human that she had lost sight of some of the more basic chimpanzee virtues. Apart from the requisite cursory grooming session on their arrival, Simon noticed that Rauhschutz hardly touched at all. Her signing was all airy-fairy, none of it truly inparted. More than that, despite the automatic rifles her camp bonobos ported and the refugees scuttling down the road from Nyarabanda

394

they were intended to fend off, the hideous massacres that were going on to the north were of no concern to her.

If she put the finger on them at all, it was only to mark some irritating fall-out from the apocalypse, in the shape of shortages of supplies, or inconvenience of travel, or – and this *really* exercised her – danger to her rehabilitated and wild human groups. Even Simon found this callous disregard for the lives of millions of her fellow chimpanzees hard to stomach, but worse was to come; because there was a caste conflict underway that *did* really upset Rauhschutz, a conflict that she thought more important and vital than any other, and that was the one between her and the international anthropological hierarchy.

'They "hooo" denote me an ugly dyke,' she stabbed at them. 'They imply that I have sexual relations with my humans "euch-euch". Isn't this just typical. Isn't this always the way that they ignore and debase females in our society "h'huuu"? I care too much about animals – therefore I must be mating with them, because, being female, my desire for sex is everything "wraaa"! So, at one fell stroke, they discredit me – and they condemn my humans, my beautiful humans, to an ultimate wilderness – a wilderness of extinction "wraaaf"!'

As if responding to this impassioned cry, there now came an answering, but far deeper vocalisation from the darkness of the surrounding jungle. A cry, which to Simon was at once remote to the point of being alien, and hauntingly familiar. All the chimps fell signless and novocal, they turned in their seats to muzzle the approximate direction of the creature who had given voice. Busner signed for all of them, 'Show me, Madam Rauhschutz, is that one of your humans now "huu"? We haven't seen any since we arrived.'

She took a long pull on her cheroot before replying, and when she signed, the accompanying vocalisations were in the form of dribbles and poots of grey smoke, that dangled from her rough chin fur like temporary beards. '"Cru-nnn" yes, that will be the humans, Dr Busner, the poor humans. The wild ones here at Gombe range far and wide, but the ones I have "chup-chupp" personally rehabilitated tend to stay near to the camp. In the late afternoon they swagger several miles off to an isolated bay, for bathing activities. They are now returning to make their night shelters. If you "aaaa" listen carefully enough, you will hear the other members of the group responding.'

The chimps squatted still novocal and signless, and listened as they had been bidden. Simon felt his hackles rise, and clutched his glass of schnapps tightly. He concentrated on the whirring of the night-time sounds, the pulse and chirrup of cicadas, the tiny whoosh of moths, then he heard it again, "Fuuuuuuckoooooooffff-Fuuuuuuckoooooooffff." It was so strange – Simon looked around the table at the other chimps. All of them were intent on the human's calls, but did they – as he did – discern within those deep, harsh cries the anger and despair that he could. They showed no sign of it.

"Fuuuuuuckoooooffff-Fuuuuuuuckoooooffff," a different human responded. Then another responded to this second animal, then a third, then a fourth, until the deep burbles of sound were coming crashing in like agglutinative waves.

This went on for some minutes, then slowly died away. There was a last, slightly higher-pitched "Fuuuuckoooooffff" then novocal. Rauhschutz, a great grin pasted across her muzzle, conducted the table, ' "Gru-nnn" the human night chorus, possibly one of the most awesome and profound noises there is in nature. Once heard – it is never forgotten. We are "chup-chupp" so privileged, my allies, to be able to witness this. Those humans were once confined in zoos, or experimental compounds. They have been infected with chimpanzee diseases and abused by chimpanzee keepers – now a chimpanzee has got them their freedom "HoooGraaa"!'

' "H'huuu" please, Madam Rauhschutz,' Busner flicked respectfully, 'did that particular set of calls have any meaning?'

Rauhschutz grinned at this enquiry and countersigned, 'Yes, it does, Dr Busner. That is the human nesting vocalisation.

It's a tender exhortation by the male humans to the females, saying that the night shelters are prepared and it is time for mating activity to begin. And, ladies and gentlechimps, it is "h'hoooo" time for nest for us too. Welcome once more to Camp Rauhschutz. Dr Busner, I will expect you and your "grnn" allies to be up at dawn. Biggles ranges some miles from here and you will need to make an early start. As for your contingent, Mr Van Grijn, I have a very thorough programme arranged for you too "HoooGraaa"!'

With this final pant-hoot, the maverick anthropologist drummed on the table top, vaulted over the veranda railing and disappeared into the stygian night, two of her tough bonobos flanking her. There was the sound of rustling in the undergrowth and she was gone.

Around the still novocal table, the members of the Busner–Dykes group exchanged meaningful looks with one another. The same thought scampering through all their low brows, brachiating in the cellular branches of their brain tissue. Could it be that Ludmilla Rauhschutz really did practise what she preached? That the male humans' cries were a summons for her – as well as their own females? That Rauhschutz, even now, was engaged in a perverse act of interspecific mating?

Busner, Dykes, Knight, Higson and Bob the gofer got bipedal, and presenting low to the Dutch chimps and the bonobos who were still lingering in the shadows, they picked their way back across the still warm expanse of muddy compound to their quarters.

Once safely inside, Busner lit the gas lamp and without any preamble they engaged in a speedy round of mating. It might have been the tense atmosphere during the meal, or the still tenser atmosphere that prevailed generally at Camp Rauhschutz, but whatever the cause Janet had within the last couple of hours begun to show – even if only very slightly, and she was more than willing to be covered by the males. Simon, thrusting, tooth-clacking and coming in a matter of seconds, was just as speedily calmed. After the crazy antics of

397

the anthropologist, and the still acquiescence of the Dutch animal rights fanatics, it was beautifully reassuring and soporific to lie in the disordered embrace of a post-coital grooming session. It was all they could manage to find their own nests and crawl under the mosquito nets before sleep enfolded them.

Chapter Twenty-Two

S imon awoke, as was the diktat of the camp commandant,
at dawn. Before he was aware of whether it was light or not,
he heard the sounds of the forest, the yammering of baboons,
the chattering of parakeets, ibises and other birds, the guttural
cries of humans – close by, and mingled with them the excited
vocalisations of chimpanzees.

Flipping back the mosquito net, Simon leapt from the nest
and pulled on his safari jacket. His horny feet clipping the
concrete, he swaggered across the hut and, seeing that his
allies were already up, swung open the door and plunged
into the harsh grey day.

The scene that met his still encrusted eyes was at first difficult
to take in. The compound was full of figures, the scampering
setiform bodies of chimpanzees and the taller, more exiguous
forms of their closest living relatives.

It was morning feeding time for the rehabilitated humans
of Camp Rauhschutz. Over by the veranda of the main hut
a feeding bin was set up. Two of Rauhschutz's bonobos
were managing this resource. The humans, moving with
their characteristic zombie-like bipedal gait, slowly emerged
from the surrounding tree cover. They ambled across the
compound and over to the bin in small knots of two or three
adults and as many sub-adults or infants.

The bonobos, using long poles, then prodded them towards
the bin. If any of the humans showed any indication of trying to

get more than its fair share of the bananas, bread and figs on offer, the bonobos would cut them out from the rest of their group and poke them away from the bin, using quite vicious thrusts of the poles, or so Simon thought.

Those humans that had secured their share of the food were standing in disordered ranks at the very edge of the compound. There must have been at least fifty or sixty of the animals, although Simon couldn't be certain as the greyness of their skins made them difficult to pick out as individuals in the crepuscular light. There was that, and there was also the sight of their lumpen bodies and the languor of their movement. For a chimpanzee, used to observing fast-moving fingers and scampering limbs, the humans required a constant kind of double-take, to check that they were still there, still standing, knock-kneed, slack-jawed,arms akimbo, eyes glazed.

In amongst this throng of ghosts were moving some of the Dutch chimps. They rubbed up against the humans, and attempted to groom them. They uttered vocalisations that they presumably hoped the humans would understand in some way; low guttural cries that approximated to those of the animals. To Simon's eye it seemed that the humans were totally unresponsive to these efforts. As he knuckle-walked closer to the scene his furled ears began to pick out the vocalisations of one species from those of the other. The Dutch chimps were grunting and pant-hooting, lip-smacking and panting, trying as best they could to impress upon the humans the joy they were experiencing at being in touch with them. While the humans, on the other hand, were merely garbling incoherently in their swinish way, "Fuckoff-fuckoff-fuckoff-fuckoff,' " over and over and over.

Simon didn't have long to absorb this spectacle, for a familiar hand grasped his scruff and inparted, ' "HooGraa" morning, Simon, up early as Madam dictated!' Simon turned to see his alpha.

Busner seemed positively buoyed up by the ambience at Camp Rauhschutz, his muzzle creased with lines of intrigue and speculation. 'Come,' he ran on, ' "grnnn" Madam awaits us on the main veranda, together with some of her "huh-huh" closer allies!'

They knuckle-walked back across the compound and swung on to the main veranda. Rauhschutz was there, wearing another vile mumu, together with a small group of humans. Simon felt quite unsettled by the proximity of the bald animals. He skulked along the edge of the veranda keeping his muzzle out. Rauhschutz was indulging in a kind of tea ceremonial, pouring out foaming tin mugs from a large aluminium pot and pushing them into the outstretched, swishing hands of the humans.

The humans did at least seem to be enjoying their tea. They knocked back the steaming fluid, their blunt muzzles pointing up to the corrugated-iron roof, heedless of the hot splashes that fell on their exposed teats. 'Tea,' Busner gently inparted Simon's wrist. 'Best drink of the day!'

Although the humans on the veranda were as diffident as their fellows across the compound, there was one who had some spunk. A short male with a red thatch of fur between his teats, and an equally revolting patch between his tuberous legs, took advantage of the brief matitudinal presenting that was going on between Busner and Rauhschutz to grab the battered bowl of sugar from the table and upend its contents into his tight, pink-lipped mouth. This male then executed what passed for a turn of speed among humankind, by swaggering off the veranda. ' "Hooo" he's got the sugar!' Rauhschutz flourished, and all the chimps followed after the rogue male.

The sugar-stealer got an instant hit from his booty. This much Simon could tell by the way he began to stagger around in small circles, mewling and bellowing, "Fuckoff-fuckoff-fuckoff." Busner, still at Simon's side, inparted, 'I think his blood-sugar level will peak fairly soon – these creatures have surprisingly fast metabolisms. They are unused to any kind of stimulus. "Grnnn" coffee and sugar can have quite dramatic effects on them.'

Simon didn't know about dramatic – but they were certainly plain to see. The sugar-stealer now fetched up by the wall of the main hut; this he proceeded to muzzle and then rhythmically bash with his hydrocephalic brow, butting the resounding metal, "Bash-bash-bash", as some giant tetrapod – an ox or a warthog – might butt a tree. Coming up beside them, the maverick anthropologist regarded the notionally rehabilitated human with an expression betokening nothing but frank admiration, before remarking, ' "Hooo" see, the force and accuracy with which he butts the wall. I think it fair to sign that he seems to have a profound comprehension of the laws of physics.'

Together with Rauhschutz was Joshua, her head bonobo assistant. The rest of the Busner–Dykes group knuckle-walked up as well. They'd been down at the lake having a morning scrape. Seeing they were all assembled Rauhschutz conducted them, ' "HoooGrann" you have been welcomed here, and I'm sure you,' she picked out Alex Knight, whose camcorder was, of course, already whirring, 'will give a sympathetic portrayal of the work we are doing "euch-euch". But for now you had better get going. The human infant you are interested in tends to range a few hours south of here. If you wish to make contact with him and get back before nightfall you had better "hooo" get going. Joshua here will act as your guide.'

They knuckle-walked and brachiated all morning. Towards noon they descended the last, steep green hillside, under the hammering sun and came to a small bay. Huddled there was a forlorn group of six or seven adult humans and a couple of infants. Joshua, who had been ranging ahead of the rest of the patrol, broke from cover with a series of loud waa-barks, and scampering this way and that, like some simian sheep pony, managed to carve one of the human infants out from the rest and herd him towards where the chimpanzee patrol was bipedal, watching.

The poor infant ambled this way and that. He really was a most sorry specimen, Simon thought, as were most of the other rehabilitated humans he'd seen in the vicinity of Camp Rauhschutz. His pitiful naked skin was scratched and grazed by the tooth-edged grass, his muzzle stippled with insect bites, his head fur was tangled and matted. When Joshua had brought the human infant to within five metres of the chimpanzees he gestured, 'Mr Dykes, this is the human that you wanted to see. The one that come to us from London. The one the boss denotes Biggles.'

Simon, squinting in the noonday equatorial glare, stared for a long time into the brutish muzzle of the human infant, who stared back at him, his white-pigmented eyes glazed and turned in on themselves. Simon took in the bare little visage, the undershot jaw and slightly goofy teeth, then he turned on all four of his heels, vocalised "H'hooo," and gestured to the rest of the patrol, 'Well, that's that then,' and they headed back towards the camp.

Late that night Simon Dykes and Zack Busner were indulging in a groom before nest on the small veranda outside their hut. The rest of the group were already asleep and their snuffles and gasps could be heard from inside the hut. The two males were squatting by a table on which a gas lantern was set, and the hissing this light made augmented the sounds of the night around them.

They were lazily passing a bottle of Scotch between them and picking over the events of the day. 'This is a good drop,' Simon signed. ' "Grnnn" Laphroaig, isn't it "huuu"?'

'That's right,' his alpha countersigned. 'I managed to pick it up in Duty Free at Dar es Salaam – have another drop.'

When they'd taken another drink, Busner squatted upright and reached out to beard Simon, inparting his chin, 'Well, old ally, so there was no hint of recognition as far as Biggles was concerned "huuu"?'

'No, none at all, he looked just like any other human to me, nasty, brutish and long of leg "huh-huh".'

'And show me.' Busner leant forward. 'Do you feel that

with this "grnnn" revelation, your delusion has dissolved "huuu"?'

'Yes, there's that and there's also this camp – that's wrought a change in me as well, seeing the lengths that that female has gone to to deny her own chimpunity.'

'You know, Simon.' Busner's signing was subtle, the lightest perturbation of the air. 'It's occurred to me for some time now that your human delusion really was not at all an ordinary psychosis "chup-chupp".'

'Really "huu"?'

'Yes, I mean to sign, your reality testing – as we psychologists like to ascript it – has, throughout all of this, been "hooo" different, rather than straightforwardly wrong. Given your preoccupation before your breakdown with the very essence of corporeality and its relation to our basic sense of chimpunity, it crossed my mind – and I hope you'll "gru-nnn" forgive me for this speculation in advance if you cannot concur – that your conviction that you were human and that the evolutionarily successful primate was the human was more in the manner of a satirical trope "huu"?'

Simon mused for some time before countersigning, then simply flicked, 'It's an image.'

For a long time afterwards, the two allies tenderly touched each other, and passed the Scotch back and forth, while all around them in the equatorial night, the humans yowled and yammered their near meaningless vocalisations, "Fuuuuuckooooffff-Fuuuuuuckooofff- Fuccckoooooffff."